Nurses to Brides

*The Peniglatt sisters find their
happily-ever-afters when wedding bells ring!*

The Peniglatt sisters
couldn't be more different—
Kira is Miss Responsible, whilst Krissy is
the family wild child! Their only similarity is
their total dedication to caring for others.

These hard-working nurses
don't have much time for love. Until
two very special men walk into their lives,
determined to sweep them off their feet!

The Doctor She Always Dreamed Of

Can Derrick tempt Kira to believe in for ever?

and

The Nurse's Newborn Gift

Will single mum Krissy let Spencer
into her life…and her heart?

You won't want to miss this
sexy and emotional duet
from the fabulous Wendy S. Marcus!

THE DOCTOR SHE
ALWAYS DREAMED OF

BY
WENDY S. MARCUS

Published in Great Britain 2016
By Mills & Boon, an imprint of HarperCollins*Publishers*
1 London Bridge Street, London, SE1 9GF

© 2016 Wendy S. Marcus

ISBN: 978-0-263-91504-4

Our policy is to use papers that are natural, renewable and recyclable
products and made from wood grown in sustainable forests.
The logging and manufacturing processes conform to the legal
environmental regulations of the country of origin.

Printed and bound in Spain
by CPI, Barcelona

Dear Reader,

I'm thrilled to be back with two brand-new Medical Romances about Kira and Krissy Peniglatt—two very special sisters who work hard to care for and give to others without expecting anything in return.

In *The Doctor She Always Dreamed Of* Kira is a no-nonsense professional, working on the business side of nursing. Rather than enjoying the glitz and glamour of New York City, she divides her time between her job as Director of Case Management at a large insurance carrier and caring for her severely brain-injured mother. With no time to spare, she gave up on finding love a long time ago. But she's never met a man like Dr Derrick Limone—a man willing to do anything to spend time with her.

In *The Nurse's Newborn Gift* Krissy is a laid-back travelling nurse who's in the process of changing her carefree life to keep a promise to her dead best friend—a soldier killed in the war. Having his baby, giving his parents the gift of a grandchild they can dote on and love in his absence, may seem extreme to some—but not to Krissy. She's waited five years, and she's ready to do it all on her own. But Spencer Penn, the baby's godfather, has other ideas.

I hope you enjoy reading Kira's and Krissy's stories as much as I enjoyed writing them! To find out about my other books visit WendySMarcus.com.

Wishing you all good things,

Wendy S. Marcus

This book is dedicated to my cousin, Justine De Leon,
in honour of her becoming a US citizen.
We love you and we're so happy you're here!

With special thanks to Barbara Kram for helping me
run through some HMO insurance fraud scenarios.
Any errors are my own.

Thank you to my wonderful editor, Flo Nicoll,
for always pushing me to do my best.

And thank you to my family,
for supporting me in all that I do.

Wendy S. Marcus is an award-winning author of
contemporary romance who lives in the beautiful
Hudson Valley region of New York, where she spends
way too much time indoors on her computer. Writing.
Really! Okay…more like where she spends way
too much time on Twitter and Facebook! To learn
more about Wendy, and the books she's managed
to write in spite of her social media addiction, visit
WendySMarcus.com.

CHAPTER ONE

"I WANT TO speak to the man in charge."

Kira Peniglatt closed her eyes and pinched the bridge of her nose. "You've reached the *woman* in charge," she told the angry older gentleman on the telephone who'd been yelling at her and making unreasonable demands for the past ten minutes. "I'm the Director of Case Management here at We Care Health Care."

No sooner were the words out of her mouth than she regretted them. *When talking with disgruntled customers, must remember to use WCHC instead.*

"We Care Health Care," he mimicked. "What a crock!"

If she had a dollar for every time she'd heard that or something similar over the past five years, she'd be a wealthy woman, retired at the age of thirty, living by a lake or a beach, somewhere far away from the crowds and smells of New York City. This job she now hated, her tightwad boss, and harassing phone calls from angry people would be nothing more than a distant, unpleasant memory.

"You don't care about me," the husband of client Daisy Limone went on. "And you sure as hell don't care about my wife or you'd be sending someone to help me take care of her. I can't do it all by myself. Three days in and my back is aching from all the lifting, my knees are swelled up from all the bending, and my hips are on fire from running up and down the stairs all day."

Kira wanted to scream, "You brought this on yourself you ornery old man, now deal with it!" But she'd always prided herself on her professionalism, regardless of the challenging circumstances. Lately circumstances had become quite challenging.

By pulling his wife—she glanced at her computer screen: Primary diagnosis: cerebrovascular accident with residual right-sided hemiparesis and expressive aphasia. Secondary diagnoses: hypertension, osteoporosis, and hypothyroidism—out of an inpatient rehabilitation facility, against medical advice, nine days into an authorized twenty-eight-day stay, he'd assumed full responsibility for her care. Before the patient's stroke she'd filled out a Health Care Proxy designating her husband as her health care agent, giving him complete control over decision-making should her doctor determine she was unable to act on her own behalf—which she wasn't. As a result, there'd been nothing the hospital staff could do.

"Mr. Limone, your wife wasn't ready to come home." He'd underestimated the amount of care she would require, despite being warned—according to hospital documentation—by the case manager, the social worker, a head nurse, and the patient's physical and occupational therapists. "Research shows, after a stroke, patients who attend independent rehabilitation facilities for intensive rehabilitation, before returning home, show much more improvement than those who don't."

"She wasn't happy there, Miss Peniglatt. She put up a fuss every time they tried to take her to therapy. She wouldn't eat or drink." Now, rather than an ornery old man, he sounded like a concerned old man in love with his wife, desperate to help her. "They were threatening to put a tube in her stomach. Neither of us wanted that. She kept saying, 'home'. She'd squeeze my hand and look into my eyes and say, 'home.' Over and over. So I took her home."

Kira's heart went out to him, really, it did. But there was nothing more she could do. "Your insurance plan won't pay for round the clock care in the home setting."

"Who's asking for round the clock? Millie James up the street, her mama's got an aide six hours a day, seven days a week, and she don't need nowhere near as much help as my Daisy."

"Do you have any family—"

"My boys don't live around here. And they're busy. They got their own lives."

Family takes care of family. Kira's mother had been telling her that, and Kira had been doing it, for as long as she could remember.

"Is there any other insurance coverage we could help you explore?" she asked.

"We don't have no other insurance. All we have is We Care Health Care. And we need for you to do what your ad says and be there for us when we need you. We need you!"

When marketing had proposed a change to We Care Health Care, We'll Be There When You Need Us, Kira had voiced her concern that the slogan might feed into unrealistic patient expectations. Case in point. "Then can you afford to pay privately for a personal care aide? I could—"

"Why should I have to pay for an aide when I've been paying you every month for years?"

He made it sound like he paid her directly. "Mr. Limone, you pay for medical insurance coverage that does not include custodial care such as bathing and dressing provided by personal care aides," Kira said, trying to keep calm. "What about a friend or a neighbor? Have you asked around? Maybe—"

"You sit there in your fancy office," he snapped, "trying to think up ways to get out of paying for the stuff you should be paying for. Then you count up the huge profits you make by withholding care from people who need it and divide the money up into big end-of-year bonus checks. You're a thief! How the hell do you sleep at night?"

Kira inhaled then exhaled. *Don't let him get to you. You do your best. You sleep fine at night.* No she didn't.

"Mr. Limone, as I explained earlier, your insurance coverage is Medicare HMO. Medicare pays for short term, intermittent, skilled care. It does not pay for personal care for bathing and dressing. We contracted with a Medicare Certified Home Health Care Agency in your area."

With a few clicks of her mouse she brought up Mrs. Limone's plan of care. "A nurse came to your home to evaluate your wife. She developed a plan of care that included physical, occupational and speech therapy visits. This plan of care was approved by your wife's physician."

Odd that no home health aide hours were recommended considering the amount of skilled services required, Kira jotted herself a note to call the agency to follow up on that.

"Well it sure as hell wasn't approved by me!" Mr. Limone yelled. "That nurse was in and out of here in under fifteen minutes. Said Daisy wasn't eligible for an aide. How could she not be eligible? She can't get out of bed by herself or eat by herself or dress herself.

And since that nurse left, no one's been here. Now she don't return my calls. You need to come up here yourself to see what I'm dealing with. I can send someone to getcha."

"Just because I haven't come to visit your home to see your wife for myself, does not mean I don't care. And it doesn't mean I don't know what is going on up there, either. My office is located a good four hours from you. I am responsible for the case management of, as of this morning, four hundred and thirty-seven patients." The highest her census had ever been.

"That's why we work with your wife's physician and contract with medical providers in your local area for home care evaluations to determine patient care requirements. If you feel there's been an acute change in your wife's health status since the nurse visited three days ago or if you are no longer willing or able to safely care for her at home, you need to dial 911 immediately and have her taken to—"

"Then your boss," he interrupted. "Put me through to your boss."

It was all Kira could do to keep from laughing. Her new, focused-on-the-bottom-line boss—the main reason she now hated her job—could care less about patient care and customer satisfaction, which put him and Kira in close to constant conflict, day in and day out, for months. It was exhausting.

Despite all of the letters that came after her name, MSN—Master's of Science in Nursing, MBA—Master's in Business Administration, and CCM—Certified Case Manager, the letters RN, for Registered Nurse, were the most important to Kira. They were the reason she always put patients first, the reason she sometimes had to get creative to maintain her patients safely in their homes. She could almost hear the CEO's booming voice when he'd found out she'd agreed to reimburse a home health aide for mileage to get her to travel to a difficult to serve area. *Guidelines for a reason. Cost containment...cut spending...budget...bottom line...blah, blah, blah...*

Case managers straddled the line that separated compassionate patient advocacy and fiscal accountability to their employer. A job made increasingly more difficult with the stringent utilization review and cost constraints of managed care.

"I report to the CEO. He doesn't accept calls from customers. However, we do have an appeals process I'd be happy to have my assistant initiate for you. Or, if you feel my staff or I have in any way treated you unprofessionally, we have a complaint process, which my assistant will also be happy to initiate for you. Let me transfer you now."

Without giving him a chance to argue, she transferred the call. Then she leaned back, let out a breath, and counted to ten.

She'd made it to seven when her office door opened to reveal her assistant, Connie. Her short black hair gelled into random spikes, a tight red blouse and black skirt clinging to her ample curves, and sexy black ankle boots—with silver chains. And a frown on her pretty, round face. "That was mean." She crossed her arms under her well-endowed breasts.

"You could not possibly have filled out the questionnaire for Mr. Limone's complaint and/or appeal in that short a time," Kira pointed out.

"I put him on hold so I could come in and yell at you."

A pint-sized dynamo, as entertaining as she was efficient, Kira loved her assistant and didn't know what she'd do without her. "I'll make it up to you tonight. Drinks are on me."

That brought a smile to Connie's face. "Good, because after the week you've had, I plan on us doing a lot of drinking."

Typically, during the few times they'd managed to go out for drinks over the past three years, Connie got drunk and Kira—ever responsible Kira—made sure she got home safely. "Your roommate's okay with me crashing on your couch tonight?" Her sister Krissy home for a rare visit, Kira would be giving up Mom duty for one whole night. Her insides tingled with glee. One night to do anything she wanted. One night to sleep without Mom waking her up, without jumping up at the slightest sound, worried Mom might try to get out of bed by herself and fall.

"She is," Connie said. "But, honey, if I have my way, you won't need to be sleeping on my couch." She winked.

"Yeah, yeah," Kira said. "Because I'm so the type to have an illicit one-night stand with a stranger." Regardless of how much she may want to, that's how women wound up dead.

Connie's phone rang out at her desk. "Shoot." She snapped her fingers. "I came in here to tell you Mr. Limone's son is on the phone. I hope you appreciate the fact that I came in here, in person, to warn you rather than just sending the call in here."

Like Kira had done to her. "You're the best assistant ever." Kira smiled. Then she glanced at the clock. "It's not even noon. Will this day ever end?"

"Do you want me to tell him you're busy?"

Kira shook her head. He'd only call back…even angrier for being put off. She'd learned that earlier this morning. Connie turned to leave.

"Do me a favor?" Kira asked.

"Anything for you." Connie turned back around with a smile. "Legal or illegal, I'm your girl."

Kira smiled back, no doubt in her mind Connie meant it. "A cup of decaf, please."

"With a shot of Baileys?" Connie asked, hopefully. "I might have some random single serving bottles in my desk drawer," she looked up toward the ceiling innocently, "that I received for Christmas and may have forgotten to bring home."

Coffee and Baileys, Kira's favorite. "Get out." She pointed to the door. "Stop putting unprofessional thoughts in my head and send me my call."

Connie shook her head and let out a disappointed sigh.

"Oh," Kira said. "And when you're done with Mr. Limone senior, would you call Myra Douglas from In Your Home Health Care Services?" Their preferred Certified Home Health Care Agency for the West Guilderford area in upstate New York, where Daisy Limone lived. "Ask her why there are no home health aide services on Daisy Limone's plan of care." Even a few hours a few times a week was better than nothing.

"Sure thing, boss," Connie said. Then with a salute she turned and left, closing the door behind her.

A few seconds later, Kira's phone rang. With a deep fortifying breath—because Mr. Limone junior was even more obnoxious than Mr. Limone senior—she answered it. "Hello, Mr. Limone. I just got off the phone with your father. Before you say one word, let me remind you of our last conversation. The first time you threaten to sue me or curse at me or call me unflattering names I am hanging up this phone. Now what can I do for you?"

"Doctor," he said.

"Excuse me?"

"*Dr.* Limone. I'm a different son."

God help me, there are two of them.

"Three actually," he said, his voice deep and tinged with a bit of humor.

Oops. She must have said that out loud.

Thank goodness Connie chose that moment to return with the coffee.

"What can I do for you, *Dr.* Limone?" She took a sip, smiled at her wonderful assistant and mouthed, "Thank you." Although the coffee wasn't near as satisfying without the Baileys.

"I'm calling to apologize, on behalf of my family. Our father can be...difficult."

So could his brother.

"But he's our father," *Dr.* Limone said. "He worked three jobs to keep a roof over our heads and see that all three of us went to college. While he worked, Mom managed the house, the finances and us boys. They got into a routine that's worked for them for fifty-four years. Since Mom's stroke, Dad's struggling to adjust. He doesn't do change very well."

Not many people did. Kira understood that. But, "You know HIPPA regulations don't allow me to discuss Mrs. Limone's care without a signed authorization."

"Please," he said. "As a professional courtesy."

In the past, on a rare occasion, Kira might have given in to a request for a professional courtesy—the unwritten understanding between doctors, nurses and the like to relax the rules of confidentiality a little bit for other health care professionals. But with all the problems she'd been having with her new boss, and with the Limones having an attorney in the family, Kira would be following company procedure to the letter. "I'm sorry, Mr. Limone. Not even as a professional courtesy. Get me a HIPPA release, signed by your father, as your mother's health care agent, specifically giving me authorization to discuss her medical status and treatment with you, by name, and then I'll be happy to speak with you."

"You're just putting me off."

"What I'm doing is following procedure which requires a signed HIPPA release, on file, designating who my staff and I may talk to regarding any specific patient, other than the patient and/or his or her physician." And just because she was in a bad mood she added, "As a physician you should be familiar with HIPPA regulations, *Dr.* Limone."

"The plan of care is inadequate," he yelled.

If the patient was still in the rehabilitation hospital, she'd be getting the round the clock care and supervision she required. "I can't discuss this with you."

"All I want is for you to explain why no home health aide services were authorized. And why hasn't therapy started yet?"

Kira would be looking into both as soon as she could get off the phone. "I can't discuss this with you."

"Damn it!"

"Get me a signed HIPPA release," Kira said.

"How the hell do you suggest I do that? My practice has exploded. Even working eighty hour weeks I can't get everything done that I need to get done. I live three hours from my parents' house. They don't have a fax machine or a scanner or even e-mail."

"You graduated from medical school," Kira said.

"Which means you must be a pretty smart guy. I'm sure you'll figure something out."

Dr. Limone slammed something close to his phone, the sound loud in Kira's ear. "You have no idea how frustratingly difficult this is," he yelled again.

"Yes," Kira said. "I do." From a professional standpoint and from personal experience.

He let out a weary breath. "I'm worried about my dad," he said, sounding exhausted. "He's not in good health. I'm worried about him or my mother falling and getting hurt because they don't have the help they need in the home."

"I understand your concern," Kira said. "From everything I've heard and read, I think you have every reason to be concerned."

"Yet you're doing nothing to ensure my mother's safety," Dr. Limone yelled.

"This case was just brought to my attention yesterday afternoon."

"My mother is not a *case*, Miss Peniglatt. She's a sweet, kind, loving woman lying helpless in her bed with no one but my elderly father to take care of her because *you* won't authorize an aide."

Kira came dangerously close to losing it. "It is not the responsibility of Medicare or WCHC, as your mother's Medicare HMO, to provide round the clock, in home care. Family takes care of family, Dr. Limone." It's why Kira needed the large salary this job paid her and why she rarely had a free moment to herself. *Family takes care of family.* Kira had grown up watching her mother live those words. So of course when Mom needed care, Kira had stepped up, happily. Being the sole dependable caregiver to a totally dependent family member was not easy, Kira knew that firsthand. And she had little tolerance for family members unwilling to pitch in and help. "If you and your brothers are as concerned for your mother and father as you say you are, then maybe you all should spend less time threatening and complaining and trying to find someone else to do it, and actually go home and help."

Kira was out of line, she knew it. But she'd reached her limit.

Apparently so had Dr. Limone, because without further comment, he slammed the phone down in her ear. Maybe it was childish, but Kira slammed down her phone right back.

The door to her office opened slightly and Connie stuck her head in. "You okay?"

No. Kira was not okay. She didn't let clients rattle her. But this guy…and his brother and father…the absolute nerve! "I'm fine."

"Mr. Jeffries wants to see you in his office," Connie said quietly.

Mr. Jeffries. The CEO. Uh oh. "Did he say why?" Kira's chest tightened.

Connie shook her head, looking grim. They both knew Mr. Jeffries never asked Kira to his office for anything good.

Kira strained to inhale, expanding her lungs to full capacity to make sure they were working as she glanced at the clock. Still not even noon and she was ready to call it a day. "When?"

"As soon as you're off the phone."

Kira stood.

"I spoke with Myra," Connie said. "She told me they don't have a Daisy Limone as a patient."

That didn't make any sense. "One more thing I'll have

to look into." Kira made a note on her ever-growing To Do list.

"She said another certified home health care agency has been approved in her area. Wants to know why all of our patients are suddenly going to them?"

A very good question that Kira would find the answer to as soon as she could find a free minute.

"Do me another favor?" she asked Connie.

"Name it."

"Tonight, at the bar, please don't let me drink too much." The way she felt right now, it was a definite possibility.

Connie gave her a "yeah, right" look. "You know, maybe if you let loose once in a while you wouldn't be wound so tight and grabbing for your chest every time Mr. Jeffries's name is mentioned."

Kira looked down at her hand resting on her sternum.

"What if tonight, *you* get rip-roaring drunk?" Connie said. "And I make sure *you* get home to my apartment safely?"

Kira shook her head. "I can't. I start administrative call at eight on Saturday morning." If her week was any indication, this weekend would likely be a nightmare. "I can't be hungover." She eyed Connie. "Sheila's the case manager on call."

"Well that sucks."

Exactly.

Sheila, who had been working at WCHC twice as long as Kira. Sheila, who had been considered for the position of Director of Case Management at the same as Kira. Sheila, who had not taken Kira's promotion well and spent a good deal of time searching out evidence of why she believed Kira should not be the Director of Case Management, which she happily shared with Mr. Jeffries. Sheila, who just happened to be Daisy Limone's case manager.

CHAPTER TWO

THIS HAD TO be the stupidest thing Dr. Derrick Limone had ever done. Considering all the crazy stuff he'd gotten himself into as a teenager that was saying something. An uncle in law enforcement had kept him out of jail. Pure dumb luck had kept him alive and in one piece.

But he'd moved past all that had gotten his life together. He was a respectable physician now, living a respectable, law-abiding life.

At least until tonight, when he'd followed Ms. Kira Peniglatt from her office to the very bar where he now sat…staring into a half empty mug of beer, contemplating the best way to snatch her away from her friend and calculating the possible consequences of doing so.

Desperation led people to do stupid things.

In the past, his stupidity could be blamed on a desperate need for excitement to alleviate the mundane boredom of small-town life.

Tonight…tonight was payback, not that he could ever fully repay his parents for all they'd done for him. But today he'd planned to travel down to the New York City office of We Care Health Care to get a start on trying.

Only a walk-in patient complaining of chest pain had made him miss his train. And an insane amount of late Friday afternoon traffic had made him too late to catch her during business hours. So when he'd seen her leaving her office building, he'd followed her. Like a deranged stalker.

She laughed, a loud, confident, bold sound that caught his attention every single time, as if there weren't dozens of other people in the crowded bar. He glanced her way to see her tossing back a third shot of Southern Comfort with lime. Apparently she hadn't stopped by for a quick drink before heading home, as he'd hoped.

The professional portrait of Ms. Kira Peniglatt, MSN, MBA, CCM, RN, Director of Case Management, on the insurance company website, where she wore conservative business attire, trendy glasses, and had her dark hair pulled back off of her face, had made it easy for Derrick to identify her leaving work. It hadn't prepared him for the smiling, laughing beauty out of her stuffy suit jacket, with her long, wavy hair hanging loose around her shoulders and a silky white sleeveless blouse leaving her firm arms bare while hugging her appealing curves. Or that skirt, clinging to her narrow hips. Or her long, slender legs. Or those fashionable four-inch black, shiny heels.

Derrick looked away, shaking his head as he did, wondering if maybe she had a twin who worked with her and he'd followed the wrong Ms. Peniglatt. Because the very appealing woman seated two tables away did not in any way resemble the uncompromising, cold-hearted female he'd spoken with on the phone that morning. The same woman who'd told him to get her a signed HIPPA form, and then, after he'd inconvenienced his uncle to drive out to his parents' house to get one signed and then fax it back to him, had not taken any of his afternoon phone calls.

"Coming down to the city was an asinine idea," Derrick mumbled to himself. Then he picked up his mug and gulped down the rest of his beer. Even if he could separate Ms. Peniglatt from her friend, after three shots of Southern Comfort and two glasses of white wine in under two hours, she'd be in no condition to talk business.

He glanced at his watch. Almost seven. If he left now he could grab a couple of slices of pizza and make it up to Mom and Dad's house before midnight. Ms. Peniglatt had been right. Family takes care of family. The least Derrick could do, in addition to getting the home care straightened out to make sure his mother received the maximum benefit allowed, was to head home for the weekend when his dad needed him. That had meant helping his overworked receptionist/medical biller to reschedule and refer his weekend patients so he could close his office on Saturday. And finding someone to cover on call for the whole weekend, which hadn't been easy.

Thinking of everything he'd done today and everything he still had to do if he wanted his new practice to be a success, exhausted him. So he stopped thinking about it. Slapping a ten dollar bill on the bar to cover his drink and a tip, Derrick stood, stretched out his sore back, and headed to the bathroom so he could hopefully make the drive without stopping.

After taking care of business, so to speak, he exited into the dimly lit hallway at the back of the bar, and walked right into... "I'm sorry." He grabbed a hold of the dark-haired woman he'd almost knocked over.

"Don't be. It's not you, it's me." She wobbled. "Or rather these heels." Leaning heavily on his arm, she reached down to adjust her shoe. "A few drinks and they've become a detriment to me and those around me." She looked up, hesitated as if trying to place his face then smiled. "Or maybe it's fate."

If so, then fate was a nasty bitch to finally give him Ms. Peniglatt's full attention, when he had a signed HIPPA form in his pocket…when she was drunk and of no use to him.

"I saw you watching me," she said.

Half the men in the bar and a good number of women were watching her. She was beautiful to look at. But Derrick knew firsthand that a total lack of compassion lurked beneath her unexpectedly appealing façade.

"Dare I take that to mean you like what you see?" She raised a pair of perfectly shaped eyebrows.

What heterosexual male wouldn't? God help him she smelled fantastic, classy, enticing.

"Are you mute?" she asked, scrunching her brow.

No, he was not mute. But like a dumbfounded idiot, he shook his head rather than responding verbally.

"I'm Kira," she introduced herself, pressing her body to his to make room in the hallway for two women to walk past, so close he could feel the swell of her breasts against his chest, the push of her hip against his… Damn. She felt even better than she smelled. His body hardened with interest, with…yearning. Not good. He tried to push her away.

But Ms. Peniglatt would have none of that. Surprisingly steady after all the liquor she'd consumed, she skillfully turned them, pinning his back to the wall. "And you are?"

"Derrick." His name came out coarse, like it was the first word he'd uttered in a decade, like he was a virgin who'd never been hit on by a beautiful woman before. Come to think of it, if he ever had, it'd been too long ago for him to remember. Between medical school, then residency and now working an insane amount of hours at his six-month-old private family practice, he didn't get out much. When he did, *he* liked to be the one to make the first move.

"Nice to meet you, Derrick." She leaned in to whisper in his ear. "Are you married, or engaged, or in a relationship?" Her hands slid up the sides of his dress shirt then back down to settle on his hips leaving a pleasing, fizzy feeling wherever she'd touched him.

He fought back a laugh. In all the possible outcomes he'd considered when first deciding to follow Ms. Peniglatt when he'd seen her hailing a cab outside of her office, he'd never once entertained the possibility she'd come on to him. Or that he'd have to fend her off or think of a way to politely turn her down, without letting her know his true identity.

"Because I've been watching you, too, Derrick," she said seductively. "And I very much like what *I* see. I've had a horrible, train wreck of a week. But at this very moment, things are looking up because here you are when I just happen to be drunk enough to pick up a total stranger in a bar."

He wasn't exactly a *total* stranger.

"So if you're interested…" She moved her mouth to his neck and set a gentle kiss just above his collar sending a flair of arousal through his system. "I'd very much like for the two of us to spend the rest of the night together." She moved her mouth back up to his ear and whispered, "Naked."

Naked. At the sound of the word, at the feel of her hot, moist breath as she said it and the enticing visual images that accompanied it, his body perked up in eager anticipation. Under normal circumstances, Derrick would like nothing more than to get naked with a woman as attractive and alluring as the woman pressed against him.

But there was nothing normal about the circumstances of their meeting.

"That feels nice," she said, setting her cheek to his shoulder.

What felt nice? Oops. Somehow his hands had wound up on her spectacular ass, which did, in fact, feel *very* nice. He couldn't help but give a little squeeze.

Remember why you're here.

He removed his hands. "I—"

"Well look at you." Kira's friend joined them. "I was wondering what was taking so long. Please tell me you know this man."

"We've just recently become acquainted," Kira said, pulling away guiltily, almost stumbling. Derrick reached out to steady her, and somehow she wound up right back where she'd started, pressed to his chest.

"Quick reflexes. Good thing. I'm Connie, Kira's assistant." She held out her hand.

Derrick shook it.

"She's also my best friend," Kira added, in a sappy drunk kind of way. "Although she's failed miserably in keeping me from getting drunk tonight."

"As your best friend," Connie said, "I consider it my responsibility to remind you that you're not the type to pick up strange men in bars." She looked up at Derrick. "You'll have to excuse her. She doesn't get out much."

"One night," Kira said sleepily, cuddling up against him. "My sister is home. I have a whole night to myself to have fun and do whatever I want and I want to spend it with Derrick."

Why did her sister need to be home for her to have a night all to herself?

"That's the alcohol talking," Connie said.

"I like what it's saying," Kira said back, looking up at Derrick. "Don't you like what it's saying, Derrick?"

He was going to hell, because for damn sure he most certainly did like what it was saying, what *she* was saying.

Connie looked conflicted. "You don't know anything about him," Connie said. Glancing up to meet his eyes she added, "No offense. I'm sure you're a great guy."

No. Tonight he wasn't. She felt so good, desire tried to overtake good moral character, screaming, "Take her to the nearest motel and give her what she wants, hard and fast. Exhaust her then leave while she's sleeping. She'll never know who you really are. First thing Monday morning, call her again like nothing happened." Common sense fought back, screaming, "You're not *that* guy. You don't take advantage of drunk women, no matter how sexy they are or how much you dislike them."

"You're the one who told me some hot sex would make me feel better," Kira said to Connie. "I've had a rotten day. I need to feel better." She wrapped her arms around his waist and squeezed. "Make me feel better, Derrick."

"She's not a big drinker," Connie explained apologetically.

All evidence to the contrary.

"Come on, Kira." Connie tugged on her arm. "Let the nice man be on his way."

Kira looked up at him, again, her expression soft and sweet. "Do you want to be on your way, Derrick?"

He *should* want to be on his way. He *needed* to be on

his way, had a long drive ahead of him. And yet, "Not, really," snuck out of his mouth, followed by, "How about we go get a cup of coffee or something to eat?"

CHAPTER THREE

KIRA CAME AWAKE to the smell of coffee. Oh, God. How did Mom get to the kitchen? She jumped out of bed and…

"Whoa," a man said. "Slow down."

She froze at the sound of a male voice in her bedroom. During that pause she noticed carpet below her bare feet. She didn't have carpet in her bedroom.

A quick perusal of her surroundings made her think she was in a child's room. One she didn't recognize. A single bed draped in a baseball-themed comforter, baseball trophies covering the desk and dresser, and posters of baseball players she didn't recognize hanging on the walls. Thumbtacks held a large periodic table on the back of the closed door. Funny, she'd done the same thing in her bedroom as a teenager, to hide her inner science geek.

But what the heck? She turned back to the handsome man before her, standing tall and solid, holding two mugs of coffee. He wore a tight white T-shirt that showcased a muscled chest and arms, and navy blue slacks. His feet were bare. Dark, mussed hair fell haphazardly over his forehead, and stuck up in spots. A day's worth of scruff covered his jaw. Kira liked scruff.

But who was he? And why did his blue eyes stare back at her with a wary edge?

She studied the face, recognizing it. Derrick. Memories of last night whooshed into her mind, seeing him at the bar, watching him as he watched her, stumbling into him, pushing him against the wall, and oh, God, propositioning him. Connie taking a picture of him and his driver's license then patting him down for weapons before walking them out to his car to check that for weapons too. She shook her head in disbelief then dropped her forehead into her palm. "I'm sorry…bad week. Too much to drink." Sexual deprivation. A night of freedom.

"So you said. Last night."

Kira could have done without the humor in his tone.

So what? She'd propositioned him. He was a good-looking guy. For sure she hadn't been the first. Embarrassment warmed her cheeks, because there was a definite chance, a small one, but a chance nonetheless, that she could have been the first woman to refuse to get out of his car until he took her somewhere they could have sex. And she'd been pretty explicit about what she'd wanted.

Yet here she stood, fully dressed in the skirt and blouse she'd worn to work yesterday. "My clothes." She looked up at him. "We didn't…?"

He shook his head.

Well that sucked. The awkward morning after without the night of hot sex that should have preceded it.

"Why not? Didn't you want to?"

Damn he had a nice smile. "Yeah, I wanted to. But it wouldn't have been right."

Wouldn't have been right? Why the hell not? Two consenting adults. Check. Mutual attraction. Hmmm.

Had their attraction been mutual? The feel of his arousal, big and hard beneath her while she'd straddled him in the front seat of his car came to mind. Oh, yeah. Their attraction had been mutual. So why—?

Someone knocked on the closed bedroom door.

Kira jumped.

"You want breakfast?" an older sounding male voice asked.

"We'll be down in a few minutes," Derrick said.

"Who was that?" Kira whispered, like whoever it was could hear her. Then she scanned the room for her shoes, messenger bag, and briefcase. Time to go.

"My dad."

She swung around to face him. "Are you kidding me? You live with your parents and you brought me home to their house?" At the age of thirty, Kira was way too old to be worried about getting caught in a boy's bedroom by his parents. Yet she found herself glancing toward the window as a means of escape.

"Second floor," Derrick said, as if he could read her mind.

But Kira was focused on what she saw outside that window…or rather what she didn't see. She stepped closer.

No big buildings, no crowded streets. No closely spaced buildings or brownstones or houses. No signs she was in New York City or any of its five boroughs. No, sirree. He'd taken her someplace rural, with lots of trees, wide open spaces, and no neighbors that she could see out of what appeared to be a back window. She squinted off into the distance. Heaven help her, was that a…cow?

Maybe fear would have been an appropriate response

right then, but Kira got mad and turned on him. "Where the hell am I?"

"I can explain," he said, holding out a cup of coffee. "You're probably going to need this."

Kira eyed the dark liquid. Last night, alcohol had allowed a far-too-long-ignored desire for sex to overtake her usually strong protective instincts. Well, this morning they were back at fully functional. She didn't know this man, didn't know what he was capable of, and would most certainly not drink a beverage she had not watched him prepare, regardless of how much she wanted it.

"It's coffee," he said. "Do you want me to take a sip before you drink it?"

"I want you to explain what's going on." Seeing her shoes, bag and briefcase lined up neatly at the foot of the bed, she bent to pick them up. "Where am I, and why is your father here?"

"Fine." He set one mug of coffee down on the dresser. "If you change your mind, help yourself." He walked over to the small desk, pulled out an old wooden chair and sat down. "Sorry, but I need to sit. I've been up watching you most of the night and I'm exhausted." He took a sip of coffee.

"Watching me? That's not at all creepy." It was totally creepy. She took one step closer to the door.

"Wrong choice of words." He ran his fingers through his hair, pushing it out of his eyes. "I've been up most of the night waiting for you to wake up. So you didn't freak out. So I could explain…"

"Go ahead then. Explain." Kira sat on the corner of the bed closest to the door, making sure she had a clear path, her hand inside the bag on her lap, her fingers wrapped around the canister of pepper spray she kept on her keychain. Just in case.

"Remember how I told you it wouldn't have been right for me to have sex with you?"

She nodded.

"That's because my being in that bar last night wasn't a random coincidence." He looked her straight in the eyes. "I'd followed you from your office."

Kira didn't wait to hear more. "That's it." She stood. "I'm out of here."

Derrick stood, too.

The movement wasn't in any way threatening, but when he reached for her Kira whipped out the pepper spray and held it few inches from his face. "Don't."

He stopped and held up both hands in surrender. "I'm not going to hurt you."

"No, you're not," Kira told him, standing tall and on guard, confident in her ability to protect herself thanks to several self-defense classes. "By the way, I've been taught that you should never trust a man who says 'I'm not going to hurt you,' because that means he's thought about it."

"Or," Derrick countered, his hands still raised up by his shoulders, "it means he realizes he's bigger and stronger and he really doesn't want you to think he's going to use his size or strength to hurt you."

He said the words matter-of-factly, but Kira could sense his tension.

"Who are you? Why were you following me?"

"I'm Derrick Limone."

Limone. Why did that name sound familiar?

"I got a HIPPA form signed and faxed it down to your office, just like you asked. Then you wouldn't take my phone calls. So late yesterday afternoon I rushed down to the city to meet you at your office to give it to you in person so you'd speak with me about my mother."

His mother. "Daisy Limone." Un-friggin'-believable.

"I missed my train," he went on. "So I drove down from White Plains, in Westchester County, where I live and work. I drove past your office just as you and Connie were getting into a cab out front…so I followed it."

"You followed it? You think that's acceptable behavior to follow me after business hours? Why on earth would you do such a thing?" Because he was a total nut job!

"You wouldn't take my calls."

He said it like it made perfect sense. It didn't. The man was obviously not right in the head. "Which son are you?" she asked. "The attorney who called me degrading names and threatened to sue me or the doctor who yelled at me and hung up on me?"

"The doctor," he admitted, looking guilty. "But in my defense, you were giving me a pretty hard time."

Not as hard as he deserved for not stepping up to take care of his mother like a good son should. *His mother.* Then it clicked. Him taking Kira to a rural location, his father knocking on the door. Her eyes went wide and she sucked in a breath. He didn't! "I'm at your parents' house? In West Guilderford?" Four hours from her home.

He just stood there.

"You really are insane." She backed toward the door. "As in mentally unhinged and in need of inpatient psychiatric therapy. Immediately."

"No. I'm not."

"You kidnapped me!"

"Kidnapped you?" He crossed his arms over his chest. "Let's talk about that, shall we?"

He seemed way too calm for a man on the verge of being arrested. *Because he's insane! Run while you can!*

Kira lunged for the doorknob.

Showing amazing speed and agility, Derrick lunged too, grabbing the pepper spray and putting his full weight against the door to keep it closed. "Not so fast," he said, looking down at her while keeping his shoulder pressed to the door. "You are not leaving this room thinking I kidnapped you."

"Let's look at the facts, shall we?" Kira held up her right index finger. "One. You followed me out to the bar last night. Two." She added her middle finger. Hmmm. How to tactfully put it? "You lured me out of that bar under false pretenses."

He actually had the nerve to laugh. "I did not *lure* you anywhere. I offered to take you for coffee and something to eat—"

"We both know you only said that to appease Connie." Kira waved him off. "I offered you sex and you accepted my offer without ever intending to follow through."

"No. I offered you coffee and something to eat and I had fully intended to follow through with *that*, but you refused to get out of the car when we got to the diner."

"Because I wanted…"

"You wanted what?"

Sex, damn it. She'd wanted sex not coffee and not something to eat.

Based on his slow, sexy smile, he knew exactly what she'd wanted.

That, and the fact he hadn't given it to her, pissed her off. So she pushed his chest. "Go to hell."

"Help me out here," he said. "Are you mad because you think I kidnapped you or because we didn't have sex?"

Both! "You're an ass."

"Maybe," he said. "But I'm not a kidnapper."

"Then how, exactly, did I wind up here at your parents' house, with no recollection of how I got here? I don't recall you asking. And I don't recall agreeing to come."

"That can easily be explained by the amount of alcohol you drank last night." With a tilted head and raised eyebrows he simply said, "You passed out."

No. Kira shook her head. No way. She had never in her life consumed enough alcohol to pass out. "Fell asleep, maybe. But I most certainly did not pass out. Okay, let's say you're telling the truth and I *fell asleep* in your car."

"I *am* telling the truth," he said confidently, still blocking her escape.

"So there I am, asleep in your car, and all you can think to do is take me on the four hour drive up to your parents' house?"

"What would you have liked me to do with you?" he challenged.

"Oh, I don't know. Maybe take me to my home?" she yelled.

"You have no memory of what happened after we got to the restaurant, do you?"

No, not really.

"You don't remember me going through your bag to find your wallet to find your driver's license?"

Nope. "If I had seen you doing that I would have told you I don't have a driver's license." She'd lived in New

York City all her life and couldn't afford to keep a car, so she'd never bothered to learn how to drive.

"I found a few college IDs, a bunch of credit cards, and insurance cards. But you know what I didn't find?" He didn't give her a chance to answer. "Anything with your current address on it."

Very possible.

"So I tried your phone, hoping I could find a home number or Connie's number."

She winced. "You need a security code to access it."

"Yes, you do." He shifted his position so his back rested against the door. "And even though I could rouse you to ask, you weren't giving up the code, any phone numbers, or your address. So there I sat, parked on Thirty-Eighth Street with a drunk woman fast asleep in my front seat."

"You could have tried harder to wake me up."

"Oh, I tried," he said. "For the record, you are very cranky when your sleep is disturbed."

That was true.

"So there I sat," he repeated. "A drunk woman fast asleep in my front seat. No idea where she lived and unable to contact anyone on her phone while the minutes ticked by. I sat there for an hour, Kira. Then I tried to wake you again. You grumbled and complained in words I couldn't understand. I asked where you lived. You refused to tell me. But you know what you did say, loud and clear?"

Kira wasn't sure she wanted to know.

Too bad, because Derrick seemed intent on telling her. "You said, 'Take me home with you. I want to go home with you.' Over and over. So you know what? That's exactly what I did. I brought you home with me."

Kira narrowed her eyes. "I don't believe you."

He reached into the front pocket of his slacks and pulled out his cell phone, pressed a few buttons, then held out the screen for her to watch and listen to him trying to get her home address and her refusing to answer.

"You took a video of me?" And not a very flattering one. Yikes!

He nodded. "You seemed like the kind of woman who'd want proof."

That she was. She'd glanced away from the screen but looked back in time to see and hear herself say, "I want to go home with you. Take me home with you."

Kira turned to face the window. "I'm never drinking alcohol out in public again."

Derrick walked up behind her. For some strange reason she didn't feel at all threatened by his closeness. "I didn't go down to the city planning to bring you up here. But I'd had every intention of heading up after I met with you. Family takes care of family. You were right. So I cleared my appointment schedule and got someone to cover for me so I could help my dad this weekend. I didn't know what else to do with you. It was getting late. My dad was depending on me to be here this morning. So I brought you with me. As soon as I spend some time with my parents and help get Mom settled for the day, I'll take you home."

Kira turned to face him. "Thank you."

"Now let's go down and have some breakfast, then you can meet Mom, last I checked, she was still sleeping."

Go down and have breakfast, as in with his father? Kira would rather starve. "Your father hates me."

Derrick smiled. "He doesn't hate you. As far as he knows you're my friend Kira who wanted to come home with me this weekend."

"*Wanted?* That's a bit of a stretch, don't you think?"

"We can go downstairs and tell him the truth if you want." Derrick headed for the door. "Your call."

"Wait. No." Kira followed him. "Let's not."

CHAPTER FOUR

"WHERE'S YOUR FRIEND?" Dad asked when Derrick entered the kitchen.

He looked old and worn-out in his standard at-home summer attire, a dingy white tank undershirt, his navy blue heavy-duty mechanic uniform pants cut off at the knee—because why waste money on shorts when you could cut up old pants?—and his black, steel toe work shoes with white socks.

"She freshening up," Derrick answered, pulling out a chair and sitting down at one of the spots Dad had set at the kitchen table. "You didn't have to go to all this trouble." Mom's sunny yellow tablecloth with matching placemats and napkins dressed up the usually bare round wooden table. And he'd put out the floral glasses Mom saved for company—because heaven forbid her rambunctious sons should break them.

"This is the first girl you've brought home since high school. It's a big deal."

Kira Peniglatt was hardly a girl. She was a full grown, much too appealing woman. "She's just a friend," he lied. Hopefully she could remain civil through breakfast and until they left. He'd have to figure out a way to break it to his mom and dad that he wouldn't be staying through Sunday as planned.

Derrick eyed the offerings on the table. Fresh croissants and Danish. Butter and a jar of Mom's homemade raspberry preserves. A fruit bowl filled with fresh peaches, plums and bananas. Dad set a casserole dish on a trivet in the center of the table. It contained scrambled eggs and bacon he'd taken from the oven where apparently he'd been keeping it hot. "Pop. You went all out. When did you have time—?"

"I asked Mrs. Holmes to run out to the store for me this morning," Dad said. Their neighbor of more than forty years was also Mom's best friend. "If your mama could, she would have done it. But she can't." Dad turned away to put the oven mitts on the counter and grab a serving spoon.

The sadness in his dad's voice squeezed Derrick's heart. His first instinct was to say something like, "She'll be back to shopping on her own in no time." But it was too early in her recovery to know that for sure. Derrick didn't want to give his dad false hope.

"Well hello, there," Dad said, surprisingly cheerful all of a sudden.

"Good morning, Mr. Limone," Derrick heard Kira say.

He stiffened. Things this morning had gone much better than he'd hoped. But how would she act toward his father? Would she keep her identity and how she'd wound up here secret?

"Thank you so much for having me on such short notice," she said, her pleasant almost friendly tone a surprise.

He relaxed then turned in his chair. She'd changed into skin tight leggings that stopped at her knees and a clingy pale pink tank top with straps too skinny to cover those from her purple bra. When she saw him looking she shrugged as if to say, "It's all I had with me. Deal with it." From the heterosexual male point of view she looked fantastic. Plus now he wouldn't have to explain why she didn't have a change of clothes with her. A win-win.

She'd washed off the mascara that'd smudged around her eyes in the night, so pretty, even without makeup. Her hair was set in a loose braid draped over her right shoulder. She looked so much softer and more approachable than her ultra-serious professional business portrait on the website. Who was the real Kira?

"Come," Dad said, motioning to the table with a spatula. "Sit down and eat before it gets cold."

"Wow." Kira took the chair across from him. "This looks delicious."

"I was hoping you weren't one of those 'just coffee for breakfast' types." Dad sat down between them. "Dig in." He handed the spatula to Kira. "Don't be shy."

Derrick watched as she served herself a small helping of eggs and one strip of bacon, wondering if she *was* one of those 'just coffee for breakfast' types. Speaking of which. "Can I pour you a cup of coffee? From the pot both my dad and I are drinking out of?" He added that last part because it was obvious she didn't trust him. Really, why should she?

"I'd love a cup." She offered him a sweet albeit fake smile. "With a splash of milk from the same container you and your father are using," she added, giving it right back to him. He kind of liked that.

"Well, I gotta hand it to you, boy," Dad said. "Whatever you said to that evil Peniglatt woman at the insurance company, really worked."

Derrick swung around and cautioned, "Dad. Kira

doesn't want to hear about your problems with the insurance company."

The topic of discussion, who sat ramrod straight at the moment, placed her napkin in her lap somewhat stiffly. "On the contrary," she said, looking straight at him in challenge. "I'd like to hear whatever your dad has to say."

Why had he traveled down to the city yesterday? Why had he brought Kira home with him? Why? Why? Why? Derrick hurried back to the table, determined to change the subject.

"My wife, Daisy, had a stroke, you see," Dad said as he loaded his plate with eggs and bacon.

"How is Mom doing this morning," Derrick asked. "Last I checked she was sleeping."

"I walked her to the bathroom earlier." Dad looked at Kira. "She's weak and gets real tired real easy. So she went back to sleep after. Which reminds me." He turned his head to Derrick. "We're getting a shipment of medical equipment this morning. So eat up quick. We may have to move some furniture around."

"Medical equipment?" Derrick asked Kira.

But Dad answered. "Like I was saying, after you let that insurance company witch have it, she got right on the ball and sent out a new nurse from a different agency to visit your mama late yesterday afternoon. A real good one. Stayed for over an hour."

Derrick looked at Kira.

"You must have given it to her but good," she said, staring straight at Derrick as she leaned back in her chair and crossed her arms over her chest.

"It's him being a doctor," Dad said around a mouthful of eggs. "Them insurance company types stand up and listen when a doctor starts talking."

"That must have been it." Kira shifted in her seat, reaching for her glass to take a sip of orange juice. "She couldn't possibly have investigated the situation, identified a problem and fixed it." She leaned in Derrick's direction. "You're a hero." Her words dripped with sarcasm…which apparently his dad missed.

"Yes he is," Dad said proudly. "Took on that heartless beast and won."

Derrick wanted to crawl under the table and become one with the floorboards.

If a stare could actually burn a hole in someone's head, Derrick would have one right between the eyes, courtesy of Miss Kira Peniglatt.

"Dad—" Derrick started, prepared to explain everything.

"Don't you 'Dad' me." Dad turned to Kira. "He is a hero. He saves lives. Lots of 'em. He's a good man who knows how to treat a woman right. Taught him how myself, I did." Dad actually puffed out his chest. Then he pointed at Kira with his fork. "He's a good catch. Any woman would be lucky to have him."

"So lucky," Kira repeated with a smirk.

Derrick lost his appetite. "Stop it, Dad. I don't need a matchmaker." All he needed was to survive this morning without Dad finding out Kira's true identity, tolerate her long enough to get her home safely, and then get back to his normal, uneventful life, where he was in control of things…at least where he used to be in control of things.

When someone knocked on the door, Derrick jumped up to answer, happy beyond belief to escape the breakfast table.

The next two hours flew by in a whirl of activity as two deliverymen from the durable medical equipment company showed up. Kira took control, ordering around four grown men with the effectiveness of a five star general. No one dared question her.

The woman was a sight to behold, in her element, knowledgeable, efficient and concise. Damn he needed someone like her in his office someone to take charge and get things running smoothly.

"She's really something," Dad said, blotting his brow with his ever present cotton handkerchief.

"Yes she is." Derrick watched her take on a man who outweighed her by at least two hundred pounds, refusing to accept a wheelchair because one of the wheel brakes didn't work to her satisfaction. "We need a replacement before the end of the day," she said.

"Sure thing, Kira," the man said, respect evident in his tone.

"I'll be calling Al on Monday to let him know how hard you both worked today and how accommodating you were." With a twenty dollar incentive for each of them, the deliverymen helped Derrick move the couches, a bed, a TV stand plus TV, and an old shelving unit packed with knickknacks so his father didn't have to do any heavy lifting. And Kira had gotten right in there to help, boxing up papers, sweeping up dust from the old wood floors after the furniture was moved, and making up the big hospital bed now sitting in the living room.

"Who's Al?" Dad asked.

"I have no idea."

"You didn't tell me she was a nurse."

A damn good one at that, an amazing one, actually. When Dad balked about them putting the hospital bed in the living room rather than in an upstairs bedroom, Kira spoke calmly and convincingly, warning him of the safety hazard of having Mom in an upstairs bedroom when she couldn't walk or manage stairs on her own. How would he get her out of the house if there was a fire? She pointed out having Mom on the main level of the house would mean less trips up and down the stairs to alleviate Dad's knee and hip discomfort. Derrick didn't even know Dad was having knee and hip discomfort.

When Dad groused about him and Mom having to sleep in separate beds in separate rooms Kira reminded him that it wasn't forever, then she demonstrated the benefits of raising and lowering an electronic bed to help alleviate the strain on Dad's back when he cared for Mom. She pointed out the positives of a more stimulating environment where Mom could watch television, visit with friends, and be with Dad while he performed his daily activities rather than being hidden away in a lonely bedroom for hours at a time. And she suggested moving one of the twin beds from upstairs down to the living room so Mom and Dad could sleep together, in the same room at least.

Dad balked at a wheelchair. He wanted his wife up and walking around so she could get stronger. Kira told him to only use the wheelchair when he could tell Mom was tired. To help her get to the small bathroom off the kitchen or out to the porch for some fresh air.

The woman was a master.

"I got an aide coming on Monday," Dad said. "Three hours a day, five days a week. She's mostly to help with exercises and therapy stuff, but the home care nurse said while she's here the aide can help your mom learn to bathe and dress herself."

"Why didn't you tell me any of this yesterday?" It would have saved Derrick a lot of time and effort.

"Didn't want to bother you at work, I figured I'd tell you when you got here."

Kira closed the door behind the deliverymen and handed Dad some paperwork. "They'll be back at some point this afternoon with a new wheelchair. The raised toilet seat has been installed in the bathroom off of the kitchen, but can be moved at any time. The commode chair by the bed is only for emergencies. There's a tub chair in the bathroom down here so Daisy can wash up at the sink. It can also be used in the tub upstairs when she gets a more thorough bath or is ready to start showering. You own all three of them. There's a sticker on the footboard of the bed. When you no longer need the wheelchair and hospital bed, just call the number and the company will return to pick them up."

"I could hug you," Dad told Kira.

"Go ahead." She held open her arms and smiled.

"Thank you," he said, hugging her tightly. "Thank you, so…much."

Over Dad's shoulder Kira's eyes met his before she quickly looked away. "You're very welcome. But it's not me you should be thanking. Miss Peniglatt got you what you need. Maybe you should give her a call to thank *her*."

"No way in hell," Dad said, stepping back. "She only done it because Derrick made her."

Not true.

"Bet it made her good and mad, too." Dad smiled. "Wish I could have been there to see it."

Derrick needed to come clean, to tell his dad the truth. But just as he was about to, a bell rang from upstairs. Dad's face brightened. "Your mama's awake." With the sole focus of getting to her, he immediately turned his back on both of them and headed for the stairs.

Kira stood there looking unsure of what to do. "See. I told you, he hates me."

"He may dislike Miss Peniglatt from We Care Health Care." Hate was such a strong word. "But he adores Kira the nurse who has been such a big help today. I can't thank you enough."

"We're the same person." Kira ignored his thanks, seeming truly bothered by what his father thought of her.

"But he doesn't know you're the same person." Not yet, anyway. At some point Derrick would tell him. Just not with her present. Dad could be…unpredictable at times. "Come upstairs and meet my mom."

Kira shook her head. "I don't think that's such a good idea. She probably hates me, too."

"Mom loves everyone. Come on." He held out his hand.

Kira stepped back.

"Do you ever visit any of the patients who receive case management services from your company?"

"I worked as a community health nurse for a year and a half before taking a job as a case manager at WCHC. I've visited plenty of patients in their homes."

"That must have been a lot of years ago. Have you visited any since? As the Director of Case Management, out in the field, following up to see how WCHC patients are faring with the services and equipment authorized?"

Kira shook her head. "Never had the time…or the opportunity."

"Well today you do."

Kira didn't respond. He had no intention of forcing her. "Hang out down here, if you like. Dad has basic cable on the TV. Remote's on the arm of his recliner." Derrick pointed. "Shower if you want."

She gave him a look that had him holding up both hands and saying, "Not that you smell or anything." Jeez. "But later on this afternoon I'd like to take you to a nice lunch." Well, as nice as they could get in these parts. "To show my appreciation for all you've done and as an apology. I misjudged you."

"There's no need to take me out to eat as a thank you for doing my job. Your mom was eligible for everything I authorized. I apologize for the fact it was not offered or recommended by the first home health care nurse to visit." Her eyes met his. "And why is it all you want to do when you're with me is eat and drink coffee?" She looked down her body. "Am I too skinny?"

Slender, yes, appealingly so. But Kira had curves in all the places he liked them. "For your information," he stared down into her eyes. "I can recall, in vivid, most enjoyable detail, the feel of your stunning body pressed up against mine last night." He lowered his voice and leaned in close to her when he added, "And straddling my lap in the car."

Kira's cheeks went pink but she maintained eye contact. Good for her.

"Trust me when I tell you," he went on. "Eating and drinking coffee are not the *only* things I want to do with you." He gave her a look to let her know exactly what he was thinking.

"Yes, well." Rather than meet his eyes she looked down, wiping some dust from her left thigh. "Now that I know who you really are, *that's* not going to happen."

"Why not?" he asked, even though he already knew the answer.

She looked straight at him. "Because you're the family member of a patient receiving case management services from a member of my staff. It's a conflict of interest and would be highly unprofessional."

Yes to both. Yet he couldn't let it drop. "But you want to," he said, watching her, needing to know for certain that her attraction to him last night was not solely the result of alcohol lowering her inhibitions.

She glanced away…hesitated…a surefire affirmative response as far as he was concerned. Yes! But before he could do anything about it, Dad called down, "Don't keep your mother waiting. She wants to see you."

"We're coming," Kira called back, hurrying toward the stairs.

Derrick watched the sway of her hips and the movement of her tight, round, sexy ass.

"Those pants, on a woman with your figure, should be illegal."

She glanced back at him with a sexy grin then took the stairs two at a time.

CHAPTER FIVE

KIRA FOLLOWED THE sound of Mr. Limone's voice to a bedroom at the end of the hallway, stopping in the doorway at the sight of him sitting on his wife's side of their full-sized bed, leaning down to kiss her on the forehead, carefully, lovingly. Kira's heart squeezed as she remembered her dad kissing her mom like that, years ago, after making her breakfast in bed for her birthday, a few months before he'd issued his ultimatum and then walked out when he didn't like Mom's choice. Back when Kira used to dream about someday finding a man who loved her as much as Dad loved Mom. Back when she'd believed in happily-ever-after and until-death-do-us-part.

"Still in love after fifty-four years of marriage," Derrick said quietly from behind her.

It was truly a beautiful scene.

Mr. Limone noticed them. "Come in." He stood. "Meet Daisy." He motioned to his wife.

Derrick skirted around her and entered the room.

Upon seeing him Daisy gave a lopsided smile due to a right-sided facial droop from her stroke, most likely. Then she started to cry.

"Don't cry, Mom," Derrick said, hurrying to the bed.

Daisy reached up to hug him with her left arm. Kira

noticed she tried to lift her right arm too, but that was the side affected by the stroke so the arm barely made if off the bed and it swayed awkwardly.

Derrick dropped to his knees by the side of the bed and Daisy hugged her son tightly with her good arm. "L-l-love," she said. "Love. Love."

"I love you, too, Mom."

Kira could hear the love in both of their voices. While she told her mother she loved her often, Kira couldn't remember the last time she'd said it back. They both had lost so much as a result of the attack.

"There's someone I want you to meet," Derrick said, bringing Kira's attention back to her present location.

She approached the bed. "Good morning, Mrs. Limone," she said formally, reaching down to squeeze her left hand. "So nice to meet you."

Daisy's eyes shifted from Kira to Derrick then back to Kira. "Day," she said, looking frustrated. "Dayyyy."

"She wants you to call her Daisy," Mr. Limone said, as if Kira couldn't figure that out. But she liked that he jumped in to help his wife communicate, although he'd have to stop doing that and let Daisy struggle to get the words out if he wanted her speech to improve. The therapist would go over that with him.

"Nice to meet you, Daisy." Kira tried to pull her hand back but Daisy held on tightly, her eyes once again moving from Kira to Derrick, back to Kira then back to Derrick, as if wondering what was going on between the two of them. "I'm a friend," Kira said, using the loosest definition of the word. "Just a friend."

Even without full movement of her facial musculature, Kira could read the disappointment on Daisy's face.

Derrick stood up. "Since I'm here, I'll be the one helping you get washed and dressed this morning."

Daisy released Kira, moved her hand with amazing speed, and jerked the bed covers up to her neck. "Noooo," she said loudly and succinctly.

Expressive aphasia aside, Daisy Limone made her opinions known.

"Please, Mom," Derrick tried to argue. "I want to help."

But Daisy wouldn't budge. "No." She made an angry face. "Noooooooooo."

Mr. Limone let out a weary, exhausted breath. "It's okay. I'll do it."

He looked drained. So Kira decided to offer up her services. Dropping to her knees beside the bed she said, "In addition to being a friend of your son's, I'm also a nurse." Daisy watched her quietly. "I have lots of experience helping women get washed up and dressed. If it's okay with you, I'm happy to help you today."

"That's not necessary," Derrick said. "I *want* to do it."

As a nurse, Kira understood both sides. She stood and turned to Derrick, speaking quietly. "I know you do. But there are some things a mother doesn't want her son to see."

Derrick nodded in understanding.

Kira turned back to the bed. "Your husband has been working hard since you came home."

Daisy's eye filled with tears as she nodded.

"He deserves a day off, don't you think?"

Daisy glanced at her husband with love, then turned back to Kira and nodded.

"I'm happy to help if you'll let me."

Daisy reached for Kira's hand and squeezed. "Love," she said.

Kira understood that was her way of expressing appreciation. "You're welcome."

The next hour spent with Daisy, helping her to wash up at the sink, washing her hair, then putting on some lipstick after she'd helped her dress, reminded Kira of why she'd become a nurse. To help people and to make a difference in their lives. As much as it pained her to admit it, after years of doing it day in and day out, caring for Mom felt like a chore. She didn't appreciate all that Kira did, her condition would never improve unless by some miracle of medicine the effects of a severe brain injury could be reversed.

"What do you think?" Kira stood behind Daisy, supporting her with the gait belt around her waist, as she looked in the full length mirror behind the door.

"Love," Daisy said, looking at herself with joy. Then her gaze shifted to Kira's and her expression changed. "Love," Daisy said, starting to tear up.

"You're very welcome. Now let's get you—"

Someone knocked on the door.

Kira helped Daisy move back. "Come in."

Derrick started to walk in then stopped in his tracks the look on his face making her wet clothing and sore back totally worth it. "What do you think?"

"I think…" He swallowed. "I think you look beautiful, Mom. Like the stroke never happened."

But the stroke had happened.

Daisy reached up to cup his cheek with her left hand.

"She's tired," Kira said to Derrick. "Daisy, do you want Derrick to carry you downstairs now or would you rather nap up here?"

Daisy took an eager step toward Derrick. He reached out to steady her.

Kira smiled. "Well, all righty then."

"Hold on. I need to talk to Kira for a minute. Grab that chair," he pointed to a wooden armchair in the corner of the room that had a bunch of male clothing draped over it. "Just throw those on the bed."

Kira did just that.

With Daisy seated, and propped with a pillow to keep her in place, Kira joined Derrick in the hallway.

"The sheriff's at the door asking to see you."

"Me?" Kira pushed some loose hairs off of her face and behind her ear. "Why?"

"He wouldn't say." Derrick looked at her accusingly.

"Well I didn't call him."

Why would the sheriff come here looking for her? Kira wondered as she hurried down the hallway and down the stairs. No one knew where she was. Seeing no one in the living room or kitchen, Kira hurried outside, where Derrick's dad stood, talking with the sheriff—a very large, very serious, very imposing man in full uniform—at the base of the porch steps. When he spotted her he asked, "Are you Kira Peniglatt?"

"Yes, officer," she answered as Mr. Limone shook his head unhappily, turned, and walked back into the house without sparing her a glance. Well she couldn't worry about him right now. "Is there a problem?"

"You tell me," he answered, studying her. "My office received a panicked phone call from a woman named," he pulled a pad out of his breast pocket and flipped to a page, "Connie, who's worried you were kidnapped and you're being held here against your will."

Kira smiled. Gotta love Connie. "I'm fine, Officer."

He looked over Kira's shoulder. She turned to see Derrick standing on the porch.

"So you weren't kidnapped?" the sheriff asked.

"No. I wasn't kidnapped." Not technically. "If Connie was worried, why didn't she just call my cell?" Kira pulled it out of the waistband of her leggings to check the screen. Almost fully charged. No messages.

"That's not going to do you any good around here," the sheriff said.

What? "Why not?"

Derrick came to stand beside her. "No cell service," he said matter-of-factly.

Wait. "What?" Kira's chest went tight and her heart started to pound. No, no, no. Her hand drifted up to her sternum. "No cell service?" She looked at the phone again. Closer this time. "That can't be. This is New York State. Everyone has cell service." But it could, in fact, be. And it was.

Kira's throat felt clogged with something big and uncomfortable.

"Welcome to the north country," Derrick said. "Hey." He bent to catch her gaze. "No worries. Use the phone in the kitchen to call her."

"No worries?" she asked, panic rising, pressure building in her head. "No worries?!" she yelled. "I'm on call this weekend. Being out of the city is no big deal, but I am required to be accessible by phone."

"On call? Why didn't you tell me?" Derrick asked.

"Why should I have to tell you? I charged my phone in your bedroom while we ate breakfast. I've been carrying it around with me all morning." She looked at the screen again. This could not be happening, not now, not after Mr. Jeffries had put her on probation yesterday afternoon.

"If you would have told me I would have told you we don't get cell service in this area."

The sheriff offered, "Some people can get a signal over in the library parking lot."

A lot of good that did Kira. "I need to make a call." She turned and ran up the porch steps.

"Your friend's waiting. Said to call her first," the sheriff called out. "Some big problem with one of your patients at work."

Of course there was. Of course the one weekend Kira didn't have cell service there would be a problem with one of her patients. When she reached the porch she stopped long enough to glance back and say, "Thank you for coming out, Sheriff. I'm sorry to have wasted your time. As you can see, I'm fine." Except for the fact she'd likely be unemployed come Monday. Mr. Jeffries had been looking for a reason to fire her for months. Unbeknownst to her, she'd just given him one.

Back inside the house Kira ran to the kitchen.

"Everything okay, *Miz Peniglatt*?" Derrick's dad asked.

Kira did not like his tone and she stopped long enough to tell him so. "Look, if you have a problem with my being here, take it up with your son. I assure you, while I am here of my own free will...now," she glared at Derrick who'd followed her in, "it was not my idea to bring me up here, and had I been included in the decision making, I would not have come. Now, I need to use your phone." She turned, added, "Please," and hurried into the kitchen, picked up the black wall-mounted phone and dialed Connie's cell phone number from memory.

She answered on the first ring. "Did you find her? Is she okay? Did you arrest that scum-sucking sonofabitch and throw him in jail?"

"I'm fine," Kira said, smiling. Only Connie could get her to smile at a time like this.

"Kira!" Connie screamed. "It's you! Oh, thank God, it's you! And you're fine! I have been scared out of my mind! When I couldn't find you on my Find My Friends App this morning I figured no biggie. You were probably too busy having spectacular sex to charge your phone last night, which hey, yay for you. But how would you do on call with a dead phone? So I figured maybe you'd gone home and were using your landline."

"Please tell me you didn't call my sister." This was getting worse by the second.

"What did you expect me to do? My best friend left the bar with a man neither of us knew, at least at the time I didn't know I knew him. Well, kind of knew him. When I couldn't reach you on your cell phone, I brought up the picture I took of Derrick's driver's license to get his address so I could look up his home phone number. That's when I recognized his full name. Do you know who he is?"

"Yes."

"No friggin' way! Did you know who he was last night when you were hanging all over him?"

Don't remind me. "No. He told me this morning. How did you figure out he brought me up to his parents' house?"

"Uh…"

"What?"

"I didn't know for sure so I sent police to his home address in White Plains first."

"You didn't."

"Sure did. His old neighbor said he didn't live there anymore but he'd talked to Derrick and he'd mentioned visiting his parents this weekend. So I logged into your work computer remotely to get Daisy Limone's address."

"Connie! You're not supposed to have that log in!"

"Well I do." Kira could almost see the stubborn look

on her assistant's face. "A good assistant needs to be prepared for anything."

Couldn't argue with that logic. Kira let out a breath. "Thank you for tracking me down."

"So," Connie said. "Did you...?"

"No. You need to call my sister and tell her you found me and I'm okay."

"No? All this trouble and you didn't—"

"No."

"Well, damn."

Yeah.

"Did you hear me?" Kira asked.

"Yes I heard you. But honestly, Krissy didn't sound all that worried. Said something like, "Kira can take care of herself," that was it."

Sounded like Krissy. She didn't worry about much, mostly because Kira took care of herself and everything having to do with their mother which allowed Krissy to live the carefree life she'd enjoyed since they were kids, only worrying about herself. Maybe she should tell Connie not to call Krissy, leave her to wonder, give her the opportunity to picture life without Kira in it.

"What's going on at work?" Kira asked.

Talkative Connie stayed quiet.

Not good. "Tell me."

"Sheila freaked when she found out you reassigned Daisy Limone to another case manager."

Kira squeezed the bridge of her nose. She'd hoped she could wait until Monday to deal with that. "How did she find out?"

"The agency she'd referred the case to initially left a message that you'd taken back the referral."

"There's something shady going on there, Con." Kira

planned to get to work very early on Monday morning to review all of Sheila's cases.

"I don't doubt it."

"Is there really a problem with one of our patients or is Sheila just making trouble?"

"I don't know. For whatever reason, she said she's been trying to get in touch with you and couldn't reach you. So of course she called—"

"Mr. Jeffries," Kira finished, the mere mention of the man's name causing a twinge of discomfort in her chest.

"Her boyfriend."

"We don't know that for certain." But most everyone in the office suspected. If the last CEO, the one who'd promoted Kira, hadn't been in his seventies and happily married, Sheila would have probably tried to seduce him for a promotion, too. She was just that type of person.

"How do you think she knows how to get in touch with him outside of work?" Connie asked. "Do all the case managers have his private phone number?"

No. They didn't. "How did you find out what's going on?"

"Mr. Jeffries called Alison to cover your on call for the rest of the weekend. She called me to see if everything was okay."

Alison, the Director of Utilization Review, a nice enough woman, but rigid and by the book. Also a nurse, she and Kira split administrative night and weekend call duty. Since Alison had a husband and two young children, the split was around Kira: eighty percent of the time and Alison: the leftover twenty percent, which wasn't such a big deal because usually on call duty was very quiet, more of a formality than a necessity.

Kira leaned her shoulder against the wall and twisted

the curly black phone cord around her fingers. "This is bad."

"Yup."

"Sorry."

"For what?"

"For making you worry," Kira said. "For giving Mr. Jeffries a reason to fire me so he can finally promote Sheila, which means come next week you'll likely be working for her."

"No way in hell that is going to happen. I'll quit."

Connie needed her job just as much as Kira did. "Let's not get ahead of ourselves. Maybe it's not as bad as it seems."

"Right," Connie said, trying to sound positive, un-convincingly so. "He can't fire you for one mistake."

No, technically he couldn't. But according to Mr. Jeffries, she'd been making lots of 'mistakes' lately. In his mind a 'mistake' consisted of any course of action he did not agree with. And he'd been sure to document each infraction. Forget the fact he wasn't a registered nurse and had no training in case management. "I'm going to have to call him."

"Or," Connie countered. "I won't tell anyone I tracked you down and you can show up to work Monday morn-ing like nothing happened. What? You couldn't reach me? Why in the world not? I had my cell phone with me the whole time."

Kira smiled again. "Nice try."

"Waiting might give him a chance to cool down."

Probably not. "You really believe that?"

Connie didn't answer right away. "Look, he's going to yell at you either way, so why not enjoy a weekend completely off duty and deal with all this on Monday?"

Connie said. "I have this number in my phone now in case I need you. When are you coming home?"

Kira glanced into the living room to see Derrick standing by Daisy's hospital bed, holding her hand, talking quietly. He was so gentle with her, so caring, such a good son. Kira felt kind of bad for being so hard on him.

"Probably tonight." Although with Krissy home and on call no longer her responsibility, Kira saw no reason to rush. Seeing how much Derrick's mom and dad were enjoying his company, she hated to be the reason he cut his visit short. "Maybe tomorrow." If she could find a local motel, since Mr. Limone would likely kick her out of the house now that he knew who she was. And if Krissy was willing to stay with Mom, two days in a row was asking a lot. "Don't bother calling Krissy. I'll give her a call now."

Then she'd call Mr. Jeffries.

CHAPTER SIX

AFTER HER CONVERSATION with Connie, Kira called her sister, Krissy.

Derrick tried not to eavesdrop, really he did. But Mom and Dad lived in a small house, the living room, where the three of them were, opened into the kitchen which held the only house phone on this level, and Kira was yelling.

"And you thought now would be a good time to tell me? Over the phone?" He could hear the frustration in her voice. "On Monday? So soon?" She went quiet for a few seconds. "So that's why you came home." The frustration in her voice turned to disappointment. "I should have known it wasn't to see me or Mom." After another few seconds she said, "Tomorrow...yes, tomorrow," she added. "I'm sorry if that means you can't hang out with your friends." She didn't sound at all sorry. "Welcome to my world." Then she lowered her voice and said a few things he couldn't make out before hanging up the phone.

"You hungry?" Derrick asked his mom, looking for an excuse to go into the kitchen to check on Kira, to start making amends.

Mom shook her head to indicate 'no.'

Out of the corner of his eyes he saw Kira staring at

the phone as if deep in thought. Then, with a swift inhalation followed by a slow, measured exhalation she stood tall, picked up the receiver and dialed another number.

"Hello, Mr. Jeffries, it's Kira," she said. "I'm so sorry—" she dropped her head forward and reached up to pinch the bridge of her nose. "Yes, sir. I know, sir. If you'd just let me explain." She stood quietly, listening. "Yes, sir. Your office, first thing on Monday morning. See you th—"

Apparently Mr. Jeffries didn't let her finish. The man was an ass. So was Derrick. By thinking only of himself and his need to get up to see his parents, he'd gotten Kira into trouble with her boss. After all she'd done for them.

When she emerged from the kitchen she walked through the living room right up the stairs, without saying a word. Derrick started after her.

"Don't." Dad grabbed his arm.

"You heard what just happened." Derrick tried to pull away.

"Have to be deaf not to." Dad looked up at him. "Fifty-four years of marriage have taught me a few things." Derrick stopped to listen so Dad released his hold. "When a woman's all fired up, especially if you're the one who got her that way, you need to give her some time alone to cool down."

Derrick looked upstairs, waiting, wondering, expecting Kira to appear at any minute, her bags and shoes in hand, demanding to be taken home. Dread filled his belly at the thought of four tension-filled hours cooped up in a car with her, especially when she had every right to be pissed at him.

Her sneakers came into view first. The rest of her

followed. She'd put her hair up into a high ponytail and added an armband above her left elbow to hold her iPhone which was attached to the white earbuds in her ears. Without looking at anyone she said, "I need to go for a run," and walked right out of the house.

Once again, Derrick started to follow.

"Leave her be," Dad said.

"She doesn't know her way around, GPS won't work."

"Town's not that big," was all Dad said.

True. But still.

Derrick hurried to the door in time to see Kira take off at a fast pace, her form excellent. Based on her physique, she jogged a lot. He watched for as long as he could, before she turned right at the end of the road and disappeared from view.

Over the next few hours, Derrick busied himself by doing laundry, helping Mom with her exercises, and then occupying her so Dad could get out for a much needed haircut in town and a few hands of cards at the firehouse. By three o'clock, though, he was done waiting for Kira to return. She could have pulled a muscle or cramped up or been hit by a car. She could be lost or injured and waiting for him to come find her.

"I'm going after her." Derrick stood.

"About time." Dad looked up from reading the newspaper he'd gotten while in town.

"About time? You're the one who told me not to go after her right away."

"Wait too long and a woman'll start thinking crazy stuff and creating problems that don't exist."

Unbelievable. "It would have been nice if you'd shared that important bit of information a little bit earlier, don't you think?" Derrick grabbed his car keys and left.

A new coffee shop had opened on Main Street about

two blocks down from a dollar store and six blocks before a fancy gas station/convenience mart. Growing up, Derrick couldn't wait to get out of this town. Now, he felt a tug of longing for the slower pace and peaceful quiet of small-town life. "Hey, Mr. Harvey." Derrick waved out his car window. The owner of the local hardware store had to be pushing ninety years old, yet there he stood, sweeping the sidewalk out in front of his store.

His old employer waved back, although Derrick got the impression he had no idea who he was waving to. After scanning the sidewalks and benches all through town, the playground at his old elementary school, and the track behind the high school, he took a right toward the park...and spotted Kira, lying on her back under a big old weeping willow tree, her legs crossed at the ankles, both hands up behind her head.

He pulled into a parking spot, shut down the engine, and climbed out of his car.

Kira rolled onto her elbow. Seeing him, she rolled right back into the position she'd been in when he'd first spotted her without so much as a wave or a smile or any sign of welcome.

He approached anyway, on guard, not sure what to expect.

"It's so peaceful here," she said, keeping her eyes closed. "I've just managed to calm myself down. Please don't ruin it."

Without saying a word he lied down next to her, assuming the same position, only eyes opened so he could watch the fluffy white clouds floating along the beautiful blue sky. He inhaled a lungful of fresh country air tinged with the scent of fresh cut grass. When was the last time he'd laid in the grass, looking up at the sky?

When was the last time he took a few minutes to appreciate a beautiful day?

He couldn't remember. Long hours at medical school and now work, both leading to exhaustion, kept him mostly indoors. His present life was so different from his life as a child, so cluttered with responsibilities, so lacking in time to relax and enjoy life.

"If I'd grown up in a place like this," she said quietly. "I never would have left."

"Trust me," he turned to face her. "If you'd grown up in this town you'd have been counting the days until you could get out same as I did." She kept her eyes closed, her pretty face turned up toward the sky. Derrick continued, talking and watching her. "After I graduated high school I couldn't pack up and get out of here quick enough. I'd even signed up to take summer classes at college. I'd told my parents it was so I could get ahead, before the fall semester started. But really, I couldn't stand the thought of another boring summer working two jobs, swimming in the same lake, playing in the same baseball league, going to the same drive-in movie place, eating the same boring burgers at the only diner in town." He closed his eyes, remembering. "Now... those are some of my happiest memories."

"I grew up in New York City, went to college there, work there, and live there." She inhaled deeply then exhaled. "It's not often I get to enjoy the fresh air and peace and quiet of a perfect summer day all by myself."

"You must get away on vacations."

She slid him a glance. "Nope. Mom does best when she sticks to her routine, when she's surrounded by what's familiar. And I can't afford what round the clock care would cost on top of vacation expenses."

Derrick rolled onto his side and pushed up onto his

elbow. "If you don't mind me asking, why does she need round the clock care?"

"Not care as much as supervision, assistance, and direction," Kira clarified, without answering his question.

So he asked again. "Why?"

"Severe traumatic brain injury and all that goes with it, memory loss, mood swings and unpredictable behavior. She's ambulatory, but with assistance."

"How'd it happen?"

She bent one leg at the knee and started rocking it from side to side. "I'd agreed to babysit my cousin, but I had a huge test the next day. I was all stressed out. Mom said she'd babysit in my place. She was attacked on her way home."

My God. "How long ago?"

"I'd just turned eighteen so twelve years ago."

Which meant her mother was most likely as good as she was going to get recovery wise.

Kira blew out a breath. "If it's okay with you, can we not talk about my mother? I'd like to go back to enjoying this beautiful day and pretending I don't have a care in the world."

Derrick wanted to know more. "What about your father?" Why did care for her mother fall all on Kira?

She closed her eyes and turned away. "Dad left when I was fourteen, Krissy was only ten. My mom was the most caring woman I knew. She looked out for everyone in the family, aunts, uncles and cousins included. If she could do something to help, she would." Kira smiled. "Or she'd send me." She turned back and opened her eyes. "Dad didn't like sharing her, but he put up with it until my grandmother had a stroke and Mom wanted to move her into our condo. Dad had a fit, said she belonged in a nursing home. Mom insisted, like she always did, "Family takes care of family." Dad issued an ultimatum. "It's your mother or me." Mom cried and pleaded, but in the end, Grandma had no one else, so Mom chose her." Kira swatted at a fly that'd landed on her forehead. "Dad packed up and left that night."

"That sucks."

Kira shrugged. "He set up very generous college accounts for my sister and me, and had his attorney send a check every month until Krissy turned eighteen."

"What about after your mom's injury?"

"Not a word, which was fine by me. I was eighteen, legal age to assume responsibility for my sister and my mother. We didn't need him."

Derrick said the only thing he could think to say. "I'm sorry." She'd been through so much at such a young age yet had managed to finish college and attend graduate school to earn not one but two masters' degrees, with no support and encouragement from loving parents, like he'd had. And while having to care for her mother and her sister. She was one strong, determined, and admirable woman.

"I'm sorry, too," she said. "He was a great dad up until he left. And my mom was a great mom. Even though she's still my mom she's not my mom like she used to be my mom...if that makes any sense."

It made perfect sense. Derrick reached over, took Kira's hand into his and held it.

And she let him.

For the next few minutes, they laid just like that, side by side, hand in hand, listening to random birds and someone hammering off in the distance. A light breeze blew past, the tree's long, graceful branches swayed back and forth, shading them from the sun. Derrick couldn't remember a more perfect late summer day, or feeling so comfortable just doing nothing with a woman.

Kira let out a sigh.

"You okay?" he asked.

"I will be," she answered.

"Do you want me to talk to your boss, to explain what happened?" He would, in a heartbeat, regardless of any possible consequences. Kira didn't deserve to suffer because of his actions.

"No." She went up onto her elbows. "I'll handle it."

Like she handled everything, he was sure, on her own. "But you shouldn't have to."

"Regardless."

"I'm sorry," he said, again. Never had he meant an apology as much as he'd meant that one.

"I know." She plopped down on her back, bending her knees, her sneakers planted on the grass.

They laid in companionable silence some more until Kira blurted out, "On top of everything else I've got going on, my sister has decided now is a good time to have a baby."

A decision Kira did not sound happy about. "Just like that? Is she married?" Not that marriage was a requirement or anything.

"Married? I don't even think she has a steady boyfriend. But I don't see her enough to know for sure."

Derrick did the math. "She must be around twenty-six years old which is old enough for her to do what she wants."

"You don't get it." Kira sat all the way up, crossing her legs, yanking on a blade of grass. "When she was nine, Krissy won a fish at a carnival in Central Park. I wound up feeding it and changing the water. When she was thirteen, Krissy insisted she was responsible enough to take care of a cat. I wound up putting out fresh food and changing the litter box. Two guesses who that damn cat still lives with." Kira pointed at her chest. "Me."

"In high school," she went on, "when the novelty of a particular boyfriend wore off and Krissy got bored, she dumped him, no warning, no negotiation, done, goodbye, moving on."

Derrick felt compelled to point out, "High school was a lot of years ago. You said yourself you don't see her that often. Maybe she's changed."

"Maybe," Kira said.

"Probably," Derrick added.

Kira glared at him. "Whose side are you on?"

He smiled. "Your side, of course. I'm just—"

"Well don't." Kira wiped dead grass from her leggings. "You stick to dealing with your family and I'll worry about mine." Kira looked off in the direction of Main Street. "You know what this town is missing?"

Derrick laughed. "Do you have any idea how long it'll take me to answer that?"

Kira smiled. God she was even prettier when she smiled. "A motel."

Funny that's the only thing she'd noticed. Wait a minute. "Why do you sound like you need one?"

"I'm no longer on call and Krissy—who I have no desire to see right now—is with my mother so there's no need for me to be back to the city today. If there was a motel in town, you could spend the evening with your parents and I could spend the night blissfully alone in my very own room."

Derrick hated the idea of her spending the night all alone in a motel room. "Don't be ridiculous. You'll stay at the house."

"Your dad doesn't want me there."

Derrick sat up too. "Then why did he tell me to pick up some steaks and whatever you want him to grill you for dinner, on our way home?"

She shrugged. "That was nice of him. But I really don't have it in me to listen to how great you are and how horrible I am."

"I told him everything, Kira."

Her eyes went wide. "Everything, everything?"

He smiled. "Okay, not *everything*. But how you wouldn't talk with me until I got the HIPPA form signed and after I got it I wasn't able to reach you so I drove down to your office and so on."

"What did he say?"

"That he owes you an apology for the heartless beast comment."

"First time anyone's ever called me that." She looked down and pulled out another blade of grass. "At least to my face."

"I doubt he would have said that to your face if he'd known who you were." Although with his dad, he couldn't be quite sure.

"To be completely honest, I'm upset with my sister and stressed about what's going to happen on Monday when I meet with my boss. I'm really not in the mood to be pleasant company." She shook her head. "A nice long hot bath, a turkey sandwich, a chilled bottle of wine and I'm good."

Not if Derrick had any say in the matter. "You have another night all to yourself. You can do anything you want and you want to spend it alone in a motel room? That doesn't sound like fun at all."

She looked over at him. "For me it is."

"It's not what you wanted last night." Last night she'd

wanted to spend the night with him…naked. And now Derrick couldn't shake that thought from his brain.

"Well, we can't always have what we want, now can we?"

"Tonight you can," he told her, wanting to show her a good time. This woman who took care of her mom, who'd taken care of his mom and had gotten her the service and equipment she needed, who rarely had a night to herself, deserved to have at least one night of fun this weekend. Derrick was determined to see that she did. "Come back to the house. We'll have dinner. Mom and Dad go to bed early. We can go out for drinks." Two glasses of wine and three shots of Southern Comfort with lime, to be exact. "Or we can swing by the liquor store now and get hammered out back by the fire pit behind the house later on." Under the stars, like he'd done so many times as a teenager. "*That* will be fun." He looked over at her. "And tonight, if you offer, I promise I won't turn you down."

CHAPTER SEVEN

KIRA SAT AT the table in the kitchen, recalling how Derrick's dad had, in fact, apologized for his 'heartless beast' comment, the minute Kira walked into the house. Then he'd thanked her again for all she'd done earlier that morning, for getting a new home health care agency to come out to visit Daisy, and for not having his idiot son arrested for kidnapping. She smiled. Thank the good Lord Derrick hadn't shared his atrocious video of her.

"You're smiling," Derrick said from across the table.

"What? A person can't smile?" Kira speared a chunk of the potato salad they'd picked up on the way home from the park earlier, a scoop of which now rested on her plate.

"You been doing it a lot," Mr. Limone pointed out around a mouthful of steak. "Sitting there all quiet, smiling."

It was the whole family togetherness thing. The four of them, Daisy propped up in her new wheelchair, sitting around the table as Derrick shared the happenings at his new family practice, his dad shared news about his friends in town, and they both argued about incidents from Derrick's youth and whose version was the true and accurate one. Mr. Limone helped Daisy, cutting her food into tiny pieces, patiently waiting while she tried to feed herself with her left hand, assisting only when she became frustrated. At times they both sat there, not eating, simply holding hands under the table, their mutual love for each other evident. Enviable. Daisy seemed so happy to be at the table, a part of their little group, smiling her half-droopy smile, actually chuckling a time or two over the antics of her husband and son.

Kira remembered dinners with her own family, Dad's hysterical impressions of his boss, Mom encouraging good manners, each one of them taking a few minutes to share the best and worst parts of their day. Entertaining Krissy would tell jokes or recount something funny that'd happened at school. They'd all laugh. Kira had felt a part of something special. Then life had changed... and then it'd changed again.

"Hey," Derrick said, reaching over to lift her chin. "I liked it better when you were smiling."

"Sorry." Kira forced out a smile. "Everything's delicious."

"So you said already," Mr. Limone pointed out.

"Dad," Derrick cautioned. "Stop it. You promised to be nice."

Even though he'd apologized and seemed to appreciate what she'd done for Daisy, he wasn't near as warm to her as he'd been prior to finding out that Kira the nurse and Miss Peniglatt were the same person. Obviously he still thought she'd only done what she'd done because his son "the doctor" had called her.

"It's okay," she told Derrick. "He's right. I did already say that." For sure she would not be saying it again. Kira focused in on eating. The sooner she was done the sooner she could leave the table and busy herself cleaning the kitchen. That'd been the deal. They'd cook while she sat with Daisy and after dinner she would clean up.

An awkward silence fell over the table.

Kira felt awful. Her presence was ruining Derrick's time with his family.

She should have insisted he take her to a motel.

"Ouch!" Mr. Limone jerked back his right hand. "Damn it, woman. You know how I hate that."

Daisy simply stared at her plate.

Derrick smiled. "Mom rarely yells," he said.

Mr. Limone added, "But she sure as heck lets you know when she's not happy with you."

"One way she does it is with a quick, hard pinch," Derrick explained.

"Which it turns out she can do just as good with her left hand as with her right." Mr. Limone rubbed his right forearm.

Daisy gave Kira a droopy yet satisfied half-smile as she slid her left hand across the table, palm up. Kira took her hand and smiled back as Daisy gave her a tight squeeze. Kira wished she could have met this sweet woman before the stroke.

Easy as that, the mood around the table changed.

Derrick said, "She's a sneaky pincher. You never saw it coming."

"Got the boys' attention, that's for sure," Mr. Limone said. "Even when they was bigger and faster, they never ran from her."

"Because she'd only get us later on," Derrick said. "At the dinner table or just as we were about to fall asleep."

Daisy said, "Nooooooo."

"Oh, yes, you did," Derrick said, with love in his eyes. "But only when we deserved it."

Daisy nodded. "Deeeserrrrrrrr…"

Turning to look at Kira, Mr. Limone asked, "So what'd your mama do to keep you in line?"

"She'd said, "Family takes care of family."'" If Kira complained about having to watch Krissy instead of getting to play with her friends, her mother would say, "Family takes care of family." If she tried to get out of helping Aunt Bernice—who was overweight and on oxygen and moved slower than a sloth—at the grocery store her mother would say, "Family takes care of family." Mom said those words and lived by them until she no longer could. Then it was Kira's turn.

Daisy gave her hand another squeeze. Kira blinked back into the present, needing some distance from this happy family time. "I'm sorry," she said, pushing back her chair. "Please excuse me." She stood. "I, um." She looked down and met each of the three pairs of eyes staring up at her. "I'm not feeling so well." She put her hand over her stomach for effect.

"Hope it wasn't my steaks," Mr. Limone said.

"No. Of course not. Everything was delicious." She stopped, realizing what she'd just said, unable to keep from smiling.

"So you said already." Mr. Limone smiled too.

They'd come full circle.

"I'm just going to," she pointed to the stairs, "lie down for a few minutes. Call me when you're done and I'll clean up." Without waiting for a response she turned and all but ran up the stairs.

Kira had just sat down on the bed when there was a knock on the door. Derrick hadn't waited long before coming after her. She didn't answer, hoping he'd go away, embarrassed by her behavior. When had she become so inept at interacting with people face-to-face? At leaving the past where it belonged, in the past? At keeping her private life private?

The door opened. "You okay?" Derrick asked.

Such a nice guy.

"Sorry." She turned to face the doorway. "It's been a while since I've sat down to a family dinner. It brought back…" Emotion clogged her throat. She tried to clear it. "…memories." She shook her head. "I don't belong here. I think you should take me to a motel."

He walked in and sat down beside her. "I'm not taking you to a motel."

"Fine. I'll call a taxi." She hesitated. "You do have taxis in this town, right?" She couldn't recall seeing any when she'd been on her jog earlier.

He thought for a few seconds then his full, kissable lips turned into a slow, sexy smile. "Nope." He shook his head. "No taxis in this town. You're stuck here."

No she wasn't. Even if he was telling the whole truth, which she didn't believe he was, after all the time they'd spent together, she was ninety-eight percent certain if she insisted, he'd take her wherever she wanted to go. But even though she probably should leave and give Derrick uninterrupted time with his parents, she'd lied earlier. While a nice long hot bath would be lovely, Kira ate too many turkey sandwiches, drank too many chilled glasses of wine without being in the company of others, and spent too many anything but blissful hours alone…with Mom, which, most of the time, was pretty much the same as being all alone.

He leaned over and bumped her playfully with his muscular shoulder. "We'll have fun."

God Kira needed a night of fun.

And tonight, if you offer, I promise I won't turn you down.

Oh, no. She jumped off of the bed, needing some distance between her and Derrick. "Fun doing what?" She turned on him. "I have no intention of having sex with you. Last night was a one-time offer." Made to a stranger, a man she'd never see again. But one day later, Derrick knew too much about her and she knew too much about him and his family. She'd actually started to like him, damn it. Sex now would…complicate things. Emotions complicated things. And Kira's life was complicated enough.

Derrick stood, too. "We'll have fun drinking and talking, drinking and roasting marshmallows for s'mores. Then we'll play drunk horseshoes and drunk cornhole in the glow of a roaring bonfire." He walked over to where she stood, looking out the window.

"I'm sensing a theme here."

He positioned himself close behind her. "Long time ago I learned, the most boring activities turn fun when you're under the influence of alcohol."

"Good to know."

"Drunk stargazing to find the constellations."

It all sounded fun.

He stepped in even closer, pressing his front to her back, too close, and leaned down, placing his mouth close to her ear as he whispered, "Drunk sex."

She turned her head slightly, trying to see his face. "Are you saying sex with you is boring and I'll need alcohol to make it fun?"

"What?" He jerked back. "Hell no."

Such a male response. "Doesn't matter, because it's not going to happen."

He turned on the charm, leaning in close again. "I bet I can get you to offer again."

Kira wasn't sure if it was his hot, moist breath hitting an over sensitive spot or the intent of his words, but a very pleasant tingle shot through her. Even so she countered, "I bet you can't."

"If I can't," he stepped back, starring down at her, so serious, "we both lose." Then, without giving her a chance to respond, he turned and walked toward the door. "Come on. I'll help you clean the kitchen."

A few hours later, after Kira had helped Daisy with some physical therapy exercises, reviewed a pack of cue cards as part of her speech therapy, and helped her get ready for bed, she followed Derrick down the back steps into the backyard. "I don't get it," he said, carrying a heavy cooler filled with ice and booze like it was nothing. "You're so good with my mother. You obviously enjoy hands-on patient care and you're damn good at it. Watch this last step."

While the light up by the back door was on and the flames blazing in the fire pit lit up part of the large yard, there was about twenty feet of total darkness between the two.

Derrick stopped and turned, waiting for her. "Take my arm."

How gentlemanly. Shifting the old comforter he'd given her to carry into her right hand, she held on to him with the left.

"Why would you want to spend your days in an office setting," he asked. "Making difficult decisions about patients you never see, being front and center in the ongoing battle between patients and their insurance carriers?"

The answer was easy enough. "I needed something with regular hours, Monday through Friday. It's too hard to schedule aides for Mom around a changing twelve hour shift schedule or on call responsibilities where I'd have to go out and see patients. WCHC pays me good money, which I need to cover all the stuff Mom's insurance doesn't pay for." But lately she'd begun to wonder if her large salary was worth all the aggravation. "Plus I like the business side of health care."

As they got closer to the fire, when Kira could see the grass under her feet again, she let go of Derrick's arm. "Nurse case managers get a bad rap." When he stopped, she dropped the blanket next to where he'd set the cooler. Then she picked up the cloth bag holding one of the collapsible chairs Derrick must have carried out earlier when he'd made the fire, dumped it out and opened it up. "Yes, we're fiscally responsible to our employer, but we're nurses first. Our priority is seeing that our patients get the quality care they need but in a cost effective manner."

"Your company makes money by limiting the care your patients receive," Derrick said, setting up the other chair.

A common misperception, Kira sat down, reached into the cooler and took out a beer. "My company makes money when our patients remain healthy. About half of my case managers are assigned to health maintenance only, reminding patients to get their physical exams and take their medications, have their blood pressure and blood sugar levels checked on a regular basis."

She twisted off the top and handed the beer to Derrick.

He took it and sat down beside her. "Thank you."

"We want our patients to be well cared for and maintained safely in their homes. Decubiti cost money. Falls resulting in fractured hips or other injuries cost money. Injury or worsening health in the primary caregiver, whether or not that primary caregiver is our client, costs money, because if they're not able to care for the patient it usually means admission to an inpatient facility which is almost always more expensive than maintaining someone in their home." Facts she'd presented to Mr. Jeffries over and over again yet he remained focused only on the cost of care.

Derrick handed her a single serve bottle of chardonnay and a wineglass. "My mom and dad were left on their own for three days, Kira. Three days."

She felt terrible about that. "We're not perfect. We've got new management focused on cost containment above all else. I'm doing my best to correct the problems as they're brought to my attention while also trying to get my boss to understand..." She twisted the top off of the bottle and poured it into her glass. "You know what? I don't want to talk about it. You promised me a night of fun, and talking about my work is not fun."

"You're right." He held up his beer. "To a night of fun."

She tapped it with her wineglass. "To a night of fun." *And tonight, if you offer, I promise I won't turn you down.* Lord help her, she needed to stop thinking about that. Kira stared into the dancing flames. "This is my first bonfire."

"What do you think so far?"

"It's beautiful." Peaceful. Relaxing. She took a sip of wine.

"So tell me more about you," Derrick said.

"Like what? You already know about my work and my family. What else is there?"

He took a swig of beer. "First kiss."

Kira had to think. "Mattie Furlander, tenth grade, during gym class, beneath the bleachers."

"Missy Kerjohnson," Derrick said. "Sixth grade, down by the water tower."

"Sixth grade?" Kira laughed. "You sure got an early start."

Derrick smiled. "I'd started chasing after her in the fifth grade. She didn't let me catch her until the sixth."

He was so handsome in the firelight, so confident and comfortable with himself, probably never felt the need to put on airs or suck up to people, like Kira had to do on a pretty regular basis these days.

"Age when you lost your V-card?" he asked, leaning back in his chair, balancing on two legs.

"My what?"

"Your virginity."

"That's a little personal, don't you think?"

"Come on. Play along. I was fifteen. She was seventeen with a pretty easy reputation, if you know what I mean." He winked. "It happened in the backseat of her car and a guy I didn't know she'd been seeing at the time beat the crap out of me afterwards." He took another swig of beer then smiled. "But damn, it'd been worth it."

Kira threw her little wine bottle at him. Too bad it was plastic...and empty.

He caught it mid-air. Impressive reflexes. "Your turn."

Fine. "Unlike you, I waited until college. Freshman year." She took a sip of wine. "There were candles and soft music." It'd been perfect. But Danny had been looking for a fun-loving college girlfriend, not one responsible for her angry and rebellious fourteen-year-old sister and her brain-injured mother, which didn't leave much time left over for fun. So he'd dumped her, same as every other boyfriend she'd had. Same as her dad had dumped her mom. For being responsible. For taking care of her family. Lesson learned. Now Kira made it a point not to get emotionally attached to men, she glanced over at Derrick, which was easier said than done sometimes.

"Ice cream," he said. "Favorite flavor. Mine's coffee. Preferably with nuts."

Happy to move on, Kira answered, "I'm not all that particular as long as it's covered in hot fudge."

"Now we're getting somewhere." Derrick finished off his beer. "Drink up, slow poke." He pointed to her almost full glass. "We can't start the fun stuff until we've got at least one drink in us or it won't be fun."

Kira sucked down two big swallows.

"Atta girl. Favorite type of music."

"Anything that isn't rap."

"I like some country and rock. I used to play drums in a band."

Of course he did. "I used to play the cello." A loud POP came from the fire pit. Kira jumped.

"Relax, City Girl. Nothing out here's gonna hurt you. And the fire should keep the skunks away."

"The what?" Kira finished off her wine for fortification then looked around. "Skunks? For real?"

Derrick didn't address her concern for skunks. Instead he laughed and said, "Sports," as he reached into the cooler.

"I think we should talk more about skunks." Kira lifted her feet onto the chair like an idiot, as if a bite to the lower extremities was the worst a skunk could do.

"Don't worry." He leaned in and patted her knee. "I'll protect you." Then he sat back. "I played baseball throughout high school."

Based on all the trophies in his bedroom, he must have been pretty good at it.

"Debate team," Kira said, reaching into the cooler for another mini bottle of wine. "Science club. Interact." Her hand settled on a large glass bottle, not the right shape to be one of Derrick's beers. She pulled it out and held it up to the fire. "Southern Comfort?"

"There's some cut up limes in a baggie in there too." He motioned to the cooler with his beer.

"Boy, while I was working with your mom you were pretty busy."

"While I wasn't in the science club, like you, because in my school, guys got beat up for stuff like being in the science club, I like science."

Which explained the periodic table on the back of his bedroom door.

"And tonight," he continued. "I'd like to conduct an experiment."

"With Southern Comfort."

He nodded. "Last night it took two glasses of wine and three shots of Southern Comfort with lime, in under two hours, to get you to come on to me."

Wow. He'd been watching her more closely than she'd thought.

"Based on that," he said. "I've created a hypothesis."

"Oh, you have, have you?" This she had to hear.

"Yes I have. If Kira drinks two glasses of wine and three shots of Southern Comfort in under two hours, she'll come on to me again tonight."

She couldn't help but laugh. "Oh, you'd like that, wouldn't you?" To be honest, if circumstances were different, she'd like it too.

"Yes, I would," he said sincerely. "But only to prove my hypothesis."

Right. "Have you considered all the possible variables? Like tonight I have a nice big dinner in my belly while last night I'd only eaten some peanuts and pretzels. That may negatively affect the outcome of your experiment."

"But tonight," he countered, "I've got a nice romantic atmosphere on my side." He motioned to the fire pit with one hand and up to the starry sky with the other. He had a point. "Plus, you like me."

So sure of himself. "You think so?"

He smiled. "I know so."

"Well you're wrong." No he wasn't. "I can barely tolerate you," she lied, liking him a little too much.

He leaned in. "How much a woman likes me is directly proportional to the amount of alcohol she consumes."

Now it was Kira's turn to smile. "Another hypothesis?"

"A fact."

"We shall see." Kira rummaged around in the cooler to find the limes and two shot glasses.

CHAPTER EIGHT

DERRICK COULDN'T REMEMBER the last time he'd laughed so hard. For sure it had nothing to do with the two beers and two shots of Southern Comfort he'd gulped down over the last hour and a half, at least he didn't think so. "In all the hundreds of times…" he fought to catch his breath "…I've played…cornhole…" he doubled over, his forearm bracing his abdomen "…I have never…" he couldn't stop "…had a corn bag…" similar to a bean-bag, only filled with dried corn kernels "…go into the fire pit." Let alone two. The second one sizzled, same as the first. Popcorn jumped out of the blaze sending another wave of laughter through him.

"I find that hard to believe." Kira stood in the shadows, facing him, about thirty-three feet away, beside the other homemade cornhole box, which was nothing more than a rectangular box, built on an angle, with a hole toward the top. "Whose idea was it to set that other box so close to the fire?"

"It's a good six feet away." He'd purposely let her pitch toward the box closer to the fire so she could see the hole better. "You can't play at night if you can't see."

Now Kira was laughing too. "Well you can't play if all your corn bags burn up, either."

God help him, his sides were starting to ache.

"I'll have you know, I have many fine qualities," she said.

"If you do say so yourself," he teased, enjoying himself immensely.

"I *do* say so myself," she said. "But athleticism isn't one of them."

"I don't know about that. You have mighty fine form when you run." He'd enjoyed every second spent watching her earlier that day.

She waved him off. "Running doesn't require any skill."

"You have to do it without twisting an ankle or getting hit by a car," he pointed out.

"I stand corrected. I am skilled at running. But a proficiency at throwing things eludes me."

"More like a proficiency for aiming at things eludes you."

"Oh, I can aim just fine," she said. "It's the actual hitting what I'm aiming at that gives me trouble. Now go on and throw your last bag, you show-off. Let's get this over with."

He held it up. "If I make this, that's three in a row. You owe me a kiss."

She planted both hands on her hips. "I think I've been hustled."

Smart girl.

He let the third corn bag fly. Swish…right into the hole.

"You and your, 'I'm rusty. I haven't played in years,'" she mimicked him. "I never would have made that bet if I'd thought you'd actually land three in a row."

Of course she wouldn't have. "A bet is a bet." To increase his odds of success, he'd fired off a bunch of practice throws while she'd been inside with Mom. Then he'd gone out of his way to pretend to suck when they'd first started playing. Did that make him a cheat? Maybe. But a man's got to do what a man's got to do to get the girl. He wanted the girl. And she wanted him.

"It was a fair bet. If I didn't get three in a row you would have gotten out of drinking that third shot." The main reason she'd likely taken the bet.

"There was nothing fair about that bet, and you know it."

He decided to ignore that comment. "I'll let you choose. Which do you want to do first? The shot or the kiss?"

"How magnanimous of you," she said sarcastically as she walked over to him, only a little unsteadily. "I'll take the shot then maybe the kiss won't be so bad."

On his way to the cooler he smiled. Nothing easy about Kira, she was a challenge. Never thought he'd enjoy spending time with a challenging woman, which is why he typically stayed away from them. But tonight he found Ms. Kira Peniglatt damn entertaining. Must be the alcohol.

"I'll pour," she said, taking the bottle from him.

"Fine. You pour." He took out two lime wedges then set up the shot glasses on top of the cooler.

Both glasses filled he squeezed a wedge of lime into each, chose one and lifted it in a toast. "To the future."

She clicked her glass to his. "May it be better than the past." Then she tossed it back like a pro and slammed the empty on top of the cooler. "Hypothesis disproved. Two glasses of wine and three shots of Southern Comfort in under two hours and I did *not* put the moves on you."

But he hadn't kissed her yet. "Too bad," he said.

"Time for horseshoes." She turned, a little too quickly and stumbled.

"Gotcha." He caught her and hauled her close, front to front. "So here we are again." Just like last night.

"I was looking forward to horseshoes." She tried to turn in his arms, straining to look toward the horseshoe pits.

"Honey, tossing around harmless little bags of corn with you is one thing. Horseshoes are heavy. In your hands they can do some damage."

"Hey." She gave his chest a push.

"Besides, you owe me a kiss." He tilted his head toward hers. "And I mean to collect," he reached down to tilt her chin up, "right," he leaned in, "now."

The second her soft lips touched his, a massive surge of yearning flooded Derrick's system. It took total concentration to keep the kiss light, to let her take the lead, when all he wanted to do was squeeze her close, slip his tongue into her mouth, and grab her sexy-as-hell ass to hold her steady while he thrust his growing erection between her sweet thighs over and over again.

Her fingers slid into his hair, angling his head, pulling him down.

Yes. More.

She tasted sweet and tart, same as her personality.

When she pushed her tongue between his lips, he sucked it in, played with it.

His hands ached to touch her, but he didn't trust himself.

Then she pressed her beautiful body to his, wrapping her arms around his neck and Derrick let instinct take over, hugging her close, driving his tongue into her heavenly mouth, again and again, thrusting his hips, showing her how much he wanted her.

She pushed him away. "Stop."

He let her go immediately and stepped away. "I'm sorry."

"I can't." In the firelight she looked just as disappointed as he felt. "As much as I may want to, I can't."

"New rule for our night of fun," he said, gently setting his hand to her cheek. She leaned into his touch. "Tonight we can be whoever we choose to be or not to be." That sounded weird. "Does that make sense?"

Kira smiled. "Oddly enough, it does."

"Tonight I choose not to be related to anyone from the Limone family. Tonight I'm a Smith. Derrick Smith."

"But you *are* related to Daisy Limone a patient of WCHC and that's not the only reason—"

"No." He held a finger to her moist lips. "Tonight I'm Derrick Smith." He held out his hand. "And you are?"

"Stop it, Derrick."

"It's just the two of us. No one will know."

She looked up at him. "I'll know."

There you have it. He pushed out a breath. "Okay. Come on then." He pointed to the blanket. "Grab that. I'll get us each another beverage and then it's time for drunk stargazing."

She placed her hand on his forearm as he reached for the cooler. "Thank you for understanding."

He hated that, as a doctor, he understood completely. "Of course." After all, he was a nice guy. A horny, nice guy who hadn't been with a woman in months and wouldn't be getting any sex tonight, but a nice guy nonetheless.

"I saw some bottles of water in there. Please grab one for me…instead of wine."

"Sure thing." He grabbed one for himself as well.

They set up the blanket far from the fire so it'd be as dark as possible for optimal stargazing conditions. After drinking down some water, Derrick lied down on his back first, immediately spotting the Little Dipper. "First one to spot the Little Dipper gets to choose what we do next."

From where she sat beside him she turned to look down at him. In the dark, he couldn't see her expression, but he had a pretty good idea the face she'd be making at him.

"You're all about the competition, aren't you?"

"Grew up with two brothers, everything was a competition. Lay down." He patted the blanket beside his hip.

After drinking some water she did. "You've already spotted the Little Dipper, haven't you?"

He smiled, hadn't taken her long to figure him out. Once again they were lying side by side, staring up at the sky.

"Little Dipper's right there." She pointed up, tracing it with her index finger.

"The North Star." Derrick pointed skyward, same as Kira. "Big Dipper." He studied the stars, looking for, "And there's Scorpius."

"Impressive knowledge of astronomy," Kira said.

Derrick would never willingly admit how many nights he'd laid in this exact spot as a kid, alone with a flashlight and the astronomy book Mom had bought him for his eighth birthday, studying the stars.

"What is Scorpius?" She slid closer. "I don't know what I'm looking for."

He moved his right arm to make room for her. She settled in with her head resting on his shoulder, pressed in tight to his side.

"Right there." He turned a little, lowering his face close to hers so they could both look up his forearm to see where he was pointing. "You see the curve of its tail?" He traced it with his finger. "Then up and around."

"I do." She sounded excited. He liked that.

Derrick pointed out a few more stars and constellations. Kira watched with interest, or at least she pretended to be interested. He appreciated that. He loved stargazing and hadn't had the chance to do it in years. After a while they both lay there quietly. Derrick looked over to see if Kira had fallen asleep.

She turned toward him. "I know I said it before, but it's so peaceful here so beautiful. Thank you for bringing me. It's such a nice change from the city."

"You're welcome." He hugged her close. "Thank you for not completely freaking out when you woke up this morning." He dropped a gentle kiss on the top of her head. "And for not telling the sheriff I kidnapped you." He'd damn near had a heart attack when he'd seen the sheriff at the door.

She turned on her side, cuddling in close. "I've had a really nice time tonight."

So had he. "See. It's the alcohol."

"No it's not." She leaned in to kiss his cheek. "It's you...Derrick Smith."

What?

She climbed on top of him, straddling his hips, lowering her chest to his. "I've never picked up a stranger in a bar before."

Hell yeah! He was totally up for some role play. "I saw you sitting there," he slid his arms around her, "and I knew I had to have you."

"What first attracted you?" She shimmied up a little to tongue his ear.

God help him his body went hard. "Your laugh," he told her honestly.

She lifted her head and smiled down at him. "My laugh?"

"Yes." He palmed her ass. "Your bold, loud, confident laugh." He bent his knees, shifting their position, to get her right where he wanted her. "And these." He cupped her breasts, running his thumbs over her nipples, loving the way they hardened from his touch. "The way your silky blouse gave hints of their shape each time you moved, fueling my imagination."

"They're small," she said.

"They're sensitive." He pinched her nipples gently causing her to suck in a sensual breath and tremble in response. Blood rushed to his groin. "They're perfect." He slid down, so he could take one into his mouth.

Through her T-shirt and bra wasn't enough. Derrick needed to feel her skin…taste her. "Your shirt." He reached down to its hem. "Take it off." Now. He started pulling it up.

Thank you God, she let him.

So damn impatient he couldn't take the time to pull it completely off, Derrick yanked up her shirt and bra just enough to expose her, straining to see her fair skin in the moonlight, before sucking a dusky nipple deep into his mouth.

"That feels…sooooo…gooood." Her voice had gone deep and throaty. When her arms gave out, he held her up, tonguing her nipple, enjoying her little twitches of pleasure before moving on to the other one. "Your mouth." She let out a breath. "I want it on me…everywhere."

Hell yeah. Derrick flipped them over, needing to be on top. "Whatever you want, baby." He kissed her lips, her chin, and up her jaw to her ear. "Anything you want."

He felt like an animal, fully clothed, rutting between her thighs, barely able to control himself, he wanted her so much. *Slow it down before you scare her away.* He tried to roll off.

"No." She held on tight. "Don't go."

"Shh." He bent down to kiss her sweet lips. "Just taking off my shirt." *And slowing things down before I come in my damn pants like a teenager.*

To his surprise, while he sat up to shuck off his shirt, Kira didn't lie there waiting for his return. She got busy pulling her own shirt over her head and unhooking the front clasp of her bra.

He smiled.

She must have seen it in the moonlight because she asked, "What?" as she removed her bra.

He lowered himself back down on top of her. "I like when a woman is an active participant." He took a few seconds to enjoy the feel of her naked chest touching his, her hardened nipples rubbing along his skin as he rocked his torso from side to side. "When she tells me what she wants, what she needs." He dropped his head down to kiss the sensitive patch of skin just below her ear. "I get the feeling," he whispered, "that you're going to be very active."

She bent her knees and opened them wide, making room for him. Then she grabbed his ass with both hands, tilting her pelvis up as she pulled him down onto her. "And very demanding."

CHAPTER NINE

THE SETTING WAS PERFECT, outdoors yet in a private, dark, and secluded spot, under the starry sky. Derrick was perfect, handsome, sexy and willing. Kira couldn't remember ever wanting a man more. And after much consideration, she'd decided she'd be a fool to let this opportunity pass her by.

It's just the two of us. No one will know.

She'd likely be fired on Monday, so professional ethics wasn't as much of an issue as she was making it out to be. But just in case, "You have to promise you will never tell anyone about this."

He stopped moving to stare deeply into her eyes. "I promise, from the bottom of my heart, I will never tell anyone about this."

So sincere, Kira's heart gave a little twitch. There was something about him…something…special. No. She couldn't let herself…feel. Sex. That's all. Tonight only. Sex with Derrick *Smith*. A stranger she'd picked up in a bar. A man she could leave without looking back.

Done thinking, more than ready to get to the good stuff, Kira set out to show Derrick just how demanding she could be, using all of her strength to try to roll them over, so she could take control.

"Nuh-uh," Derrick said, a large, heavy, immovable

weight on top of her. "I'm in charge." He kissed down the side of her neck.

"You see, that's not going to work for me." She struggled beneath him. "I like to be on top."

"Tell me what you want," he said, sliding down her body, setting a kiss on her clavicle before sliding lower. "What you need. I'll take care of you."

"I want to be on top." He didn't seem to hear, apparently too busy giving her left nipple some attention. He sucked it into his hot, wet mouth, hard. Wow! Tingles of pleasure shot inward, straight to her core. "After you're done with that, I mean." No need to rush. The man was a master, an absolute master.

"Tell me what you need," he said seconds before he sucked her right nipple into his mouth. Her body actually spasmed it felt so good.

"On top," she said, having a difficult time focusing on anything but the absolute wonderfulness of his mouth. "Need to be on top." The only way she could achieve orgasm with a man.

"Why?" He slid further down her body, his tongue leaving a cool, wet trail leading to her belly button, then lower.

"I won't come otherwise." No reason to lie. She needed to come, needed release so bad she'd kill for it. Well... maybe not kill, but—

He reached the elastic waistband of her leggings. "Oh, you're going to come."

She appreciated his confidence, but—

"First from my tongue." He sat up, inserted a finger into her waistband at each hip. "Lift up."

In a move that was totally out of character, she did, without question, without argument.

"Good girl." He started to pull down her leggings.

"The second time, you'll come while I'm pounding into you. Sneakers."

She toed them off. "You're a confident one, aren't you?" *Please God, if you're listening, let him be telling the truth, let him have the skill to make his words a reality.*

He yanked the stretchy black fabric and her underwear over her ankles, tossing them to the side. "After that," he pushed her bare legs apart, crawled in between them and laid down on his stomach, "you can come any way you want."

Then he was done talking, couldn't talk if he'd wanted to, his mouth on her sex, feasting, devouring, ravenous. Fabulous. To say she'd never been on the receiving end of oral sex before would be a lie. But she'd never, ever, enjoyed it as much as she was enjoying it right then, the sensation unleashing a groan from the depths of her soul. It was too much. It wasn't enough.

Kira bent her knees, lifted them, spread them even wider, giving him room. "That feels so good." So very, very good. She rocked and twisted and pinched her own nipples. His tongue shot inside of her. "Yes." She lunged up with her hips, needing to feel him deeper. "More."

He lifted his mouth.

No!

"You have no idea how much I want to bury myself inside of you right now," he said.

"Do it. Please. I'm ready." So ready. Past ready. Lord help her. Begging. She was actually begging…and couldn't quite muster the energy to care.

"Not yet." He shoved a finger deep inside of her.

"Yes."

He moved it in and out. Added another one, so good.

"More," she said, her voice not sounding like her own. "You wanted me to tell you what I need. I need more."

He gave it to her, setting his mouth on her again, even more aggressively than before, moving his head from side to side, licking, drawing her sensitized flesh into his mouth. Kira felt her orgasm starting to build "Like that." She pumped her hips. "Just like that." She reached for his head, holding him where she needed him. "Don't stop. Don't stop."

He didn't stop, licking and sucking, plunging his fingers deep.

"I'm—" was all the warning Kira could manage before her mind shattered and her body blew apart and all she could do was let it happen, enjoy the exquisiteness, ride a wave of pleasure more forceful and intense than anything she'd ever experienced before.

If out of body experiences were a thing, than Kira had just had one, floating back to reality slowly, unhappily, not wanting to leave that place of absolute delight and contentment.

"Hey," Derrick said quietly, his voice deep and quiet, and very close to her ear.

"Hey," Kira replied, stretching, ready for a nap.

"Sorry, but if I don't get inside of you soon I think I may suffer permanent damage."

Kira smiled as much as she could manage with her facial muscles still all tingly. "Gotta warn you, I'm not feeling like much of an active participant at the moment. Feel free to go ahead and do your thing, though."

"Bet I can have you actively participating in under three minutes." He moved around beside her, probably taking off his pants.

Kira smiled big this time. "You even bet on sex?"

He climbed over her, the hair on his bare legs tickling her. "I'll bet on anything as long as I know I'll win."

"Condom?"

"Always," he said as he slowly lowered himself on top of her.

Once again, Kira bent her legs and spread them wide to make room for him. "What are the terms of the bet?"

He set the tip of his erection at her opening. "If I can't get you actively participating in under three minutes…" He dipped inside. "Anything." He pushed deeper, stretching her, filling her…so…good… "Anything you want that's within my power to give."

"Deal." Either way she came out a winner. Kira wrapped her arms and legs around him, holding on as she rocked her pelvis, all the way up, all the way back in long, slow strokes until she took his full length.

Her vibrator got the job done. But damn, nothing compared to this. She flexed her internal muscles, gripping him tight.

He went still. "Don't do that."

"Why?" She did it again. "You don't like it?"

"Too much. I like it too much." He dropped his head to her shoulder and let out a breath. "I think we need to renegotiate the terms of our bet."

She rocked against him, clamping down on him with her internal muscles as she did.

"You are an evil woman." He pulled out and thrust back in.

"What are the new terms?"

"I can get you actively participating in three minutes only if I last for a whole three minutes." He pulled out and thrust back in again, his body rigid, like he was barely holding on to control. "I'll do better next time. Promise."

Next time. Only if their next time took place tonight. Kira had accepted her fate when she'd taken on the responsibility for her mother. Rather than letting it make her sad, it made her determined. Determined to enjoy herself and to see that Derrick enjoyed himself, too, in the short amount of time they had together.

"Forget about the bet." She planted her feet on the ground and started to move beneath him. "Go as fast or as slow as you want. I had my turn, this time it's all about you."

"Oh, thank God." He thrust his hips, fast and hard. "You feel so good." His breathing came out choppy. "It's been so long." He kissed her neck. "Feel so good. Damn." He started to laugh. "I'm so far gone I'm repeating myself."

Kira laughed too, couldn't remember the last time she'd laughed as much as she had tonight. If circumstances were different, she'd want to see more of him.

"You feel good, too." He'd started rotating his hips, faster, deeper. Something wonderful flared inside of her and this time she let out a, "damn," of her own. "What was that?"

"Found it," he said, pounding that same spot over and over.

The North Star. It felt like the North Star was flaring to life inside of her.

They pulled back then slammed together again and again.

Derrick's mouth found her ear, panting. "I can't wait."

"Don't wait."

"It's too good."

Amazingly good. "Come for me," she said. "Show me how good."

Three more thrusts, so hard they moved her up the comforter, and his body went stiff as he groaned out his release, thrust again, stiffened and groaned, again, then a third time.

That third time sent Kira over the edge with him.

Derrick Limone was a man of his word.

Thank God for that.

She came back to her senses when Derrick rolled off of her, the cool night air hitting her sweaty skin, making her shiver.

"Here." He curled the comforter over them. Then he cuddled into her side, nuzzling in close to her ear. "Thank you. I needed that so much." He wrapped his arms around her and slid his knee over her hips. "I needed *you* so much."

He didn't need her. He'd needed sex, same as she'd needed sex. "Glad to be of service." *Glad to be of service? What a moronic thing to say.* Kira didn't do cuddling or pillow talk, made her uncomfortable. She didn't offer empty, sappy endearments simply because the moment seemed to call for them. They'd shared something special. But now they were done.

Only Derrick didn't seem intent on moving any time soon.

Kira tried to relax and enjoy the feel of a satisfied male body partially wrapped around her, to appreciate this intimate contact with another human being, but to what end? Tomorrow she'd be back to sleeping alone. She wasn't going to ever see Derrick again. Best to pull away now, to not get attached or start thinking about things that could never be.

She tried to roll away.

"Not yet," he said, holding her close.

"I need to use the bathroom." True, but not an emergency.

"What are your dreams for the future?" he asked.

"Dreaming is a waste of time." They never came true, so why bother?

"So cynical," he said sleepily. "Do you ever plan on getting married or having children?"

"No." She had enough to deal with. And what man would want to take on her and her mom?

"Too bad," he said, matter-of-factly. "Because you're perfect for me."

Time to go. "No." She fought her way out of his hold. "I'm not. Where are my pants?" She looked around the shadowed grass.

"I want to see you again." He sat up, calm as can be.

"No." Spotting a dark blob, she prayed was not a skunk, she reached for it. "You don't." Pants in hand, she stood and put them on.

"Yes, I do." Still on his back, he slid into his pants.

Kira found her bra and shirt. "Well we can't."

"Why?"

Because he didn't live in the city. Because she didn't have the time or energy to put into a relationship that wouldn't last anyway. Because of her mother, it always came down to Mom. "Don't do this, Derrick." Now fully dressed, she bent to pick up her sneakers. "I had a fun night. Thank you for that. But tomorrow you're going to drive me home and drop me off. Then you'll go back to your life and I'll go back mine." That's the way it had to be. Without waiting for him to respond, Kira walked to the back porch, up the stairs, and into the house.

CHAPTER TEN

On Sunday afternoon, Kira entered her two bedroom condo, tired and cranky and in no mood to deal with her sister. Standing in the entryway she was hit by the stale odor of sickness and age. She missed the fresh air of the North Country, as Derrick had called it. Derrick, who'd barely spoken to her during the tension-filled four-hour ride home, other than to ask if she was hungry or needed to use the restroom and to confirm directions once they'd gotten into the city. Kira could have apologized for walking away like she had, only it was easier this way.

Keep telling yourself that.

"I'm home," she called out.

Her sister ambled out of the bathroom, towel drying her short dark hair. Aside from their hair color, eye color, and height, there was little resemblance between them. Krissy's figure was full, her temperament carefree and happy, and her attitude positive. "Mom's taking a nap."

Damn it. "Why is Mom sleeping in the afternoon?"

"Because she was tired," Krissy said, like it made perfect sense. She chucked her towel onto the bathroom floor.

"Now she's going to be up all night." And Kira would

be up with her, not Krissy. She eyed the sink full of dirty dishes. "You couldn't wash the dishes?"

Krissy ducked back into the bathroom to put on some eyeliner and lip gloss. "I'll do them when I get back."

"Get back? Where are you going? We need to talk."

Krissy slipped in a pair of hoop earrings. "There's nothing to talk about."

"Nothing to talk about? You hit me with you're planning to have a baby and you have an appointment for artificial insemination scheduled for tomorrow morning, and we have nothing to talk about?"

"Right." Krissy emerged, finger combing her hair.

"Why now? Why so sudden? You don't have a steady job."

She jerked her head up to stare Kira down. "Yes I do."

"Working as a traveling nurse, moving from assignment to assignment across the country and to international parts unknown, is not what I consider to be a steady job."

"Well who cares what you think?"

"Where are you going to live?"

Krissy's eyes darted to the living room.

Oh, no. "You can't possibly think you're going to raise a child here, with Mom the way she is. It's not safe."

"I'll work it out."

"I know you will, Krissy." Kira hated fighting with her sister, hated that she still fell into the mother role when both of them really needed a sister. "You're smart. You're a hard worker. All I'm asking is that you wait a little while. Save up some money. Find an apartment and a steady job that keeps you in one spot and has good benefits."

"My appointment is tomorrow and that's that." Krissy walked toward the door and started putting on a pair of black leather sandals. "I have been cooped up in this condo for two days." She grabbed her pocketbook from where she'd left it hanging on the front door knob. "You're back and I'm out of here." She opened the door, and without another word, she left.

On Monday, Kira arrived at her office a few minutes before five o'clock in the morning. So she was there waiting when Connie showed up, dressed in sweatpants, looking half asleep and not at all happy, at a quarter to six. "Only for you would I drag myself out of bed so early."

She set two very large takeout coffee cups and a white bakery bag on the corner of her desk.

"You're the best assistant ever." Too bad, after today, she'd likely be someone else's assistant. Kira hadn't wanted to involve Connie in her investigation of Sheila, but when she'd tried to log in to her system remotely from home, she'd been locked out. And when she'd arrived at work this morning, she found she'd been denied access to certain programs. A surefire sign she would be let go today.

Well she wasn't leaving without finding out what Sheila was up to.

Connie sat in her chair and booted up her computer.

Kira rolled her chair over and sat down beside her, looking at the screen. "I need you to get me into the case management program so I can bring up a list of Sheila's case management patients."

Connie entered in her password, clicked a few keys then used her mouse. "You know, technically speaking, I don't have access to that program."

Patient confidentiality limited access to files containing medical information. Kira smiled at Connie's use of 'technically speaking.' "I also know you have something going on with Richie down in IT. And you've got crazy amazing computer skills. And between the two of you, you'd figure out a way to get me in."

"Yeah, I'm thinking after I called him for help at five o'clock this morning, Richie will probably be expecting a blow job or something." She shook her head. "The things I do for you."

"Oh, no." Kira laughed. "I'm not taking the rap for that. You know I would never expect you to perform sexual favors for me." She glanced at Connie out of the corner of her eyes. "You like him."

"He's a pretty cool guy, if you can get past the way he dresses." She clicked her mouse. "Okay. You're in."

"Scoot over."

For the next two hours, Kira reviewed a sampling of Sheila's cases, old and new, and couldn't believe what she'd found. "Here's another one. Same Medicare certified home health care agency."

Connie, who'd changed in the bathroom and was now professionally dressed and ready to start her work day, looked over Kira's shoulder.

"Based on the hospital documentation," Kira explained, "physical therapy three times per week and fifteen hours of home health aide services per week were recommended."

Connie pointed to the screen. "But that says two physical therapy visits and I don't see anything about home health aide services."

"Right. It looks like the nurse from this new agency Sheila is using, without my approval, submitted a revised plan of care with one less physical therapy visit per week and no home health aide visits, and sent that to the patient's primary care physician to sign off on."

"Why would she do that?"

"I don't know. Maybe they didn't have the staff available." Which was a totally unacceptable reason to revise a plan of care. "Or maybe it's something more sinister. I need more time to figure it out." Kira brought up a document she'd hastily put together. "I searched by diagnosis and reviewed five cases, all fractured right hips, all female, all within a five-year age range. Two managed by Sheila. The other three managed by three different case managers. Sheila's patients received significantly less home care services and durable medical equipment than the other patients. And since WCHC is paid a predetermined monthly amount for each client, independent of the services used, Sheila's patients will cost us less than the patients managed by the other case managers."

"So WCHC makes more of a profit on those patients."

"In theory. There are other variables to consider, but yes. That about sums it up."

"It's not right."

It's unconscionable.

"Why aren't those patients complaining?" Connie asked.

A very good question. "They may not know they have the right to appeal." Or they may be appealing and Sheila wasn't following company protocol for handling patient complaints/appeals.

"What are you going to do about it?" Connie asked.

"I need more time to review more cases, to compile a good sampling of data and analyze it." Time, the one thing she didn't have. She glanced at the clock. Almost eight o'clock. Mr. Jeffries would be in any minute. "Would you do me a favor?"

"You even have to ask? Later on I'll be giving Richie a blow job for you." Her assistant winked.

"No," Kira stood. "Later on, if you do wind up giving Richie a blow job, it'll be because you want to, not because of me."

Connie smiled. "You're no fun."

No. She wasn't.

"Please copy all these open files to a data stick," Kira said. "The best I can do is summarize what I've found so far and forward it to the board of directors along with my concerns. Then I've done my due diligence. I've identified a potential problem and forwarded it on for investigation, since I won't be here to investigate it myself. The rest will be up to them." She wouldn't forward it to Mr. Jeffries for investigation because she couldn't shake the feeling he and Sheila were somehow working together to bilk patients out of care they're entitled to.

Connie lunged in for a hug. "Maybe he won't fire you." She sniffled.

Oh, he was going to fire her. It was just a question of how he'd do it and when. Oddly enough, when she was able to tamp down the panic of being unemployed and losing her weekly paycheck, with all the financial responsibilities she had resting so heavily on her shoulders, she felt relieved. Her job had become almost unbearable of late. Kira couldn't work for a company that put profits ahead of patient care. Fighting about it, daily, was as exhausting as it was futile. She'd find another job. A better job. God willing, she'd find it quickly.

Kira hugged Connie back. "You know all the times I've told you you're the best assistant ever?"

Connie nodded.

"I've meant it, from the bottom of my heart. Anything you need, preferably legal, I'll help in any way I can."

Kira was summoned to Mr. Jeffries's office at three minutes after eight o'clock.

She knocked on his door two minutes later, surprised when Sheila opened it.

"Since no one from the Human Resource Department was available this early, I've asked Sheila to sit in as a witness," Mr. Jeffries said from behind his excessively large mahogany desk, his partially bald head shiny, his plump face in its usual scowl.

How convenient. "Good morning, Sheila."

The aging, well-dressed blonde tilted her head in acknowledgment. If Kira didn't have such good self-control, she'd have slapped the self-satisfied grin right off of Sheila's face.

"Please sit." Mr. Jeffries motioned to a chair in front of his desk.

Kira sat.

Rather than sitting in the chair beside Kira, Sheila stood just to the side of Mr. Jeffries's chair, looking down on her.

"I'm sure you know why you're here," Mr. Jeffries said, getting right down to it.

"Yes, sir. And if you'd give me—"

"There is no acceptable explanation for a gross dereliction of duty, Miss Peniglatt."

Gross dereliction my ass.

But Mr. Jeffries wasn't done. "You hold yourself up as the epitome of patient advocacy, yet you abandoned your beloved patients by failing to work on call as assigned, to be there for them when they needed you."

"Mr. Jeffries, if you'll recall," Kira said, sitting up

taller, knowing it wouldn't be enough to save her job, but she had to try, "because of the situation with my mother, I have a system in place for just this type of incident. If, for any reason, the administrator on call cannot be reached, the case manager on call is to contact the other name on the call list, which is Alison, who you called, who was available, and who happily covered on call for me."

"But what if she wasn't?" Sheila asked.

Kira wanted to point out she was only there as a witness and not a participant. Instead she stared directly at Sheila and simply stated, "But she was."

"None of that matters, Miss Peniglatt," Mr. Jeffries said. "Your dereliction of duty this past weekend showed poor judgement." He opened a file on his desk. "I have here documentation of numerous incidences demonstrating your lack of commitment to our new management philosophy." He lifted up several sheets of paper then let them fall to the desk. "And your job performance has not improved, despite a counseling session for each infraction, performed by me, to help promote change and bring you on board."

Counseling session, right, if counseling session meant him yelling and not giving her a chance to speak. Although she did provide the rationale to justify every one of his 'infractions' in the space provided on the counseling sheet…if he'd bothered to read them, which he probably hadn't.

"Mr. Jeffries, I've made it clear that as a nurse, I cannot, in good conscience, be a part of a management philosophy that puts profit ahead of patient care," Kira said. Especially after hearing Mr. Limone's struggles and meeting Daisy.

"That is not what we're doing," Mr. Jeffries yelled.

Sheila put a calming hand on his shoulder.

He let out a breath. "I'll remind you, We Care Health Care is in business to make money."

Well here goes. "I'll remind *you*," Kira said. "That you work in health care now. You're no longer dealing with carbonated beverages or computers. You're dealing with human beings who are entitled to certain care as determined by Medicare." Boy it felt good to get that out.

Mr. Jeffries looked up at Sheila. "You see how she talks to me? Make a note to add insubordination to her termination documentation."

"Of course," Sheila said oh, so helpfully.

"So that's it." Kira stood. "If you're going to fire me, then do it."

"You're fired," Mr. Jeffries said.

Kira spoke to Sheila. "At least I can walk out of here with my head held high knowing I've worked hard and done my best to ensure our patients received the quality care they deserve."

"What about your responsibility to your employer, Miss Peniglatt?" Mr. Jeffries asked.

"I have had excellent reviews, every one of my years here at WCHC. Up until your arrival, Mr. Jeffries." She looked down at him.

"The cost of patient care is up eighteen percent this year."

"And my census is the highest it's ever been. Our patients are older and sicker. I have tried to show you that the majority of patients who are well cared for recover quicker and suffer less falls and re-hospitalizations, yet all you remain focused on is the cost of care. We will never see eye to eye." She turned and walked to the door, stopping long enough to say, "I'll be sure to swing by Human Resources on my way out to complete my exit interview," before leaving his office for the last time.

CHAPTER ELEVEN

DERRICK FOUND THE address Connie had given him easily. Finding a parking spot on the tree-lined streets of the Murray Hill neighborhood had been a different story. But Kira wouldn't answer his calls? Again? Well then she should expect a visit.

Why couldn't anything with her be easy? He didn't need this hassle, didn't need this guilt, had no time…

He entered the lobby of her building, walked over to where the doorman sat behind a small desk, and held up the manila envelope filled with blank computer paper Connie had told him to bring. "Delivery for Kira Peniglatt," he said the words Connie had told him to say. "From Connie at her office."

The older man held out his hand. "I'll see that she gets them."

Derrick held the folder back. "It's a confidential file. I was given strict instructions to deliver it to her myself."

"No men allowed up there," the doorman said.

"Connie called," Derrick lied. "She's expecting me. I'll stay in the hallway." *Please don't pick up the phone and call her.*

"Go on up then," he motioned with his head. "Third floor. To the left. Look for C."

"Thank you." Rather than risk waiting for the elevator, he took the stairs.

Derrick wasn't that familiar with the city, and wasn't sure exactly what to expect when it came to Kira's apartment, but based on her high paying job and her nice clothes, he'd expected better than this. Sure, she lived in what looked like an okay part of town, in a building with a doorman, but everything looked old and dingy. And it wasn't as clean as it could have been.

He found the apartment easily and knocked on the door.

When no one answered, he knocked harder.

The door swung open. "Did you forget your—?" Kira took one look at him and tried to slam the door in his face. Well he wasn't having any of that. She'd been fired today, because of him. He was damn well going to talk to her about it. So he pushed his way inside.

"Kira," he said, stopping immediately at the look of panic on her face.

"Nooooo," a female voice screamed from behind him, fear evident in her tone. "Nooooo." Something started to thump.

"Wait outside," Kira said.

"But—"

"Please." She pushed at him, hard, then looked over her shoulder and yelled, "It's okay, Mom."

Thump. Thump. Thump.

Derrick backed into the hallway, listening through the partially opened door.

"Mom," Kira said her voice calm. "Don't do that. You'll hurt yourself."

The thumping stopped.

"Nooooo," her mom yelled.

"Shh," Kira comforted her. "He's gone. I won't let anyone hurt you."

"No men," her mother said, sounding calmer. "No."

"How about some Oreo cookies," Kira suggested. "And milk."

"I like Oreo cookies." Simple as that, her mother sounded happy again, like the last few minutes never happened.

"I know," Kira said. "Sit right here and I'll get them for you."

"Well what have we here?" A woman with short dark hair asked as she walked down the hallway in his direction. "A Peeping Tom?"

Her hair was the same color and texture as Kira's, her blue eyes similar, yet while this woman's sparkled with playfulness, Kira's were more…burdened, for lack of a better word. "You must be Krissy." He held out his hand.

She shook it, holding on a little too long. "You must be…" She studied his face. "I have absolutely no idea who you must be because Kira has never mentioned you. Or any other man for that matter, so don't feel bad." She looked him over.

"Stop it, Krissy," Kira said as she joined them. Then she focused in on him. "You need to leave."

"We need to talk," he told her.

"No we don't."

"You got fired today. Because of me."

Kira let out a breath. "Connie must have called you. She shouldn't have."

"Wait," Krissy said. "What?" She looked at Kira. "You got fired? From your job?"

"No." Kira crossed her arms over her chest. "From a cannon," she said, completely deadpan. "I got fired from a cannon."

"Oh, no!" Krissy said, glancing into the condo. "What are you going to do?"

"Don't you worry yourself one bit," Kira snapped at Krissy. "Your life will not be affected in the least. I'll take care of Mom and me and everything else without asking for or expecting a damn thing from you or anyone else!" Her eyes filled with tears. She turned away as she wiped at them. "I'm sorry. It's been a difficult day."

Derrick got the feeling her life was filled with difficult days.

"I'm not a crier." She glared at Krissy. "But I was up most of the night with Mom." She turned her gaze to him. "I left for work very early this morning. I'm exhausted, and I really can't deal with this right now. Please go." She turned away, wiping at her eyes again. "Just go."

No way in hell. He took a step toward her. "Kira." He tried to convey his understanding and concern with nothing more than the tone of his voice and a comforting hand placed on her shoulder.

He wasn't prepared for her to turn into his arms, but when she did, he hugged her tightly, holding her while she cried.

Poor Krissy, sarcastic and playful moments ago, looked lost and unsure at the sight of her big sister crying.

"More Oreos," their mother said from inside. "More."

"I'll get them," Krissy said, eyeing her sister with concern. "Go take a walk or something. You look like you could use one. I'll watch Mom."

A chair scraped along the floor.

"Go!" Krissy hurried inside.

"Shoes," Kira said.

A pair of black flip-flops flew into the hallway. The door slammed shut.

Derrick released Kira just long enough to pick them up. Then he put his arm around her shoulders and started walking toward the elevator. "Come on. I'll buy you a cup of coffee."

She looked up at him with teary eyes and a small smile. "Again with the coffee?"

He gave her a one-armed squeeze. "Would you rather we find a bar for two glasses of wine and three shots of Southern Comfort?" he teased.

She elbowed him in the side. "You'd like that, wouldn't you?"

Damn right he would, but now didn't seem like the right time to mention it. He pressed the button for the elevator.

She slipped on her flip-flops. "Since her attack, Mom suffers from an intense fear of men, all men, regardless of age or ethnicity."

Understandable. But, "What I don't get, is why Connie would send me here if she knew—" Derrick stopped, figuring it out for himself. "She doesn't know."

Kira shook her head. "She knows my mom sustained a traumatic brain injury years ago, but she doesn't know anything about how it happened or the extent of her cognitive or behavioral changes." She looked down at her feet. "It's not something I talk about."

The elevator doors opened and he followed her inside. She stood leaning against the back wall. "Now you see why I have to keep Mom with me, why I can't take her out in public, and why I never invite men to my home. Sometimes, if a man gets too close, she'll fly into a rage and go on the attack. Other times, like today, she'll bang a body part on whatever hard surface is closest."

He nodded.

When they reached the lobby he put out his hand to keep the door from closing on her. He waited until they were out on the street before talking again. "There are new medications coming out all the time." For PTSD and anxiety.

She stopped and looked up at him. "I know you're only trying to help, but trust me, if there was a medication that worked, that I could afford, and that I could get her to take on a daily basis, she would be taking it."

"When was the last time you tried?"

"A few years ago." She started to walk. "Can we please not talk about this?"

He fell into step beside her, walking slowly. "I want to talk about it. I want to understand," why she'd stopped trying. "What if there's a medication out there that will help?" He planned to begin researching that possibility as soon as he got home. "You could get her into a day program or a facility. It would take the burden off of—"

She stopped so short, a man walking behind them almost plowed into her. "Sorry," she said as he grumbled past. Then she turned to Derrick. "My mother is not a burden. She's my mother. My family. And family takes care of family."

"But—"

"There are no buts." Kira looked up at him, standing tall and proud. "What if it had been me that night?"

"Is that what this is about? Guilt?" He stared into her eyes. "Kira, you have to know what happened to your mother is not your fault."

"I know that." She stared right back. "But what if it *had* been me? What if I was the one who'd gotten attacked and suffered a severe brain injury as a result? There is no doubt in my mind that my mother would have taken care of me until the day she died. And I will do the same for her."

He respected that, but, "Even if that means you can't have a man in your life? No husband? No children?"

Kira didn't even hesitate. "It's my choice, my responsibility. My mother is happy with me...well, as happy as she's capable of being. She's safe with me. I have three fantastic women who help me. I pay them a fortune, but they're worth every penny."

Wait. "You mean you pay privately?"

"They're very good at what they do." She took a hair band off of her wrist and started putting her hair up into a ponytail. "When you're as good as they are, you can charge what you want and insist on cash." She looked up at him. "But they put my mind at ease. My mother trusts them. I trust them. When I'm not home I don't worry. I know they'll call me if they need me. And they're a bargain compared to the female doctor and female neuropsychologist who come to the condo."

He could only imagine.

And now she was out of a job.

"You told me not to call your employer and I haven't, but I really think you should reconsider. Maybe I can—"

"Stop." She placed her hand on his arm. "If my boss didn't fire me for the on call issue, he would have found another reason to fire me. It's not your fault. And even though being unemployed makes my life infinitely more complicated at the moment, it was for the best. I firmly believe that." She turned and started walking again. "The good news is I'm a nurse. I can always find work."

"Come work for me," he blurted out the thought that'd been on his mind since he'd received Connie's call.

She stepped in front of him to avoid a dog peeing on a mailbox. "Up in Westchester County?"

She said it like he'd asked her to commute to China. "The Metro North train from Grand Central Terminal to White Plains only takes around forty minutes." Usually.

"This way." She pointed to the right and they crossed the street. "Let me get this straight. You want me to travel a good hour, each way, to work for you, because that's what it'll take, door to door, when I add in time to get to Grand Central then to my train. What exactly would I be doing?"

"Office manager. Nurse Manager. Savior of my fledgling family practice." He smiled. "I got the doctor part covered. I need help with everything else."

"I don't know anything about managing a physician's office."

They turned down a side street. "You're smart, I can tell. You'll pick it right up, I know you will."

"How many staff do you have?"

"One receptionist slash biller who doesn't have time to bill, one nurse who's threatening to quit if I don't hire another nurse to help her, and me."

"So you want me to be your nurse?"

"I want you to hire a nurse, ASAP, and manage the office. You'll be great at it. You know the business side of things, you can handle insurance companies, you're good with patients. You're perfect for the job." And the job was the perfect way to get to see her every day, to spend time with her and get to know her better, which he really wanted to do.

"You can afford to pay me one hundred and five thousand dollars a year?"

What? "You make one hundred and five thousand dollars a year?"

"I did."

"I can pay you half that, to start." If he paid himself

less. "Once things at my office are working smoother and I have the staff I need, I can take on more patients. As soon as I'm able, I'll give you a raise."

She shook her head. "I can't survive on fifty thousand dollars a year."

"Work for me while you're looking for your next job. A few weeks, a few months." *Anything.* "Start tomorrow. You won't miss a paycheck." *And I won't feel so terrible about being partially responsible for you getting fired.* "You'll be making more than you would on unemployment. If you need a day off to go on an interview, no problem."

She was still shaking her head. "I don't like the idea of working so far from home."

"You'd only be an hour away. You trust your mom's aides, you said so yourself. Surely they could handle any situation until you got there."

She walked along looking deep in thought.

Hmmm. What would get her to agree? Then it came to him. "I'll throw in free medical care for you, your mom and your sister."

"My mom needs a female doctor."

"I'll wear a dress." At this point, he'd do anything.

She laughed. "You. You'll wear a dress." She looked him up and down as if trying to imagine it.

"And full makeup and a wig, whatever it'll take for me to pass as a woman. I need you that much." He also wanted to help her with her mom the way she'd helped him with his.

"I don't drive. How will I get from the train station to your office? Next block." She pointed. "See that red sign?"

It read Phil's Tavern. He nodded. "I'll pick you up every morning and drop you off every night." *Happily.*

"You need a nurse, too." She looked up at him. "Full time?"

"You'd be in charge of scheduling. But yes, I'm pretty sure I need both positions full time. Maybe even a nurse practitioner or physician's assistant to help me with patients. Maybe you could research salary ranges and which would be a better fit for my practice."

She stopped in front of a heavy wooden door. "Benefits?"

"Medical and dental."

"And free health care for me, Mom, Krissy *and* her baby, when and if she has one? Even if I only work for you for a short time then come back to the city to work?"

"Yes." So he'd have a reason to keep on seeing her, so she'd always have someone to call if she needed help.

She nodded, a hint of a smile on her face, as she pulled open the door. "That might work. Let me think about it."

CHAPTER TWELVE

THE TRAIN RIDE up to White Plains wasn't as bad as Kira had thought it would be. Forty minutes of time to herself was an absolute luxury. But the book on her iPad didn't hold her attention. She glanced over to Krissy who sat next to her, staring out the window.

"Don't sulk. It's not forever," Kira said. "All I asked is that you give it a try." Maybe she'd like working in a doctor's office. A set schedule and reasonable hours would make it easier to coordinate child care, when and if she needed it.

"I'm not sulking, I'm thinking," Krissy said without looking at her.

They returned to sitting in silence.

Kira had managed to read three uneventful pages when Krissy said, "You know. I'm not the waste of life you think I am."

Kira set her iPad down in her lap. "I don't think you're a waste of life."

"I can't do what you do," Krissy said. "With Mom. I can't…" She shook her head, turning to look out the window again.

Kira reached for her hand and held it.

"It's too hard," Krissy said.

Indeed, it was hard.

Krissy turned back to look at Kira. "Seeing you sacrifice your life—"

"I'm not—"

"Let me finish." Krissy added her other hand and held Kira's hand in both of hers. "Seeing you give up... so much makes me so...angry. She doesn't know who we are. She's not our mother and yet you're—"

"She *is* our mother," Kira said quietly. "Even though she doesn't look the same or act the same, every now and then she'll do something or say something that reminds me of who she used to be. And if God forbid, anything horrific ever happened to you, I'd take care of you just like I'm doing my best to take care of her."

"I know you would. And I love you, for it."

"I love you, too."

"I know it makes me a terrible person, but I don't like spending time with Mom," Krissy said. "It's hard to see her like that."

"For me, too."

"But that's not the only reason I don't come around more often." Krissy looked down at her lap. "I've always felt like you don't need my help, or want it. But yesterday...when I saw you lose it in Derrick's arms, I realized how wrong I was to not even try." She looked Kira in the eyes. "I'm sorry I haven't been around more, made more of an effort."

Kira turned in her seat. "It was my decision to bring Mom home. So it's my responsibility to care for her. I want you to live life to its fullest, for both of us." She squeezed Krissy's hand. "But I'd love it if we could see more of each other throughout the year."

"I'm glad you said that." Krissy turned in her seat too. "I think I'd like to stick around a while." She placed a hand on her belly. "To see if the pregnancy takes but also to help out."

"I'd like that."

"And for your information, I do have money. A lot of it actually." She handed Kira what looked like a receipt of some sort. "Yesterday I went to the bank and paid your mortgage for the next three months."

What? "You—"

Krissy jabbed a finger in Kira's direction. "Don't you dare tell me I didn't have to, I know I didn't have to. I *wanted* to."

"That's over eleven thousand dollars," Kira said. "Where did you get that kind of money?"

"It doesn't matter." Krissy looked ready to do battle if Kira pushed the issue, so she didn't. "All that matters is now you have one less thing to worry about." Then her expression softened. "I got your back, sis."

The gesture reminded Kira of the sweet, generous child Krissy had been prior to Mom's injury, before Kira had been forced to transition from sister to parent.

"You know a thank you would be nice."

Kira did better than that. She grabbed her sister and hugged her tight. "Thank you."

"You're welcome," Krissy said, trying to get her arms free. When she did she hugged Kira back. "Now knock it off." She pushed away. "We're almost to our stop."

When they arrived a few minutes later, Derrick was standing there waiting for them, just like he'd said he'd be. "Good morning." He smiled at them over the roof of his car. "How was the trip?"

Kira glanced at Krissy. "Good. The trip was good." It'd given them uninterrupted, Mom-free time together. A little more, and maybe there'd be hope for their relationship after all.

Derrick gave Krissy's multicolored scrub top and maroon scrub pants a quick look before his gaze settled on Kira. "You look nice." The heat in his eyes when he looked at her was totally inappropriate, and yet she liked seeing it here.

Her elegant white blouse, sleek beige pencil skirt, and matching patent pumps might be total overkill for her temporary new job, but, "My wardrobe consists of outfits like these or shorts, T-shirts, and leggings. I figured a skirt was the way to go." Besides, the professional look had given her a boost of confidence she'd really needed this morning. What did she know about running a medical practice? Nothing. But the challenge of doing something new, after so many years of working in case management, had sparked an excitement she hadn't felt in a long time. Maybe, just maybe, the opportunity to see Derrick on a regular basis had a little something to do with that.

The drive to Derrick's office took roughly ten minutes. Kira watched the route carefully. She could walk it if she had to.

"Limone Family Medicine. Walk-ins welcome," Krissy read the red, white and blue sign above Derrick's strip mall office.

"The walk-ins are killing me," he said.

"Look, there's a deli in the next plaza over," Krissy blurted out. "And a donut shop. Sweet."

"What do you think?" Derrick asked Kira, as he pulled into the farthest spot in the lot. She liked how he left the spots out front for his patients.

"I think it's an excellent location." On a busy road. She climbed out of his car. As they walked closer she studied the other occupants of the strip mall. On the left corner was a podiatrist, then Derrick's office, an otolaryngologist, an audiologist, an orthopedist and a diagnostic imaging facility on the far end. "You're certainly in good company."

While he unlocked the door, Kira looked through the glass wall into the waiting room. Neat. Functional.

"Sara and Bonnie will be here by eight thirty. Office hours start at nine. We have a full schedule today. Lots of parents left their back-to-school physicals for the last minute. Let me put this down in my office," he held up a plastic grocery bag. "Then I'll give you a tour."

The office was set up in a rectangle with the waiting room at the top then a large reception area. There were ten exam rooms placed around the perimeter, four decorated specifically for young children. In the far left corner was Derrick's office. Beside that was Kira's office, which had been turned into a storage room of sorts. A small lab area and a medication/supply room took up the space in the center. In the top corner, facing the parking lot, a staff breakroom had a partial kitchen area with a coffeemaker, a microwave and a small refrigerator. There was also a water cooler and an oval table that could seat six.

"I can't thank you both enough," Derrick said.

"On account of you're paying us, we should probably be thanking *you*," Krissy replied.

Actually, it seemed their arrangement would work out well for all three of them, at least for the time being.

When Sara arrived, Kira partnered with her in the front to learn patient sign in and check out procedures, and the phones. When Bonnie arrived, Krissy partnered with her for a quick intro to the lab, the computer system, and everything she'd need to handle the back-to-school physicals.

By eleven o'clock, Kira was proud to note, each of them were functioning independently. Kira working the phones and reception/checkout, freed up Sara to start catching up on billing.

Just before noon, Derrick walked behind the desk to hand her a form, looking so professional in his long white lab coat with his stethoscope around his neck. "How's it going?"

Sara answered. "She's doing great. I've finally gotten through the mail from the last three weeks." She held up a stack of checks. "I'll be making a nice deposit today, boss."

"Good to hear." He smiled then turned back to Kira. "Thanks for pitching in. I know you didn't come all the way up here to answer phones."

"She's doing a lot more than answering the phones," Sara said.

"If I'm to be an effective office manager," Kira said. "I have to understand all the jobs I'm expected to supervise. No better way than to jump in and do them."

After lunch, compliments of her new boss, Kira's job responsibilities expanded when she picked up an internal call and Derrick said, "Kira, I need help in room seven."

On her way back she realized working in a patient care setting meant she could be called on to assist with a medical emergency at any time. Time to get her CPR certification updated. When she reached room seven she knocked.

Derrick called out, "Come in."

A young woman with black hair sat on the exam table, her legs hanging over the side, a little girl in pigtails dressed in head-to-toe pink, who looked to be around two years old, not that Kira had much experience with young children, had her arms wrapped around the woman's neck, her legs wrapped around her waist, and was clinging to her chest.

"I need to examine Mom," Derrick said. "But little Isabelle here is intent on playing baby koala."

Little Isabelle buried her head in the side of her mom's neck.

"Maybe you could take her to see the secret box of stickers and surprises I keep in my office for special little girls who let me examine their mommies."

Little Isabelle wasn't interested.

So Kira sweetened the pot. "I think I saw lollipops in there." While she didn't have much experience with children, she had lots of experience with distracting and bribing her mother.

Isabelle lifted her head.

Kira held out her hands. "Shall we go see?" She glanced at Mom. "Is it okay if Isabelle has a lollipop? Or maybe a candy necklace? I think I saw some of those, too." Derrick had quite a few things stashed in there.

Isabelle looked up at her mother, unsure.

"Go ahead, honey," her mom said with a tired smile.

"We'll only be a few steps down the hall." Kira held out her arms again.

This time Isabelle reached for them and let Kira pick her up. Without even thinking about it, she settled the girl on her hip like it was the most natural thing to do. Odd, because she rarely came in contact with children, let alone picked one up. Unlike other women, she never dreamed about one day being a mom. Not with everything she had going on in her life. Yet there she stood, liking the feel of a tiny child in her arms. Something inside of her shifted.

"Kira?" Derrick's voice brought her back. "You okay?"

"Yes. Sorry." Her face heated. "We're off to the secret box." Without looking at Derrick, she exited the room.

At the end of the day, while waiting for Krissy to

finish up with her last patient, Kira sat at the desk in her cluttered office, thinking about all she'd done since eight thirty that morning. She'd enjoyed interacting with the patients and helping out wherever she was needed.

Derrick was great with the patients, young and old. Professional and hardworking, friendly and caring, everyone loved him. Kira could see the potential in his practice, would have loved to help it grow and be a part of its success…if only it was located closer to her home. For now she'd have to settle for helping him find qualified staff and putting procedures into place that would help everything run smoothly.

A knock brought her attention to the doorway where Derrick stood, still in his lab coat, so handsome.

"Busy day." He walked in, moved a box, and sat down in a chair.

"Busy is good." Her mom always used to say that.

"What did you think?" He took off his stethoscope and set it on her desk. "You coming back tomorrow?"

"I enjoyed it." She smiled. "Of course I'll be coming back tomorrow." Then she got serious. "I'll give you as much notice as I can if and when I find something else."

"Thank you." He studied her.

"What?"

"Something happened when you picked up Isabelle today."

Of course he'd noticed. "I'm not used to being around children, that's all."

"You were a natural."

God she didn't want to hear that, didn't want to start thinking about things she had no business thinking about. "Oh. While you're here." She held up a manila envelope, changing the subject. "I found these keys, but they're not labeled."

"Those are to the front and back doors. There should be a paper with the alarm code in there. I figured whenever I got an office manager he or she would need them so I left them on the desk."

Kira opened a drawer and stuck the envelope inside of it. "Don't want to leave that lying around where anyone can find it."

Krissy joined them. "All done."

Kira looked at her sister feeling such pride. "I realize today was the first time I've ever seen you on the job. You were incredible." Except for a quick lunch break, Kira hadn't seen her sister sit down once. "You acclimated so quickly. It was like you've been working here for months."

"As a traveling nurse I have to adapt quickly to new situations. But bottom line, patients are patients and nursing is nursing, doesn't matter where you do it." She looked at her watch. "We've gotta bolt or we'll miss our train."

CHAPTER THIRTEEN

ON SUNDAY MORNING Derrick woke and glanced at the clock. Almost eleven. He hadn't allowed himself the luxury of sleeping in for months. He stretched, feeling completely relaxed for the first time in a long time.

He owed it all to Kira.

Things were stable up with Mom and Dad. The new home health care agency she'd brought in was providing quality aides and therapists and they were showing up as scheduled. According to Dad, Mom was improving a little bit each day.

In the office, it'd only taken Kira one week to straighten things out. Not even a week, four days. Patient billing was all caught up, the medication nook had been organized alphabetically, and any expired doses discarded. There were no longer boxes stacked in his hallways or dozens of messages piled on his desk, waiting for a response. She effectively and efficiently screened his calls, dealt with problems, and managed the patients, the staff, and him with ease. She'd even negotiated two contracts for pre-employment physicals and drug screening, getting him a higher rate than he'd gotten on the one he'd negotiated on his own last month.

And she sure prettied up his work environment in her classy clothes and sexy shoes.

He turned onto his side, wondering what he'd do with an entire free day now that he didn't have to deal with paying bills, managing supplies, and catching up on paperwork.

A noise in the hallway caught his attention. He listened, heard it again and jumped out of bed. Someone was definitely out there. Damn alarm system. A total waste of money. It should be blaring to scare off the intruder. It wasn't.

He scanned the room, looking for something he could use as a weapon. Heart pounding he ran to his desk. Where the hell was his letter opener? He moved some papers around, uncovered the stapler, and picked it up.

Great idea, idiot, a staple to the side of the head would surely incapacitate a big, burly criminal. He heard another noise, saw the tape dispenser, picked it up and checked the weight. It'd have to do. Maybe if he could catch the intruder off guard he could slam him in the side of the head with it. He grabbed the stapler, too, backup, just in case. Then he crept to the door.

Footsteps were coming closer.

He turned the knob, carefully, as quietly as he could, and slid the door open, slowly, just a crack, enough to see a body passing by. Perfect timing! He whipped the door open, sending it slamming into the wall, raised the heavy tape dispenser high into the air and oomph…took an elbow right to the ribs. Ouch.

The intruder was small, but quick and after that lightning-fast jab he took off running. Derrick gave chase, following as he rounded the corner heading back to the waiting room. The guy's ponytail swished back and forth, long for a man. Leggings cut off at the knees cupped a very fine, and if he wasn't mistaken, very female ass. An ass he recognized. "Kira?"

She jerked to a stop and turned to face him, doubling over, a hand cupped to her chest. "Jeez," she said, panting. "You scared me."

"*I* scared *you*?" Now that he'd stopped he noticed the pain in his ribs and rubbed the area where she'd struck him. "You hit me."

"You tried to attack me from behind..." she glanced at one of his hands "...with a tape dispenser?" Then she glanced at the other. "And a stapler?"

Yes, well, no need to dwell on those poor choices. He set them down on the counter to his right, behind a box of tissues. "How did you get here?"

"The train."

"I mean to the office?"

She lifted up her sneaker and wiggled her foot. "I walked. We city girls are big walkers."

"What are you doing here on a Sunday?"

Apparently done answering questions, she just stood there, staring back at him, her gaze traveling down.

Ah yes. That's the moment he remembered he hadn't taken the time to slip on pants prior to confronting his burglar, and there he stood, in the hallway of his office, wearing nothing but a pair of boxer shorts.

"You live here?" she asked.

"Give me a minute to put some clothes on then I'll explain." He returned to his office/bedroom and pulled on a pair of sweatpants and a T-shirt. While there, he also grabbed the two prescriptions he'd planned to give her on Monday.

He found Kira in the staff lounge making a pot of coffee and took a minute to admire her sexy figure from the doorway. While naked would be his first choice, he sure liked it when she wore those tight fitting leggings. "You first," he said.

Taking two mugs down from the cabinet she said, "My office is a mess." She turned to face him, leaning her hip against the counter, crossing her hands in front of her. "I ordered two metal shelving units to use for storage. You approved the purchase."

"I did."

"Well, they were delivered on Friday. Since Krissy's around to watch Mom today and there weren't any patients scheduled, I figured I'd come up in clothes I can get dirty in, put the shelving units together, sort through all the papers and supply boxes, and get everything organized."

"Why didn't you ask me to put them together for you?"

She looked up at him. "Because I don't need a man to do things for me, because you're even busier during the week than I am, and I thought you were supposed to be visiting your parents this weekend."

"Change of plans." He walked into the lounge, pulled out a chair and sat down at the table. "My brother, the one finishing up his doctorate in physical therapy, flew in to meet with the physical therapist taking care of Mom."

"Oh, boy."

"Not to make trouble. Just to check on Mom's progress and collaborate on the exercise plan." He held up both hands. "At least that's what he told me."

The coffee started coming out. Kira moved the glass pot to fill one mug then the other before sliding it back under the dripping brew. Then she prepared his coffee the way he liked it, same as she'd done for him all week. A man could get used to a woman taking such good care of him.

She joined him at the table.

He slid the prescriptions toward her.

She stared down at them.

"For your mom. Relatively new on the market. Both effective for anti-anxiety and PTSD."

"Derrick—"

He didn't let her finish. "I numbered them. First one had a seventy-two percent success rate in clinical trials, very few side effects. The second one had an eighty-four percent success rate, more side effects, but easily managed with other medications."

She set her hand on his. "I know you want to help, but you have no idea what I've been through. I finally have Mom in a manageable place. The tiniest change to our routine can ruin everything." She picked up the prescriptions and tapped them on the table. "Mom's smart. I try to slip in a medication she doesn't recognize and she'll refuse to take all of her meds. It'll be a fight, morning and night, for days, until I can get her back into a routine." She sat back. "It's exhausting."

He could only imagine.

"She'll accuse me of trying to poison her. She could get agitated and aggressive."

"You have the prescriptions," he told her. "Research the medications. See what you think. Try one. Don't try one. The choice is yours. I just thought it'd be nice if you could invite a guy over to dinner sometime, if you wanted to."

"Yeah, right. What guy in his right mind would want to have dinner at my place with me and Mom?"

He looked her straight in the eyes. "I would." She gave him a smile so sad he felt compelled to lighten the mood. "I mean I'd invite you to my place." He used both hands to display his surroundings. "But I don't have a stove. And since you work here all week, you probably wouldn't find it all that exciting."

That got a happy smile out of her. He liked making her smile, a challenge, so rewarding when he succeeded.

"Thank you." She held up the prescriptions. "Really." She set them back down. "Now enough about me. Your turn. Why are you living in your office?"

He looked down into his mug. "I'll start off by saying everyone seems to think doctors are rich. Plenty are, but they're usually the ones who have been doing it for a while. Most of us relatively new ones are trying to dig out of massive debt from student loans." He took a sip of coffee.

"All through medical school I knew I wanted to own my own family practice. For years I've scrimped and saved what money I could to make that dream a reality. Even with a loan from my parents, when my accountant and I looked at all the numbers I realized I couldn't afford rent on this place and an apartment in addition to all of my other expenses. So I decided to stick a pull-out sofa in my office, add a shower to my private bathroom, and live here for a while, with no one the wiser."

"Until an employee snuck in here on her day off."

He was so happy to see her, to get to spend the day alone with her, he couldn't care less that she'd caught him.

"I figured it'd take at least a year before I could get my own place." He took another sip of coffee. "A house this time, something small, but with a yard where I can set up cornhole and dig out a fire pit, like at my parents' place. But the practice took off and it's doing so much better than I'd hoped it'd be doing at this time." He set down his mug. "Now I have money for a small down payment, but no time to go looking for a place."

"You could do it today," she suggested.

"No I can't. I need to stay here to help you." *I want to stay here and help you.*

She tilted her head to the side. "I thought we already established I don't need your help."

Well, she was going to get it whether she needed it or not. "You said there were two shelving units. How about we make it fun?" He rubbed both hands together. "You put together one. I'll do the other. Bet I can get mine finished before you can."

"You and your betting." She shook her head. "What are the stakes?"

Hmmm. "Winner gets to choose what we do after we're done." He gave her a look that made his choice of activity clear. Speaking of which, he'd better run and change the sheets on his bed.

"Right. Like I'll take that bet."

"You're not working for WCHC anymore," he pointed out. "Can't use that as an excuse."

"Derrick." Her voice took on a parent scolding a child tone. "You are my boss. Propositioning me is wrong on so many levels."

"The way you've taken charge of things around here, I don't feel like your boss at all. I feel like *you're my* boss, which I'm perfectly okay with, by the way." He set his arms on the table and leaned in toward her. "Lucky for us, *I* have no qualms about sleeping with *my* boss."

"Stop it."

"Fine." He sat back. "Then you choose."

She thought about it. "Okay. Got it." She pushed back her chair and stood.

"Wait." He stood too. "Aren't you going to tell me?"

She took off running down the hall, yelling over her shoulder, "I'll tell you when I win."

* * *

"Easy, no tool assembly, my ass," Kira said, frustrated, the thumb she'd just pinched in the stupid shelving unit starting to throb. "Mine is obviously defective." She glared at Derrick who sat in front of the unit he'd put together quickly and easily, smiling.

"I offered to help you."

"I don't need your help," she snapped. Then she apologized. "Sorry."

"Hey." He crawled over to her. "There's nothing wrong with needing help sometimes." He took the shelf from her hands, turned it around and snapped it into place then gave her a side-eyed glance. "Men are just better at some things than women."

She gave him a shove.

"Not a lot of things, mind you," he said, teasing. "But stuff like assembling shelving units." He moved out of reach. "Changing tires. Barbequing."

"Being obnoxious."

"Definitely being obnoxious," he said, nodding with a big grin on his face.

Easy as that her frustration disappeared. "Okay. You can help me."

"What? No please?"

Damn him. "How about I give you a—"

"Kiss?" he finished, rolling onto his back and pulling her on top of him. "Of course you can give me a kiss."

She'd missed this playful side of him and having fun with him. And man, oh, man had she missed the feel of his body pressed to hers, or, as in their present position, her body pressed to his. But kissing him was a terrible idea, no matter how much she wanted to.

He shifted beneath her, sliding her legs to the side so she straddled his hips. "I'm waiting," he said.

She dropped her forehead to his shoulder. "This is a bad idea."

He wrapped his arms around her. "On that we'll have to agree to disagree."

"We have no future together." It would never work.

"All I want is a kiss."

He wanted more, a point he'd made clear after they'd had sex in his parents' yard. She lifted her head so she could stare into his beautiful blue eyes. "What happens after the kiss?"

He cupped the back of her head, applying a gentle downward pressure. "Let's find out."

Their lips touched and Kira's resistance melted. "Damn you." She kissed him again, deeper this time. He hardened beneath her, his sweatpants and her leggings allowing her to feel the full firm length of him. Kira took full advantage of it, sitting up, resting her hands on his shoulders, rocking her hips, rubbing all the way up, then all the way down, slowly, again and again. So good.

"Atta girl." Derrick cupped her breasts. "Use me. Take what you want. I'm all yours."

Boy did she like the sound of that. "Take off your shirt."

He did.

"I didn't get to see you last time." In the dark, away from the bonfire. She ran her hands over his dark nipples, through the dusting of hair on his chest, down along his ribs. "You obviously make time to work out." She caressed his muscled abdomen.

"My second favorite type of stress release." He reached for the hem of her shirt and started to lift it up. "Want to know what my first is? Take this off."

She did.

"So pretty." He fingered her black lacy bra. "Please tell me your panties match."

"You'll have to wait and see," she teased.

In an instant he had her on her back. "I'm not a big fan of waiting." He went up on his knees, slid his fingers into the waistband of her leggings and pulled them down to her thighs. Kira loved his urgency…and the way he went still, staring down at her body with a look of awe. "You are…stunning." He ran his fingers over her matching panties.

He made her feel stunning, and valued, and cared about. Things Kira hadn't felt in a very long time. "So are you," she said because he was, so big and strong.

He moved to the side so he could slip off her sneakers then her leggings.

While he did, Kira asked, "Remember how earlier you said I could choose the stakes of our bet?"

He nodded.

"Well, I chose loser gets her choice of position."

He smiled. "Oh, you did, did you?"

She nodded.

"I want to be on top this time." She waited to see if he'd argue. Surprise, surprise, he didn't.

But he did say, "Lucky for you I like the bottom, too," as he laid down on his back. "Now get over here." He reached for her.

"Nuh-uh-uh." She scooted out of reach. "I'm in charge."

He went up on his elbows. "No one said anything about you being in charge."

"Well, I'm saying it now." God how she wanted to be in charge of him, to bring him to the brink of orgasm again and again before letting him come. "Lay down, big guy." She pushed on his shoulder. "I think you'll like me being in charge."

"We'll see. And I get to be in charge next time."

She tugged on the waistband of his sweats. He lifted his butt so she could pull them down.

She kissed his erection through the fabric of his boxers, looking up at him as she did. "Next time?"

Still up on his elbows, he watched her every move. "Yeah, next time."

So confident. She reached in through the opening, pulled him out, and took him between her lips. She swirled her tongue around his sensitive tip again and again before taking him deep once, twice, three times, her hand working in tandem with her mouth.

He closed his eyes, dropped his head back and drew in a long, deep breath.

She lifted off of him. "You think you'll have energy left over for a next time?" She cupped his balls, rolled them then squeezed them oh, so gently.

He opened his legs wider then flashed her a sexy grin. "Baby, we've got all afternoon."

Hours later Kira lay wrapped in Derrick's arms, in his bed, exhausted, but the best kind of exhausted, content, and…happy.

"That makes three next times," he said groggily and proudly at the same time.

After giving her control the first time, he'd taken control each of the three times after that, and Kira hadn't minded one bit. "You're the man," she teased.

"Damn right I am." He hugged her close, his front pressed to her back.

In between rounds two and three they'd cleaned up her office. Between rounds three and four they'd ordered in Chinese food. But now it was getting late. "I've got to go."

He held her tight. "No."

"Really." She tapped his arm.

He didn't budge. "Stay the night. Krissy can bring you clothes tomorrow."

Kira had already spent too much time away from home over the past week. If Mom's increased agitation was any indication, she'd noticed. "I can't."

He released her.

Forty minutes later he walked her to the train platform. "I hate the idea of you having to travel back to the city alone at night."

"I'll be fine." Appreciating his concern she gave him a big hug.

He nuzzled in close to her ear. "I wish you could have stayed the night with me."

"In your office?" she teased.

"In my bed."

She'd already spent too much time in his bed...too much time thinking about all the things she liked about him...wondering... It had to stop. Or she would get her heart broken for sure.

Men didn't stick around, not in Kira's world.

"Next weekend," he said. "We'll plan ahead. Ask Krissy to watch your mom."

The train whistle sounded, signaling its approach.

"I can't."

The front of the train rumbled past.

"Can't or won't?" he yelled over the noise.

The doors opened. Passengers exited. As soon as she could, Kira boarded, without answering Derrick's question.

CHAPTER FOURTEEN

ON MONDAY MORNING Kira arrived at work and greeted Derrick like nothing had happened between them, like she hadn't spent hours in his arms, naked and breathless, the day before. On Tuesday and Wednesday she did her job and looked after him like nothing had changed. But something *had* changed. Derrick wanted more, the intensity of his desire was so strong it was starting to become a dangerous distraction. Seeing her every day and not being able to touch her was pure...torture.

By Thursday, after two patients, one pharmaceutical sales rep, and his old neighbor Jeff, who'd stopped by to borrow his car, all inquired about the availability of his sexy new office manager, Derrick had had enough.

She wasn't available, damn it. If she was, she'd be his—despite all the challenges they'd have to overcome to be together. He'd make it work. He'd compromise. He'd do...anything. A primal urge to claim her raged inside of him. He paced his office, antsy, needing an outlet, a release.

Someone knocked on his door.

He called out, "Come in."

Kira stuck her head in. "Last patient is out, phones are on answering service, and the front door is locked. We are officially closed for lunch."

"I need you."

She looked over her shoulder. "I was going to run to the deli with Krissy. Can it wait?"

In two big strides he reached her, pulled her into his office, and shut the door. "No." He pushed her up against the wall, his body flush with hers, and kissed her, hard. Needy.

She wouldn't give him more than sex? Fine. He'd take sex. Now.

Hands clamped to her ass he lifted her and carried her to his desk.

"What are you doing?"

He pushed aside papers, his inbox and outbox, and whatever else was in the way to make a clear space for her.

"Derrick."

He set her down, looked deep into her eyes. "I need you," he said again. "Now."

"No."

"Yes." He clutched the sides of her head, kissing her again, deeper this time. He slid his leg between her thighs, tried to spread them wide, to let her feel his erection, to show her how much he burned for her, to make her burn for him.

For the first time since he'd seen her in one, he hated the tight, figure hugging skirts she wore.

"Derrick, stop," she said, so calm while he felt on the verge of losing it.

He didn't want to stop, damn it! But he forced himself to step back, couldn't look at her, didn't want to watch her leave.

She picked up his phone. "Hey, Krissy. Derrick and I need to go over a few things. Would you bring us back two of the specials?"

What? He turned.

She winked at him. "Just put them in the kitchen." Phone balanced between her shoulder and her ear, she used both hands to start unbuttoning her blouse. "We'll be out in a little bit."

Derrick ripped off his lab coat like it had caught fire and tossed it onto the couch.

"The door," she whispered, pointing, as she hung her shirt on the back of his chair. "Honestly," she said, undoing the back of her skirt. "As if I'd let you get me all wrinkly." She slipped it off, draped it neatly over the arm of the chair, then stood tall wearing nothing but a satiny light purple bra and pantie set, a pair of killer black heels, and a smile. "I'm guessing you'd like me to keep the heels on."

Derrick felt about to explode. "You're damn right I would." He picked her up. "Wrap your legs around me." She did. He palmed her ass, pulled her close, and thrust his rock hard erection against her. "You feel what you do to me? How much I need you?"

She ran her fingers through his hair, angling his head. Leaning in she whispered, "That's quite a hard-on you've got going there. What do you plan to do with it?"

He laid her down on the desk, ran his hand over her breasts, across her flat abdomen, beneath the waistband of her pretty panties, down between her silky, wet lips. "I'm going to put it right here." He slid a finger inside of her, finding her hot, wet and ready. His balls tingled with anticipation.

"Do it." She spread her legs wide. "Now."

Derrick unbuttoned his pants with shaky hands, letting them fall to the ground so he could kick them off. That's when he remembered. "Do. Not. Move." He ran to the bathroom, sliding off his underwear with one hand and grabbing a condom from the drawer in the vanity with the other. On his way back he ripped the damn thing open with his teeth and started rolling it on.

He returned to find her naked, her body absolute perfection.

The condom securely on, he pushed between her legs then inside of her, fast and deep, knowing she was ready, unable to take it slow. "God help me you feel good." In and out, in and out, over and over.

She reached down between her legs and fondled herself. He watched, seeing what she liked before pushing her hands away and taking over.

"Yes," she said, clamping her legs around him. "Like that."

He moved his fingers and hips, his body a machine, programmed to give pleasure and receive pleasure. Right now those were the only two things that mattered.

His orgasm started to build. He could feel it, wanted it, *needed* it.

"Come on, baby." He moved his hips and fingers faster. "Come for me."

Her breathing heavy, Kira rocked up and down, bit her lip and moved her head from side to side.

In and out, in and out, again and again.

When she arched her back, stiffened and let out the most gratifying of groans, Derrick let go, pouring himself into her, wishing she could feel it, that there was no barrier between them.

His heart pounding, his body spent, he laid his upper body on top of her, his elbows taking most of his weight, still buried deep inside of her. He kissed her cheek. "Thank you."

"Did something happen?" she asked, running her fingernails up and down his back.

He didn't want to talk about it.

"Hey." She bucked her hips. "Look at me."

He lifted his head.

She studied his face. "Something upset you."

"I don't like other men asking about you." He leaned down to tongue her ear. "I want to tell them you're mine." He moved down to kiss her neck. "I want you to actually *be* mine."

With a hand on each side of his head she lifted him. "If you want me, I can be yours between the hours of nine to five, Monday through Friday. That's the best I can do."

It wasn't enough, but he'd take it, for now. "I want you."

Usually Derrick didn't settle, he identified what he wanted—in this case Kira—then went after it with unbridled determination. But that approach wouldn't work with Kira. So he'd be patient, bide his time until he could figure out a way to get more. He had no doubt the wait would be worth it.

For the next two and a half weeks he and Kira 'ate lunch' in his office, most every day. The staff probably had a good idea of what they were really doing, but they had too much respect for Kira, and maybe for him too, to say anything about it. At night and on the weekends, he and Kira talked for hours, about so many different things, some funny, some sad, everything but the future. Every time he brought it up she stopped talking.

And he began to wonder if agreeing to her terms was a good idea. He wasn't any closer to figuring out a way for them to be together than he'd been two and a half weeks ago. Every request to see more of her, denied. Every suggestion for change, shot down. And while, with each passing day, Derrick fell more in love,

Kira showed him nothing more than a hot sexual attraction, which, with another woman, would have been great. But he wanted Kira long term. A man of his age and experience knew when he'd found the woman he wanted to spend the rest of his life with. Only he could feel himself running out of time, and he didn't like that feeling one bit.

Late on Thursday afternoon, when he couldn't find Kira anywhere, he searched out Krissy. "Did Kira run out for something?"

"Shoot." Krissy shifted the blood-draw carry-all into one hand and her laptop into the other. "You were in with a patient. Then I got crazy busy. She told me to tell you she had to run home. The aide called. Mom spiked a temperature or something and was acting all crazy."

Jeez. "How did she get to the train?"

"Sara took her."

Good. "Do you need to go, too? We can manage—"

Krissy shook her head. "Don't look so worried. Kira will handle it."

For as much as he liked Krissy and appreciated all of her hard work on the job, he hated that her laissez-faire attitude let responsibility for their mother fall solely on Kira's shoulders, part of the reason he and Kira couldn't be together like a normal couple. "I get that Kira will handle it, but she shouldn't have to do it all alone."

Krissy looked up at him. "I've got dinner plans. Kira said—"

"Let me guess. She said, "Don't worry. I'll handle it." Like she always does. And you let her, because that's what *you* always do."

"Wait just a minute—"

No. He would not wait just a minute. Enough was enough. "If you think going out to dinner with your friends is more important than helping your sister take care of your mother, fine. That's your decision. But you won't be going out to dinner until after you help me with something, and you can't help me until after we finish with our patients, so back to work." He turned and left without giving her a chance to respond. But for the rest of the day he couldn't shake the feeling something bad was about to happen.

Around six thirty, Kira looked down at her cell phone, expecting to see Derrick's number come up—after talking with him briefly earlier, he'd promised to call back after work. But she was equally happy to see Connie's smiling face on her screen, something her old assistant had programmed to happen every time she called.

Of course Kira accepted the call. "Hey, Connie."

"Hey, hon. How's it going?"

"Not so good." She looked over to where Mom sat in her recliner chair, watching television. "Mom's sick."

"That sucks. Then you won't be able to meet up with me to celebrate?"

"Celebrate what?"

"Mr. Jeffries got fired today," Connie said. "I heard they threatened him with legal action if he didn't leave quietly."

What? Kira had received a call from her old boss, Mr. Regis, the CEO prior to Mr. Jeffries, who'd agreed to come out of retirement, along with Kira's predecessor, April Weir, to perform a covert audit based on the documentation she'd sent to the board of directors. He'd asked her dozens of questions, which she'd answered honestly, and then…nothing.

"What happened?"

"Word is…"

Kira smiled. Of course Connie had the inside scoop.

"…was in the process of forming alliances or something with the heads of home health care agencies around the state. Apparently he offered to make them preferred providers so they'd get first dibs on WCHC referrals along with kickbacks in return for limiting home health care services and medical equipment referrals wherever they could."

The bastard. "What about Sheila?"

"At first she claimed she didn't know anything about it, the skeezeball. Then Richie told me that Michael told him that while he was doing some random computer stuff next door to the conference room he overheard Mr. Regis confront Sheila about a bunch of statements from patients who said they'd filed complaints and appeals with her and then heard nothing back. Mr. Regis pointed out he couldn't find any of those complaints or appeals. Well, knowing she was caught, Sheila turned on Mr. Jeffries like the rat that she is, claiming he used sex to manipulate her and she felt her job would be in jeopardy if she didn't go along. You have no idea how much I hate her. Anyway, now she's sucking up to anyone in power who will listen, vowing to clean up the case management department, blah, blah, blah, make me sick."

Needing to move, Kira walked out of the living room and started to pace up and down the hallway. "Do you think they'd honestly promote her?" For some reason, Mr. Jeffries hadn't given Sheila the Director of Case Management position.

"No way in hell. Mr. Regis agreed to serve as interim CEO until a replacement can be found. Richie says they probably want to handle things internally, keep it from going public."

Kira's phone buzzed. She moved it from her ear to look at the screen, her heart skipping a beat. "Connie, I've got to go. Mr. Regis is calling me."

An hour later, Kira sat in the chair beside her mom's recliner, reeling over what her old boss had told her. And what he'd offered her.

The house phone rang. Kira got up and hurried into the kitchen to answer it, expecting Derrick. But why would he be calling on her house phone? "Hello?"

"Miss Peniglatt? This is Harold downstairs at the desk. A Dr. Limone is here to see you."

Derrick? Here? She glanced at Mom, finally calm. Krissy had gone to dinner with friends straight from work. Kira couldn't leave. "Please tell him—"

"Don't you mean her?" Harold asked.

"Her?"

"Yes, Miss. This here Dr. Limone is a she."

Kira smiled as she remembered.

"I'll throw in free medical care for you, your mom and your sister."

"My mom needs a female doctor."

"I'll wear a dress."

Her eyes filled with tears. He'd come. Just like he'd said he would. Without her even asking. "Please." She sniffled. "Send her up." She loved him so much her heart actually hurt. Although she couldn't be quite certain whether the hurt was caused by so much love or the pain of knowing nothing would ever come of it. The closer they got, the more she knew she needed to put a stop to their lunchtime trysts and intimate phone calls. It wasn't fair to him...or to her.

She opened the door and stood in the hallway, waiting, completely unprepared for the sight of him walking toward her, his gait in no way feminine, carrying his briefcase. He wore a flowy, multicolored dress that fell to a few inches above his ankles, which were covered in thick navy blue tights that disappeared into his sneakers.

"I know," he said, looking down. "The sneakers don't match." He said it like he'd really wanted to match, and she fell a little bit more in love with him. "But I have size thirteen feet. That's a men's thirteen. We tried dozens of pairs of women's shoes and couldn't find any suitable ones that fit, except for a pair of bright red heels, if you can believe that. But no way am I wearing heels."

She ran to hug him. "We?"

"I made Krissy come to Goodwill to help me put an outfit together." He hugged her back. "It was the least she could do."

"She *did* ask if I wanted her to come right home." Kira wasn't ready to release him yet, so she didn't. "But I knew she had plans to meet up with some friends she hasn't seen in a while. Why should we both have to sit around the condo?"

"You're too nice." He gave her a squeeze. "How's your mom?"

"Resting." She stepped back to get a good look at his face. Foundation covered any hint of razor stubble. Black liner and purple shadow highlighted his eyes, blush brightened his cheekbones, and a red lipstick colored his lips. "I like you better as a man, but you make an okay looking woman." Not drag queen pretty, but passable. Her gaze dropped to his breasts.

"I know." He nodded proudly as he caressed his womanly form. "They look real, right?"

She couldn't help but laugh.

"What?" he asked, obviously offended.

"So big?"

"Krissy and I decided I was a big guy so I needed a big rack." He adjusted his rack. "You should see the size of the bra I've got on. I could launch watermelons with it." He twisted. "It looks cool, but it's not all that comfortable. I don't know how you women do it."

She poked one of his boobs. "What have you got in there?"

"Socks," he said, itching his head through a black page boy wig then fussing with his synthetic bangs. "The lady at Goodwill is going to have one very un-happy customer at her register first thing tomorrow morning if I find anything crawling on my scalp when I take this wig off later."

Kira covered her mouth to keep from howling in laughter.

"Yeah, very funny. I did all this for you." He motioned up and down in front of himself. "You should see the contraption we had to rig up to keep the tights from falling down around my ankles. The crotch is hanging down by my knees."

Kira couldn't hold it in any longer. She laughed out loud. It felt especially good after all the stress and worry of the past few hours. She wanted to tell him how much she appreciated him and loved him. But admitting that would be a huge mistake. So she settled for a sincere, "Thank you." It wasn't enough. *It'll have to do.*

"You're welcome." He looked down at her. "You going to let me in?"

That's when Kira realized she was blocking the door. "I don't know." She glanced over her shoulder. "I just got her quieted down."

"Let me in," he said, his voice calm, his big warm hand cupping her cheek. "Let me examine her."

"But what if…" she recognized that he was a man. "She might…" hurt him or hurt herself.

"It's going to be fine," he said, so sure of himself. "At least let me try."

She wanted him to try, really, but…

He placed his hand on her arm and applied a gentle pressure. "You're going to need to move."

"Wait. Let me get something." Kira ran to her room, unlocked the cabinet where she kept Mom's meds, and grabbed an injectable sedative and a syringe, just in case. Then she returned to the door. "Okay." She held up her hand.

"You're not going to need that."

"Let's hope you're right." Better to be prepared than unprepared.

Derrick followed her into the living room. Lord help her, he was taller than any woman Kira had ever met. *Please don't let Mom notice.*

When they reached Mom's recliner, Kira said, "Mom, the doctor's here to see you."

Mom turned her head slowly, blinking, as if trying to focus.

Please don't focus too hard.

"Mrs. Peniglatt," Derrick said. His voice came out deep.

Mom's eyes went wide and wary as she shifted in her chair, moving away from him.

Kira clutched the syringe.

Derrick cleared his throat. The next attempt came out higher, like a woman with a head cold accompanied by a sore throat. "I'm De…Debbie Limone. Dr. Debbie Limone. Kira said you weren't feeling well."

Mom glanced at Kira nervously.

"It's okay," Kira told her. "I'll be right here the whole time."

With that reassurance, Mom relaxed a little bit. And Derrick got to work. He took his time and explained what he was about to do before he did it. So kind and gentle. Mom watched his every move, staring at his face, his eyes in particular, concentrating longer and harder than she had in years. Derrick spoke softly in his strange new voice, the sound almost mesmerizing Mom. She didn't fight or argue. Just kept staring.

Before Kira knew it, Derrick was packing up. "It was very nice meeting you, Mrs. Peniglatt," he said.

Mom turned her attention back to the television.

"We can talk in the kitchen." Kira walked that way. Derrick walked beside her, a big, cocky smile on his face. "What?" she asked.

"Your mom totally bought it." He'd lowered his voice back to normal.

"Shh." Kira pushed him into the kitchen then peeked around the corner. Thank goodness Mom hadn't heard. When she turned around Derrick was there, pulling her into a hug.

"And how are you?" he asked as he dropped a kiss on the top of her head.

She cuddled into his embrace, loving the feel of his strong arms wrapped around her, trying to ignore the feel of his 'big rack' pressing up against her chest. "I'm fine." Now. "Thank you for coming."

"I promised I would," he said, lifting her chin, looking into her eyes. "I'll always be here for you if you need me. No matter what."

The honesty in his eyes and the sincerity in his tone gave Kira a sense of security she hadn't felt in over a decade.

CHAPTER FIFTEEN

On Monday morning, Derrick busied himself at his desk, waiting for Kira, looking forward to her arrival as much as he was dreading it.

On exam, her mother's lungs had been clear, her abdomen soft with good bowel sounds, and her ears, nose, and throat within normal limits. She was urinating and moving her bowels regularly without complaint. His initial thought was she'd picked up a virus of some sort that would run its course and in a few days she'd be back to her usual self.

That'd gotten Kira nervous about what types of germs she and Krissy were bringing home as a result of working in a doctor's office. At which time Derrick took the opportunity to remind her she had three different aides caring for her mother. Any one of them could have unknowingly exposed her mother to a virus.

On Friday, her mom still running a temperature, Kira had taken the day off.

Fine. No problem.

On Saturday, Krissy had pulled him aside to see if he and Kira were fighting. Apparently she'd been especially quiet and withdrawn on Friday night.

Not a good sign.

While writing a note to remind himself to call Mr.

Simmons about his liver function tests, Derrick felt someone watching him. He looked up to see Kira standing in his doorway.

"Morning." She gave him a small smile that didn't reach her tired eyes. She held a business-sized white envelope in her hands. A resignation letter, he had no doubt. "Do you have a few minutes?"

Don't do this.

He wanted to say, "No, now get to work," then avoid her all day, all week if necessary, just so he wouldn't have to hear what she was about to say. But eventually she'd track him down. So he said, "Sure," motioning to the chairs in front of his desk. The desk where he'd made frenzied love to her not too long ago. "Sit."

"I'd rather stand." She reached out to hand him the envelope.

He didn't take it.

She set it down in front of him. "I'm giving notice."

"God, Kira." He stood. "Don't do this."

"I can't be so far away from my mother."

"The aide called. You rushed home. Everything worked out fine."

"But what if it was something more serious?" She looked up at him. "I paced that platform for twenty minutes waiting for the train, worrying myself sick. What if she flew into a rage and hurt herself or heaven forbid the aide? What if she needed emergency care and the aide had to call an ambulance and it took me an hour to get to her? What then?"

"You can't be with her twenty-four hours a day," he pointed out. "Even if you were working in the city it would take you time to get to her."

"Yes, but I'd be a taxi or subway ride away. I wouldn't have to beg for a ride then wait for the train and sit there all stressed out while it made stop after stop, each one delaying my arrival to the city where I'd then have to grab a cab or catch the subway to get home. Have you ever tried to catch a cab outside of Grand Central Station? Good luck."

"So that's it, then. Your mind is made up."

She wouldn't look at him. "I'll stay until I've hired and trained my replacement."

He didn't want a replacement. He wanted her. "What will you do for a job?"

She walked over to his bookcase and pushed in a medical journal that didn't line up with the rest. "WCHC offered me my job back." She glanced over. "With a raise."

He plopped down into his chair, realizing he would never be able to pay her what she's worth...and he wasn't enough to make her stay.

"It's too good an offer to pass up," she said, staring at the row of journals.

"Of course it is." He didn't care, but asked anyway, "What happened?"

"Your mother's inadequate home health care plan alerted me to a bigger problem within the company. I was only able to do a preliminary investigation before my boss fired me, but I'd forwarded what I had to the board of directors. They investigated further. The results of that investigation led them to terminate the CEO and offer me my job back."

"With a raise." Lucky Kira. He should be happy for her, but he couldn't get past the misery of losing her. Because no doubt in his mind, today, when she left his office, it'd be for the last time. And not only would she leave her office manager's job behind. She'd also be leaving him.

"With a raise," she repeated quietly.

"What about us?"

"I told you we had no future, Derrick," she answered. "This is for the best."

"No it's not."

She still wouldn't look at him. "Better to end things now, before it gets any harder."

"It can't possibly get any harder." He stood again. "I'm in love with you." He walked toward her. "I love you, Kira." He took her hands in his, bringing them up to his mouth for a kiss. "We can figure out a way to make this work." *Fight for us, damn it.*

"We can't." She shook her head. "I have a responsibility to take care of my mother. She will always come first in my life."

"What life?" he raged. "You have no life. You go from work to home and home to work. You can't be happy."

"I'm not *un*happy," she said calmly.

"And that's good enough for you? To live a life that's not unhappy as opposed to one that's happy? One that includes a man who loves you? A man who understands your responsibility to your mother, who accepts it and wants to help? We can find a way—"

"No."

Damn it. Derrick wanted to shake her. "You won't even try?"

"Don't you get it?" She threw up her hands. "I *have* tried. Not recently, but early on."

"None of those men were me," he told her.

"I know you think you're different." Her eyes softened. "In many ways, you are. But over time you'll want to see more of me. You'll start to resent all the time I spend with my mother, time you can't be a part of. We'll fight. And just when I allow myself to believe it will work, just when I allow myself to fall in love and dream of a future with you, you'll leave."

"No I won't."

"You will!" Tears filled her eyes. "Like every man in my life before you has, and I can't go through that again." She shook her head. "I won't. It's too…hard. We end now. Today."

"If you need to go back to work in the city, fine. I understand. But why do we have to end? I can visit as Debbie. We can get your mom used to me. Then gradually I'll transition into Derrick. Step by step. Lose the boobs one week the skirt the next. The wig."

She shook her head, blotting her eyes with a tissue she'd taken from his desk. "For a normal person, sure, great idea, but my mother's memory is impaired. She won't remember. Each time you come to visit will be like the first time she's met you. It won't work."

How could she be sure if she wouldn't even try? Damn frustrating woman. And that made him mad. He strode to his desk, picked up her resignation letter and ripped it down the middle. "Fine. If you're worried about being so far from your mom, if you're so certain I'm like every other man before me that you won't even give me a chance to prove you wrong, then leave today. There's no need for you to stay." He couldn't bear the thought of seeing her every day and not being able to taste her or touch her, of knowing she didn't care for him as much as he cared for her, knowing her presence had an end date and there was nothing he could do to make her stay.

"But—"

"You have a great job waiting for you. Go," he said, louder than he'd intended. "I managed to get by without

you when I started my practice, I can do it again now."
Of course it'd be easier now after all the hard work she'd
done to get things organized and running smoothly.

"I'm sorry," she said again.

And he lost it. "Not sorry enough to try anything
that might give us a chance." He loved her and hated
her at the same time.

"You don't understand." She sounded weary. "I *have*
tried. And I don't have it in me to try again. My heart…"
she clutched her hand to her chest, "my heart can't handle another failed attempt."

He didn't want to hear anymore. "Get out." He pointed
to the door.

She just stood there.

"Fine. You're fired. Your services are no longer needed.
I'll send your final check home with your sister. Goodbye. Have a nice life." Since she wouldn't leave his office, he did.

As mad as he was, he didn't want Kira walking to
the train station in rush hour traffic. So he asked Sara
to drive her and Bonnie to cover the desk while she did.

Kira returned to her job at WCHC on Wednesday. Although she'd been thrilled to see Connie and most of the
members of her staff again, by the following Wednesday
she missed working at the family practice something
fierce. She missed riding the train with Krissy, missed
Sara and Bonnie, missed the patients. But most of all,
she missed Derrick.

"For the record, I think you're an idiot," Krissy said,
from across their kitchen table. "Derrick is a great guy.
He's crazy about you and you dumped him like yesterday's
trash."

Kira could have argued, but she didn't have the energy. "How is he?"

"Grumpy." Kira pushed away her plate and sat back in her chair. "Same as you."

"It was for the best." Maybe if she said it enough times she'd believe it.

Krissy shot her a knowing look. "Thinking that help you sleep better at night?"

Despite feeling a bone deep exhaustion, all the time, Kira couldn't sleep. Somehow Krissy knew.

"Damn it, Kira." Krissy crumpled up her napkin and threw it onto the table. "You're the smartest, strongest, most resourceful person I know. If anyone could find a way for you and Derrick to be together, you can. Yet you won't." Krissy studied her with narrowed eyes, as if trying to see deep into her mind. "Why?"

Because she loved Derrick, because the longer their relationship lasted the more that love would grow…the more it would hurt when he left, like all the men in her life always did. But she wouldn't share that fear with Krissy. Instead she said, "For starters, how about he lives and works up in Westchester County and Mom and I live here?"

"So you move." Krissy made it sound like it was no big deal. "What's keeping you here?"

"Martha, Ingrid, and Tippy." The three aides who covered the shifts working with Mom.

"You're nice to them and you talk to them but you're always so busy planning, managing and scheduling you don't really listen, do you?" Krissy crossed her arms over her chest.

Feeling parched, Kira reached for her glass and took a sip of iced tea. "What are you talking about?"

"Tippy. She's been here the longest. She loves you like a daughter and for some reason she loves Mom, too."

"So?"

"Her son went into the Navy."

"I know that."

"She's lonely in her apartment without him. Says she's thinking of moving upstate to be with her sister. Get out of the city, fresh air, yada, yada, yada."

"Oh, my God." Kira's brain went into overdrive. "What will I do without Tippy?"

"See?" Krissy slapped her palm on the table. "That's your problem. Right away you're so worried about your precious schedule of coverage that you're missing out on a potential opportunity."

"And what might that be?"

"Now hear me out." She held up both hands. "What if you decide to move up to Westchester?"

"I can't—"

Krissy held up a finger. "I said to hear me out, now listen. I could tell how much you loved managing Derrick's office. You were damn good at it, too. What if you moved up there? What if you asked Tippy to move in with you as a live-in caregiver? That would get her out of her apartment filled with memories of her son. She wouldn't be lonely. She'd be in the country."

"Someplace with a fenced-in yard." Kira warmed to the idea. "Where Mom could get outside and maybe have a garden."

"That's right," Krissy said, nodding dreamily, as if lost in a memory. "I remember Mom saying one day she wanted to move to the country so she could have a big beautiful garden."

If only. Kira shook her head. "This is silly." To hope. To allow herself to dream of something she could never have. "So many things would have to happen for me to be able to pull that off. Even if I could, Derrick probably hates me anyway." Her heart twitched uncomfortably at the thought.

"He doesn't hate you," Krissy said.

How could she be so sure?

"All I'm suggesting," she went on. "Is rather than flat out saying no, it will never work, give you and Derrick and a future together some more thought. And you, uh," she stood and carried her dishes to the sink, "may want to figure it out sooner rather than later."

"Why?" Kira stacked Mom's plate and utensils onto her own plate.

"Because…I'm leaving."

Kira shot out of her chair. "You're what? When?" Kira had gotten used to having her around. "Why?" When they were finally starting to get along?

"First time's a charm," Krissy said, holding her arms out at her sides. "I'm pregnant."

Kira knew she should be happy for her sister but she just…couldn't…

"Don't look so sad," Krissy said. "This is a good thing." If it was so good, why did her smile look forced? "My friend Zac scored us two primo assignments on Oahu. Hawaii, baby." She made that hang loose sign with both hands and wiggled them. "I am going to have some fun in the sun while I can still rock my bikini."

"Krissy—"

"Three months with an option for three more." She slid the tips of her fingers into the front pockets of her tight jeans. "Then I'll come back to New York. I'll find a nice steady job that keeps me in one place, just like you want. I'll get my very own apartment where I will finally settle down as I prepare for motherhood."

She made it sound like she'd be serving out a sentence under house arrest. Which made no sense, didn't she want to be pregnant? "Krissy—"

Without waiting to hear what Kira had to say, Krissy turned and walked out of the kitchen toward the bedroom they were currently sharing.

Kira followed. "Krissy," she said again. "What about your job with Derrick?"

"That's all you're worried about?" She dropped down on her hands and knees to drag her duffle bag out from under her bed. "I'd thought for sure you'd get on me about prenatal care and not doing anything stupid while I'm pregnant." She stood and plopped the duffle onto the bed.

Kira let out a breath. "You're an adult and a nurse. I know you know you need good prenatal care. And I know you're responsible enough not to do anything stupid while you're pregnant." But maybe she should mention... "Like surfing. You probably shouldn't try surfing."

Krissy stopped, holding a stack of T-shirts she'd just taken out of her drawer, and smiled. "There's the overprotective sister I know and love."

"And heavy lifting," Kira added. "Make sure you get someone to help you with lifting."

"I will." Krissy packed the T-shirts in her duffle. "Don't worry about me. I promise to take good care of myself." She returned to the dresser and pulled open her pajama/sweats drawer. "As far as Derrick, I talked to him. He didn't have any problem with me leaving. Said he'd get along just fine. Frankly," she stopped what she was doing and looked at Kira. "I think I reminded him of you and he was glad to be rid of me."

"So you're done? You didn't even give him notice?"

Krissy shrugged. "I offered to stay on for a couple of more days, but he said no need. So I told Zac to book us on the first flight he could get." Her eyes met Kira's. "We're leaving tomorrow afternoon."

So soon? One more day? Then Krissy would be off on yet another adventure while Kira remained at home. Alone with Mom. And with Krissy gone, Kira knew she'd feel the loss of Derrick even more. She felt tears collecting in her eyes. She quickly turned so Krissy wouldn't see.

Her sister's arms came around her in a great big hug. "It's only for a few months." She squeezed. "Then I'll be back. Promise."

Too choked up to talk, all Kira could do was nod.

CHAPTER SIXTEEN

ON THURSDAY MORNING, before any of his staff arrived, Derrick sat out at the reception desk, looking over his schedule of patients, dreading the insanely busy day ahead and missing Kira. He stared down at a picture of her on his phone. She'd been asleep in his bed, so peaceful. He brought up another one of her sitting in the exact same spot where he was sitting, with a big, beautiful smile on her pretty face. His heart squeezed.

It hadn't even been two whole weeks, and he missed her so much. But he'd made it clear he wanted to try. She'd made it clear she didn't. If they were to have any hope of a future together, the next move would have to be hers.

He looked around the messy desk. Kira wouldn't have allowed it. He needed to find a new office manager, but couldn't bring himself to do it. A small, irrational part of him still clung to the hope that if the position remained open, maybe she'd come back to work…back to him.

Stupid.

And now he needed to find a nurse to replace Krissy, too.

God help him. Short-staffed again. Too much work. No fun. He'd come full circle.

Someone knocked on the glass door. Derrick looked up to see a thirtysomething woman with short blonde hair, wearing light blue scrub pants, a multicolored scrub top, and a pink stethoscope around her neck.

Was she lost? Derrick stood and answered the door. "May I help you?"

"My name is Andrea. My friends call me Andy." She held out her hand.

Derrick shook it.

Andrea went on, "A few weeks ago I brought my nephew in. He'd fallen off of his bike. You took him as a walk-in."

Derrick tried to place her, but couldn't.

"You were great with him. The staff was nice. I'm new to the area so I talked with Kira to see if you had any RN work available. At the time she'd told me no, but she had me fill out an application."

Derrick started to feel a glimmer of hope.

"Anyway, she tracked me down last night to tell me a nursing position opened up, and if I could start immediately, it's mine." She held up a paper lunch sack. "So here I am."

Derrick's cell phone rang. He pulled it out of his pocket and glanced at the screen. Kira. "Come in." He invited Andrea in. Partly because it was the polite thing to do, partly so he could close the door with her inside so she wouldn't think about leaving. "Give me a minute to take this call."

"Sure thing."

Derrick accepted the call. "Hello?"

"It's Kira. Don't hang up."

"I know it's you," he said. "That's why I answered the call. What's up?"

"I have a nurse coming into the office today. Her

name is Andrea. I already did her interview and checked her references. You can find the paperwork in the top drawer of my…of the file cabinet in my…in the office manager's office, in a file labeled Excellent Nursing Candidates. All you need to do is make a copy of her nursing license, which I told her to bring with her, and fill out the new hire paperwork that's in the same drawer in a file labeled New Hire Paperwork. I left a bunch of packets paper clipped together."

Typical Kira. So organized and right on top of things. Derrick couldn't help but smile. "She's already here."

"Oh. Sorry. I'd hoped to catch you before she arrived. But hey, she showed up early. That's a good thing."

"Yes it is."

"Tells you what kind of employee she'll be," Kira said. "I knew I liked her."

"I do, too."

The silence that followed grew awkward, until Kira broke it. "Well, that's it then."

Andrea stood a few feet away, looking around, trying to pretend she couldn't hear his every word. But Derrick wasn't ready to end the call. He turned and walked to the far end of the waiting room. "How are you?"

"I'm doing well. How are you?"

"Better now that Andrea's here," he told her the truth.

"I'm glad."

She sounded glad for real. "Thank you for looking out for me," he said, touched by what she'd done.

"You're welcome."

He probably should have ended the call there but he couldn't say goodbye without letting her know, "I miss you."

She didn't respond at first, but then she said, "I miss you, too." Her voice so low he could hardly hear her.

More silence followed.

Derrick would have been content to stand there all day maintaining the connection between them. But he had so much to do. "I really need to—"

"Me, too."

"Call me sometime," he said before he could stop himself.

"Goodbye, Derrick."

He hated the finality of her tone.

"Goodbye."

Andrea proved to be a nice addition to his staff. She worked hard, got along well with Sara and Bonnie, and had no problem covering the reception desk when asked. His business thriving, he was making money and paying down his loans faster than he'd imagined possible. Sure, he worked his ass off, but what else did he have to do?

One week passed in a blur of patients and paperwork, then two, then three.

He got up to visit Mom and Dad once to see first-hand how well Mom was doing.

Kira never called.

He was finally getting used to life without her—to the point late one Saturday afternoon, after office hours, he'd pulled out her file labeled Excellent Office Manager Candidates and started looking for her replacement—when Krissy called.

Saturday night Kira sat at her kitchen table, sipping a glass of wine, scanning through the real estate listings she'd printed out at work, condos and small houses for sale within half an hour of Derrick's office. If she bought a house, she'd need to worry about mowing the grass in the summer and plowing snow from the driveway in the winter. A condo would be easier, but then Mom wouldn't have a private yard for her garden. Up in Westchester County she'd need a car, another expense. And she'd need to learn how to drive.

She took a few more sips, okay, more like large swallows of wine, then refilled her glass. It'd taken three weeks, but Kira, with Tippy's happy agreement to relocate with them, had figured out a doable plan that just might work. Assuming Derrick hadn't moved on. Assuming he still wanted her in his life and as his office manager.

"Three weeks." She took another sip of wine, staring at her phone. "Idiot." Why hadn't she called him? "Because you pushed him away and compared him to all the losers that'd come before him. He has every right to hate you now. And you're too much of a coward to call him, to admit you were wrong and you want another chance. Which is why you're sitting here talking to yourself rather than to him."

Last night, after refusing to discuss the topic during her prior phone calls with Krissy, Kira finally admitted that she'd never told Derrick of her plans to move so she could be closer to him. Why get his hopes up if she couldn't make it happen? And now, three weeks later, she was worried too much time had passed, that she'd missed her opportunity. Typical Krissy, she'd freaked out saying—

Someone knocked on her door.

Kira glanced at the clock. Who would be knocking at her door at eight o'clock at night? She stood, glanced into the living room to make sure Mom was occupied, then headed to the door. She looked through the peephole and sucked in a breath...could not believe her eye.

She opened the door.

There stood Derrick dressed as Debbie, carrying his briefcase.

"What are you doing here?"

"You going to let me in?" he asked in his Debbie voice.

Kira nodded and made room for him to enter.

Once inside Derrick said, "Krissy called. She said your mom was sick again and you were being too pig-headed to call me because you didn't want to bother me."

Sounded like something Krissy would do. Sweet, interfering Krissy.

"And you came?"

He stared deeply into her eyes as he cupped her cheek. "Of course I came. I'll always come if you need me. Never worry about bothering me."

God she loved him. Kira flung her arms around his neck. "Thank you."

He wrapped his arms around her waist and hugged her back. "So what's going on?"

Kira stepped back. "Nothing." She motioned into the living room. "Mom's fine. Watching television with the volume on low in a dimly lit room as usual."

"Then why—?"

"Come." Kira held out her hand. He took it and she led him into the kitchen. "Can I get you something to drink?"

He eyed her glass of wine. "I'm driving so maybe a cup of coffee if you have?"

Kira opened the refrigerator. "Instant okay?"

"Instant's fine."

While Kira took out a mug, filled it with water and set it in the microwave, Derrick set his briefcase on the floor, pulled out a chair and took a seat at the table. "What's all this?"

Her back to him, Kira froze.

She heard him moving around the papers.

Well… She turned. Krissy had gotten him here, the rest was up to Kira. "I'm guessing all this," she pointed to the papers on the table, "is the reason Krissy had you come all the way down here. Because it'd been so long since we'd spoken and I was nervous to call you…"

"Houses in Mount Kisco? Somers? Golden's Bridge?"

The microwave pinged. Kira made Derrick's coffee like she had so many times at work. Then she put together a small plate of the Oreos she always kept on hand for Mom and delivered both to the table. "I guess none of that matters if you've filled your office manager position." Kira sat down across from him.

Eyes filled with caring, affection, and hope, met hers. "I haven't."

Thank you! "And would you be willing to keep it unfilled for a little while longer until I can find a place up in Westchester, sell my condo, and move Mom and me up there?"

Still staring at her, he nodded. "But what about your high-paying job with WCHC?"

Kira smiled. "Turns out I like the perks of working for you more than a big salary."

He slid his chair back and held out his arms. "Come here."

She didn't hesitate, straddling his lap, hugging him close. "God I've missed you."

He squeezed her tightly. "I've missed you, too." He pulled back to look at her. "So. Damn. Much." He moved some hair from the side of her face, then slid his hand to the back of her head, and pulled her in for a deep, loving, wonderful kiss.

"I smell Oreos," Mom called out from the other room.

Kira stiffened. Not now.

"Go," Derrick said.

"I'm sorry." Kira climbed off of his lap.

"Don't be."

She called out to Mom, "Be right there." Then to Derrick she said, "This is my life. Even with Tippy working as a live-in, she's going to need help, and time off. And I'll need to—"

"I understand, Kira," Derrick said. "I only wish I could help, that everything didn't fall on you."

How had she gotten so lucky? Kira took the package of Oreos down from the top shelf of the closet where she hid them. "After Mom gets settled in our new place, and I honestly have no idea how long that will take, maybe I can introduce a new caregiver. But even then—"

"I know what I'm getting into." Derrick stood. "I'm going into this relationship with my eyes wide open." He walked up behind her. "I can deal with sharing you." He leaned in and set a tender kiss on the side of her neck. "It's not having you in my life that's giving me trouble." He pressed in close. "Not having you in my bed." He thrust his pelvis against her butt. "Not seeing you every day or being able to talk with you."

"Oreos!" Mom yelled.

Kira turned in his arms, went up on her tippy toes and gave him a kiss on the cheek. "Hold that thought." She opened the refrigerator, grabbed the milk, and poured Mom a glass. "Be right back."

Mom taken care of, Kira returned to find Derrick leaning against the counter, still decked out as Debbie, waiting for her. She walked right into his arms, wrapping hers around his waist, setting her cheek to his chest. "I know there are no guarantees in life, but I need some assurance you're not going to change your mind, that you won't, at some point demand more than I can give you, that you—"

"I'm not going to change my mind—"

"Because I love you and I'm letting myself think about a happy future, for the first time in a long time. A future with you and I know I'm getting totally ahead of myself, but maybe a baby. And if you have any concerns, any doubts…" She'd rather know now than have her heart broken later. "Because I'll be uprooting my life, and my mom's life. For you."

He lifted her chin and stared down into her eyes. "I have no doubts, Kira. I love you. I want you in my life, in my future." He sealed his words with a kiss. "I say we get working on that baby sooner rather than later." He thrust the bulge of his erection against her.

Kira laughed.

"That wasn't quite the reaction I was hoping for."

She laughed again. "It's your dress." She palmed his fake breasts. "And these."

He leaned in close to her ear and whispered, "Would you like to join me in your bedroom so I can take them off?"

Arousal surged through her system. She leaned against him. "You have no idea how much."

He thrust against her again, his erection even bigger and harder than before. Okay, maybe he did have an idea how much.

His hands caressed up her sides, stopping to cup her breasts before traveling back down to her butt. "When do you put your mother to bed?" He held her in place as he thrust his hips again. Lord help her.

Kira glanced at the clock. "Around ten." A whole hour and a half. "But maybe I can get started a little early tonight."

"You do that." He kissed her. Then, his lips still pressed to hers, he said, "I'll be waiting for you in your bed." As if that wasn't alluring enough he added, "Naked."

"I'll hurry." Kira turned to leave.

Derrick stopped her, reaching out to grab her arm. "Don't hurry," he said. "Do what you need to do. Take your time." He winked. "You're worth the wait."

In that instant Kira fell even more in love with him. He understood. He accepted that her mother had to come first. God willing, that would never change. "Thank you." She turned away, vowing from tonight on, she would make sure to always be worth the wait, so he would never stop waiting for her.

EPILOGUE

Six months later

KIRA HUNG UP the phone.

"Everything okay?" Derrick asked, walking over to hand her a glass of wine.

Kira set it down on the counter. "Krissy was crying so hard all I could make out is the baby is fine and she'll be home tomorrow as planned." And something about Zac being a jerk and life sucking and a huge mistake. "Thank you for offering to drive me down to Newark Liberty International Airport to pick her up. I would have driven myself but..." Driving around town and to work was one thing. Down to a bustling airport? Not ready for that yet.

Derrick held up his beer mug in a toast. "Happy to do it." Then he returned to his seat on the couch and picked up the medical journal he'd been reading when the phone rang.

Kira looked around the home they'd purchased, decorated, and had been living in together for the past three weeks, happier than she'd ever been. After much research, they'd found the perfect mother-daughter setup with three bedrooms and two bathrooms in the main living area, and a private apartment with one large bedroom, that they divided into two, and a separate entrance for Mom and Tippy. With the money Kira got from selling her condo in the city, they were able to put down a big deposit and still have enough left over for all new furniture.

She walked over to the sliding door that led to the deck and stared out into their large yard. "They did a beautiful job on the fence." A high wooden privacy fence that split the yard in two so Derrick could have his fire pit and cornhole and Mom could go outside to garden any time she wanted.

Her fiancé of three weeks—he'd proposed with a beautiful ring on their first night in their new home—walked up behind her, pressed in close, and kissed her neck—something he did often. "Can't wait to get you out there for some drunk stargazing."

Sober stargazing would likely have to do for the next nine months. "As soon as the April showers head out and the ground dries." Kira leaned back against his firm, broad chest. "Are you sure you're okay with Krissy living here until she finds her own place?" Especially on account of she'd be working at the family practice, too.

"Your family is my family."

Poor man, he'd really taken on a lot when he'd taken on Kira. She turned in his arms and looked up at him. "There's something I've been putting off telling you."

He looked down at her with concern. "What?"

"It may be just stress from the move and work being so busy and all the problems I've been having getting Mom settled in. But…I'm late."

It took him a few seconds to figure out what that meant. "You mean?"

She nodded. "Our crazy family may be getting bigger."

He picked her up and spun her around.

Kira laughed. "So I take that to mean you're happy about the news?"

He walked them over to the couch and sat down, settling Kira in his lap. "I am ecstatic about the news." He smiled. Then he kissed her.

Kira was ecstatic, too. They'd only been together for a few months, but Derrick had already given her a future filled with more happiness than she'd thought possible. "Thank you for coming down to the city to yell at me." She shifted around until she was straddling his lap, one of her favorite places to be.

"I didn't—"

She put her finger to his lips. "Yes, you did."

He smiled. "You're right. I did."

"And thank you for following me to that bar, and dragging me up to your parents' house, and coming to my condo when Mom was sick." She rocked along the growing length of him. "Thank you for loving me enough to put up with a life that includes my mother and my sister."

He started to move beneath her.

"Thank you for giving me a job I love that makes it possible for me to spend so much time with the man I love." She leaned in and kissed him.

"I love you, too." He held her tightly. "Now let's go to the bedroom so I can show you how much."

He showed her every day, in *and* out of the bedroom. Kira climbed off of his lap. "Bet I can make you come first."

Derrick scooped her up into his arms and ran down the hall. "Bet I can make *you* come first."

Twenty minutes later, Derrick won. And Kira was perfectly okay with that.

* * * * *

Look out for the next great story in the
NURSES TO BRIDES *duet*
THE NURSE'S NEWBORN GIFT.

And if you enjoyed this story, check out these other great reads from Wendy S. Marcus:

NYC ANGELS: TEMPTING NURSE SCARLET
CRAVING HER SOLDIER'S TOUCH
SECRETS OF A SHY SOCIALITE
THE NURSE'S NOT-SO-SECRET SCANDAL

All available now!

THE NURSE'S
NEWBORN GIFT

BY
WENDY S. MARCUS

Published in Great Britain 2016
By Mills & Boon, an imprint of HarperCollins*Publishers*
1 London Bridge Street, London, SE1 9GF

© 2016 Wendy S. Marcus

ISBN: 978-0-263-91504-4

Our policy is to use papers that are natural, renewable and recyclable
products and made from wood grown in sustainable forests.
The logging and manufacturing processes conform to the legal
environmental regulations of the country of origin.

Printed and bound in Spain
by CPI, Barcelona

This book is dedicated to my readers.
Thank you for reading and reviewing my books.
I love chatting with you on social media!

With special thanks to my son, who didn't want to have
his name mentioned in one of my books,
for helping me with the athletic training aspects
of this story. Any errors are my own.

Thank you to my wonderful editor, Flo Nicoll,
for always pushing me to do my best.

And thank you to my family,
for supporting me in all that I do.

KRISSY PENIGLATT REMEMBERED the middle-of-the-night telephone conversation like it'd taken place yesterday as opposed to two years ago. Her best friend in the whole world, Jarrod, had called two days before he was scheduled to deploy for his first tour of duty overseas in the Middle East. A courageous U.S. Army soldier, prepared to give his life for his country, his nineteen-year-old self struggling a bit with the finality of the deed should he be unlucky enough to perish in battle.

"Promise me, if I manage to get myself killed, you'll do it."

He'd been there for her after her father had left when she was ten years old and after her mother's attack and subsequent severe traumatic brain injury shortly after she'd turned fourteen. He'd comforted her and consoled her and cheered her up time and time again, year after year, asking for and expecting nothing in return.

Of course, Krissy would do anything he asked of her, anything to put his mind at ease, to keep him focused on staying alive rather than what would happen if he... didn't. But, *"You're not going to get yourself killed,"* she'd told him. The response had been automatic. She'd refused to even consider the possibility of a life without Jarrod in it. They'd been inseparable for over a decade.

Sure, her leaving for college and him enlisting in the army right out of high school would change things between them. To be expected. But it was only supposed to be temporary. A few years apart, then they'd be ready to start their adult lives, together.

Well, not *together*, together, but inseparable once again, maybe living in the same apartment building, or in the same town at the very least.

"My mom can't stop crying," Jarrod had said. *"My dad can barely look at me without tearing up."*

They were such a kind and caring couple. An only child, Jarrod's parents' lives revolved around him. No parents loved their son more than Jarrod's parents loved him. Lucky for Krissy that love had extended to Jarrod's best friends as well. On some level, she'd actually felt closer to his parents than to her own. She owed them so much.

"I need to know," he'd said, uncharacteristically emotional, *"if my life is cut short, that some part of me lives on, that my parents have a grandchild to love and spoil. Because losing me..."*

He didn't need to finish. Losing him would be devastating, to his parents and to her.

The anguish in his voice had made her willing to say anything, to *do* anything to make it go away, to bring back the kind, happy, always joking boy she'd loved like a brother. So even though she'd never expected to ever have to follow through, she'd agreed.

"Okay. I'll do it, but only if you manage to get yourself killed, which you aren't going to do, so this conversation is a total waste of time."

A short two years later, twenty-one-year-old Krissy stood all alone, her body feeling weighted down by

hundred pound blocks of ice, the chill in her bones in
direct contrast to the beautiful, bright sunshiny spring
day, as she stared at the casket that held the remains
of her best friend in the whole world. The service long
over, only a few mourners remained, mulling around
over by their cars. But Krissy couldn't bring herself to
leave, knowing once she did, the workmen standing
off in the distance would lower Jarrod's body into the
cold, dark ground, and she'd never again be as close to
him as she now stood.

Her heart ached, literally hurt, every time she thought
about never seeing him again, never being on the receiving end of one of his powerful hugs, never hearing his
annoying snort-laugh that always got her snort-laughing
too.

A tear trickled down her cheek.

Who would she share good news with? Who could
she count on to cheer her up when she had a bad day?
Whose visits and phone calls would give her something
to look forward to? Who would ever understand her and
love her and accept her, as is, like Jarrod had?

No one.

Out of the corner of her eye, Krissy saw Jarrod's
mother, Patti, walking toward her. A quiet, plain woman,
with short darkish hair, a figure that tended to run toward chubby, and a heart filled with love, she looked
like she'd aged twenty years in the past two. "Come on,
honey." She put her arm around Krissy's shoulders and
tried to steer her away. "We have a room reserved at
a local restaurant. Jarrod wanted a party, so we'll give
him a party."

"And it's not a party…" Krissy started.

"Without Mom's caramel, fudge brownies with walnuts for dessert," Patti finished sadly, repeating what

Jarrod would have said if he'd been alive and able to talk.

The fact that he wasn't, and never would be again, sent another wave of tears flooding Krissy's raw, sore eyes.

Patti pulled her into a hug, not as wonderful as one of Jarrod's, but close. "I swear that boy could eat a whole pan by himself." She rubbed Krissy's back. "I put a batch in the casket with him," she said quietly, almost numbly. "Along with a picture of the two of you from graduation. Gosh darn it, this is so unfair."

"I know." Krissy squeezed her tight, well acquainted with the unfairness of life.

"Come on, you two," Jarrod's dad, Bart, said. A tall, solid man, like his son, he put a strong arm around each of them. "Time to go." He walked them away from the casket that held her best friend, away from the grave where he would lay for eternity…alone. "He lives on in our hearts," Bart said, walking slowly. "We may not have a piece of him to hold on to, but as long as we think about him and remember him, he'll never be fully gone from our lives."

But they *could* have a piece of him to hold on to, if Krissy did what she'd promised to do.

CHAPTER ONE

Five years and seven and a half months later

KRISSY SAT ON the bed in her temporary bedroom at her sister Kira's house in White Plains, New York, home from a mostly fantastic six-month assignment, that'd actually turned into seven months, in Hawaii, sorting through a mess of papers. She moved the real estate listings into one pile, time to find a place of her own and set down some roots. Help Wanted printouts got their own stack, her days as a traveling nurse over, it was time to figure out what she wanted to do going forward, in a job that would keep her in one place, but no rush on that. For the time being she was happy to work as an office nurse in her soon-to-be brother-in-law's family practice.

That left pictures and mementos of all the fun times she'd had with Zac, her ex-traveling nurse buddy/friend with benefits/almost but not quite a boyfriend. She scooped those up and dumped them in the trash basket on the floor, time to move on.

Krissy had waited long enough. She had a promise to keep.

And Zac, for as often as he'd professed his love for her, which happened pretty regularly after orgasms—

back when they used to have sex, before her successful artificial insemination—didn't love her enough to give up his carefree existence to settle down with her and start a family. Especially, he'd made sure to point out, a family that included another man's child.

Which was probably a good thing since Zac was everything Jarrod had hated in Krissy's boyfriends. Stuff that made him fun—he partied hard, didn't take life too seriously, and couldn't care less what people thought of him—would have made him a bad parent. Which is probably why, while their last goodbye had caused some tears—seemed tears came rather easily these days—the ache in her heart had been short-lived.

Krissy found the manila folder she'd been looking for when she'd first gotten the bright idea to dump out the box. The sight of her name written in Jarrod's scrawl still gave her a pang of loss in her chest, bringing on the memory of his funeral, the party afterward, where she'd sat in the back and kept to herself, and the talk she'd had with his parents before heading home.

"He left it all to you," Patti had said, handing Krissy the manila envelope she now held in her hands. *"His savings, some certificates of deposit, and his car. And you're the sole beneficiary on his military life insurance policy."* Patti had stared into Krissy's eyes, looking for answers. One question was obvious: Why would he leave everything to you?

At the time, Krissy couldn't do more than stare right back in bewilderment, shocked and overwhelmed by what Jarrod had done. For her. For the son or daughter he would never know. His confidence that she would do what she'd promised to do had made her love him and miss him even more.

When Krissy had regained her composure, she'd

briefly considered telling Jarrod's parents of her promise. But she'd decided against it, wasn't ready to make the commitment, or to get their hopes up. She'd only been twenty-one years old, for God's sake, just starting out, and in no way ready to have a baby.

But now, at twenty-six, almost twenty-seven years old she felt...ready. Well, as ready as a woman about to become solely responsible for the life of another human being could feel. Sure, it would have been nice to have a man who loved her and was eager to accompany her on this journey, but three boyfriends had been quick to skedaddle upon learning of her plans to have her dead best friend's baby. Fine. She never loved any of them as much as she'd loved Jarrod, anyway. And settling for Zac would have been a horrible mistake. Thank goodness he'd seen that, when she'd been too worried about the responsibility of caring for and raising a child, alone, to see it for herself.

"I *can* do it on my own," she told the baby in her belly, hoping it couldn't sense her self-doubt. "I'm going to be a great mom," she told herself, remembering what a wonderful mother her own mom had been, before the brain injury. If Krissy could manage to be half as wonderful, it'd be enough.

"I *will* do it on my own." She'd given herself five years to mature and prepare. Five years to travel and have fun and live life to its fullest before settling down to raise her child. Five years to find a man worthy of being her baby's surrogate daddy. Didn't happen.

"Alone is fine." Thanks to Jarrod and years of hard work and careful spending, she had plenty of money. She was used to living independently and had excellent nursing skills, which would surely come in handy during any bouts of baby choking or illness. Not that she planned on having to do everything on her own forever.

Surely Jarrod's parents would help with babysitting… if they were still local. She swallowed back the guilt of waiting so long as she opened the large tan envelope and pulled out the letters inside, all but one still sealed, each labeled by Jarrod with specific instructions.

#1—For Krissy—Open after my funeral

She'd read that letter so many times she could recite it from memory.

#2—For Spencer—When you're ready to give it to him

Spencer, of all people! Why did he want Spencer to be the baby's godfather? Spencer hated her. And, as of junior year of high school, the feeling was mutual.

#3—For my mom and dad—To explain our agree-ment

She planned to hand-deliver that one after the birth of the baby.

#4—To my son on his tenth birthday
#4—To my daughter on her tenth birthday

She caressed her pregnant belly, knowing that it would be Jarrod's son who would be getting letter number four on his tenth birthday.

"Stop putting it off." Krissy reached inside to pull out a piece of paper that had Jarrod's parents' home telephone number on it. God willing it hadn't changed. With a deep, fortifying breath, she picked up her cell phone and dialed the number.

First ring.

She twirled the post earring in her left ear, an annoying nervous habit Jarrod would have been sure to point out.

Second ring.

Suddenly parched, she reached for the glass beside her bed and took a sip of water.

Third ring.

She started to plan her message. *Hello Mr. and Mrs. Sadler. It's—*

"Hello?"

Krissy recognized Patti's voice immediately, so familiar it brought on a rush of emotion. She swallowed. Wasn't ready—

"Hello?" Patti said again.

Stop being an idiot. "Hi, Mrs. Sadler," Krissy said. "It's me—"

"Krissy! Oh, my word. How are you, honey? It's been… so long." Patti may have started out happy to hear from Krissy, but the sadness tinged with disappointment and hurt in her 'It's been…so long' was unmistakable.

"I know," Krissy said. "I'm sorry. I…" How did one adequately apologize for failing to keep in touch with a woman who'd been like a mother to her throughout high school? For failing to be there for a woman who had been there for Krissy when her own mother couldn't be? For failing to offer her love and support to a sweet and caring woman who'd been dealing with the worst tragedy a mother could face, the death of a child?

"I…" Krissy tried again. But how could she adequately explain that she'd tried to stay in touch, and she had, for a good year after Jarrod's death. But hearing the complete desolation in Patti's voice during each phone call had been too difficult? That it made Krissy feel things she didn't want to feel when she'd been trying so hard to move past the pain? That knowing she held the key to Patti and Bart's happiness, in the form of a grandbaby fathered by their beloved son, but not feeling ready to give up her freedom to have that baby at such a young age, made her feel guilty and selfish and just plain terrible?

"I'm sorry," she said again. It would have to do until she could explain further.

"I'm sorry, too," Patti said. "I've missed you. Now tell me everything. What have you been up to?"

Easy as that, sweet Patti moved past what a terrible friend Krissy had been.

An hour later they were all caught up—getting caught up on the happenings of Patti and Bart had taken less than five minutes, because not much new had happened in their lives. They were in the same apartment, working in the same jobs, still mourning the loss of their son. They were going through the motions of life but not really living. It would have broken Jarrod's heart to know. It made Krissy feel even more awful for waiting so long to give them a grandchild to dote on.

But in six weeks, all that would change. She wanted to tell Patti, wanted to hear the joy in her voice and give her something to finally be happy about, but not yet. Not until Patti could hold a happy, healthy baby in her arms. Mr. and Mrs. Sadler had been through too much, couldn't handle any more sadness if anything were to go wrong with the birth, or God forbid, if the baby wasn't born healthy.

Krissy forced out the question she'd called to ask.

"I'm wondering if you know how I can reach Spencer Penn?"

"Of course. Spencer is such a dear. He stops by for Sunday dinner every couple of months."

Shoot. Leave it to Spencer to screw up her plans. "I thought he was living out in California. Wasn't that why he hadn't attended Jarrod's funeral?"

"Oh, no. He was only out there for a week or two, taking his sister to look at colleges. I told him not to cancel his plans that Jarrod would understand. Now hold on a minute. Let me get his number from my address book."

Take all the time you need. Can't find it? No worries. Krissy was in no rush. She'd already put this off longer than she probably should have.

"Here it is." Patti read off the number. "If you don't mind me asking, why do you need it?"

Because your son has a sick sense of humor and I'm trying to do the right thing and abide by his wishes for Spencer to be our baby's godfather, even though the thought made her a bit nauseous.

"I was under the impression," Patti went on, "that the two of you weren't friends anymore."

No. They weren't. Not since that night... "I need to talk to him about something important," was all Krissy said, hoping Patti would leave it at that.

Thank goodness she did. "Don't be a stranger," Patti said. "If you have some time, we'd love to see you."

Soon, if things went as planned, they'd be seeing quite a lot of her. "I'd like that. I'll be in touch." *After your grandson is born.*

A week later, on a Friday evening after work, Krissy sat in her parked car, watching the clock, not wanting to show up too early. She'd kept the heat on, because an April evening in New York was not near as warm as an April evening in Hawaii. Or maybe it was nerves giving her a chill.

It'd taken days of back and forth messages to set up a meeting with Spencer, the pain in the butt. He kept suggesting various bars in White Plains, all relatively close to where she worked, saying a neutral location with lots of witnesses was safest for both of them. Seemed the years hadn't managed to mature him any.

Regardless of the fact she wasn't drinking any alcohol these days, the topic they needed to discuss would be better dealt with in private. So Krissy had insisted on meeting him at his apartment—which, as it turned out, was also relatively close to where she worked.

Learning that had been a bit unsettling.

The christening, the confirmation, and maybe a few milestone birthday parties was all the time she'd planned to have to tolerate Spencer. The bare minimum required for her son to get to know his godfather. Heaven forbid Spencer wanted to play a bigger role in her child's life.

No. Tonight she'd set some ground rules.

Krissy eyed the clock then the distance between her parking spot and the front door of Spencer's fancy high rise. Six minutes should do it, only because she wasn't walking all that fast these days.

At seven o'clock, on the dot, Krissy knocked on Spencer's door.

A few seconds later, it opened and ho-lee cow. The years had been good to the now very handsome Spencer Penn. He must have grown a foot since high school. His lean, teenage soccer player physique? Gone, replaced by muscles, defined, sexy, desirable muscles that were prominent beneath the short-sleeved black polo shirt and tight fitting khaki pants he wore. His thick, wavy, always mussed—in a lead singer of a boy band kind of way—dark hair? Gone, replaced by a shortish, surprisingly appealing, buzz cut. His smooth, boyish face? Gone, replaced by sculpted cheekbones, sexy scruff, and full, kissable lips…that were smiling as part of a 'You like what you see?' expression.

Shoot. Krissy focused in on his light brown eyes, smart eyes that, like Jarrod's, could always seem to tell what she was thinking.

Spencer looked her up and down his gaze settling on her midsection, "Still have a sweet tooth I see."

Any attraction she may have been feeling vanished. Poof! Gone. "Can you manage to *not* be obnoxious, for at least the next five minutes?" If she'd cared one bit what Spencer thought of her, she'd have changed out of her work scrubs and freshened her makeup or run some gel through her short hair. But she didn't care. Krissy handed him Jarrod's letter. "This is why I'm here. And I have no intention of standing out in the hallway like an annoying salesman while you read it. So either invite me in or I'm gone."

Without saying a word, he stepped aside and Krissy walked into his apartment. Feeling awkward, and not wanting to stand there while he read Jarrod's letter, Krissy asked, "Where's your bathroom?"

Spencer looked up from the envelope he'd been staring at but hadn't yet opened and pointed down the hallway to the right. So that's where Krissy headed.

Since she had some time to kill to make her visit believable, she spent it snooping. One toothbrush in the holder. Basic man stuff neatly stashed in the medicine cabinet. An electric beard trimmer. Deodorant. A small box of condoms. Mostly empty drawers. No tampons, or hair paraphernalia, or any signs the same woman visited on a regular basis. Rather than think too hard on why that made her happy, Krissy flushed the toilet, washed her hands, and walked back into the hallway.

Seeing Spencer sitting at the kitchen table, fully engrossed by his letter, Krissy took a few minutes to admire his apartment, neat, modern, and nicely furnished in tans and blacks, so different from the cluttered, messy bedroom of his youth. In the living room he had a bunch of thick textbooks stacked on a low shelf. Krissy walked closer. Anatomy and Physiology. Nutrition. Relaxation. Strength and Conditioning. Athletic Training.

Then she saw it, at eye level, a full color picture of the three of them in a plain black frame, Jarrod on one side, Spencer on the other, and Krissy in the middle. It'd been taken in Central Park, during the winter. They'd been all smiles, with red cheeks, disheveled hats and coats, and covered in snow. Happier times. The good old days, always together…until junior year, when everything had changed.

Beside it were a bunch of pictures of Spencer wearing the same clothes he wore now, posing with various adult male soccer players. "What's with all these soccer pictures?"

"I'm an assistant athletic trainer with the NYC United," he answered, his eyes never leaving the letter. "A semi-pro, United Soccer League team."

Pretty cool, but she'd never tell *him* that. Krissy remembered her sister Kira telling her there was a semi-pro soccer team in their area. They practiced and played at one of the local colleges, which explained why Spencer now lived so close to her. "That's what you went to school for?"

"Got my master's degree in it."

"What does an assistant athletic trainer do exactly?"

"Athletic trainers deal with prevention, acute care and rehabilitation of sports injuries."

Other pictures caught her attention. Spencer hiking. Spencer skiing. Spencer on the beach with a bunch of his good looking friends. *My God!* Krissy looked away. "No pictures of your girlfriend?"

"I don't have a girlfriend."

Good to know.

Why is that good to know?

Hmmm.

Before she could come up with an answer, Spencer interrupted.

"You're pregnant?" he yelled from the kitchen, in a tone that seemed to indicate women like Krissy shouldn't procreate. Really, he felt it necessary to yell? The apartment wasn't all that big.

"Yes," Krissy said, keeping her voice uninterested and her back to him as she perused the other pictures on the shelf. "Sorry you wasted a perfectly good insult."

"With Jarrod's baby?" he asked.

The disbelief in his tone had her swinging around to face him. "Yes with Jarrod's baby."

From where he sat, Spencer looked up from the letter. "How do I know?"

"How do you know *what*?"

He stood. "How do I know that's Jarrod's baby in here," he motioned to her belly, "and not some other guy's?" He walked closer. "How do I know you didn't get yourself knocked up and now you're digging out these letters Jarrod left you so you can get me, Patti and Bart involved so you don't have to raise the kid on your own? Do they know?"

A rage like she hadn't felt in years, quite possibly

since the last time she'd seen Spencer, surged through her. How dare he insinuate… "As if I would waste one minute looking for you if Jarrod hadn't asked me to. As if I would want someone like you in my life, in my baby's life, if Jarrod hadn't specifically stated he wanted you to be his baby's godfather. God I hate you. This was a mistake." She stomped toward the door. "I don't know what Jarrod was thinking." She bent to pick up her pocketbook—no easy task considering she'd soon be entering her ninth month of pregnancy, but no way would she ask Spencer for help. "And, no, Patti and Bart don't know. Not yet. I'm waiting until after the baby's born. To save them from worry…or having to grieve another loss if something goes wrong."

"Wait," he said, sounding tired.

No way would she wait simply because he wanted her to. But she could slow down long enough to let him have it. "You may not believe this is Jarrod's baby, and frankly, I don't care whether you do or you don't. I did what he asked me to do, out of love for him, but I won't—"

"Love." Spencer let out a cruel laugh. "You don't know the meaning of the word. If you loved Jarrod so much, why'd you flirt with him and tease and then flaunt all your boyfriends in front of him?"

Yes, she'd teased and joked. But she most certainly had not flirted with Jarrod. "I did not—"

Apparently ready for a fight, he set his hands on his hips and leaned in. "Oh, yes, you did. Holding their hands in front of him, sucking face in front of him, telling him the intimate details of your sex life, breaking his heart over and over again."

Breaking his heart? "I did not break his heart. We were pals, best friends. We talked about everything."

Although to be honest, usually Krissy had done most of the talking while Jarrod had done most of the listening.

"He didn't want to be your best friend. At least that's not *all* he wanted to be. I never understood how you couldn't see it? Except that you were always too absorbed in yourself and what was going on in your life to notice much about anyone else."

Even though that had been true, Krissy told him to, "Go to hell." She didn't want to relive those days. She'd moved on. She was a better person now. She was doing the right thing by having Jarrod's baby, following through with his wishes. But she refused to stand here and listen to one more word out of Spencer's mouth. She turned to the door.

"All the times you ran to him when you were upset, cried on his shoulder, let him hold you and console you. You gave him just enough to keep him content with the scraps of affection you tossed in his direction, to make him hopeful that maybe someday…"

"Shut up." Krissy's chest started to ache.

"He loved you," Spencer said. "Boyfriend, girlfriend loved you."

No.

"But you came after me." His words dripped with resentment. "Kissed me on some whim, without a care who saw you, without a care for my friendship with Jarrod or how much it would hurt him if he found out."

"What's the matter, Krissy?" Spencer had said to her that night. *"Getting desperate? Every other guy at the party turned you down?"* Like she was a common slut, like she'd only gone after him because no one else would have her. He had no idea how long it'd taken her to finally act on her feelings for him. If anyone had gotten hurt that night it'd been her.

Krissy turned back around to face him. "Jarrod and I were friends. Best friends. That's all."

"He wanted more." Spencer stared her down. "Why do you think he kissed you?"

An innocent peck on the lips, in the tenth grade, beneath the bleachers at a basketball game. "He said he liked me better than any other girl at school and he just wanted to see..." But there'd been nothing. No tingle. No spark. No desire to take the kiss deeper, for either of them...or so she'd thought...so he'd led her to believe. Why?

"Did you have to laugh afterward?" Spencer asked, doing nothing to hide his contempt, as he walked back to the kitchen, folded Jarrod's letter and stuffed it back in the envelope.

The whole kiss thing had made her feel weird and out of sorts. So yeah, she'd laughed. A nervous kind of laugh, because she didn't know what else to do, the two them standing there, alone... "He told you about that?"

Spencer nodded. Then he shrugged. "You confided in him and he confided in me. After you went off with your friends, like nothing had happened, he sent me a text." Spencer looked down at his feet. "I found him crying in the third floor bathroom."

"You told me he went home because he wasn't feeling well."

"He *wasn't* feeling well. He was heartbroken. He'd finally kissed the girl he'd secretly loved for years and she'd laughed in his face."

Krissy's stomach churned.

Spencer folded the envelope and slid it into his back pocket, casual as can be, while Krissy felt like the very foundation of her life was crumbling beneath her feet.

"The next day, after he'd calmed down he decided he

could be patient." Spencer's eyes met hers. "That you were worth the wait. That eventually he'd win you over, but you didn't make it easy on him, did you?"

Had she really hurt her best friend again and again? God help her. All the things she'd confided in him. Vomit started to creep up to the back of her throat. "I had no idea." Absolutely no idea at all or she never would have—

"Why do you think he went into the army?" Spencer looked at her with such anger, such…hatred. "To impress *you*."

No! "Don't you dare belittle his decision," she jabbed her index finger in Spencer's direction, "his commitment and dedication or how hard he'd worked to get into shape. He enlisted because he wanted to serve his country."

"He enlisted to impress *you*." Spencer shook his head. "There was no talking him out of it, believe me, I tried. After hearing you gush about that Martinez kid who'd joined the marines, Jarrod got it into his head that he'd join the military, too. So you'd gush about *him*. He'd planned to come home a war hero so you'd finally see him as a man."

What? "Are you saying…?" The ache in her chest worsened. The floor seemed to undulate beneath her feet. Krissy grabbed on to the wall for stability. "He joined the military because of me?" A sharp pain stabbed at the right side of her belly. "Ow." She rubbed the area, tears forming in her eyes. It couldn't be. "That he's dead…" Her whole abdomen tightened uncomfortably. "He's dead…" She couldn't breathe. "…because of me?"

Fluid gushed between her legs. "No." She clamped them closed.

"What's wrong?" Spencer ran toward her. He looked

down. Then he ran back to the kitchen, grabbed a chair and ran back. "Sit."

She wanted to yell, "I am not a dog," because Spencer brought out the fight in her. But if she didn't sit right then there was a good chance she'd collapse to the floor. "I can't have this baby. Not yet." She rubbed her belly, wasn't ready. "It's too soon." The baby kicked. At least that was a good sign.

Krissy could hear Spencer talking but she paid no attention to what he was saying, thoughts of Jarrod swirling in her head. He'd gone into the army because of her. He'd been killed because of her. *I'm sorry. So sorry.*

Spencer knelt down beside her. "How far along are you?"

"I'm due in five weeks." He repeated what she'd told him into his cell phone. "Who are you talking to?"

"An ambulance is on the way."

CHAPTER TWO

UPON THEIR ARRIVAL at the hospital, the ambulance crew whisked them right up to the Labor and Delivery floor where Spencer stood by helplessly—something he was not used to and did not like one bit—while the doctor examined Krissy and the nurse hooked her up to a fetal monitor. Forty-five minutes later, they were alone, Spencer sitting in a guest chair, holding on to a black and white sonogram picture. Krissy in a hospital gown, lying on her side in the bed, facing away from him. The sound of her baby's rapid heartbeat—correction: her *and Jarrod's* baby's rapid heartbeat—filled the tense silence between them.

What had Jarrod been thinking, asking someone as irresponsible and self-centered as Krissy to have his baby, especially when he wouldn't be here to, at the very least, keep an eye on her? And now he expected Spencer to do it? He shifted in the uncomfortable plastic chair. Friendship had limits. Even after death.

Ten years.

For the past ten years, since his father had collapsed on a subway platform and died of a massive heart attack when Spencer was only seventeen, he'd been the man of the family, helping his mother, looking out for his two younger sisters. Finally, just this year, with Reagan in graduate school out in California, Tara finishing her first year of college in Massachusetts, and Mom moved out of their old apartment and into a smaller, more affordable one close to her new boyfriend, he'd earned his freedom.

He had his own place, outside of New York City where his mother still lived, could come and go as he pleased without having to check in with anyone. In the off season he could spend the winter skiing in Utah or on the beach in the Caribbean. Or he could do both! He was responsible for no one but himself...finally.

And now this. Krissy was having a baby, and Jarrod expected Spencer to look after them both? He wanted to run from the room screaming, *Noooooooooo.*

Seeing her for the first time since high school—her face fuller, but still beautiful, the blue eyes that used to haunt his teenage dreams, her breasts looking even more voluptuous beneath her baggy scrubs—had been like a punch to the gut. And the way she'd been looking him over, with lust in her eyes.

Why couldn't she have looked at him like that back in high school? Why couldn't she have set Jarrod straight all those years ago? Told him, in no uncertain terms, that they'd never be more than friends? Then Jarrod could have gotten a real girlfriend and he wouldn't have gone into the army and he wouldn't be dead! Long buried anger, frustration, and blame had resurfaced. He'd wanted to hurt her, like she'd hurt Jarrod, so many times, like she'd hurt him. So Spencer had emptied the load he'd been carrying, telling her everything.

It was as if nine years had not gone by, as if he hadn't changed at all. As if he was still the antagonistic jerk he'd turned into all those years ago.

But this evening's little bit of bad behavior aside, he

had changed. He was more tolerant and understanding, at least he tried to be…usually. Now, when he wanted something, he went after it, regardless of who else wanted it.

Maybe she had changed, too, at least a little. While the girl she'd been wouldn't have thought twice about making an empty promise to her best friend, old Krissy probably wouldn't have made good on that promise, especially when it involved something as huge and life altering as getting pregnant and having a baby on her own.

That Jarrod had gone as far as to ask wasn't as much of a shock as Krissy agreeing, and actually following through, especially with Jarrod gone. Their agreement could have died with him. No one would have known.

She could have taken all the money Jarrod had left her—a decision that finally made sense—and lived quite comfortably without having to work. Yet she hadn't. According to Jarrod's mom, Krissy had said she'd been working as a traveling nurse. Maybe she wasn't the conniving opportunist he'd thought her to be all these years.

A nicely dressed woman in a pair of killer heels hurried into the room. Tall and thin, the opposite of Krissy, but with the same blue eyes and dark hair, only hers was long and up in a ponytail, it had to be Krissy's sister, Kira. "My, God." She walked past the foot of the bed to the side Krissy was facing. "Are you okay? The baby? What happened?"

A tall man with dark hair followed her in. "Give her a chance to answer."

Whereas Kira didn't notice Spencer, the man with her held out his hand. "Derrick Limone, Kira's fiancé."

According to Jarrod's mom, Krissy had mentioned working for her future brother-in-law, the doctor, at

Limone Family Practice. Spencer liked that the man didn't throw his title around. "Spencer Penn." Spencer shook his hand. Then, feeling the need to justify his presence, without admitting to most likely being the reason for Krissy's trip to the hospital, he added, "Baby's godfather."

"Spencer Penn?" Kira asked, and not fondly. "From high school?"

Yeah, *that* Spencer Penn.

Krissy turned onto her back and struggled to sit up.

Without giving it a second thought, Spencer rushed over to help her, for the first time noticing how tired she looked. No wonder. According to what she'd told the doctor and nurse, she'd just recently returned from an assignment in Hawaii, was already working full time while in the process of looking for an apartment, and had not yet had time to visit a local OB-GYN or attend a birthing class.

For a woman as pregnant as Krissy, shouldn't finding a local OB-GYN and attending a birthing class have been the first two things she'd done upon arriving in the area where she'd be having her baby?

"What are you doing here?" Krissy asked Kira.

"A nurse called me."

"Why did a nurse call you? I didn't ask a nurse to call you." She directed her question and statement to Kira. But she directed one heck of a look at Spencer.

Yes. He'd asked the nurse to call Krissy's sister. A woman, in the hospital, possibly about to lose her baby would *want* her sister with her, wouldn't she? Based on the look she'd given him, apparently not.

"Why did a nurse call me?" Kira said. "Maybe because my sister is in the hospital and couldn't be bothered to call me herself, that's why. What happened?"

"Don't look so worried," Krissy said to Kira. "I'm fine."

"You are not fine," Kira said, her eyes roaming over the fetal monitor reading then up to the cardiac monitor. "I told you to get in to see a local OB-GYN as soon as possible."

"Exactly!"

Krissy shot him a glare so fierce it would have burned all the flesh from his face, if such a thing were possible. Okay, so he probably should have kept his opinion to himself. *You're just screwing up left and right today, aren't you?*

To his surprise, rather than lay into him, Krissy turned to Kira and calmly said, "I didn't call because I didn't want you to worry. I didn't want you to drop everything and run over here, which is exactly what I knew you'd do." She reached out and held Kira's hand. "Between managing Derrick's office and helping Tippy care for Mom and being pregnant yourself, you have enough to deal with. I told you I could do this on my own and I will."

A snippet from Jarrod's letter flashed in his mind.

> *Krissy will try to do everything on her own, but she can't. She'll need help. And since I'm not there, I expect you, my oldest and best friend, my blood brother since the third grade, to be there for her.*

"I don't want to be another burden," Krissy went on.

"You're not a burden," Kira said. "You have never been a burden. You're my sister and I love you." She bent down to hug Krissy.

Krissy hugged her back. "I love you, too. And I *did* listen to you. I visited my doctor in Hawaii the day before I left. He examined me and said everything was fine. He recommended to follow up in two to three weeks. I've been researching doctors and asking around. As luck would have it, the doctor who saw me today was one of the ones I was considering. He's agreed to take me on as a patient. So there, you see?" She lifted her hands off of the bed. "No need for you to worry about me."

Then she whipped her evil eyes back to Spencer. "Now that my sister's here, you can go." Krissy dismissed him. "She'll give me a ride home."

"But the doctor—" Spencer tried.

"Don't." The about-to-commit-murder expression she gave him softened when she turned to look at Derrick. "You'll talk to the doctor," she said sweetly, "and get him to let me go home tonight, won't you Derrick?"

"Why wouldn't he let you go home tonight?" Kira asked, obviously worried.

"Because she came in hypertensive," Spencer answered.

"It's not a big deal," Krissy said to Kira. "Really. As if all the hideous and uncomfortable changes your body goes through during pregnancy aren't enough, a new fun fact I learned today, is that when your baby gets to be a certain size, he can kick your bladder and make you pee yourself and think your water's broken and you're going into early labor. I panicked. That's all. My blood pressure shot up and now it's back down. It's been stable throughout my pregnancy. Today was a fluke, a one-time response to an upsetting event."

She'd failed to mention the sharp pain and resulting abdominal tightness she'd felt just prior to her thinking her water had broken. This time he kept quiet. But even that didn't save him.

"Part of the reason I came in hypertensive," she said to Spencer, looking like she was trying very hard to stay in control, "is because *you* made me go hypertensive." She jabbed her index finger in his direction. "The doctor said I need to stay calm and I can't stay calm when you're here because every time you open your mouth you upset me. Now get out of here." She pointed to the door rather aggressively. "Before you make me burst a blood vessel in my head and have a stroke and you kill me *and* my baby."

Spencer couldn't help it. He crossed his arms over his chest and smiled. "Still have a flair for the dramatic, I see."

Krissy threw her plastic cup of water at him. Luckily she had lousy aim. And there wasn't much water in it.

"On a serious note." Derrick took on what Spencer figured was his Dr. Limone voice. When he had everyone's attention, he pointed at Krissy's cardiac monitor.

Her heart rate and blood pressure, which had, in fact, returned to within normal limits soon after she'd learned her baby was okay, were both back on the rise. Riling her up in high school had provided him with hours of entertainment. Riling her up when she was pregnant and in the hospital? He needed to be more careful. "I'm sorry," he said, forcing as much sincerity as he could into his tone, because he *was* sorry, for real, and for more than teasing her in that moment.

"Why is he even here?" Kira asked. "What would make you pick Spencer Penn, of all people, to be your baby's godfather?" She looked over at him. "No offense, Spencer. But last I remember, Krissy didn't think all that highly of you."

She probably didn't think all that highly of him now, either. Justifiably so.

"Because that's what Jarrod wanted," Krissy said.

"Jarrod?" Kira asked. "What's he got to do with this?"

"This is his baby." Krissy caressed her large belly over the monitor straps, looking down at it, her expression soft and loving and so unexpected, as was the warmth that spread through him when he saw it. "A little boy," she said, with a small smile. "Not to jinx anything, but I've already decided to name him Jarrod Junior and call him J.J."

J.J. Spencer liked it. Jarrod would have liked it too. He imagined a little boy with Jarrod's mischievous smile and dimples running around and getting into trouble. Between that little bit of imagery and the baby's heart beating loudly through the monitor, reality gave Spencer a second punch to the gut. Like it or not, Jarrod's baby would soon be coming into the world. And he'd need a good man in his life.

Spencer glanced at the bed, at Krissy's hands in particular. No wedding or engagement ring. Did she already have a man in her life? If so, she didn't call him to tell him she was in the hospital. And she'd put Kira down as her emergency contact.

Not that it mattered. Spencer would be there too. To tell little J.J. all about his dad, to introduce him to the banana splits with chocolate sprinkles his dad had loved, to take him to baseball games and introduce him to rock music and teach him all the things he knew Jarrod would want his son to know.

"This is Jarrod's baby?" Kira asked.

Surprising that Krissy hadn't shared that bit of information with her sister.

"Wait a minute," Kira added. "Your artificial insemination was done with Jarrod's sperm? He had his sperm frozen before he died? And you..."

Krissy nodded.

Spencer had been cruel to insinuate Krissy would try to pass off another man's baby as Jarrod's. Deep down, he didn't believe she'd do such a thing. But Kira mentioning Krissy's artificial insemination put an immediate halt to any lingering question he may have had.

Krissy yawned, a big, totally exhausted looking yawn. "I'll tell you everything. Later. I promise." She repositioned herself in the bed. "Right now, I really need to close my eyes for a few minutes." She found the bed controller and lowered the head of the bed.

"I'm going to go track down her doctor," Derrick said as he left the room.

"I'm going to go grab a cup of coffee," Spencer said, knowing Kira would be in the room if Krissy should need anything. But when he left the room, he didn't go to grab a cup of coffee. He followed Derrick, hoping to listen in on his conversation with Krissy's doctor.

CHAPTER THREE

ON MONDAY MORNING, Krissy sat at the reception desk at Derrick's office, helping Sara with answering phones and checking in/checking out patients, while Kira covered most of her nursing duties in the back. It was that or use a valuable sick day to stay home alone and rest, which would no doubt give her too much time to think about all she had to do before the baby came and worry about the actual giving birth part, which would be anything but restful. So Krissy had given in and agreed to Kira's terms.

The good news, she was getting paid. With her delivery date fast approaching, every penny counted. Working the desk wasn't so bad. And since Kira had been spending her time on the business side of nursing for the past few years, prior to taking on the job of office manager at Derrick's family practice, her nursing skills were a little rusty, which meant Krissy still got to work with patients who needed injections, blood draws, and/or EKGs.

Krissy had just checked out a mother and her newborn baby following her first checkup when Spencer walked in followed by a thinner but equally fit and equally good looking man. Lord help her. Spencer in khakis and a polo shirt looked good. But Spencer in black dress slacks, a crisp white fitted dress shirt and a black tie was off the chart hot. To the point his hotness was making her hot…and bothered.

Based on the 'You like what you see?' expression on his face, again, he knew exactly what she'd been thinking. The man was too cocky for his own good.

Krissy tilted her head down and pretended to look for something on the desk in front of her. "Stupid pregnancy hormones would have me doing the deed with the devil himself just to get some satisfaction." Good thing Krissy had more self-control than that.

"So I'm the devil?" Spencer asked, standing right in front of her, with a way too amused smile on his nauseatingly handsome face. He handed her a folder.

Krissy took it. "You weren't supposed to hear that." Heck, she hadn't even realized she'd said the words out loud. "I blame pregnancy brain."

The look he gave her screamed, "You're a total nut job," although without words.

Maybe she was. "It's a real thing. Look it up. It's like a pregnant woman's body is so busy growing another human being, the brain gets overloaded and doesn't filter stuff that shouldn't come out of her mouth or remember stuff she's supposed to do. It doesn't comprehend the same or think the same. I hope it goes back to working normally once all this is over."

His smile made her insides feel all fluttery.

Then he opened his mouth. "Your brain never worked normally."

"Careful," she gave him the stink eye. "Or I'll call Kira and tell her you're upsetting me. She's gotten even more overprotective now that I'm pregnant." And more bossy and more opinionated and more of a pain in the butt—who Krissy loved dearly, but still a pain in the butt, which was why Krissy needed to find the energy to go apartment hunting.

"Hmmm," Spencer said. "It's not like you to let Kira fight your battles. You going to blame that on pregnancy brain too?"

"No. I'm going to blame that on mother-protecting-the-health-of-her-unborn-baby brain. Stop trying to upset me, Spencer. What do you want?"

He had the good sense to look contrite. "You're right. I'm sorry." He leaned in and added, "And I'm sorry about the other day. When I told you—"

"Don't." She held up her hand to get him to stop talking. "You already apologized." About ten times in ten different messages on her cell phone. "I don't want to talk about it." Or think about it. "So if that's the only reason you're here, you can take your friend and leave now."

He looked at the man standing beside him. "This is Alfonso Gianelli, a newly acquired player with NYC United. He just arrived from Italy. I spoke with Derrick and then Kira yesterday. She said she could get him in for a full physical this morning. We'd like him to be able to start practicing with the team as soon as possible."

Nice of her darling sister not to mention a word about it. Krissy held out her hand. "Nice to meet you."

Alfonso smiled a charming smile, brought her hand to his lips and kissed her knuckles.

Spencer flashed him an annoyed look and said something in what sounded like Italian. Alfonso dropped her hand.

Killjoy.

"He doesn't speak much English," Spencer said.

Krissy looked Alfonso over and smiled. "He doesn't need to."

"Is Kira here?"

"She's in the back." Krissy checked the spelling of Alfonso's name on the paperwork Spencer had given her then wrote it on the label of a specimen cup and handed it to the patient along with two antiseptic cleansing wipes. "We'll need a specimen for a basic urinalysis," she told Spencer. "Does he need a drug screen?"

"Already done."

"Bathroom's over there." Krissy pointed.

Spencer spoke to Alfonso in Italian and the other man walked toward the bathroom.

Krissy couldn't stop herself from watching him walk away, even if she wanted to, which she didn't. "That is one fine backside on that man." Tight and round and just begging to be squeezed.

"Stop trying to make me jealous," Spencer snapped.

"I'm not trying to make you jealous." For that to happen he'd have to care about her, even the tiniest bit, which he didn't. "I'm merely stating my opinion." If verbalizing her opinion bothered Spencer, well, bonus points for that!

"How are you feeling?" he asked.

Now he was going to be nice? Which meant she should be nice too? Fine. "I'm feeling well. No more pains. Derrick has been checking my blood pressure three times a day. Mornings and afternoons it's been running around one hundred and thirty-eight systolic, seventy-four diastolic. In the evenings it's been spiking a bit. But I think that's because by the evening time I've taken all I can handle of Kira commenting on everything I do and eat and telling me what I should be doing and eating." She lowered her voice and looked him straight in the eye when she added, "While I know she loves me and just wants what's best for me, she is absolutely driving me crazy, more crazy than you drive me, which is something I'd never thought possible. If I don't find an apartment soon there's a good chance I might wind up back in the hospital strapped to a bed in an isolation room for the rest of my pregnancy."

And he was smiling again. Frustrating man. "You find something amusing about me being strapped to a bed in an isolation room for the rest of my pregnancy?"

His smile grew. He didn't even try to hide it. "I find *you* amusing, Krissy. Always have."

She looked away. "Not always."

A woman carrying a small child walked in and got in line behind Spencer. Krissy leaned to the side to see her. "May I help you?" She needed a little break from the soon-to-be godfather of her baby.

Spencer stepped away, far enough to respect the woman's privacy while Krissy checked her in. "You're all set." Krissy gave the woman a friendly smile as she handed back her insurance card. "A nurse will be with you in a few minutes."

No sooner had the woman left to find a seat in the waiting room, Alfonso returned. Perfect timing. Krissy held out a little plastic tray and he set his urine specimen on it. Then she placed their new patient paperwork on a clipboard, hooked on a pen, and handed it to Spencer. "Do the best you can to help him fill this out. When you're done, I'll take you back."

While Spencer and Alfonso took two chairs in the waiting room, Krissy accessed the computer system to see if Kira had already set up a new patient file for Alfonso. Of course her ever efficient sister had. Then she walked Alfonso's urine specimen back to their small lab, slid on a pair of latex gloves, and completed a dipstick urinalysis. After waiting the required length of time, she loaded the normal results into the computer on the counter.

"Hey," Kira said from behind her. "Why aren't you out at the desk?"

Krissy turned around to face her. "Why didn't you warn me Spencer was coming in today?"

Kira walked over to grab the phlebotomy tray. "Because I didn't know *he'd* be here. He called the answering service over the weekend. They've been having problems getting immediate appointments with the general practitioner they'd been using. He asked if we could complete a physical exam on a new player today. He said someone on the athletic training staff would be bringing him over." She handed the phlebotomy tray to Krissy. "Since you're here, I need blood drawn in room three. Orders are here." Kira handed Krissy her laptop. "I'll go get started on the physical exam for Spencer's soccer player."

"No need." Krissy stood. "I'll do it."

"You sure you feel up to it?" Kira studied her. "When I say feel up to it, I mean mentally and emotionally. He had you pretty upset the other day."

"If Spencer is going to be a part of my baby's life, I need to learn how to deal with him." She walked toward the door. "Best I do it in a medical setting where there's resuscitative equipment available."

After drawing five tubes of blood from a middle-aged female and packaging them to be picked up for processing, Krissy freshened the paper liner on the exam table in room nine then returned to the waiting room. "Alfonso Gianelli," she called out.

Alfonso smiled and stood. Spencer stood, too. When

the men approached, Krissy said to Alfonso, "Are you okay with him going in with you?"

Alfonso looked at Spencer who said something in Italian.

Alfonso turned back to Krissy and said, "Yes."

Krissy looked up at Spencer. "How do I know what he's saying 'yes' to?"

"I'm here to translate," Spencer said. "Word for word." He walked past her. "Where do you want us?"

Krissy walked them back to the scale and took Alfonso's height and weight. Then, with his back to the eye chart—because Krissy didn't trust him not to cheat—Spencer helped translate Alfonso's letters for the eye exam. After that Krissy walked them to the exam room where she completed a hearing exam and took Alfonso's temperature, pulse, respirations, and blood pressure. Spencer watched every move she made.

After going through the physical exam health screening questions—with Spencer's help—and entering all of the information into her laptop, Krissy took an exam gown from the drawer and handed it to Alfonso. "Please tell him to take everything off. The gown opens in the back."

No sooner had she escaped to the hallway, Spencer caught up with her. "Hey," he said, gently taking her by the arm. "Is there someplace we can talk in private?"

"I'm working." Krissy tried to pull away.

He released her. "I know. So am I. It'll only take a few minutes."

Fine. Krissy switched the plastic markers to the right of the door to red, indicating the patient was ready to be seen by the doctor. Then she led Spencer into the staff lunchroom. Once inside she closed the door, picked up the receiver on the wall-mounted phone, and called the front desk. "I'm taking a break in the lunchroom if anyone needs me."

After hanging up, she crossed her arms over her large belly and turned to look at Spencer. "You have two minutes." She glanced at the clock on the microwave. "Go."

He reached into the front pocket of his slacks and took out a folded up sheet of paper. "I know you're supposed to be resting. Which I hope you're doing?"

Since he looked more concerned than confrontational, she told him, "I am. And I'm taking it easy at work, too. Believe me, Kira makes sure of it."

"Good. Figuring you might be too tired to do it yourself, I did some research," he held up the paper. "From what I've read, a woman in her third trimester of pregnancy, which you're in, should take Lamaze classes to learn how to breathe and cope with contractions, even if she's thinking of getting an epidural."

Wow. Of all the words that could have come out of Spencer Penn's mouth at that moment, Krissy never would have expected to hear 'Lamaze classes' and 'epidural' tossed into a conversation.

When she didn't respond, because, wow, she was still trying to process what'd just happened, Spencer kept right on talking. "This is a list of local hospitals and their birthing classes, everything from baby care to breastfeeding."

Krissy fought back a smile. Did Spencer Penn really just say the word breastfeeding? This entire encounter could only be described as bizarre.

Either he didn't pick up on her amusement or he didn't care. "Your doctor's office probably gives Lamaze classes, most do. You should find out about that when you go for your first appointment there. Is Kira going to be your coach?"

"My coach?"

"Come on, Krissy. You're killing me."

He rubbed his hand over his head and Krissy wondered if his hair was as soft as it looked. Jeez. Where the heck had that come from? She shook her head to clear her wayward thoughts and get back on topic.

"Haven't you thought about who's going to be in the delivery room with you?"

No, she hadn't. In fact, she purposely worked very hard to occupy her mind so she didn't have to think about it, which was getting tougher and tougher as her delivery date approached. Of course Kira would do it if she asked, but her sister already had so many responsibilities. Too many responsibilities. Yet the thought of going through it alone…she looked away from him through the window to the parking lot outside so he couldn't see her fear. "Boy, you're taking this godfather stuff pretty seriously. I'd kind of figured your responsibilities wouldn't start until after the baby is born. So you can relax." And back off. Unless…she swung back around. "Unless you don't trust me to do what's best for my baby." That had to be it. "Unless you don't think I'm capable of managing—"

"Whoa." He held up both hands. "Calm down. I'm not here to upset you, I'm trying to help."

"Well I don't need your help. And I don't need Kira's help. I'm going to do this on my own. I *can* do it on my own. I *will* do it on my own." She repeated her mantra of late.

"But you don't have to do it on your own, Krissy. Jarrod wouldn't want you to go through all of this on your own."

Jarrod. God how she missed him, how she wished he was here. Tears pricked her eyes.

"Let me help you."

"Why would you want to help me?" she snapped. "You blame me for Jarrod's death." Now *she* blamed herself, too. "You hate me."

"I don't hate you."

Even though he towered over her, Krissy stared him down. "Liar."

"I don't. I know you're not responsible for Jarrod's death. He was an adult. He made his own decisions, however misguided they may have been. I'm sorry for what I said and how I acted when you came to my apartment. I was mean. You didn't deserve it. Seems I had some unresolved issues where Jarrod's death was concerned. But I'm over them now." He motioned to a chair. "Please, sit down. You look ready to collapse."

Now that he mentioned it, she kind of felt ready to collapse, too. Probably because this was the most energy she'd exerted since she'd left the hospital three days ago. So she sat.

Spencer sat, too.

"Glad I was available to help you resolve your issues," Krissy said, even if, as a result, she now felt even more weighted down by guilt. "Happy to be of service." In truth she wasn't happy at all. Rather than look at him, Krissy reached to take a packet of artificial sweetener from the basket in the center of the table and started flipping it between her fingers.

"Hey." Spencer reached over, slid a knuckle under her chin, and tilted her face up so she had to look at him. "I'm sorry, truly sorry, from the bottom of my cold, unfeeling heart," he said, with such sincerity she believed him. But the damage was done, the truth had come out— about Jarrod and about what Spencer really thought of her—and there'd be no unhearing it.

Only moving her eyes, Krissy glanced at the clock on the microwave. "You've exceeded your two minutes." She didn't like this nice, self-deprecating version of Spencer, didn't like the way it made her feel, didn't know how to respond to it.

Spencer released her chin and held out his hand. "Can we have a truce? Maybe start fresh?"

"Why?"

He reached down to her lap and took her hand into his. "We were friends once, good friends for a long time."

But they weren't friends anymore.

"And that's my best friend's baby in there." He pointed to her belly. "Can't we put our differences aside and do what's best for Jarrod's baby?"

Rather than remind him that little J.J. was part her baby too, Krissy thought about his proposal. She'd spent most of the last five and a half years traveling from place to place and had no local friends, as in good friends she'd feel comfortable calling for help in the middle of the night, in White Plains, where she now lived to be close to her sister. It'd be nice to know, in case of emergency, she had someone she could call aside from Kira and Derrick.

"Come on," Spencer said with a handsome smile. He let go of her hand and held his out. "Friends?"

After a brief hesitation, more to make him wait than anything else, Krissy shook it. "Friends."

"Good." Spencer unfolded the paper he'd set down on the table and turned it so she could read what he'd written.

"On top," he pointed, "is the hospital information. Down here," he moved his finger lower, "is the rental agent for my building."

"Whoa." Krissy sat back. "No."

"It's not my intent to overstep, but you mentioned you needed an apartment."

"I am not moving into your building."

He looked offended. "Why not? It's nice. It has security. It has ample parking and is close to shopping, Derrick's office, and White Plains Hospital. Also, I checked, they have two one bedroom units and three two bedroom units available for immediate occupancy. With a recommendation from me, you could probably be in by the end of this week, early next, assuming your credit's okay."

While Krissy liked the sound of 'immediate occupancy', "I can't afford it."

"I happen to know you were the sole beneficiary of a huge life insurance policy. You couldn't possibly have…" He hesitated, his eyes studying her face as he seemed to be trying to figure out the safest way to finish his statement.

Krissy stared back, at a crossroad. She could pounce on him for even thinking she'd blow through all the money Jarrod had left her. Or she could avoid confrontation and take the high road, so to speak, which is what she decided to do. After all, Spencer was trying to be nice. She could try too. "I have every cent Jarrod left me, and it's been accruing interest for the past five years."

Spencer let out a relieved breath. "Good. Then you can afford—"

"No I can't. I need someplace cheap. What if my baby is a genius and wants to go to an Ivy League college? I want to be able to send him. Then there's graduate school or medical school."

Spencer smiled. "Getting a little ahead of yourself

there, aren't you? The baby's not even born yet and you're planning his college education?"

"No. I'm being a responsible parent and trying to ensure the best future I can give my and Jarrod's son."

Spencer simply stared at her with an odd look on his face.

"What?"

"Nothing," he answered, glancing away. "I just… didn't…"

Krissy finished for him, "Expect I'd want to be a good, responsible parent?" She could have gotten offended. Instead she looked down at her belly and rubbed each side. "Jarrod entrusted me with a part of him. He believed in me, believed I'd make a good mother for his child. I'm honored to have his baby, to give his parents a grandson. I loved him, maybe not the same way he loved me," she wiped at a tear threatening to spill out of her right eye, "but I did love him. And I love our baby and will do everything in my power to see he grows up happy and healthy and is afforded every opportunity I can give him."

She lifted her eyes to Spencer. "I'm not the same person I was in high school. I may not do things according to everyone else's schedule, but I do what needs to be done by the time it needs to be done."

She pushed back from the table and stood. "Thank you for this information." She picked the paper up from the table, folded it, and slid it into the pocket of her scrub top.

Spencer stood, too. "I picked my apartment building, because I'm there. Well, not all the time. It's soccer season now, so I'm busier than during off season. I rotate traveling to away games with another assistant athletic trainer." He slid his hands into the front pockets in his slacks, the move relaxed and confident and oh, so sexy. "What I'm trying to say is, I thought it would be nice for you to have a friend close by just in case. Middle of the night? I can hop on the elevator, be there in minutes, rather than getting into the car and driving to wherever you are. Unless there's some other guy you'd rather call, then by all means, call him. Either way, I don't plan on bothering you."

"Or checking up on me?" Like Kira tended to do.

"Not up, but checking *in* on you, to make sure you're okay, to see if you need anything." He held up both hands. "That's all. I promise to respect your privacy. And I won't ever come over without being invited."

Maybe that'd work, if the rents were reasonable, and until she figured out what she wanted to do and where she wanted to be long term, after J.J.'s birth. Maybe she'd move back to New York City to be closer to Jarrod's parents. "Thank you, Spencer. Really." She looked up into his eyes. "For the record, no, there is no other guy I'd rather call. Well, except for Derrick, but then Kira would come too, and I'm trying to avoid bothering her. And, yes. I'll think about looking into available apartments in your building."

Someone knocked on the door.

As Krissy went to answer it Spencer said, "Great. And if you need a Lamaze coach…"

"Absolutely not."

CHAPTER FOUR

FIVE DAYS LATER, on Saturday morning, Spencer found himself driving to Lamaze class with an unhappy Krissy in the front passenger seat of his car.

"How do you like your new place?" he asked, trying to make conversation.

"It's fine," she answered, sounding bored, as she looked out the window.

Much better than fine, her one-bedroom apartment in his building—because the rent on the one-bedroom was less than the rent on the two-bedroom—was beautiful. Spacious, with freshly painted walls, refurbished hardwood floors and an updated kitchen. He knew the details for certain, because he'd helped Derrick and Kira move her in on Thursday night, not that she'd required much help since all she'd brought with her were two duffle bags, five or six boxes, and a small, twin-size bed.

Now, every time he rode the elevator past the fourth floor, to or from his apartment on the sixth floor, he thought about her, wondered if she was okay, if she needed anything.

Yes, as she'd pointed out during their chat in the staff lunchroom at Derrick's office, Jarrod had entrusted her with a part of himself. Well, Jarrod had also entrusted

Spencer to look after and help the woman he'd loved completely and the child he'd entrusted her with. Spencer took his responsibilities very seriously, always had. Jarrod knew that, had seen Spencer step up after his father had died, keeping a close eye on his younger sisters, protecting and guiding them, like his father would have. Better than his father would have.

As much as Spencer had been looking forward to his newfound freedom from his mother and sisters, the truth was he'd been feeling a little lost for the past few months. No way he wanted to take on the responsibility of another woman in his life, one mother and two sisters were enough, thank you very much. But the more he thought about it, the more the idea of helping and looking after Krissy and her baby, at least for now, until they were both settled, started to grow on him. It gave him a purpose, made him feel needed again. And just like researching future occupations, scholarships and colleges with his sisters, and helping his mom figure out college loans and investment strategies for retirement planning, Spencer had put in the hours to research pregnancy, labor and delivery, and caring for a newborn.

The timing worked.

During soccer season he could be around for Krissy, help her out. After she had the baby he could stop in here and there, make sure little J.J. was well cared for. Then, at the end of soccer season, he'd take off for a few weeks of rest and relaxation.

Playing the role of godfather to Krissy and Jarrod's baby didn't have to ruin his plans.

"I really appreciate you coming with me today," Krissy said, again, for the... Spencer had lost track of how many times she'd said it. "I have lots of friends down in New York City. But Kira moved herself and my mom up to White Plains while I was out in Hawaii. I don't know many people here yet."

She repositioned herself in her seat, again, either uncomfortable or antsy. He couldn't tell which.

"No problem," he answered, again, like he'd answered each time she'd stated her appreciation. The crash course version of Lamaze—three hours on Saturday morning and three hours on Sunday afternoon—worked out perfectly with his work schedule. Luckily he hadn't been scheduled to travel to Canada with the team. Only a few injured players had stayed behind for rehab so he could easily flex his schedule.

"Kira had to work today. I'm sure if I'd asked, she would have come tomorrow."

"But I insisted on going both days because—"

"Attending only half of the class won't make either one of you a proficient coach," she finished. "That makes sense. If you're even around when I go into labor."

"I'll be around."

"What if you're traveling with the team?"

He wouldn't be. Come Monday he'd be talking to management about his need to stay local for the next few weeks. "Even when the team is out of town, one assistant athletic trainer stays behind to work with the players who are injured. And not all of the guys travel with the team. The ones who remain here still practice, so an athletic trainer needs to be on site."

"Don't go changing your schedule at work because of me. I mean it's not like I *need* a coach." She continued to stare out the window as Spencer pulled into the parking lot behind her doctor's office. "I mean I *am* a nurse. I *did* do a labor and delivery rotation as a nursing student. I *know* what Lamaze is."

She demonstrated a breathing sequence he recognized from the Lamaze research he'd done online to prepare for the class. "During which phase of labor are you supposed to use that particular breathing technique?"

Still looking out the window, she crossed her arms over her chest, defiant, and said, "When it hurts, that's when."

Spencer pulled into a vacant spot, turned off the car, and removed his seat belt. Then he shifted in his seat to face her. "What's the matter?"

"Nothing's the matter." She wouldn't look at him.

"You're all sulky."

That got a rise out of her and she swung around to face him. "I am *not* all sulky."

Oh, yes, she was. It's not like he'd never seen her sulky before. This was her standard MO back in high school, every time he and/or Jarrod had tried to get her to do something she didn't want to do—like go to geometry class, stay after school for extra help in U.S. History, or walk directly home with them rather than getting into trouble with the kids who hung out at the deli on the corner.

In the past he'd have made a joke or poked fun to get her riled up. But not today. Today was too important. "What's wrong, Krissy?"

She turned back to the window. "I don't want to be here."

Now they were getting somewhere. "Why not?"

Shoulders hunched, she shrugged and mumbled something.

"What?"

"I'm not ready," she said quietly. "For the whole giving birth thing."

"You're not ready? I've got news for you. This baby's going to be coming in the next couple of weeks whether you're ready or not so you'd better get yourself ready."

She turned on him. "Don't be mean to me, Spencer. I really can't handle you being mean to me right now." Her voice sounded like she might be on the verge of tears as she turned to look down at her hands fidgeting in her lap.

A moment of vulnerability from the tough-talking, fiercely independent and confident Krissy took him by surprise.

"I didn't think this whole 'have Jarrod's baby' idea through carefully enough," she went on. "The pregnancy itself? Not totally awful. Raising little J.J.?" She caressed her belly lovingly. "I'm sure I'll get the hang of it."

Get the hang of it?

Her eyes met his again. "It's the getting the baby from in here," she pointed to her belly, "out into the world that's giving me some trouble."

"Krissy—"

"I have four weeks left until my due date," she cut him off. "In four weeks I'll have to be ready and I will be ready. Until then I don't want to talk about it or think about it or worry about it."

He reached for her hand, finding it ice cold. Whoa. "Hey." He gave it a squeeze. "You know it's normal to be scared." For sure he would be. "But women have been having babies for centuries, a lot of them over and over again. It's a very natural process."

"Says a man who has never experienced and will never have to experience the act of pushing a fifteen pound baby out of an opening the size of a walnut."

Smiling probably wasn't the best response, but he smiled anyway. "You're not having a fifteen pound baby."

She slid him a look. "You don't know that."

That's right. He didn't, at least not for sure. But according to his research, the average birth weight for babies was seven and a half pounds, with a range of five and a half pounds on the low end of normal and ten pounds on the high end. Since, even pregnant, Krissy was on the small side, he'd guess her baby would be on the small side too.

"All this talk about individualized birth plans and creating the experience you want. A bunch of bull." She waved off the idea. "I told my doctor I wanted the unconscious plan. A scheduled cesarean, so I know when J.J. is coming. General anesthesia, so I can sleep through the painful parts and wake up relaxed and happy and ready to get started on the mother son bonding."

She may be scared, but she managed to be amusing at the same time. "General anesthesia, that's your birth plan." She had to be kidding. Although she didn't look like she was kidding at all.

"Don't judge me, Spencer. I don't like pain. Pain hurts. And to have to endure it for hours and hours and maybe days." She wrapped her arms around herself and shivered. Then she shook her head. "Nuh-uh. Not for me."

"How'd your doctor respond to your request for general anesthesia?"

"He laughed." She looked like she couldn't believe he'd had the nerve. "Like I was joking around. Well I wasn't. I was totally serious." She fidgeted with her necklace. "Then he told the nurse to sign me up for the next Lamaze class. I told him I wasn't available this weekend but he told me to make myself available that he expected me to be here and would be very disappointed if I didn't show up. Like a parent tells a child. 'I'll be very disappointed if you don't show up,'" she mimicked in a deep, authoritative voice. Then she turned to look out the window. "I really don't want to disappoint him but...maybe I should find a new doctor."

"You don't need a new doctor." Spencer liked the guy, especially since he seemed to know how to handle patients like Krissy. "Maybe he wanted you to take this weekend's class because he thinks you're going to deliver early."

Krissy's eyes went wide and all the color drained from her face. "Don't say that. Don't even think it."

"Lamaze is supposed to teach you how to cope with the discomfort of contractions," Spencer said, keeping his voice calm. "Give the class a chance. Maybe you'll learn something. Maybe it'll alleviate some of your fears."

"I doubt that."

He gave her hand a shake. "I promise to take you for a hot fudge sundae when it's all over." Her favorite, at least it used to be.

"No." She shook her head and pulled her hand from his. "I've made up my mind. If my current OB-GYN won't knock me out with medication, I'm going to find one who will. So all this Lamaze stuff is going to be a total waste of time that could be much better spent shopping for furniture and baby stuff."

"As a nurse you know natural childbirth is best for the baby."

She turned to look at him, or, more specifically, to stare down at his crotch. "Hmmm. What do you think we could do to you to simulate what natural childbirth might feel like?" She smiled sweetly. "Then we can talk about natural childbirth."

Okay. Not going there.

"I have seen women give birth," she said. "I have listened to their screams on the Labor and Delivery floor. I have actually witnessed the birthing process, live and in person. I can tell you, in no uncertain terms, nothing short of knowing I will be heavily medicated so I can sleep through delivery, will put my mind at ease."

"Krissy," he cautioned.

"What?" she snapped.

Good lord. The woman was stubborn to the end. "We're going to Lamaze class," he told her calmly. Even if he had to drag her. "Just give it a try. That's all I ask. If you hate it and find it not at all helpful, we'll leave." Not before he did his absolute best to convince her to stay. Hopefully once he got her inside she'd calm down.

"You're not going to leave me alone about this, are you?"

He shook his head. No. He wasn't.

"Fine." She threw open the door. "Let's go waste the next three hours of our lives. Time we will never get back, by the way." She slammed the door shut behind her.

Spencer didn't care. She'd gotten out of the car, and that's all that mattered. Reaching into the backseat, he grabbed his pad and pen and the two pillows Krissy had brought, then he climbed out, too.

One look at what he held in his hands and Krissy slammed her hands on her hips. "Really? A pad and pen? You plan to take notes?"

Just to get a rise out of her he said, "I plan to study them, too."

"Poindexter." She turned to walk up the sidewalk. "Some things never change."

He smiled as he followed, hadn't been called that name in years and he liked hearing it, especially in Krissy's annoyed voice. Just like old times. "Call me what you will, but when you're ready to give birth, I'll be ready to coach you through it."

"I plan to be *sleeping* through it." She glanced back. "But thanks."

Two hours later, in a large, dimly lit room, with Krissy laying on her side on a mat with a pillow under her head and one between her legs, Spencer, and the couples around them, got an earful of how Krissy likely sounded and acted during sex.

Vocal—gratifyingly so, a total ego boost. He dug his thumbs into her low back.

"That feels sooooo good," she moaned.

Demanding—better to know than to have to guess and hope you get it right.

"Lower. Right there. Harder." She let out a deep satisfied breath. "Don't stop."

An active participant—the very best kind of bed partner.

She rolled her hips and arched her back. "Up a little. No, down."

He slid his hands up, then down, following her directions.

After her "Aaahhh," accompanied by a pleasure-filled exhalation, Spencer actually found himself getting a little aroused by it all.

The teacher, a tall, slender, middle-aged woman wearing a lab coat over street clothes, said, "Okay, time to change positions."

"Nooooo," Krissy whined loudly. "I like this position."

The teacher smiled at Spencer. "Looks like someone has the magic touch."

Why thank you, thank you very much.

Krissy turned onto her back. "Don't look so proud of yourself." She whacked him in the face with the pillow that'd been between her knees. "It's only because I haven't...been touched...in a long time."

The teacher called out, "Next position I want my partners to take a seat on the floor, backs straight, legs opened, knees bent."

Shoot, just when things were starting to get interesting.

The teacher continued, "Now I want my mamas to sit between their partner's legs, back to their chests, and rest your head on their shoulder."

Krissy maneuvered into position.

"Partners," the teacher said. "Slide your arms under and around," she demonstrated on another couple, "then clasp your fingers together on the top of her belly."

Spencer did as instructed.

Krissy felt so good and smelled so good. Her soft, fragrant hair tickled his cheek. Her body heated his wherever they touched, which felt like everywhere. How many times had his teenage self dreamed of holding her this close?

She wiggled her bottom then stiffened.

Krissy may have been clueless about Jarrod's true feelings for her, but she didn't miss the key indicator of how Spencer was feeling about her at that particular moment.

She wiggled her bottom against his arousal again then turned her head close to his ear and whispered, "Really, Spencer? I'm big as a manatee and we're at Lamaze class of all places."

She wasn't big as a manatee. She was full and lush and even sexier than she'd been in high school. "Sorry," he said. Thinking fast he added, "It's only because I haven't…been touched…in a long time."

Krissy pinched his thigh.

He tried to muffle his laugh in the side of her neck.

Then she wiggled against him again.

The minx probably planned to torture him for the rest of the class. Well, no way he'd allow that. Determined to put a stop to it, Spencer leaned in close, moved his mouth to her ear and quietly warned, "Don't start something you can't finish."

Krissy stiffened.

Then she pulled his head down and whispered back, "Oh, I can finish, Spencer, in so many different ways. FYI, those rumors back in high school were true." She licked his ear. "I give an amazing blow job."

Lord help him.

A rookie mistake. He should have known Krissy would take his words as a challenge and use her confident sexuality to say something outrageous that would give her the upper hand.

It'd worked, too. The image of a naked Krissy, on her knees at his feet, looking up at him as she took his erection into her hot, wet mouth filled his mind. At the anticipated feel of her sucking him deep into the back of her throat, over and over, he grew bigger, and harder, and more aroused.

She slid her backside in even closer, readjusting her position again, rubbing from side to side against him until all Spencer could think about was lifting her onto his lap, lowering her leggings and his zipper, and entering her from behind, thrusting up into her, again and again until…

This had to stop.

Spencer wasn't a sexually inexperienced teenager anymore. He was a man who liked to take charge and be in control.

So he called her bluff, leaning down to whisper, "Maybe I didn't get much action back in high school, but I've made up for it in adulthood." Not really, but what he lacked in quantity he'd made up for in quality. "You're not the only one with amazing talent. In fact, if you can keep quiet, I bet I can get you off in minutes, right here, right now, in this room full of people, without anyone knowing."

There. Take that! And just to give his words some added oomph, he ran his tongue around the rim of her ear eliciting a small but most rewarding tremble from her.

Krissy let out a breath and melted into him.

"What do you say?" He took things one step further, moving one of the pillows partially into her lap to hide what he was about to do from those around them. Then he slid his hand up her inner thigh, slowly, waiting for her to stop him, knowing she would.

"Krissy and Spencer," the instructor called out in an unpleasant, disciplinary voice, her eyes focused in on the pillow between Krissy's legs as if she could tell what he was doing underneath it.

Busted!

"Sorry," Spencer said. "Krissy had an itch she couldn't reach."

Based on her expression, the instructor wasn't buying it.

"I'm sorry, too," Krissy said, repositioning herself, again, in a move that made it perfectly clear to Spencer that she wasn't sorry at all. "Spencer had a question about your diagram. I was trying to answer it as best I could."

The instructor turned back to her oversize poster of the female genitalia. "Would you like to share your question with the class?" she asked Spencer.

"No." Spencer shook his head, feeling his face heat.

A few of the men in the room laughed.

"Okay, then," the teacher said. "As I was saying…"

With the attention no longer on them, Krissy whispered, "Just like high school, you're always getting me into trouble."

It was all Spencer could do not to laugh out loud. Invoking quite a bit of self-control to keep his indignation from showing, he whispered, "*Me* getting *you* into trouble? I don't think so! Not then and not now. You and your moaning." He moved in close to her ear to mimic, "'That feels soooooo good.'"

She gave him a tiny elbow to the ribs. "Well I'm sorry for moaning. I promise to be quiet from now on."

He didn't want her sorry and he didn't want her quiet. He wanted her as aroused and off-kilter as he was feeling. So he pressed his mouth to her ear and told her, "Never apologize for moaning when I make you feel good. I like making women moan in pleasure, means I have them right where I want them."

Krissy pinched his thigh. A lot harder that time.

Ouch! He resisted the urge to rub it.

"Pay attention," she snapped. "You're the reason we're here."

Right. Lamaze class. Birth coach. Huge responsibility.

Spencer needed every bit of willpower, determination and concentration in his possession to ignore the sensual woman between his legs and turn his attention back to Lamaze class. But he did it. Thank goodness the class ended twenty-five minutes later.

CHAPTER FIVE

KRISSY CAME AWAKE to someone knocking on the door to her apartment, but was too exhausted to get up from the couch to answer it. When the knocking stopped, she closed her eyes and started to sink back into sleep.

Until her cell phone rang.

She picked it up from the coffee table. Seeing Spencer's name and number on the screen she accepted the call. "Sorry. I completely forgot you were planning to stop by. Did you win?" His soccer team had played a Saturday afternoon game.

"Yeah. Three to one. Where are you?" he asked. "Your car's parked in your spot but you're not answering your door."

"Because I'm sleeping." She stretched. "At least I was sleeping until *someone* started knocking on my door."

"Open up," he said. "I have a surprise for you."

She wanted to, really she did. Even though he'd made it a point to call her every night around eight o'clock—a call she'd started to look forward to—due to their busy schedules, she hadn't seen him in almost a week, since Sunday's Lamaze class. But as much as she'd like to show off her handiwork in putting together J.J.'s crib all by herself, she just couldn't muster the energy to walk to the door. "Come back later."

"It's ice cream," he sing-songed.

Krissy's stomach growled. "What kind of ice cream?" No way she'd put forth the monumental effort to heft her massive body off of the couch for anything less than a hot fudge sundae or banana split.

"A hot fudge sundae, just like I promised."

After all the sexual back and forth during Lamaze class on Saturday, Spencer had gone quiet, making things feel weird between them. So Krissy had claimed she needed a nap and asked for a rain check on the ice cream, eager to put a little distance between them. On Sunday, Spencer didn't have time for ice cream because he had to head straight to work—after dropping her back home—for some late treatments.

Krissy's mouth started to water. "Give me a sec." She rolled onto her side and hauled herself into a sitting position, her arms and upper body feeling almost too heavy to lift. *Hot fudge sundae.* She set her hands on her knees, leaned forward and pushed up.

When she opened the door Spencer said, "You look exhausted."

"I *am* exhausted." Down to her bones. Too exhausted to remain upright, so Krissy turned around and headed back to the couch. "Which is why I was sleeping." She sat then lied down on her side and closed her eyes again. "Put the ice cream in the freezer, will you? I'll eat it later. Thank you."

"Are you feeling okay?"

She appreciated the concern in his voice. "Just a very busy week catching up with me." Tippy, Mom's caregiver over at Kira's house, hadn't been feeling well so Krissy had been helping out over there in the evenings after work so Kira could spend some alone time with Derrick before she went down to spend the night.

"Today I worked until three in the afternoon then I came home did some laundry, cleaned the bathroom and got involved in putting J.J.'s crib together." What a nightmare that had been.

She heard Spencer open her freezer. "I told you I'd put the crib together."

"And *I* told *you* I could do it myself."

"You know it's okay to let people help you."

"I know." But since the age of fourteen, since Mom's brain injury, Krissy had gotten used to doing things for herself. With her father no longer a part of their family, an eighteen-year-old Kira had been stretched thin, going to college while managing the expenses, the condo, and Mom's care. Krissy tried hard not to be an additional burden, to anyone, even though Kira might tell a different tale.

She heard Spencer walk into the living room. Something rattled. "Looks nice. But what's with that pile of screws and springs on the floor?"

Krissy yawned. "They were left over after I finished."

Spencer let out a breath.

Krissy didn't have the energy to read into it and start a fight.

"Have you eaten dinner?" he asked.

"I will when I wake up." Krissy yawned again, thankful Spencer had stopped talking, thankful for the quiet, thankful to be able to go back...to...sleep...

Sometime later Krissy opened her eyes to darkness and the smell of—she inhaled to be sure—Chinese stir-fry chicken. Hunger made her empty stomach ache. She turned to see the light on in her kitchen and someone moving around in there. "Spencer?" Who else could it be?

"Hey," he said, coming to stand in the doorway. "You're awake. I thought I was going to have to eat without you."

"What time is it?" Krissy sat up.

"Almost eight-thirty." Spencer walked into the living room and held out his hand.

Krissy latched on to it and he pulled her up. "Thank you."

He bowed at the waist then motioned to the kitchen. "Dinner is served."

As much as she wanted to eat, "Bathroom first." She hurried down the hall. One glance in the mirror and, "My God!" A wild woman looked back at her. Hair matted on one side, sticking out in all directions on the other. Eye makeup smudged. And drool, she wiped her mouth. Thank goodness the living room had been dark.

How she looked shouldn't matter. It was only Spencer, after all. But for some reason it did matter. He always managed to look good and she wanted to look good too. So after she emptied her overfull bladder, she took a few minutes to freshen up.

In the kitchen Spencer greeted her with a smile. "Feel better?"

She smiled back, feeling uncharacteristically shy. "Yes. Much." He'd been busy while she was sleeping. "Wow. You went all out." The table neatly set, all the pots washed and in the drain board, a yummy looking chicken stir fry with vegetables beautifully plated over brown rice and ready to be eaten. "I know for sure I didn't have broccoli or red peppers," she pointed out.

He pulled out a chair. "You had chicken breast, carrots and soy sauce. I combined that with some stuff I had and voilà!" He motioned to the serving dish. "A healthy dinner for two and two-thirds."

She smiled again at him referring to J.J. as two-thirds.

"We make a good team," he added as he sat beside her.

They'd made a good team at Lamaze class, too. "I'm impressed." She inhaled deeply. "I hope it tastes as good as it looks."

"It does." He served them both.

So confident. Wait a minute. "Let me guess. Cooking classes?"

He wouldn't look at her. "It was something to do."

"Good place to pick up women?" she teased.

"Good place to learn to make healthy food taste good," he countered. "Now eat." He pointed to her plate with his fork. "Before it gets cold."

Typical Spencer. Always learning, always taking classes or workshops to be the best he could be. As she enjoyed her first delicious mouthful, Krissy was glad he hadn't changed in that regard. "It's fantastic. You can cook for me anytime."

"I like your new table and chairs."

Of course he did, since he's the one who'd made her get them, even though she'd insisted she didn't need them because she mostly ate on the couch in front of the television...that is, when she ate at home, which she'd likely be doing much more of once she had little J.J.

"Good thing you have them so we can have this nice dinner together," he said. "And they fit perfectly in your kitchen."

Just like he'd said they would.

She looked up at him. "You were right, okay? There, I said it. Happy now?"

He smiled his handsome smile and Krissy's insides warmed. "As a matter of fact, yes I am."

"...you're not the only one with amazing talent... I bet I can get you off in minutes, right here, right now, in this room full of people, without anyone knowing."

Starting the ninth month of her pregnancy, with another man's baby, and she couldn't get Spencer's words out of her head, couldn't move past the way his touch had made her feel…so alive…so needy. A tingle of intrigue buzzed around her insides, settling between her legs.

"Hey." He ducked his head to catch her line of sight. "You okay?"

Nope. Not at all. "Yup." She forced a smile and stuffed more food into her mouth so she wouldn't be expected to say anything else. While she chewed she looked at Spencer, so neatly put together in a very virile package. Then she looked around her now neat kitchen. In so many ways he reminded her of Kira, organized, prompt, smart, and loyal, a know-it-all who usually turned out to be right. It irked her a bit. But he'd been so nice over the past two weeks, she could overlook it…as long as she didn't spend too much time thinking about it. So she changed the subject to something neutral. "How was work today?"

"Busy." He took a sip of water. "I've got to go in tomorrow morning. Not too early, but for a few hours."

He'd told her that during the soccer season, more often than not, he went into work seven days a week. "How's Alfonso doing?" Maybe she'd only met the new star player of NYC United once, when she'd helped with his physical exam, but she'd seen him almost naked, which put them on first name basis, as far as she was concerned. "I saw him go in for that header at the same time as the player from the other team." She cringed. "It looked bad." He'd gone down hard and had needed to be helped off the field.

"I didn't know you were a soccer fan."

She wasn't. At least she hadn't been prior to learning of Spencer's job with NYC United. Now, whenever she could, she watched the games, hoping for a glimpse of Spencer on the sidelines, or better yet, seeing him in action on the field. Not that she'd tell *him* that. "I'm a fan of the Italian hottie, Alfonso Gianelli."

"You and hundreds of other women." Spencer sounded peeved. "He's a player, and I'm not talking about his skills with a soccer ball." He looked up from his plate. "Stay away from him."

"As if he'd have any interest in me now." Thirty pounds heavier than normal, which even before her pregnancy tended to run toward full-figured. But she appreciated the hint of something...concern, maybe jealousy in his voice.

Spencer's eyes met hers. "Knock it off. You're beautiful and sexy and you know it."

"I'm fat," came out of her mouth before she even had a chance to process what Spencer had said.

"You're pregnant. There's a difference."

Whoa. "You think I'm beautiful and sexy?" She stood to remind him what she looked like, arching her back to make her oversize belly protrude even more than usual. "Almost nine months pregnant." She tilted her head as she stared down at him. "Have you been drinking? I mean I know I don't have any booze down here, but did you toss back a few beers up at your place when you went to raid your fridge?"

His expression totally serious, Spencer said, "No, I haven't been drinking. And yes, even at almost nine months pregnant. Now stop looking for compliments and finish eating. I'm ready for my ice cream."

Oh, no. She liked this topic of conversation and wanted to spend a little more time on it. "Hmmm." She tapped her chin. "So it was me, in all my pregnant glory, who turned you on at Lamaze class?" How flattering. "You hadn't been thinking of someone else?

That impressive hard-on wasn't only because you hadn't had full body contact with a woman in a while?" A topic worthy of further discussion at a later time. "It wasn't being in a room with all those hormonal pregnant women that got you going? Tell me the truth. Do you have some kind of pregnancy fetish? Is that why you were so determined to get me to go to that class?" Krissy teased.

Fork halfway up to his mouth, Spencer froze. Then his heated gaze locked on hers. "You found my...hard-on, as you so eloquently put it, impressive?"

Out of everything she'd just said, he'd chosen that one thing to focus in on. Such a guy. "*Now* who's looking for compliments?" God Krissy had missed this, had missed Spencer and this crazy banter between them.

Oh, so casually he removed the napkin from his lap and blotted his mouth. "As a matter of fact I *was* thinking of another woman."

Way to ruin her fun.

"Or at least another time." He stood, cleared his dishes and placed them in the sink. "You were a teenage boy's wet dream." He turned to face her, leaning his hip against the counter. "The way you teased and flirted. Your body." He shook his head. "Seeing you again...it's sent me back in time. I'm sorry. It won't happen again."

What? No need to apologize. Wait a minute. "A teenage boy's wet dream? *Your* wet dream?" She couldn't believe it. "Then why...?" When she'd offered herself to him... "Why...?" Had he been so mean, so...hurtful?

"It's a long story," he said, turning around, giving her his back.

"Tell me. I've got time."

He ran the water and soaped up the sponge. "No."

She recognized the finality of that tone, knew there'd be nothing she could do to get him to talk more on that subject. At least not right now. Krissy could be patient, could wait for a better time to bring it up. She stood and walked her dishes over to the sink. "Don't want to talk about that? How about we talk about you not being touched in a while." Standing next to him, her back to the counter, she looked up. "You know, like exactly how long 'a while' has been and why?"

"Or," in the process of rinsing a glass, he turned his head to face her. "We can talk about exactly how long 'a while' has been for *you*, and why."

Nah. That would require bringing up her relationship with Zac, and how, upon learning she was pregnant, he'd refused to do anything more than hold her hand, which she had no desire to do.

"So work it is." She returned to the table, clearing Spencer's delicious entrée. "What's the final diagnosis on Alfonso? Concussion?" She took the plastic wrap from a drawer.

"You know I can't discuss my patients with you," he said.

Right. The rules of confidentiality applied to all health care professionals, not just doctors and nurses. "So what *can* you tell me?" She wrapped up the leftovers and put them in the refrigerator, kind of liking this bit of shared domesticity and having someone to talk to. "Describe a typical work day."

"First thing we do is get the water together to keep the athletes hydrated during practices and games." He continued washing the dishes while he talked. Krissy picked up a towel and started to dry. "We stock the med kits with appropriate medical supplies. Then the athletes start coming in for pre-practice or pre-game treatments consisting of modalities such as therapeutic ultrasound or electrical stimulation—for pain control or edema reduction, manual therapy, anything from stretching to spinal and/or joint mobilization. In soccer we tape a lot of ankles as a preventative measure to avoid injuries. We attend all practices and games to handle any medical emergencies."

"What types of medical emergencies have you dealt with?"

"You name it, I've probably seen it. Everything from orthopedic injuries, sprains, strains and fractures, to head injuries, to lacerations and contusions. Heat stroke, hypoglycemic shock. Cardiac emergencies like commotio cordis."

"Commotio what?"

"A disruption of the heart rhythm as a result of a strong blow to the chest directly over the heart."

"Yikes. What do you do for that?"

"Apply an AED—automated external defibrillator—as soon as possible and activate emergency medical services to get the player to the hospital. The one time I had to deal with it, the player lived. Not all of them do."

The kitchen clean and their conversation winding down, Krissy realized she'd been enjoying their visit and didn't want him to leave. "If you don't have plans tonight, would you want to hang out and watch a movie?" she asked, turning on the light in her sparsely furnished living room then retrieving the remote from the coffee table. "We could rent something On Demand." In the fully lit room, Krissy noticed the crib, or more precisely, the missing pile of leftover pieces she'd stacked beneath it. "Hey. Did you work on the crib while I was sleeping?"

"Yeah," he called from the kitchen.

"You know I had every intention of going back over the directions to see where I went wrong. I wouldn't put J.J. in an unsafe crib."

Standing in the doorway to the kitchen, wiping his

hands on a towel, Spencer said, "I know you wouldn't put J.J. in an unsafe crib."

At least that was something.

"But I wanted to help and you were sleeping so I helped."

Thank goodness. Even though she had, in fact, planned to retrace her assembly steps, she wasn't looking forward to it.

"I put together the changing table too."

Krissy lifted the box to find it empty.

"I moved it into your bedroom, but I can put it anywhere you'd like."

"Thank you," she said, meaning it. "Bedroom's fine."

"I'll put the crib in there too if that's where you want it."

"I can wheel it in there."

"So ice cream and a movie?" he asked.

Sounded great to her, she clicked on the television. But when she turned around to set the remote back down on the coffee table, her eyes slid over her small couch, the only place to sit in the living room, other than the floor. A niggling worry in the back of her mind had her thinking maybe being alone with Spencer, on the same couch, wasn't such a great idea.

"What?" he asked, still able to read her better than most.

"Uh." How to explain? She pointed to the couch. "That's the only thing I have to sit on."

"So?"

She pointed back and forth between them. "There seems to be some latent sexual chemistry between us that's, I don't know, come back to life or something."

He crossed his arms over his chest and leaned against the doorway, looking amused.

"Stop it," she snapped.

"Worried you won't be able to resist me?"

So cocky. "Worried I won't be able to resist smacking you is more like it." She stormed past him into the kitchen and yanked open her freezer.

"Krissy," he said.

"Don't." She found the sundae he'd brought for her, set it on the counter and reached into an upper cabinet for a bowl. Then she pulled out the silverware drawer and took out a sharp knife and a spoon.

"Krissy," he said again, standing closer this time.

She ignored him, ripping a banana from one of the two big bunches on her counter, peeling it, slicing it and placing the pieces into the bottom of the bowl. Then she opened the refrigerator and pulled out a container of fresh strawberries. "I'm kind of tired," she lied as she washed and sliced a few, placing them in the bowl too. "You should probably go." She scooped half of the ice cream and fudge topping into the bowl then put the rest back into the freezer.

That's when she noticed Spencer staring at her with an odd expression on his face.

"What?"

"Strawberries and bananas."

Jarrod's favorite fruits.

"Back in high school you wouldn't eat strawberries because you didn't like it when the tiny seeds got stuck in your teeth."

Still didn't like it.

"And you hated bananas, used to give Jarrod such a hard time whenever he ate one in front of you, said you couldn't even stand the smell."

Or the way they got so mushy. "Yeah. In some sick turn of events, since my morning sickness ended I crave them, can't get enough of them." She looked up at the ceiling. "I bet Jarrod's up in heaven laughing himself sick about it."

Spencer smiled. "Probably."

Krissy took a spoonful of ice cream, making sure to include some banana, some strawberry and some fudge. The flavors converged on her taste buds. Amazingly fantastic. Better than sex. Not really. Not even close. She turned to Spencer. "Why are you still here?"

"What's wrong?"

She shoved another perfectly composed spoonful of ice cream into her mouth to put off having to answer.

All too soon her mouth was empty. But when she tried to fill it again, Spencer put a hand on her forearm to stop her. "Talk to me."

Lord help her. Talking was the last thing she wanted to do with him.

Needing to say something, she looked down at her melting ice cream and shrugged. "Since Lamaze class I'm..." How to put it... "I feel..." Tense and horny and frustratingly unsatisfied.

"How do you feel?" Spencer asked quietly.

She shrugged again. "It doesn't matter." She wouldn't let it matter. "You should go."

He didn't go. "Tell me," he said, like he already knew, like he understood.

But she wouldn't be fooled. "So you can tease me?" So he could reject her again?

He shook his head, so serious.

Oh, how she wished Jarrod were here. She used to be able to tell him anything, everything. But Jarrod wasn't here. Only Spencer was, as was a lingering attraction from her youth.

An attraction she couldn't act on. He needed to go. And the best way to ensure he'd leave? Tell him the truth. In Krissy's experience, nothing made a man leave quicker than when a woman shared her innermost feelings. So she stood tall, looked him straight in the eyes, and told him the truth. "I feel tense and horny and frustratingly unsatisfied." There. Done.

She braced herself for the sting of his comeback, totally unprepared when he pulled her into his arms and said, "Me too," milliseconds before he lowered his mouth to hers.

Oh. My. God.

His lips felt warm and soft, his arms big and strong as he held her close, while being careful not to squeeze her pregnant belly.

He tightened his hold on her, moved his mouth and deepened the kiss. Pleasure took over. Need. Krissy reached up, clasped her hands around his neck and held on for the ride. This kiss had everything her kiss with Jarrod had lacked. This kiss…this soul-scorching, life-changing, earth-shattering kiss bombarded her senses like no other kiss ever had, made her feel so many things, too many things. An overwhelming intensity. An excited thrill. Affection. Lust. Anticipation. Desire. And fear.

It was too intense, too…perfect. It felt too…right, when it couldn't be right. Not with Spencer, not after all they'd been through, not after finding out what he thought of her.

She pushed him away, both of them breathing heavily.

"We shouldn't," she said. No matter how much she may have wanted to, and she *really* wanted to, taking things one step further would make an already complicated relationship significantly more complicated.

Spencer must have thought so too because he responded with an, "I know." Then, without another word, he turned away, walked to the door, and left her apartment.

CHAPTER SIX

THE NEXT DAY, it took a monumental effort, but Spencer pushed his stupidity from the prior evening out of his mind to focus on his work. The current player on his exam table, Sergio, one of their top defenders, was suffering from an adductor strain, two weeks post injury, almost ready to return to play. Dressed in a pair of black shorts he laid on his back with his right leg bent and externally rotated, his knee propped on a balled-up towel for comfort. "How's it been feeling?" Spencer lifted the heat pack from his patient's groin.

"Better."

Most of the guys rarely complained, didn't want to spend too much time out of the lineup. Spencer would be sure to pay special attention to the patient's range of motion tolerance at the end of their session.

"Time for some therapeutic ultrasound." He reached for the transducer. "With one finger, point to where you have the most pain."

"I don't have much pain anymore," Sergio said. "But when I do, it's here." He pointed.

Spencer spread gel on the flat transducer head and on the area Sergio had identified as most painful. Then he placed the transducer on his patient's skin, turned on the machine and set the ultrasound parameters. Keeping the transducer moving, he maintained constant contact with the skin over the localized area.

"You still taking ibuprofen?" Spencer asked.

"Every morning before coming in."

"Good."

Andres, their top scorer, recovering from a grade one inversion ankle sprain, stuck his head into the training room. "I'm finished with my exercises."

Earlier Spencer had progressed him to resistance band training. "How'd it go?"

"Still sore."

Busy with the ultrasound, Spencer told him to, "Make yourself an ice bag and ice it for fifteen minutes."

Andres did as instructed, taking the treatment table beside Sergio.

The timer dinged and the ultrasound machine shut off. Spencer wiped off the transducer head then handed the player the towel to wipe the gel from his leg. That done, he repositioned Sergio's leg and began passive stretching. "Tell me when you feel a stretch. You shouldn't feel pain."

As he applied tension, he counted off fifteen seconds then ten seconds for each rest before starting again. He pushed hard today, testing flexibility. "How's that feel?"

"Fine."

"No pain?"

"None at all."

"Good. I think tomorrow we'll head out to the field and do some work with the ball."

"Sounds good to me."

Spencer finished up then went to the sink to wash his hands. "Head on over to the weight room and get started on your exercise plan. I'll be in to check on you in a few minutes."

Around two o'clock that afternoon, Spencer had just started to clean up the athletic training room, when his cell phone buzzed in his pocket. Seeing Krissy's name and number on the screen, he hesitated. He'd acted like a jerk last night, walking out on her without taking the time to explain…again. He debated not answering, needed more time to figure out how to apologize, how to put everything he was feeling into words, if that was even possible.

But she rarely called him. What if…? He accepted the call. "Hello?"

"Spencer Penn?"

A woman spoke. It wasn't Krissy.

"Who is this?"

"I'm calling from White Plains Hospital."

Spencer froze. "Is Krissy okay?"

Hearing a pained yell in the background, he dug into his pocket to grab his office keys and headed out the door.

"She wants to talk to you. Please hold on. A contraction took her by surprise."

Phone to his ear, Spencer hurried down the long hallway to the large lunch/meeting room, listening to Krissy's pained groans along the way. Why wasn't the nurse coaching her in Lamaze breathing?

Three of the players he'd just finished working with stood at the far table autographing shirts and soccer balls for fans. The strength and conditioning coach sat reading the newspaper.

"Al," Spencer called to him. "I've got to take off. You'll lock up?"

"Is it time?" he asked with a smile.

A good friend, Spencer had filled him in on the situation with Krissy. "Think so."

"Good luck, man. Don't worry. I got you covered here."

"Thanks."

Brandon, the athletic training intern scheduled to work with him, sat eating a sandwich. "Everything okay?" he asked.

Phone still to his ear, trying to make out what Krissy was saying in the background, Spencer shifted the mouthpiece to answer. "Have to run." He tossed the college student his keys. "Please clean up and restock the A.T. room. Just like I've showed you." The kid had been there for six weeks. He knew what to do. "You okay on your own?"

"Yeah."

"Lock up when you're done," he said loud enough for Al to hear. Lots of expensive rehab equipment in the A.T. room.

Al gave him a thumb's up.

"Spencer?" Krissy's voice cracked.

"I'm here."

"I know you don't want anything to do with me."

"That's not—"

She cut him off. "Déjà vu, right? Junior year of high school all over again."

"Krissy—"

"It's just, I know you're at work, but if you could spare some time. I need…" She started to cry and Spencer's heart broke. "I need…" She sniffled. "I thought I could do it on my own but…" She sniffled again in between hiccupping breaths. "Maybe you could talk to me for a few minutes, tell some jokes or something."

"Honey, it's not that I don't want anything to do with you." It was so much more complicated than that. Kissing Krissy had felt strangely dishonorable, even with

Jarrod dead, same as it had so many years ago. His head and his body were not in agreement on how to proceed. He needed time to figure things out.

Time he didn't have apparently.

He turned and headed for the stairs. "How far apart are the contractions?"

"A few minutes. Oh, God. Here comes another one."

"Already?" He took the stairs two at a time. "When did you get to the hospital?"

"A few hours ago."

"A few hours? Christ, Krissy." He reached the main floor, pushed out the door, and broke into a run toward the parking lot. "Why didn't you call me?"

"Ow, ow, ow. Spencer!"

"Breathe, honey. Like this." He demonstrated, not an easy thing considering he was running as fast as he could at the same time.

"I can't," she cried out.

"You can." He reached his car, jimmed his key into the lock and opened the door. "Just like this. Do it with me." He demonstrated again.

Krissy breathed with him, her breaths strained and mixed with pained moans.

"Did you find a focal point?"

"Yes. A picture. Brought it from home."

"Good." Spencer turned on his car and hooked up his phone so he could talk hands-free. That done, he shifted his car into drive, slammed his foot down on the gas pedal, and peeled out of his parking spot. "I can be there in fifteen minutes." If he drove through yellow lights, yielded at stop signs and ignored the posted speed limits, which he was fully prepared to do.

"Don't," she panted. "Come."

"I'm coming." He breathed with her again. "That's good. You're doing great."

"I am *not* doing great, Spencer," she yelled.

Maybe she didn't think so, but her fighting spirit told him she was doing just fine.

"It hurts." She groaned loudly.

He coached her through the pain as he pulled onto the main road. "You can do it."

"I'm so tired," she said, starting to cry again.

He hated hearing her so upset, hating knowing she had no family or friends there to offer their support. "What about pain medication? Or an epidural?"

"Natural childbirth is best for the baby," she snapped. "You know that."

Atta girl. He smiled. "So all that stuff about the unconscious birth plan?"

"Stupid coping mechanism," she said. "It's less stressful to think about taking the easy way out. But in the end, it's more important to do the right thing, which, in this case, is what's best for J.J."

Old Krissy would have taken the easy way out, regardless. "Contraction over?"

"Yes. But another one will be coming soon. My back hurts so bad."

"As soon as I get there I'll rub it."

"No, Spencer. Really. Don't come. It's too... Just talk to me. That's enough."

No it wasn't. Looking both ways, he coasted through a stop sign. "I'm coming." And that's that.

He listened on the phone, hearing only the rapid beat of the fetal heart monitor. He knew she needed to rest between contractions but couldn't stop himself from asking, "You there?"

"Of course I'm here. Where else would I be? I'm having a baby."

Spencer smiled again. "Why didn't you call me when the contractions started?"

"Because things got weird last night. Then I woke up in pain around four in the morning."

Spencer glanced at the clock on his dashboard. She'd been in labor for almost ten hours.

"How did you get to the hospital?"

"I took a taxi."

A taxi. Spencer wanted to scream. But what good would that do now? So he kept the conversation light. "Has the doctor been in?"

"I met his partner. Oh, no. Oh, God. Here comes another one."

Spencer slammed on his brakes and laid on his horn as a car came to short stop in front of him. "Idiot," he yelled.

"What?"

"Not you, honey. Bad driver." He steered around the car, sped up then stopped again, absolutely hating city traffic, even though White Plains traffic was much better than New York City traffic. "A few more minutes."

The sound of Krissy breathing through the contraction, exactly as he'd demonstrated earlier, came through his car speakers, making him so proud of her. Would this red light ever turn green? When it did he peeled out again, driving up the hill, weaving in and out of traffic. "I can see the hospital."

"Something's happening," Krissy yelled. "I have to push."

"Don't push," Spencer said at the same time a female voice, he assumed the nurse in the room with her, said the same thing. He made a sharp right then sped to the parking garage. "Breathe." He got his ticket then screeched into the structure to look for a spot. "Hang on, honey. I'm almost there."

"I'm. Not. Waiting," she said, her voice strained.

Spencer heard a male voice.

"I have to—" A loud thud cut off Krissy's words.

"Krissy? Krissy! What happened?"

All he heard were muted sounds.

The next few minutes passed in a blur of stressful, heart pounding activity. Somehow Spencer managed to make it to Krissy's room before J.J. entered the world, an event he felt obligated to attend, for Krissy as much as for Jarrod.

"That's it." A male doctor, mid-fifties or early sixties, dressed in blue hospital scrubs, stood at the foot of the bed, looking down between Krissy's legs. "Keep pushing. I see the head. Push, push, push, push."

Spencer's heart started to pound for a different reason. This was really happening. Krissy was about to give birth to Jarrod's son, to Spencer's godson. The magnitude of this moment stopped him in his tracks.

"Come on, Dad," one of the nurses said. "Wash your hands then come hold her leg."

Spencer rushed to the sink without taking the time to clarify his role in all this.

He noticed Krissy didn't correct her either. Considering she was mid-contraction, she no doubt had a lot of other stuff on her mind. An intravenous ran into Krissy's right arm and an oxygen mask hung loosely around her neck. A nurse blotted sweat from her brow, something Spencer should be doing so he dried his hands, hurried to the bed, and took over for the nurse closest to him.

"Push, push, push, push," the nurse holding the other leg said.

"Come on, Krissy. You can do this," Spencer said, noticing a high school picture of him and Jarrod on the rolling table beside the bed. Had that been the item she'd chosen as her focal point?

Krissy strained and pushed.

"The head is out," the doctor said. "Stop pushing."

Spencer fought the urge to look, it just didn't feel right to be looking down there.

"I need to be done," Krissy said.

"Hey. Eyes on me," Spencer said. When her eyes met his, he said, "You're almost done. Breathe like this." He demonstrated.

She stared at his mouth and followed his lead. So focused. Absolutely amazing.

"Oh, God," she looked away. "Here comes another one."

"Give me a good push," the doctor said. "Hard as you can."

Krissy looked exhausted, but determined as she pushed harder than he'd ever seen a woman push in his life.

"You're doing it." The doctor tilted the baby and his little face came into Spencer's view, followed by his tiny body.

Unbelievable.

"It's a boy," the doctor said, placing little J.J. on paper toweling the nurse had spread on Krissy's belly.

"It's a boy," Krissy repeated, still breathing heavily, tears sliding down her cheeks. "I did it." She reached out protectively to hold J.J. steady as he cried.

"You did it." Spencer bent down to kiss her forehead. "Jarrod would have been so proud." Jarrod. The best friend he'd ever had. Jarrod, who should be here experiencing the birth of his son. This was Jarrod's dream, not Spencer's.

But Jarrod was dead.

"Want to cut the cord?" The doctor held out a pair of scissors.

With an uncomfortable hollow feeling in his gut, Spencer did what was expected of him.

An hour later, after giving Krissy privacy to clean up and breastfeed J.J. for the first time, Spencer returned to her room to find the curtain drawn around her bed.

"Oh, Krissy. He's beautiful."

He's handsome, Spencer thought, recognizing Kira's voice. Men are handsome, women are beautiful.

"I can't believe he's finally here," Krissy said, sounding tired but happy. "Mommy's going to take such good care of you," Krissy said in that voice adults used when speaking to babies.

Would she take good care of him? Or would she fall into her old party-girl ways? Time would tell.

"When you get bigger," Krissy went on. "I'll sign you up for karate classes and soccer, just like your daddy used to take."

His daddy, who wasn't Spencer.

"But only if you want to." Her grown up voice came back. "I'm not going to force him into anything just because Jarrod liked to do it." After a brief silence, Krissy said, "What?"

"You're going to be a great mother, just like Mom was," Kira said.

"I hope so."

Spencer hoped so, too.

Through the curtain he heard J.J. start to fuss.

"Look at that face," Krissy said. "I know it makes no sense, and you're going to think I'm insane, but J.J. reminds me of Jarrod already. He makes me feel… I don't know. Having him here is…comforting. It's like a void within me has somehow been filled." She sniffled.

"Ah, honey," Kira said.

If Spencer could see through the curtain he'd bet Krissy and Kira were hugging.

"It makes complete sense," Kira said. "You and Jarrod were so close. I'm sure you miss him very much."

"Every day. I'll see something, hear something, or inhale a certain scent and I think of him."

Same thing happened to Spencer.

"I'll make sure Jarrod is never forgotten," Krissy said. "J.J. will know his daddy, he will always be his father's son, no matter what."

Spencer felt like an unnecessary outsider, an intruder, rudely eavesdropping. He should go. But there were a few things he needed to check on first. How was Krissy getting home from the hospital? Did she have everything she needed for the baby, a safe, new car seat? Diapers? Wipes? Clothes?

After something that sounded like a yawn, Krissy said, "Sorry."

"Don't be. I'm going to head to the nursery. Derrick had another newborn to visit. He should be about done. Here, let me take the baby with me. You need to rest."

Shoot, Derrick was here too? Spencer looked over his shoulder, debated the best course of action to keep from getting caught, briefly considered leaving and coming back in.

But Krissy's voice stopped him. "Derrick will do the circumcision in the morning?"

Number two on Spencer's list.

"Yes," Kira said. "Very early. Before office hours. Do you know when you and J.J. will be released?"

"I'm not sure. Probably sometime tomorrow morning."

"Call me," Kira said.

"But—"

Or she could call Spencer. He'd work it out so he could bring her home.

"Call me," Kira said again. "When you call, I'll come. I want to."

"Thank you. Here." Something jingled. "Take my keys. The car seat is in a box in the trunk."

Number one on Spencer's list, because he hadn't seen a car seat in her car or her apartment. Yeah, he'd checked. Jarrod would have wanted him to.

"Do you think Derrick will have time to install it tonight?"

Spencer had time.

"Of course," Kira said. "We'll go over when we leave the hospital and I'll drive your car here tomorrow. What else do you need?"

"Pads to put in my bra so my breasts don't leak all over."

Spencer tried to scrub that image from his brain.

"Let me write that down," Kira said.

"You and your lists," Krissy teased.

What was wrong with lists? Spencer loved lists. Speaking of which, he mentally checked off the things he'd wanted to ask Krissy that she'd already answered.

"You have a diaper pail? A baby bath?"

"No and no."

"What?" Kira asked, with the same amount of disbelief Spencer would have used had he been the one asking.

"If taking the garbage out every day doesn't work, I'll get a diaper pail," Krissy said calmly. "And for now I plan to bathe J.J. in the sink. If that doesn't work, I'll get a baby bathtub. Don't worry. I got this."

At least she'd thought it all out.

"You're good with baby clothes and supplies?" Kira asked.

"Stop," Krissy said. "A few friends had a little baby shower for me before I left Hawaii. I have what I need for now. As things come up, I'll run to the store."

Not how Spencer would have done it, but he was a planner, liked to have everything available just in case. One of the reasons he was so good at his job.

Krissy was more of a 'deal with it when you have to' kind of person.

As much as Spencer struggled with the idea of not being prepared for every possible situation, it was Krissy's life, not his. For now, she seemed to have everything under control. He wasn't needed. He wasn't the baby's father, wasn't family, or a boyfriend, had no reason to still be there. Krissy needed to rest. So he set the flowers, the "It's a Boy" balloon, and the package of chocolates he'd picked up for her at the gift shop, down on the floor, and left the room.

CHAPTER SEVEN

TWO WEEKS LATER, Krissy stood in the doorway to her kitchen watching Kira go through the bags she'd lugged in and set on the table. She took out a quart of milk and put it in the refrigerator.

"I told you the last time you brought me milk that I don't drink milk."

"Breastfeeding women need to drink milk."

"No. They don't."

"Well, at least I know you have it available if you want it."

She wouldn't want it. She didn't like it.

Next Kira put a package of Swiss cheese in the refrigerator.

Krissy preferred American cheese, when she ate cheese, which wasn't often. "I don't like you wasting money on food I won't eat and things I don't need."

Kira held up a bag of salad and a bottle of light balsamic vinaigrette dressing.

"Okay. Fine. Yes," Krissy admitted, even though she didn't want to do anything to encourage her. "I like salad and that's my favorite dressing."

Looking as if she'd triumphed in battle, Kira dug into the next bag. "Look at this adorable pacifier." She held it up. "It has a baseball on the end."

"I told you I don't believe in pacifiers."

"It helps babies calm themselves down."

"So does sucking their thumb." Or in J.J.'s case, his knuckles.

Krissy struggled to generate more patience as Kira pulled out the next item, a plastic bib big enough for a toddler. "Plastic is partially responsible for destroying our environment." No, she wasn't an environmental activist to the point she'd use cloth diapers, but she limited her use of plastic when possible.

"It will keep his clothes dry when he starts teething. It was on sale," Kira said. "I couldn't resist." She held up a book on parenting. "When you're done, I'll take it."

Krissy noted the colorful strips of paper sticking out from between the pages where Kira no doubt highlighted whole sections of outdated parenting techniques. "I will raise J.J. the way I think he should be raised, not according to rules in a book that can't possibly take into consideration the unique needs of each individual child."

This interference had to stop. The time had come for Krissy to take a stand. For days she'd been trying to figure out how to broach the topic in a way that wouldn't make her seem ungrateful. They were finally on good terms and Krissy didn't want to ruin that by starting an argument. But she didn't have room for all the stuff Kira had been bringing over. She preferred to do her own grocery shopping, hated wasting the food Kira brought for her. And she would raise her son the way she darn well pleased.

"Just give it a quick browse," Kira said. "At least the chapters on teething, toilet training, and discipline. Maybe you'll learn something helpful."

Settling on the straightforward approach, Krissy

started an open and honest conversation, hoping for the best. "You want to know why I decided to follow you and make a home for myself in White Plains?" At least for now.

Kira stopped what she was doing and looked up.

"To be more of a help with Mom," Krissy explained. A responsibility she'd neglected, leaving the burden on Kira for way too many years. "To be close to my only family when I gave birth to J.J. in case something horrible happened and I didn't survive, so he wouldn't be all alone. And while I appreciate every single thing you have done for me since I had J.J., I did not come here because I need you to take care of me."

"Fine." Kira started collecting the plastic bags strewn on the floor. "I won't—"

"Stop."

Kira didn't stop. "If you don't want my help," she balled up the bags and shoved them under the kitchen sink, "then I won't help."

Krissy had hurt her sister's feelings. The very last thing she'd wanted to do. "You're wonderful," Krissy told her, because she was.

Kira stopped.

"The most wonderful sister in the world." If not for Kira's fierce determination and willingness to go against the recommendations of several social workers, when she'd been only eighteen, Krissy could have been forced into foster care after their mother's severe brain injury. But Kira had held their little family together. Krissy still didn't know where she'd found the courage and stamina to do it. "But this is starting to feel like Murray all over again, and I have no intention of giving you J.J."

"Murray? My cat?"

"*My* cat," Krissy clarified. "Or at least that's how he'd started out." Krissy sat down at the table and motioned for Kira to do the same. When she did, Krissy went on, "Until you decided he should have canned food instead of dry food and he should be allowed to sleep in a bed even though I didn't want him sleeping in my bed. Until you decided I didn't buy him the right kind of toys or scoop his litter often enough or brush him often enough and you took over all of his care. Then, when we'd get into a fight, you'd bring up Murray and accuse me of being irresponsible. Well I'm not irresponsible. I just have my own way of doing things. And just because it's not the same as your way doesn't mean it's the wrong way."

Kira stared down at the table, looking deep in thought.

"When I was younger? You didn't like the way I was doing something so you took over and started doing it yourself? Fine, it was easier to let you do it than fight about it." She leaned down to catch her sister's eyes. "But I'm an adult now. It has to stop."

"I am not trying to take over. I'm only trying to help."

"By buying me milk I don't drink and cheese I don't eat."

"You're breastfeeding. You need to eat and drink healthy food. Last time I was here all you had in your refrigerator was ketchup, mayonnaise and yogurt."

"I'm only one person. I like yogurt. And when I need food I'll run to the store to get it. Or I'll order it."

Kira looked ready to argue so Krissy set her hand on Kira's forearm. "You work all day then you run to the store then you come here for a visit. Then you run home, make dinner, and spend some quiet time with Derrick before heading downstairs to Mom's apartment to check in on her. You're running yourself ragged. I know you're exhausted and more often than not, queasy. I was just recently pregnant myself, remember? I know how awful the first three months can be. And yet you're still pushing yourself. My point is, I don't want you running yourself ragged because of me. I love seeing you, but we don't have to see each other every day and you don't always have to come here. I can come to you. You don't have to make a special trip to the store for me. I'm fine. J.J.'s fine. I won't let either of us starve. I will always have a clean diaper available." And if she didn't, she'd improvise. "And if there is ever a time when we really do need something, I will call you and ask for your help." She placed her hand over her heart. "I promise."

Kira let out a weary breath. "I'm sorry. All I ever wanted to do was make your life easier than mine was."

"You have." Even if Krissy had never asked her to and she sometimes threw it back in Krissy's face. "And I love you for it. But you can stop now. I'm all grown up."

"Yes you are." Kira leaned in to hug her. "I'm so proud of the independent, competent, and hard-working person you've become."

Those words, coming from Kira, meant so much. "Thank you." Krissy hugged her back. "When you have your baby, I'm going to be there for you like you've been here for me. Every day for the first two weeks. I'm going to cook for you, shop for you, and drive you absolutely crazy with all my suggestions. Because I will finally know more about two things than you do, actual hands on taking care of a newborn and breastfeeding."

"I look forward to it."

"We'll see."

"How's it going, the breastfeeding?"

Krissy tried not to think about her cracked, sore nipples. "Let's just say it's not as natural or as easy as you'd think."

"You could…" Kira started then stopped even though Krissy could tell she really wanted to continue.

"Thank you for your restraint." Krissy smiled. "I have an appointment with a lactation consultant tomorrow."

"Good. You'll tell me how it goes?"

"Sure." Krissy glanced at the clock on the microwave. J.J. would be waking up for his next feeding any minute. "You can take back the diaper pail and baby bathtub you dropped off after I got home. I don't need them." She stood. "They're unused so you can save them for your baby. But I'm keeping the long-sleeve onesies and sleepers and the towel set."

Kira looked confused. "I didn't bring you a diaper pail or baby bath. You said if you needed them you'd buy them."

Yes, she had.

"I didn't get the other stuff, either."

"Then who?" Spencer.

Kira said his name at the same time Krissy thought it. "Spencer. At the hospital. He didn't just drop off the flowers."

And the thoughtful balloon and yummy chocolates. "He must have stuck around for a few minutes, listening." Krissy thought back on their conversation when Kira had visited her after J.J. was born, hoping she hadn't said anything about Spencer, coming to the thankful conclusion she hadn't, at least she was pretty sure she hadn't, hoped she hadn't.

"I know you had some concerns about moving into his building. Does he stop by often?" Kira asked.

Krissy shook her head. "He doesn't stop by at all."

It was like he'd helped her through labor and delivery and his job was done. While part of her felt relief to not have to deal with him dogging her every move, part of her felt...deserted. Which made no sense, Spencer didn't owe her anything and they were hardly even friends. And yet...

"Not at all?" Kira clarified.

Krissy shook her head again. "But he texts me every night to see how we're doing and if we need anything, then I text him back that we're fine and don't need anything." She shrugged. "That's it." As much as she hated to admit it, she missed him. "Anyway," Krissy went on. "I'm feeling better and I'd really like to bring J.J. down to meet his grandparents."

"That's going to be such a wonderful surprise for them."

Krissy hoped so, had always thought so. But lately self-doubt had crept in, overshadowing her excitement. Should she have discussed Jarrod's request with his parents *before* she'd gone through with the artificial insemination? Should she have told them about the pregnancy *before* she'd given birth?

Too late now, she'd made her decisions and now had to live with them. "I was thinking of asking Spencer to drive me into the city. He's kept in touch with them more than I have. And I don't want to take J.J. on the train."

"I wouldn't either," Kira agreed. "If you want Derrick and me to go with you, just say the word." Kira smiled. "I'd offer to take you myself but, and I have a very hard time admitting this, I'm not a great driver and don't think I'm ready to drive into the city."

Unlike Krissy, who'd gone to college and worked outside of the city, which required she get her driver's license, Kira had lived and worked in the city up until her move to White Plains a few months ago and, thanks to public transportation, she hadn't needed a driver's license prior to that.

"Thank you." As much as she hated bothering Kira, knowing she could always count on her sister meant everything to Krissy. If J.J.'s big reveal didn't go as planned, no way she wanted to be down at Patti and Bart's apartment alone. "I'll let you know what he says." Krissy rolled her post earring between her fingers. "There's something I wanted to talk to you about," she said. Now was as good a time as any.

"Of course."

Krissy had given this a lot of thought and really wanted to know Kira's opinion. "I'd like to introduce J.J. to Mom." She shrugged. "Not that Mom recognizes me or knows she's my mom, or that she has any understanding of what it means to be a grandmother." The traumatic brain injury had taken away so much. Krissy looked down at the table. "I just want…" *Want her to see what I've accomplished, that I'm a mother now, like her. And a good one, like she'd been. I want her to be proud of me.*

"You want…"

"Nothing," Krissy said, knowing Mom was no longer capable of noticing an accomplishment, or being proud, and she could no longer recognize the difference between a good mother and a bad mother. All she cared about were her television shows, painting and now gardening, and her beloved Oreos. Regardless, she was still Krissy's mother and Krissy wanted her mother to be a part of her son's life.

"Do you ever wonder…?" Krissy started. Then stopped, feeling foolish.

"What?" Kira asked. "Talk to me."

"Do you ever wonder if meeting our children, if finding out she's a grandma, hearing the word, will somehow trigger something deep inside…" Her eyes met Kira's. "…and bring her back to us?"

"Brain injuries are so complex. You just never know." Kira gave a slow shake of her head. "But I really don't think so."

Even though Krissy didn't think so either, hearing Kira agree wiped out the little bit of hope she'd been holding on to. "Mom would have loved being a grandmother. She'd have been fantastic at it."

Kira reached out and took Krissy's hand into hers. "It makes me sad to think our children won't know the smart, loving, exceptional woman she used to be."

Krissy blinked back tears. "That they won't get to bake cookies with her before Christmas."

"That they won't get to go out on special lunch dates with her," Kira added.

Mom had gone out of her way to make both of her daughters feel special, and loved.

"What do you think?" Krissy asked. "Is introducing J.J. to Mom a horrible idea?"

"I think…" Kira hesitated. "I think if you want to introduce J.J. to Mom, then of course you should." She released Krissy's hand and sat back. "We'll make sure to do it on one of her good days."

"How do you think she'll react?"

Now it was Kira's turn to look down at the table. "With Mom, you never know." Then she looked up. "Let's give her a few more weeks to get adjusted to her new home. Then we'll pick a time when you, me, Derrick and Tippy can all be there."

Kira didn't say it, but Krissy knew they all needed

to be present in case J.J.'s presence caused Mom to act out…or become violent, which rarely happened anymore, thanks to her daily medications and the fact they'd all become so in tuned to her moods and triggers. But introducing a baby was an unknown. Who knew how Mom would react? "As much as I want to do this, I won't unless I'm sure J.J. will be safe."

"He will be," Kira said, with a confidence that put Krissy's mind at ease. "We'll all make sure of it."

The little man in question started to cry.

"Oh, good." Kira jumped up and hurried to the sink to wash her hands. "A quickie hello and cuddle with my favorite nephew then I'll leave you two in peace."

Later that evening, when Krissy received Spencer's nightly text, she responded with a return call. He answered on the first ring, "What's wrong?"

"Nothing's wrong. You asked if I needed anything and there's something I wanted to ask you."

A response would have been nice, maybe a "Sure, ask me anything." All Krissy got was silence. So she kept on talking. "I'm feeling much better now and I'd really like to take J.J. down to meet Patti and Bart. I don't want to take him on the train, and I'm not comfortable making a long trip with him in the backseat where I can't see him or take care of him if he needs me. I know this is your busy time at work, but do you think you may have a free Sunday afternoon coming up? And if you do, would you be willing to drive us in? I'd have to work it out with Patti, of course."

"Let me take a look at my schedule. If it's okay with you, I'll call Patti directly to set something up. Then I'll let you know."

"That'd be great. Thank you." Krissy hated how things felt so strained between them now. No laughing. No banter. "Don't mention J.J." Good or bad, Krissy wanted to be there in person, to see their reaction as well as to render first aid if one of them collapsed in shock.

"I won't." After a pause he added, "Thanks for asking me."

"Thanks for agreeing. And thanks for the baby bath and the diaper pail. I would have thanked you sooner if I'd known they were from you. I thought they were from Kira. We'd discussed them at the hospital."

"Uh, yeah, about that. I um…"

"No worries." She gave him an out.

He took it. "Whew. Okay, then. Well, I guess I'll be in touch with the date and time."

"Talk to you then."

Only she didn't talk to him then, because late one night about a week later, she received a text.

3 p.m. next Sunday. Pick you up at 2 p.m. Spencer.

CHAPTER EIGHT

SPENCER GLANCED AT the time on his cell phone then settled back onto his sofa. He had half an hour before he needed to head down to Krissy's apartment to get her and J.J. down to Patti and Bart's by three o'clock. He tapped his 'Find Friends' app to find her down in her apartment, where she spent most of her time, taking care of her newborn baby like a good mother should.

Maybe it'd been wrong to load the app onto her phone and accept the terms on her behalf, especially within minutes of her giving birth. But when she'd asked him to find the cell phone she'd dropped during labor, he couldn't bring himself to pass up the opportunity. When she'd moved into his building, he'd promised to respect her privacy and not to stop by without an invite. 'Find Friends' allowed him to keep tabs on her without intruding in her life, without putting them in close proximity, which would no doubt lead to more kissing, which would no doubt lead to…complications he didn't need in his life right now. The app served his needs perfectly. God willing she wouldn't notice the icon amongst the dozens already on her phone.

For all the time he spent on 'Find Friends', you'd think he was tracking more than one friend. Well, maybe tracking wasn't the best word to represent his purpose. Some might see tracking someone's movements as stalkerish behavior.

He wasn't a stalker.

He was a concerned friend, a godfather responsible for the well-being of his godson, a man trying to do the right thing while distancing himself from temptation. Yet the more he'd checked on her location over the past month, the more he'd thought about her. And the more he'd thought about her, the more he'd started to miss her. He glanced at the time again, the buzz of excitement zinging around his belly. The time had come. Today he would see her. In twenty-six minutes, to be exact. Only he didn't want to wait twenty-six more minutes. He didn't want to wait one more minute. So he stood and grabbed his keys and walked to the door.

As he left his apartment he wondered how he'd be received. After texting her every evening since she'd given birth, to see how she was doing and if she needed anything, not once had she invited him over. He should be happy, relieved even. Instead it irked him. He didn't like being shut out of her life. In the elevator he wondered if she'd be happy to see him, or angry that he showed up early, or frazzled and thankful for an extra pair of hands?

As much as he'd been thinking about her and trying to imagine what she'd look like without her pregnant belly, when she opened her door, nothing could have prepared him for the sight of her big, welcoming smile and the vision of her beautiful, voluptuous figure in a pale peach baby doll type dress, tight on top, flowy on the bottom, stopping a couple of inches above her bare knees.

All the air whooshed out of his lungs.

She looked...stunning, had lost all of her baby

weight, at least as far as he could tell. But her breasts, her big, beautiful breasts had grown even larger. Spencer swallowed to keep from drooling. He couldn't look away, couldn't keep himself from thinking about dropping his head into her deep cleavage, from wondering what the soft heat of that creamy white skin surrounding his face would feel like?

"I know," she said, looking down. "They're freakishly huge."

"They're…awesome," slipped out of Spencer's mouth before he could stop himself. Thinking it made him a typical guy. Saying it out loud made him sound like a jerk.

He was on the verge of apologizing when, Krissy smiled. He took that as a 'no apology needed.'

"Come on in." She stepped aside. "We're almost ready."

The apartment wasn't as neat as it could have been, but Krissy had a diaper bag, her pocketbook, and the car seat ready and waiting by the door. J.J. looked neat and clean and way too adorable for words lying on his back on a cushiony baby comforter on the floor in the living room, just off the entryway. It didn't escape his notice that Krissy had dressed the baby in the light blue sleeper with the baseball emblem on the chest that Spencer had bought. "Wow, he's really filled out." And he was alert, his eyes opened and looking around, his little legs bending and straightening, his tiny hands clenched into fists, one shoved half into his mouth.

"He's a breast man, too," she teased, coming to stand beside Spencer. "Every two to three hours. Which means we'd better get on the road soon in case we hit traffic."

Right. But before they left, he took a few seconds to be impressed by how calm and organized she seemed.

Krissy went down on her knees and carefully scooped J.J. into her arms.

"What can I do to help?" he asked as she placed J.J. into his car seat on the floor and buckled him in.

"If you'd carry the car seat down, that'd be a big help. Usually I put him in a baby carrier thing that I wear. But since you're here I will shamelessly take advantage of your big, strong muscles."

"Happy to help," he said, meaning it. He missed helping her as much as just being around her.

On their way out the door Krissy stopped and ran back into the kitchen. "Almost forgot." She opened the refrigerator and took out a plastic bowl. "I made a fruit salad."

That she'd even thought of that, with all she had to do, impressed him even more. "With lots of bananas and strawberries?" he teased.

"Oh, my God, don't even bring them up." The bowl in her right arm, her pocketbook and diaper bag draped over her left shoulder, she walked toward the door. "I'll start retching. Can't stand to even look at them. J.J. left my body and took those awful cravings with him." She glanced up at Spencer. "I'm hoping he doesn't develop a taste for them when he starts on solid food."

With Jarrod as his dad, chances were pretty good that he would.

Down at the parking lot, Spencer moved the base for J.J.'s car seat into his SUV. Ten minutes later they were on their way.

"I'm going to start out in the front seat," Krissy said, "So you don't feel like a chauffeur. But if J.J. starts to fuss, I may need you to pull over so I can move into the back."

"No problem."

"I hate that he has to face backward so I can't see his face."

Spencer didn't like that either. He recalled seeing a mirror that could be placed on the seat so you could see the baby's face from the front seat and in the rear view mirror. Later on he'd do an Internet search to see where he could buy one.

After he'd run out on Krissy post-kiss, then left the hospital without saying good bye, and then went a full month without seeing her, Spencer had been concerned things might be a little strained between them. But Krissy kept the conversation going, sharing stories from J.J.'s first month of life, until about halfway through their trip, when she stopped talking, mid-sentence.

Spencer looked over to see she'd fallen asleep.

So exhausted, and yet she never asked for help. Krissy was so different from his needy mother and sisters. She was so different from his last few girlfriends, too. He got the feeling Krissy wouldn't complain about his long hours on the job or days away when he traveled with the team. Krissy wouldn't demand his time and attention, wouldn't expect him to buy her expensive things she didn't need. Krissy wouldn't clam up and give him the silent treatment, either.

He smiled.

She didn't play girlie mind games. She was angry? She came right out and told you so…loudly. That'd been one of the things he'd liked most about her.

Ten minutes from Patti and Bart's house he woke her. "Krissy," he said quietly as he gently shook her shoulder.

She jerked awake, would have sprung out of her seat

if not for the seat belt. "J.J." She looked around, seeming confused.

"He's in the back. Haven't heard a peep out of him." He'd been driving with the radio off to make sure he didn't miss even the tiniest whimper. "We should be there in ten minutes."

Krissy's hand went up to twirl her post earring, a nervous gesture Jarrod used to tease her about back in high school. "You okay?"

She sat staring out the window, same as prior to Lamaze class.

He waited her out.

Still staring out the window she eventually said, "Maybe I should have checked with Patti and Bart before I went through with the artificial insemination. I mean sure, Jarrod wanted to leave a part of himself behind, wanted his parents to have a grandchild to dote on. And I grew to love the idea of having his baby, of having Patti and Bart's grandbaby. For a long time, they were more mother and father to me than my own mother and father were. But what if they don't want a grandchild? I never once took that into consideration. What if they—?"

"Stop getting yourself all worked up. There are no two people on the planet who deserve to be and would love to be grandparents more than Patti and Bart."

"But what if—?"

"They're going to be thrilled," he told her. No doubt in his mind. "Word of advice. When Patti goes in to hug you, which she will no doubt do, I'd bet in all her excitement she's going to put some power behind that squeeze. My suggestion, take a deep breath before she grabs on to you."

Krissy's small smile warmed him.

When they reached the old neighborhood, Spencer circled the block to find parking. "I'm not going to find anything close. You want me to drop you—?"

"No," shot from her mouth before he could even finish. Seeming to realize her exaggerated response, she took a breath and calmed it down. "I mean, no thank you. I like to walk. Walking is good. If J.J.'s car seat is too heavy for you to carry, I'll carry it."

As if seven *maybe* eight pounds of baby and a plastic car seat would be too heavy for him to carry. Heck, he could carry Krissy and the diaper bag too without breaking a sweat. "I can handle it."

Fifteen minutes later Spencer pressed the intercom button for Patti and Bart's apartment.

"Do I look okay?" Krissy asked nervously, trying to rub some wrinkles from the front of her dress. "Do I look like a woman you'd want raising your grandchild?" she asked, without giving him a chance to respond to her first question.

"Hey," he said, lifting her chin so she had to look at him. "I know telling you not to be nervous isn't going to stop you from being nervous, but trust me, it's wasted energy. Patti and Bart love you, they've always loved you. You look beautiful. And while I find you way too sexy to want you to raise *my* grandchild, I think Patti and Bart will be perfectly fine with it."

She smacked his arm, the one holding J.J.'s car seat.

"Hey," he said. "You're going to make me drop the baby." Not likely.

Her eyes went wide.

He smiled.

She smacked him again.

Just like old times.

The intercom buzzed them in and Spencer opened the door.

"The hallway looks and smells the same," Krissy said.

Dimly lit, off-white walls with various nicks and scratches, and worn carpeting that could quite possibly be the same carpet his eleven-year-old feet had walked on so many years ago. The scents of fried food and garlic and tomato sauce lingered in the air. Coming for a visit was a journey back in time.

He tried to be a gentleman and let Krissy precede him up the stairs to the second floor, but she insisted he go first. When they reached apartment 2F, Krissy stood there, looking like she'd seen a ghost.

"You okay?" he asked her again.

"So many memories," was all she said.

So many memories indeed, delicious food, fun times and so much laughter…followed by such heart-wrenching sorrow.

After a few seconds Krissy straightened to her full height and, shoulders back, lifted her fist to knock.

Only she didn't knock. "I should probably…" She dug into her purse to take out a white business sized envelope similar to the one Jarrod had left for him. Made sense he'd leave one for his parents too. She pulled out two other papers then lifted her fist to knock again.

She hesitated.

"You want me to do it?"

She nodded.

Spencer knocked.

Bart must have been standing in wait because the door flew open. "Look at you," he said to Krissy. "Pretty as ever." He pulled her into a hug. "Haven't changed a bit."

Actually, in Spencer's estimation, she'd changed quite a bit. Adult Krissy was so much more than a pretty face, a hot body, and a fun time. She was strong and determined, yet at times, vulnerable. She was competent and responsible, yet not afraid to ask for help when she needed it. And most importantly of all, she seemed to be a great mother.

"Let them in you big oaf," Patti said from behind Bart, hitting his shoulder with a dish towel. No sooner did Bart step aside, Patti's eyes went straight to J.J., who was fast asleep in the car seat carrier dangling from Derrick's hand, and everyone went silent.

CHAPTER NINE

KRISSY SET HER hand to her chest, hoping to keep her heart from banging through her sternum, as she watched Patti set her eyes on J.J. for the first time. So many times she'd tried to visualize this moment, what Bart would say, how Patti would react. Deep down, in the tiny, still pure, believe-in-fairy-tale-endings, part of her brain that somehow remained unaffected by her years as a weary realist, Krissy had let herself believe that Patti would somehow take one look at J.J. and just know he was her grandson, that she'd feel an instant connection to Jarrod's son, an immediate grandma-grandson bond that defied rational explanation.

So Krissy wouldn't have to explain, wouldn't have to risk them not believing her. Like Spencer had.

But one look at the confusion and disbelief on Patti's face told Krissy today would not be the day for fairy-tale endings.

Tears filled her eyes as all her dreams for the future, for happy family get-togethers, visits to grandma and grandpa's place, and over-the-top celebrations courtesy of Patti, started to flicker.

No!

In Patti and Bart's silence, Krissy couldn't help but wonder, yet again, if she'd waited too long, had missed that window of opportunity when they would have welcomed Jarrod's son? When having a grandson would have made a difference in their lives. How could she have been so stupid to automatically assume Patti and Bart would accept her child into their hearts without Jarrod being there?

Patti pointed between Krissy and Spencer. "You and Spencer…?"

"What? Me? No!" Spencer blurted. "I'm not the father."

Could he be any more insulting? He made it sound like being J.J.'s father would be the worst thing in the world. That sent tears flowing down her cheeks. She did not need Spencer tainting their view of her, making them question Jarrod's choice of a mother for his son.

She was a good mother. Maybe she didn't know it all, but every day she learned something knew, every day she strived to be better than she'd been the day before.

"Ah, honey," Patti said. "Don't cry." She held open her arms, and Krissy couldn't resist walking into them, accepting the comfort they offered.

The feel of her, so soft and cushiony, the smell of her, an elusive hint of fragrance, had Krissy feeling sixteen years old again, wanting to absorb as much of Patti's loving care as she could, to hold her through until the next time she came to visit. "I'm sorry," Krissy said, trying to keep control of all the emotion churning inside of her, looking for an outlet.

"There. There." Patti rubbed her back. "Nothing to be sorry about, having a baby is a wonderful thing. I only thought Spencer because you called looking for him. But if he's not the daddy, who is? And why didn't you bring him with you?"

Because J.J.'s daddy is dead.

With that thought the floodgates opened and months of worry and fear poured out of her, to the point she couldn't stop crying even if she wanted to. God help her it felt good, felt necessary. "I'm sorry." Her words came out between hiccupping breaths. "I waited...so long. Too long. But I...wasn't ready." She couldn't get enough air. But short of passing out from lack of oxygen, she would not stop talking, not yet, not until she said everything she needed to say. "And that I...didn't check...with you and... Bart first. But Jarrod wanted... and I agreed...and I hope..." she said, sobbing more than talking.

"Calm down, honey," Patti said. "It's okay. Everything is going to be okay."

It didn't feel okay, didn't feel like it was ever going to be okay again and Krissy's heart started to ache. What if—?

Someone walked up behind her. She heard Spencer's soft voice close to her ear, a much kinder version than when he'd balked at someone thinking he was J.J.'s dad. Heaven forbid!

"Give them the letter," he said.

Right. The letter she held in a death grip behind Patti's back. The letter that, in seeing Patti's face, she'd forgotten all about.

Krissy nodded. *Get it together.* She wiped her eyes, inhaled a shaky, yet somewhat fortifying breath and stepped away from Patti's embrace, standing tall, trying to be strong for her son. Whatever happened she'd deal with it.

Krissy handed Patti the letter. "It's from Jarrod."

From the look on Patti's face, she'd already recognized the handwriting.

"Maybe you should sit down when you read it," Spencer suggested.

Yes. Right. They should both sit down. Just in case. "In the living room?" Where she, Jarrod and Spencer had spent so many hours hanging out, watching movies or playing video games. It looked exactly the same. Pictures of Jarrod covering the far wall, his trophies and other memorabilia lining the shelving below. Bookcases filled with books lined the other wall.

As if in slow motion, Patti followed Bart into the living room and they sat down on the sofa. Wanting to give them privacy, and needing something to do, Krissy went down on her knees to unbuckle J.J. from his car seat.

Under normal circumstances, she'd have let him sleep.

These were not normal circumstances.

She needed his warmth, needed to feel him in her arms, needed to feel some connection to Jarrod. "Come on, sweetie," she whispered as he stretched and let out his little baby moans. "Time to meet your grandma and grandpa." Grabbing a shoulder cloth from the diaper bag, she lifted him. Cuddling him close to her chest, she joined Spencer by the entrance to the living room, happy to stand and sway with J.J., to burn off her nervous energy, rather than sit.

Still on the first page of the two page letter Patti looked up at Krissy. "You mean you…?"

Her expression was filled with such wonder, such hope. Krissy's eyes filled with tears again as she nodded.

"That's…" Patti brought her fingertips to her lips, her now tear-filled eyes stared at J.J.

"Jarrod's baby," Krissy said, turning J.J. to hold him in front of her, facing his grandparents, so they could get a good look at him. "Your grandson."

A jolt of fear had Krissy remembering Spencer's disbelief when she'd told him she was carrying Jarrod's baby. Not wanting to experience the same response from Patti and Bart, Krissy had come prepared. "Here." She walked to where Patti sat on the couch. "This is the documentation from the clinic where I had the artificial insemination performed, confirming the use of Jarrod's sperm. I'm not sure what he told you in the letter, but he had it frozen before his first deployment." She handed over the paper, fighting panic. *Please believe me.* "And this is the baby's birth certificate." She handed that to Patti too, not that a birth certificate served to verify paternity, but it had to mean something that she'd named the baby after Jarrod? Right?

Patti didn't scrutinize the papers like Krissy had hoped she would. Instead she handed them to Bart, still looking confused and uncertain, her eyes locked on J.J.

Krissy's hope from a moment ago turned to dread. Is this where they'd tell her they didn't believe her? Where they'd accuse her of trying to pass off another man's baby as Jarrod's, just like Spencer had? Krissy bounced J.J. while she waited for Bart to read the papers, her heart pounding in her chest once again.

"This is all my fault," Spencer said, coming to stand beside her. "Krissy's worried you're not going to believe that the baby is Jarrod's because when she told me I gave her a hard time."

A *really* hard time.

He looked down at her. "I'm sorry. Again."

"Thank you." For coming to her rescue and for the apology, but it didn't wipe his harsh words from her mind, didn't stop her from worrying.

Without a word Bart got up from the couch and left the room.

Oh, no. She glanced over to Spencer and shot him a non-verbal, *What's going on?*

Spencer shrugged but didn't look concerned.

Patti's voice interrupted the silence. "Jarrod Spencer Sadler Junior," she read from the birth certificate.

"I call him J.J."

"You gave him my name?" Spencer asked.

It'd seemed like a good idea at the time. Now? Not so much. "You're the godfather. Jarrod's other best friend. I thought…" It'd be an honor, that he'd appreciate the gesture. Apparently not.

Bart returned to the room holding a large, framed, wall-hanging picture. "Look." Patti held up the birth certificate for him to read.

The big man looked like he was barely keeping it together. "Sadler." His eyes met Krissy's. "You gave him our last name."

Of course she had. "He's Jarrod's son, Jarrod's legacy."

Bart turned the picture so Spencer and Krissy could see it. "This is Jarrod at a few weeks old."

Oh, my goodness. "They could be twins." She'd hoped there'd be a resemblance, but never did she think they'd look so much alike so early on.

"I don't need any papers to tell me that's Jarrod's child," Bart said. "I can tell from just looking at him."

Krissy thought she might melt with relief. "Thank you." Wouldn't you know it? Tears filled up her eyes again. "I'm sorry." She wiped them away, one-handed. "My emotions are all over the place lately."

"May I hold him?" Patti asked quietly, still staring at J.J., but now with such longing.

As she prepared to hand over her baby, as Patti reached out her hands to take him, Krissy saw what she'd been hoping for, waiting for. Patti looked at her grandson with so much love and pure joy it made all of Krissy's nervous concern vanish.

She handed her son to his grandma and he cuddled his little face into the base of her neck like that space had been created just for him and he'd been there a thousand times before. Patti held him close as she rocked him, eyes closed as if savoring the moment. "It feels so good to be holding a baby, again."

"To be holding your grandson, you mean," Bart said.

Tears streaming down her cheeks, Patti nodded.

"And you can hold him all you want after I get a turn." Bart held out his large hands. "Easy to forget how little they are." But he handled his grandbaby with the skill of a seasoned grandpa, and J.J. settled right in against Bart's chest, completely content.

Spencer said, "He was six pounds, two ounces when he was born."

"You were there?" Patti asked.

"Considering he bullied me into attending Lamaze classes, it seemed only fair to make him be my coach," Krissy said.

"Good for you, Spencer," Patti said. "You always were such a levelheaded boy."

Spencer smiled proudly, tauntingly, in Krissy's direction.

Krissy got the urge to stick her tongue at him in response, but she refrained.

"Oh, how I would have loved to have been there," Patti said dreamily.

"I'd gone back and forth about telling you sooner," Krissy admitted. "But I didn't want to risk you having to deal with the loss of another family member if something went wrong. So I decided to wait."

Patti stood up and gave Krissy a hug. "For as much as Spencer was the levelheaded one of your little group, you were always the thoughtful one."

She'd tried to be, still tried to be.

"You have given us the most thoughtful gift of all." Patti squeezed her tightly. "Thank you, honey. A grandchild! I can't believe it." She squeezed her even tighter. "I'm a grandma. Thank you." She kissed her cheek. "Thank you so much."

Krissy's heart swelled with love. This is the response she'd been hoping for. "You're welcome."

"Now tell me," Patti took a step back. "What do you need from us? Anything, doesn't matter how big, Bart and I will take care of it."

God how she loved this woman.

"I don't *need* you to do anything. I purposely waited until I was mature enough and financially secure enough to raise J.J. on my own, without having to depend on anyone else. But if you *want* to do something for us, and you by no means have to, so don't feel under any pressure. I'd love it if we could get together for Sunday dinners, like we used to." Years ago.

"You don't have to go crazy cooking," Krissy told Patti. "Grilled cheese sandwiches are fine. Or take out. And it doesn't always have to be here. You could come up to my place in White Plains. It's not that far. And I have this great kitchen table we could all sit at." She slid a small smile to Spencer.

He smiled back.

"The important thing is that we're together, like family. Not that I'm family or anything," Krissy backtracked. "But J.J.—"

Patti pulled her into another hug. "I've always thought of you as family, honey, the daughter of my heart." She reached out to Spencer to include him in the hug. "And you're like a second son to me," she told him.

Spencer stepped into the hug.

Krissy started to tear up. But she had to stay strong, had to get out what she wanted to say without falling apart again. So she stepped back and looked at Bart. "We may not *need* anything, but I'd love it if you'd teach J.J. about sports, and maybe take him to football games and baseball games." Jarrod had always looked forward to that. "And if you'd help him plan out and construct his Halloween costumes." Jarrod always had the best costumes.

"It'll be my pleasure," Bart said, cuddling his grandson close.

Krissy turned to Patti. "I'd love it if you'd make all of J.J.'s birthday cakes." Patti baked and decorated the best cakes. "And help me make his parties special. If you'd bake him your caramel fudge brownies with walnuts to celebrate soccer wins and placing in the science fair or to cheer him up after some disappointment."

Patti blotted her eyes and nodded. "Of course I will."

"But most of all, I hope your home will be a place where J.J. knows, no matter how bad life gets, he will always be welcome, he will always be safe, and most importantly, he will always be loved, like I was."

"Always," Patti said, wiping at the corners of her eyes again.

Bart sniffled and, looking down at J.J., mumbled his own, "Always."

Pure joy flowed through her veins. This was what she wanted, what she'd hoped for.

J.J. started to fuss.

"He's probably getting hungry." Krissy took him from Bart. "Is there someplace I can feed him?" She glanced between Bart and Spencer. "In private. I'm breastfeeding."

"Of course you are," Patti said. "Come." She walked toward the stairs. "You can sit in our bedroom, there's a glider rocker in there."

"Oh. I've been thinking about getting one of those."

"Well, don't you dare, Bart and I will get you one."

"You don't—"

Patti stopped and turned. "We *want* to." She placed special emphasis on 'want.' "It's the least we can do."

CHAPTER TEN

AFTER THE WOMEN retreated upstairs, Bart headed into the kitchen. He opened the oven door to peek inside, sending the delicious smell of roasting meat into the air. "She went all out for the two of you."

Spencer's empty stomach growled. "She always goes all out for company."

"Pot roast and potatoes. I can't remember the last time she made pot roast and potatoes." Bart motioned to the coffee machine on the counter. "Want a cup?"

God yes, he'd barely slept last night, thinking about today. "That'd be great."

Bart took a mug from a cabinet and handed it to Spencer. "You know your way around."

That he did.

When Spencer finished, Bart made his own cup of coffee. Then they both sat down at the table. Something about Bart's expression made Spencer uneasy. Before he could excuse himself to go…anywhere else, Bart asked, "So what's going on between the two of you?" He followed the question with his most serious stare, the one where he locked eyes with you, trying to detect an uneasy blink, or twitch, or bead of sweat, anything that may give the slightest hint you're even considering not telling the truth.

"Nothing, sir." The truth.

Bart studied him. "Do you want there to be?"

A question that kept him up more nights than he'd ever admit. Leave it to Bart to get right to the heart of the matter. Spencer broke eye contact, dropping his head to blow on his coffee, lifting the mug to take a sip, drawing both out while considering his options, deciding there'd be no use in lying. Bart knew him too well. "Honestly?" He met the man's eyes head on. "I don't know. But for there to be something between us, she'd have to show some interest. And she hasn't." Except briefly, during their kiss.

"You've got to make her interested," Bart said, adding, "Again," in a much quieter voice.

"Again?"

"Patti and I always wondered how you could miss the way Krissy used to look at you. Weren't sure if you were too dumb to notice, or too smart to let on that you knew."

Too dumb to notice apparently. "How did she used to look at me?"

Bart looked out the kitchen window. "Like a girl in love."

Nuh-uh. No way. She'd been a flirt, a tease. She probably looked at lots of guys like a fickle girl in love.

"Oh, she loved Jarrod, too. No doubt about that. But she never looked at our son the way she looked at you." He shook his head. "The hours I had to listen to Patti fret over that. How she would have loved to have Krissy as a daughter-in-law. Alas," he took a sip of coffee. "It wasn't meant to be."

"No," Spencer said, looking into his mug. "You've got it all wrong."

"Just because you missed it, doesn't mean others didn't see it. Like Jarrod. He knew."

Spencer lifted his head.

"But he was determined, that boy of mine, thought he could create something that wasn't there."

Spencer watched him. Did Bart know Jarrod had gone into the military to impress Krissy? Yes, he did. Either Jarrod had told him or he'd figured it out, but somehow he knew.

"For a lot of years, I blamed Krissy for Jarrod's death," Spencer admitted, not able to meet the eyes of the man he'd looked up to as a surrogate father after his own father had passed away. He would be ashamed of Spencer's behavior if he knew. "When she showed up at my door, I let her know it. I was...horrible to her." He couldn't bring himself to admit the depth of just how horrible, horrible enough to send her to the hospital.

"You over it?" Bart asked with his typical straight-forward approach.

Spencer nodded. "But I'm not sure she is."

"She's a tough one," Bart said. "No doubt about that. Fiercely independent. Has been for as long as I've known her. But the tough ones are worth the effort." He winked. "Make the effort." After a brief hesitation he added, "In his letter, Jarrod made it clear, if he couldn't be with Krissy, there's no one he'd want her to be with more than you."

But it wasn't up to Jarrod. "He mentioned that in my letter, too." And he just had to share that with his parents, nothing like putting Spencer under even more pressure. *Thanks, old pal.*

"Her crush on you aside, she didn't used to have great taste in men."

On that they could agree.

Without warning, Patti swooped into the kitchen. "Krissy will be down in a minute." She went straight to the drawer by the stove to take out a pad and a pen.

"Uh-oh," Bart said. "Here we go."

"You stop it." Patti sat down at the table, unfazed by her husband's teasing, and started to write. "Krissy loved the glider rocking chair that I used to rock Jarrod in."

"So give it to her," Bart said. "We don't need it."

Spencer could probably fit it in the back of his SUV. But before he had the chance to do any more than think it, Patti said, "Yes we do. For when Krissy comes to visit and when we babysit."

Bart leaned back in his chair and crossed his arms over his chest. "So it begins."

"So what begins?" Spencer couldn't help but ask.

"The lists. Everything we need to buy and everything I need to do." Bart motioned to the list Patti was feverishly making.

Spencer read: *Crib. Playpen. High chair. Bibs. Bedding. Car seat. Stroller.*

"By now she probably has all that stuff," Spencer said, even though he couldn't be sure.

Krissy entered the kitchen with a very contented looking J.J. in her arms. "All what stuff?"

"Oh, it's not for her," Bart told Spencer. "It's for here."

"What's for here?" Krissy asked, trying to catch up. Although Spencer had been present for the entire conversation and still wasn't sure what was going on.

"Go on," Bart said to Patti. "Tell them."

"All the stuff we're going to need to set up a nursery for J.J," Patti explained. "For when you come to visit."

She looked over at Krissy. "For when we babysit. So you don't have to schlep."

"Give me my grandson." Bart walked over to Krissy, holding out his hands.

Krissy looked hesitant. "He hasn't burped yet."

"I'll get a burp out of him."

"Oh, he will, too," Patti said. "He's wonderful with babies."

Bart sat back down, settled J.J. against his chest with the baby's head on his shoulder, and started to pat his back very gently. Spencer watched and learned, so he'd be ready when he got a turn to hold J.J. Not today. Today was all about Patti and Bart, but someday very soon.

"So about this babysitting." Krissy pulled out the chair next to Spencer and sat down.

"We're here whenever you need us," Patti said. "Will you be going back to work?"

Without hesitation Krissy answered, "Yes. My sister has been stopping by to visit pretty much every day, but I'm not used to spending so much time at home. I need adult interaction. To be honest, I'm starting to go a little stir crazy."

Wait a minute. "I message you every evening to see if you need anything," Spencer said. "Why didn't you tell me you needed adult interaction? I would have stopped by. It's not like I have to go much out of my way or anything." Patti made a questioning face. "We're living in the same building," Spencer explained. The knowing expression on Bart's face and the hopeful expression on Patti's face had Spencer looking anywhere but at them.

Krissy said, "You always ask if I need anything, and I appreciate knowing that if and when I do, like a ride down to visit Patti and Bart for instance, I can count on you. But in the normal course of the day, I don't *need* anything. I know you're busy and you have your own life. Asking you to take time out of your day to stop by because I'm bored or lonely is selfish. Asking you to do things for me simply because I'm tired and would rather nap is inconsiderate. Regardless of what you may think of me, I'm neither of those things."

No, she wasn't, not anymore.

"I'm not your responsibility, Spencer. I don't want to be a burden."

"You're not—"

She crossed her arms over her chest. "Well then what am I? Not a friend. If I was a friend, you wouldn't have left the hospital without saying goodbye."

"You needed your rest." It sounded lame, even to his own ears.

"If I was a friend," she went on. "You would have stopped by my apartment to visit me, and I haven't seen you in a month…not until I *needed* you for something."

Oh, no. "I was trying not to bother you. I was respecting your privacy and waiting for you to invite me over, like I'd promised I would do when you moved into my building."

She studied him. "You mean you *wanted* to…?"

He nodded.

She smiled. "Then instead of texting me to see what I need, you should have sent me a text that said: No plans tonight, you want to do pizza and a movie at your place? And I would most likely have responded with a: Heck yeah! What time?"

Good to know.

"What will you do for child care?" Patti asked.

"Well that's the million-dollar question, isn't it?" Krissy said. "I'm lucky that Jarrod's generosity has given me a financial cushion so I don't have to go back to work right away. But I enjoy working as a nurse and I'm eager to get back to it. Plus I want to save as much of that money as I can for J.J.'s future."

"I wish we lived closer," Patti said. "I would give up my job to babysit my grandson in a heartbeat."

The two women chattered like they were the only two in the room, like they used to years ago, while Spencer and Jarrod played video games and Bart, when he was home, sat in his recliner chair, reading. Back then, Spencer had listened with half an ear, if he'd listened at all. Today he paid close attention.

"Would I be a terrible person if I admitted to hoping you'd feel that way?" Krissy asked. "But I know. The distance is a problem. I've thought about moving back to the city, maybe getting a place close by."

What? No. Spencer didn't like the thought of that at all. He liked seeing her car in the parking lot, being able to check the tires and registration/inspection stickers to make sure she was driving little J.J. around in a safe vehicle. He liked being close by, liked knowing that her levelheaded sister played a big role in her life.

"But that'd be expensive," Krissy noted.

Right. Very expensive. Don't do it.

"My sister is pregnant," she went on. "My mom lives with her and I really feel the need to be close to both of them, if I can manage it."

Oh, she'd be able to manage it. Spencer would see to it. Somehow.

Patti shared a look with Bart that Spencer couldn't quite read. But Bart's nod showed he understood and agreed.

"You've got time, honey." Patti reached out to pat Krissy's hand. "Don't rush into anything. Let us know

before you make any major decisions. I bet between us
we can figure something out."

J.J. let out a loud, rather impressive, burp.

"Atta boy," Bart said every bit the proud grandpa.

"Well done," Patti said. And she actually clapped.

"Hey." Spencer would have none of that. "Since when
is it acceptable to burp at your table?" More than a few
times he and/or Jarrod had been banished to the living room as punishment for burping, even when they
hadn't done it on purpose. He turned to Krissy. "My
how things have changed."

Making her smile was fast becoming his new favorite thing.

Patti waved a threatening finger at him. "Now don't
you go thinking *you* can do it!"

The grandbaby fed, changed, and burped, they were
finally ready to adjourn to the dining room for dinner. A
brief argument ended with Krissy convincing Patti she
needed two hands to eat and J.J. would be fine laying on
a cushiony blanket on the floor between them, set back
a little from the table so nothing would spill on him.

Spencer had attended Sunday dinner at Patti and
Bart's numerous times over the years since Jarrod had
died, and no dinner had been more enjoyable than this
one. Adding Krissy and J.J. to the mix lifted the mood
and increased the fun factor considerably.

But all too soon it was time to say goodbye.

Patti and Bart walked them to the car, probably to
spend every minute they could with J.J. which was fine
with Spencer, since Bart carried the car seat and all he
had to carry was the leftovers.

Back in his SUV, with Krissy settled into the front
passenger seat, Spencer said, "That went pretty well,
don't you think?"

Her head back against the seat, she nodded, looking tired.

"Did Patti really ask if she could Skype with J.J.?"

Krissy smiled and nodded again. "Yup."

"Don't worry." He patted her thigh. "It's all so unexpected and new. They'll calm down." Eventually.

"I hope not. I want them involved. I want J.J. to have what Jarrod had." She took his hand—which somehow still rested on the bare skin just above her knee—and held it. "Thank you so much for coming with me." She looked up at him. "I really needed you there."

"Happy to be of service." What an asinine thing to say. He squeezed her hand. "Thank you for asking me to go with you. I really wanted to be there."

Krissy covered her mouth with her free hand as she yawned. "Sorry. J.J.'s still getting up two, sometimes three times a night. Derrick suggested I consider giving him a bottle of formula at bedtime to see if he'll feel fuller and sleep longer. But I'm not ready for that." She yawned again. "Last night I couldn't get myself back to sleep between feedings. Worried about today."

Understandable. "Go to sleep." He released her hand. "If J.J. needs you, I'll wake you up."

She looked up at him with sleepy eyes. "Thank you."

"Oh, before I forget."

She opened her eyes.

"Thank you for giving J.J. my name, too." After hearing that, he felt even more of a bond between him and his godson. "It really means a lot." More than she could ever know.

She smiled. "I'm glad. You're going to be a great godfather, Spencer."

He planned to be.

Her eyes drifted closed again, and she slept for the rest of the trip.

After carrying J.J. up to Krissy's apartment and saying good night to both of them, Spencer stood in the hallway outside of her door and took out his phone to text her.

No plans Tuesday night. You want to do pizza and a movie at your place?

He hit send.
She responded before he made it to the elevator.

Heck, yeah. What time?

He smiled.

7:30. I'll bring the pizza.

It's a date! See you then.

CHAPTER ELEVEN

IT'S A DATE. Why the heck did she have to call tonight a date? Krissy hurried around her apartment, plucking clothing and assorted baby paraphernalia from the couch, floor, and basically every flat surface around her apartment. Did Spencer think it was a date? She walked into her bedroom and dumped everything on the bed.

Did he want it to be a date?

Did she?

The memory of that kiss they'd shared in her kitchen sent warm tingles of joy and anticipation pulsing through her body. Part of her, a long neglected part, sure wanted tonight to be a date.

"Stop it," she whispered so as not to wake J.J. who lay napping in his crib in the bedroom they shared. "It's not a date."

But then she turned and caught a glimpse of herself in the mirror, hair scrunched perfectly, cute little pink sundress, and makeup. Yes, she'd actually made time to apply makeup and shave and paint her toenails. She looked down to admire her skill, such a pretty shade of pink.

"I should change," she told her reflection in the mirror above the dresser. "Into sweats." As quietly as she could, she eased out a drawer. "Something that'll make it clear I'm not trying to impress him." Only she was trying to impress him.

A knock on her front door brought the decision of what to change into to a halt. She glanced at her alarm clock. "What is it with that man always coming early?" She left the room, leaving the door ajar, and then went to greet Spencer.

Deciding it didn't matter how she looked or what she wore as long as she set him straight right from the start, Krissy opened the door, and before saying 'Come in' or 'That pizza smells great' or even 'Hello,' she said, "This is not a date. I know in my text message I said it's a date, but it's not a date."

Spencer stared at her.

His lack of response sent her into full babble. "Unless you want it to be a date, in which case I guess it could be a date." She looked up at him. "Did you want it to be a date?"

"I want it to be whatever you want it to be," he said calmly, almost cautiously, as if worried saying the wrong thing might launch her into crazy town.

"All right then." She took a deep breath then let it out. "Not a date." She stepped back to let him in. "Just dinner and a movie with a friend. Purely platonic."

"Works for me." He walked into the kitchen and set the pizza box on the counter. "Where's the little man?"

She liked that, 'the little man.' "He's totally off schedule today. I have no idea why or how long we'll have until he wakes up. We can eat in here and I doubt I'll make it through the whole movie without having to feed him. Or we can eat on the coffee table and start the movie now."

"Let's eat in the kitchen. I don't mind pausing the movie later on if we need to."

She appreciated that.

While he washed his hands, she set the table. They both reached for the pizza box at the same time, in the exact same spot where he'd kissed her. Krissy froze, which was odd, considering everything inside of her warmed most pleasantly.

Spencer went still.

He looked down.

She looked up.

Their eyes met.

"You worried I'm going to kiss you again?" he asked.

"More like worried you're *not* going to kiss me again."

He smiled.

Uhhh… "Did I say that out loud?"

His smile widened. "Yes, you did."

She blamed, "Pregnancy brain. I'm breastfeeding so things aren't back to normal yet."

He leaned in, slowly, no longer smiling, his mouth getting closer.

She should stop him, stop this craziness. This kiss, that she wanted with every fiber of her being, could ruin the fragile friendship between them. If he walked out on her again… His lips millimeters from hers she said, "A word of warning, Spencer."

He stopped, but held his position.

"If you kiss me and leave again, I'll consider this your third and final strike. I will never again give you the opportunity—"

He closed the small distance between them, setting his lips to hers, gently, sweetly, but oh, so enticingly.

It wasn't enough.

Krissy's body screaming for more, she went up on her tiptoes, wrapped her arms around his neck, and pulled him close.

Much better.

Spencer's hands caressed down her back to cup her butt. "Too much?" he asked against her lips.

"No." She answered. *More.*

He yanked her hips in tight to his.

Just right.

Or so she'd thought, until he dipped his tongue into her mouth again and again, tasting her, and, she'd like to think maybe savoring her a little, too.

Perfect.

But all too soon the kissing stopped and Spencer moved his mouth along her jaw, to her ear. "Pizza's getting cold," he whispered.

His scruff tickled her skin. That combined with the aftermath of their kiss and his heated breath on the inner rim of her ear made her eyes go blurry. She tried to focus. "There's pizza?" Pizza was not what her body wanted at the moment.

Spencer smiled against her cheek. "Come on." He left her to carry the box over to the table. "Let's eat."

But Krissy wasn't able to change gears so quickly. "That was some kiss." She traced her still tingling lips with her index finger.

"There's more where that came from," Spencer said as he served himself a slice of pizza then put one on her plate as well. "But I figure it's best we stop now, since tonight we're keeping things platonic."

He deserved a nice, hard pinch, and Krissy was more than willing to give him one. Instead she goaded him right back. "Interesting plan." She sat down. "Although most men I know take what they can get when they can get it."

"I'm not most men."

No. He certainly was not. Most men would not accompany a woman they hadn't seen in years, and didn't much like, to Lamaze class. Most men would not leave work and speed across town to attend the birth of a baby that wasn't theirs. Most men would not give up their very limited free time to drive a friend into the city then stick around for the emotional tear-fest when she introduced her baby to his grandparents for the first time. "No." She met his eyes. "You're not most men."

"Thank you for noticing." He took a bite of pizza.

For some reason she hadn't noticed…until that moment. Sure, she'd found him physically attractive from the start. But noticing his other very attractive qualities, his confidence, dependability, and attentiveness had taken a bit longer. Needing to process that bit of newly recognized information, Krissy took a bite of her own pizza so she wouldn't have to talk.

Spencer filled the quiet. "So how is it a pretty, fun, sassy woman such as yourself doesn't have a grown-up man in her life?"

Unfortunately that was easy enough to answer. "I've had a few boyfriends over the years, some relationships longer and more serious than others." She took a sip of water. "Some didn't work out. Others…who I thought maybe…dumped me when I told them about Jarrod and my plan to have his baby."

"A bunch of idiots." He took a bite of pizza.

How sweet of him to say so. "Jarrod would have thought so, too. Now your turn." She looked him in the eyes. "You're good looking and you've got the whole good-guy vibe buzzing around you. How come no woman has claimed you as hers?"

He raised both eyebrows and tilted his head at her. "Good-guy vibe?"

"I know." Krissy took a small bite of her own pizza.

"Caught me by surprise too." And very recently, as a matter of fact.

"I dated my last girlfriend for two years."

That shouldn't make Krissy jealous, yet it did.

"A year and a half too long," he admitted.

That made her feel better.

"She started out sweet. But the longer we were together the more demanding she got, always nagging me to spend more time with her. The needier she got, always asking me to do things for her. Between her, my mom and my sisters, and my new job with NYC United, something had to give. So I broke up with her."

"Two things I will never be, demanding and needy." Krissy felt his stare and looked up. "What?"

"Two things you will never be, demanding and needy?"

"I said that out loud?"

He nodded, looking way too amused. "Apparently so, because I heard it. And it's got me wondering why you'd be comparing yourself to my last girlfriend?"

Krissy shrugged. No particular reason.

Spencer studied her, waiting for a response.

Krissy didn't have a good response available at the moment, so she pretended to listen carefully, going as far as to squint her eyes and turn her ear toward the hallway. "I think I hear J.J." She stood and left the kitchen. Not because she'd heard J.J., who lay sleeping in his crib like a little angel, but because she needed a few minutes to regroup.

Why on earth had she compared herself to Spencer's last girlfriend? That answer came easily enough: To tell him she'd never be demanding and needy. Why did she want him to know she'd never be demanding and needy? No way. She refused to accept the first answer that came to her. Maybe standing alone thinking wasn't the best course of action at the moment.

Returning to the kitchen, Spencer's expression told her he knew exactly why she'd left. But he played along anyway. "Everything okay with J.J.?"

"Yup." She sat back down, no sense saying any more. He'd know she was lying. "So how's work?" Soccer was a much safer topic than past relationships. "The team's playing well. Alfonso has made a huge improvement to your wins and losses record."

Luckily Spencer loved talking about soccer, and Krissy knew just enough to ask the right questions to keep the conversation going. Before long they'd wrapped up the leftover pizza, cleaned the kitchen, and were on the couch ready to start the movie.

Turning off the lights in the living room and closing the blinds in an attempt to recreate an actual movie-going experience, sans the massive screen and surround sound, had seemed like a good idea...until Krissy seated herself next to Spencer, the two of them alone, in a room lit only by her television screen.

She'd let him pick the movie, didn't really matter what they watched on account of she felt hot and horny and all she could think about was how easy it'd be to straddle his lap to rock and rub...

"You don't like the movie," he said.

"The movie is fine." It was his proximity that was giving her trouble. Like in Lamaze class, proximity had given him an impressive erection. Proximity had him claiming he could get her off in minutes, in a room full of people without anyone knowing. Right now, the 'get her off in minutes' part had her concentrating on that possibility rather than the movie.

Spencer laughed.

Krissy looked at the television.

"You didn't laugh," Spencer said. "Everyone laughs at that part."

She hadn't laughed because she hadn't seen or heard what had happened on screen because she'd been too busy imagining what it'd feel like to have Spencer's hand in her panties, to have his erection deep inside of her, pumping… She inhaled a shaky breath.

This had to stop.

Spencer picked up the remote control from the coffee table and paused the movie. Then he turned to look at her. "What's wrong?"

Shrugging seemed easier than having to answer, so that's what she did.

"Not good enough," Spencer said.

Pain in the butt. "Just thinking about something, that's all."

Please leave it at that. Please leave it at that.

He didn't leave it at that. "Thinking about what?"

Of course he'd ask. And you know what? Of course she'd answer. With the truth. Krissy didn't let guys get her all…befuddled. What the—? Krissy also never used the word befuddled. "Fine. You want to know what's on my mind?"

He nodded. "Yes. That's why I asked."

Well get ready for an honest response. She looked him straight in the eyes. "At Lamaze class, you said you could get me off in minutes, in a room full of people without anyone knowing. Were you serious?"

"That's what you're sitting here thinking about? Me getting you off?"

Not proud of it, at all, but yup.

"Good," he said. "You and your 'Those rumors back in high school were true. I give an amazing blow job.'

How is a man supposed to sit next to you, in the dark, without thinking about that? But you said platonic." He threw that back at her.

Staring straight ahead she asked, "What if I changed my mind?" Out of necessity. Out of desperation.

Spencer shifted on the couch, ever so slightly. "Then I'd say, for the record, I told you I could get you off in minutes, in a room full of people if you could keep it quiet, which I seriously doubt."

Was that a challenge? "Oh, I can keep quiet if I want to keep quiet." Except where was the fun in that?

"Really?" He moved fast, reaching out, lifting her onto his lap, facing toward the television. "Let's see." He draped her legs over his then started to spread them, slowly, carefully. "This okay?"

"Yes."

He kept going until her legs were spread as wide as they could go. "Lean back."

Primed and eager to see where this would lead, she did, resting her back on his chest, her head on his shoulder.

A moment of hesitation, of worry that letting Spencer proceed was a mistake of epic proportions, fled the instant his warm fingers took a gentle glide from her inner knees up the sensitive insides of her thighs to the elastic leg openings of her panties. Yay for wearing a dress!

"Is it okay if I touch you?"

"Yes." Please do, right away, and hurry it up if you don't mind.

He dipped beneath the elastic, following it up to her hips then down as low as he could reach.

It was all Krissy could do not to cry out at the overwhelming sensation of being touched by a man's hands, so intimately after so long. But she wanted more, needed more, now, so she tried to shift on his lap, to get him to—

"Nu, uh, uh," he said quietly, his mouth next to her ear. "I'm in charge."

Oh, no, sirree. Krissy tried to sit up. She had no intention of letting him—

"You want me to stop?" he asked.

God, no. Her body plopped back down of its own accord. "I'm not one to just lie in one spot without moving."

"Shh…" he whispered. "Pretend we're in a room full of people. No moving and no talking."

"Then hurry up," she whispered back, losing patience with this game, ready to excuse herself to the bathroom to take care of things on her own.

"Tsk, tsk, tsk," he moved his hands, sliding both down beneath the top of her panties this time. "And you told me you weren't demanding."

She rocked her hips, urging them upward, inviting him in, so close. "I'm usually not. But sometimes…"

He pushed forward, between the seam of her lips to her opening and Krissy lost all control, needed this, so bad. "Yes. Like that." She moved up he moved down. She moved down he moved up, over and over again. "Soooo good." He spread her wetness, moved his hand faster, in circles.

Absolutely shameless, Krissy rocked her hips, rolled her hips, arched her back, getting closer. "I need more."

"Tell me what you need."

"Harder. Move faster, side to side." He did. "Inside. I need you inside."

He stopped.

"Noooo!"

"Is it okay?"

"Yes. It's okay. Please."

"Have you been to the doctor? Did *he* say it's okay?"

"God, I hate you."

She tried to sit up.

He threw his arms around her and held her tight. "Don't go. Let me take care of you." He slid one hand back between her legs, swirling the tips of his fingers around her opening, turning Krissy into a limp rag of compliance.

"That's my girl."

She wasn't a girl, only she couldn't muster the muscle control necessary for speech to tell him so. Later. She'd tell him later. Much later. Right now... "God that feels good. Don't stop."

He didn't stop.

Lungs heaving, orgasm building, Krissy lost herself in the pleasure, moving as her body needed to move, moaning when she needed to moan, until it happened, that burst of wonderfulness that had her crying out, "Yes! Oh, God, yesssssss!"

"Shh," he said, but he kept moving until every last bit of pleasure had been drained from her sated body, until Krissy drifted off into a blissful place she never wanted to leave.

Spencer's kisses to her cheek and neck brought her back, which was when she noticed the swell of his erection beneath her butt.

His turn.

She got up carefully, making sure her legs would hold her, before she stood and stripped off her saturated panties.

"We can't," Spencer said.

As much as she wanted to, she hadn't been to the doctor yet, hadn't been given the all clear to resume sexual activity. So she dropped to her knees at his feet, pushing his legs apart to make room for herself.

"What are you doing?" he asked, watching her every move.

She let her actions answer, unsnapping the button of his jeans, working down the zipper, and exposing the tip of his cotton covered sex. She dropped her mouth down to kiss it. "Getting acquainted."

CHAPTER TWELVE

GETTING ACQUAINTED? KRISSY blew out a hot breath, barely filtered through his cotton briefs, and Spencer thought both of his heads might explode. "You don't have to." But every single cell in his body wanted her to, needed her to.

"Lift up."

At this point he'd do anything, absolutely anything, to feel her hot, wet mouth on the bare skin of his erection. He followed her instruction, lifting up and helping her slide his jeans and underwear over his hips, exposing that part of him, allowing it to stand tall and proud, eager and ready.

"Well look at you." Krissy caressed him with her soft hand, from tip to base, applying just the right amount of pressure. "Spencer Penn is all grown up."

In the process of formulating a comeback, his mind went immediately blank when she sucked him deep, taking all of him, and holding him there, squeezing him there, down into her throat.

Spencer fought to remain still, when every part of him wanted to thrust into her, hard and fast.

When she started to move, Spencer thought he might weep with joy. And he was *not* the weep with joy type. Krissy moved on him like a woman on a mission, a mission he fully condoned and was thrilled to be a part of, taking him deep again and again.

"That feels…" No word seemed adequate. He settled on, "Fantastic." He didn't want to waste valuable energy thinking.

Her hands worked in tandem with her mouth, her talented tongue swirling around his tip before she dove back down his length.

He fisted his hands on the couch, didn't want to touch her, didn't want to do anything that might interfere with the perfection of her mouth on him and the rhythm she'd set, a perfect rhythm that had his balls starting to tingle a most enjoyable warning of spectacular things to come. So good, too good. "I'm not going to last." He didn't want to last, not this time.

God love her, she seemed okay with that.

Spencer lost the battle to control his hands and they gripped her head as his hips lifted in jerky little thrusts, up and in, a little deeper each time, he couldn't help it. "Oh, God." Feet planted on the floor, he moved faster, couldn't stop. "Oh, God. Here it comes." He tried to lift her off of him but she fought back, sucking him deep again and again until he gave her every bit he had to offer, the intensity of his orgasm draining him of the ability to do anything but exist in a place of overwhelming contentment.

Until J.J. started to cry.

"Perfect timing," Krissy said, standing up.

Spencer forced his eyes open to see her wiping her mouth.

"No time for first time post orgasm awkwardness with a baby in the next room." She forced a playful smile, all lips.

She looked nervous and uncomfortable and Spencer hated that.

"Come here." He grabbed her hand and pulled her down for a kiss. "I like tasting myself when I kiss you."

She pushed away and stood. "You probably want to get going." She bent to pick her underwear up from the floor.

"Don't do this," Spencer said, not when their shared intimacy had made it clear he could have a relationship with her based on more than Jarrod wanting them together and Spencer's feeling responsible for J.J. He tugged his briefs and pants back up. He'd grown to like her again, but more importantly, he'd grown to respect her. Friendship, respect, and mutual attraction made a strong foundation for a lasting relationship. This could work. "I'm not feeling awkward." He was feeling supremely satisfied, hopeful for the future, and maybe a little sleepy, but most definitely not awkward. "You shouldn't feel awkward either."

"I'm not sure how to do this," she said.

"I beg to differ." He stood. "In my opinion you were great at it." He kissed the top of her head then moved to see her face, liking the shy smile he saw there.

"Yeah, I guess you were pretty good at it, too. But I was talking about us." She motioned between them. "You and me and whatever's happening between us. What if—?"

J.J. started to cry louder.

"Go take care of him," Spencer said. "We can talk more when you're done."

"I have to change him and feed him. It takes a while."

"If you feed him out here, on the couch, I promise not to look." She had no idea the magnitude of restraint that would require. He'd been dreaming about her breasts, seeing them bare before him, touching them and sucking their nipples, since he'd hit puberty.

He started to get hard all over again just thinking about it.

While Krissy took care of J.J., Spencer took some time to clean up and get himself back under control. Apparently that took the same amount of time as a diaper change because he returned to the living room at the same time Krissy exited her bedroom carrying a wide awake J.J.

"Hey there, big guy." Spencer rubbed his back. "Hungry?"

J.J. started to squirm.

Krissy walked toward the couch. "He's not much for social interaction when his stomach's empty."

Spencer turned on the movie, but lowered the sound, not so he could listen to J.J. feeding. That was an added bonus.

He sat there, staring at the television, not watching the action on the screen, lost in thought, feeling… He couldn't quite summarize how he was feeling. Content. Happy. Protective. *Is this how men feel while sitting beside their wives, listening to their son's voraciously taking nourishment from their wives' bodies?* It felt good.

Except Krissy wasn't his wife, and J.J. wasn't his son, and this had been Jarrod's dream, not his. But Jarrod wasn't here to live out his dream. Could Spencer take it on as his own?

"You're staring."

Unintentionally. Somehow it'd just happened. Rather than delve into the thoughts racing through his mind, thoughts that had somehow, unbeknownst to him, turned his head, he decided to make light of getting caught. But not until he took a moment to really see the beautiful sight before him. The top of Krissy's dress unbuttoned, her left breast exposed with J.J. latched on to the nipple. "Can you believe I'm jealous of a five-week-old baby? What does that say about me?"

Krissy smiled. "That you're a breast man?"

Oh, yeah. For sure. He nodded, preferring to think about that rather than all the other stuff.

"Well, sorry to say," she looked down at her son and caressed the top of his head lovingly. "Right now my boobs are for nutritional enrichment only."

"I'm a patient man," he told her, even though right now he didn't feel like a patient man. "I can wait." And dream and anticipate and plan all the things he would do when he could finally see them, feel them and taste them.

Since thinking carnal thoughts of a breastfeeding mother felt wrong, on so many levels, Spencer turned his attention back to the television set, and raised the volume enough to cancel out the sounds coming from beside him. Eyes focused straight ahead, Spencer tried to ignore Krissy removing J.J. from her breast and shifting him to feed on the other side. He only knew what was happening thanks to his excellent peripheral vision.

The baby's soft head brushed up against his a forearm.

"Sorry," Krissy said. "I'm not used to doing this while someone else is on the couch."

He wanted to say, "Well get used to it because I plan to be hanging around a lot more often." Instead he said, "No worries."

A few minutes later, movement caught his attention again. "Is it okay to look?"

"I'm…almost…yes."

He turned to see her buttoning her dress. "Do you want me to burp him?"

She'd gone from them fooling around on the couch to change J.J. then back to the couch to feed him without ever using the bathroom, putting the needs of her son ahead of her own. "You don't mind?"

"Of course not." He'd do whatever he could to help her.

With a relieved smile she said, "That'd be great." She handed him a white cloth. "Put this on your shoulder."

Spencer thought back to how Bart had done it, and when Krissy handed him J.J., he held the baby the exact same way.

"Just rub and pat."

Spencer rubbed and patted.

"He won't break."

"Good to know."

With another beautiful smile, she turned and after going into her bedroom for a moment, she walked across the hall into the bathroom.

"Just you and me," he told J.J., feeling a little nervous about holding his godson in his arms for the very first time, not that he'd ever tell Krissy that. He rubbed and patted and nothing happened.

J.J. started to fuss.

Spencer stood, swaying in place like he'd seen Krissy do down at Patti and Bart's. He continued rubbing and patting and was rewarded with a very loud burp.

"Good job." J.J. calmed right down after that, and Spencer felt quite a sense of accomplishment. It felt good to hold a baby and take care of him, and not just any baby, Krissy and Jarrod's baby. His godson. "If there was any way your daddy could be here with you right now, he would be. But don't you worry that he's not here, because I am and I'll always be here for you."

A noise brought his attention to the hallway, where Krissy stood, watching him from the shadows.

"Sorry," he said, because an apology felt necessary for some reason. "I didn't mean—" that he planned to replace Jarrod or…

Before he could finish that thought Krissy was hugging him. "Thank you."

Thank you? "For what?"

"For showing me the kind of godfather you plan to be, for talking to J.J. about his dad. For coming to hang out with me tonight, and not leaving when I had to nurse, and…for everything else."

Holding J.J. in his left arm and Krissy in his right, Spencer felt a part of something special, a part of this little family. And he liked it.

Krissy said, "Let's see if you can put J.J. down in his crib without him waking up."

Spencer felt like he could do anything.

Except, it seemed putting a baby down into a crib, without waking him, required special skills. Luckily, Krissy possessed those skills, and quickly took over, whispering, "Wait for me in the living room," as she quieted her crying baby.

Okay. Spencer walked into the hallway. He wasn't a perfect surrogate parent, not yet, anyway. It would take time. He had no problem putting in the time it would take to master the task, in fact, he looked forward to it.

Krissy emerged from the bedroom a few minutes later, looking tired. "If you're okay with me possibly falling asleep on you, you're welcome to stay and finish the movie."

He didn't care about the movie. But cuddling on the

couch with a sleepy Krissy sounded most appealing. "Sure." Since he was already sitting on the couch he lifted his arm, inviting her to slide on in next to him.

She did, setting her head on his shoulder, fitting in beside him like the curves of his body had been created just for her. He clicked on the movie, but didn't watch. Instead he closed his eyes, savoring this moment of absolute perfection.

Krissy dozed off within seconds of sitting down.

Spencer sat there, holding her, eventually shifting their positions so she laid half on top of him. He would have stayed there, just like that, all night, but he had to work in the morning. Planning to carry her to bed, Spencer slid off the couch, trying not to wake her.

"What?" Krissy sat up.

"Sorry. I tried not to wake you."

She rubbed her eyes. "What time is it?"

"A little after midnight, I've got to get going."

Krissy stood. "I'll walk you to the door."

"We have a rare Wednesday night game tomorrow so I won't be home until late. Are you free Thursday? I could pick up dinner and—"

Krissy put her hand on his chest. "I don't expect you to stop by every night to see me. Don't feel like you have to explain your schedule to me. We fooled around, that's it, nothing more."

It meant more to him. But he wasn't ready to tell her that just yet. "While I appreciate you not expecting me to stop by every night, I'd like to stop by when I can. Would that be okay? If I check with you first?" He didn't want to crowd her.

She nodded. "That'd be great."

Good. "So." He tried to sound casual. "Any doctor's

appointments coming up?" He slipped on his shoes to avoid looking at her.

J.J. would be turning six weeks old next week which meant Krissy should be due for her six week checkup at the OB-GYN. According to his research, that's the appointment where a woman who had a normal vaginal delivery was usually cleared to resume sexual intercourse.

When he looked up, Krissy smiled. "Why Spencer Penn, are you asking because you want to have sex with me?"

Heck yeah! "After tonight, there should be no doubt in your mind that I'm attracted to you. God's honest truth, I want to make love to you more than I've ever wanted to make love to any other woman in my entire life. That doesn't mean I'm going to pressure you or expect anything based on tonight's…fun. It's just, if we should wind up alone and in the mood, *again*, and we both want to take things further than we did tonight, I want to know that you've been medically cleared to do so. That's all."

"Since you're planning to stop by a lot more often, I'm guessing chances are high we'll wind up alone and in the mood again soon."

"Exactly." Whoa. "Wait a minute. That's not why—"

Krissy smiled. "I know, Spencer." Then she wrapped her arms around his neck, went up on her tiptoes and whispered, "I have an appointment next Thursday." She tongued his ear. "And I'd love for you to be the first guy I'm with post baby. I trust that you'll, you know, take it easy until we're sure everything on the inside is all healed up and back to working like it should."

First guy? First *and* last he thought, feeling rather

territorial even though he had no right to be. He hugged her close. "You know I will."

"You have any plans for Thursday night?"

Didn't matter, if he did, he'd cancel them. "Now I do."

"Bring condoms."

Lots and lots of condoms. Check!

She released him. "And Spencer?"

"Yeah."

Her eyes met his. "If we take this next step, please promise me that, no matter what happens, you won't start to hate me again."

"I promise." On Jarrod's grave, he promised.

After that, Spencer visited Krissy almost every night. They ate dinner together, talked about their days, and laughed, a lot. Then they cuddled on the couch, exploring each other's bodies, never to the point of orgasm. They'd agreed to save that for when he could be buried deep inside her.

At Sunday dinner with Patti and Bart, they acted like there was nothing starting up between them. Krissy had felt it was too new, she didn't want the pressure of Patti and Bart hoping for something permanent between them. It was too late for him to escape it. At least he could save her for the time being. So he'd played along while under Patti and Bart's watchful eyes. But he'd held her hand during the car ride down and then back home again. And when they'd slipped out to take a walk to the local park, just the two of them, he'd kissed her under the tree where she, he, and Jarrod used to hang out as pre-teens, acting too old for the swings and slide.

On Thursday, Spencer made sure to clear his schedule around noon, expecting to hear from Krissy. When his cell phone vibrated in his pocket, he jammed his hand in there to retrieve it.

Just saw the doctor. We're good to go. Still on for tonight?

Oh, yeah. He replied.

I want to come now.

Me too!!!!

He smiled as he texted back.

Don't you dare. Not without me there. I'll make it worth the wait.

I know you will.

He appreciated her confidence in him, her trusting him with her body.

See you soon.

Not soon enough.

CHAPTER THIRTEEN

AFTER HER APPOINTMENT with the doctor, Krissy drove to the plaza across the street for another motherhood first: Perusing sexy undergarments while lugging a six-week-old baby in a car seat.

"Welcome!" A nicely dressed woman with neatly styled blonde hair, maybe in her mid-thirties greeted Krissy as she entered the lingerie store. One look at J.J. and she added, "Let me guess. Gearing up for first time after baby sex?"

Krissy nodded. "First time with the new man in my life sex, too." And not just any man. Spencer. Over the years she'd had a lot of drunk sex, no seduction required. But Spencer was different than the man-boys she typically dated, and she wanted their relationship to be different.

Their relationship.

Thinking that had her feeling euphoric yet frightened at the same time.

"Well then we'll have to find you something extra special," the saleswoman said with a smile. "Follow me. You breastfeeding?"

Holding the car seat in front of her, Krissy navigated between rack after rack of lacy, silky, sexy outfits. "Yes."

"So we'll need to cover your bra." The saleswoman stopped then looked Krissy over. "I have just the thing."

Seven hours later, dressed in her new sexy lingerie, a silky, deep red outfit sure to drive Spencer wild, Krissy had a bottle of wine chilling, candles out and ready to be lit, and a platter of assorted veggies, crackers, and humus for sustenance, when disaster struck.

"Why tonight? Of all nights?" she asked as she stripped off J.J.'s soiled sleeper. "What did I eat to make this smell so bad?" She undid the tabs of his diaper, taking a moment to mentally prep before opening it. "Good Lord." She held her breath until she couldn't hold it anymore. "The green bean salad I picked up at the deli. Never again."

This mess required more cleansing power than baby wipes. And Spencer, who always came early, would likely be here any minute.

"Oh, well," Krissy told J.J., dropping a kiss on his forehead. "He'll just have to wait." And so would she.

Wrapping J.J. in a towel she picked him up, walked to the bathroom and set him down on the mat while she readied his bath. No sooner did she put him in the baby bathtub, Spencer knocked on her front door. Knowing he'd worry if she didn't answer, and knowing she couldn't leave J.J. unattended in the tub, she scooped him up, covered him with a towel, and went to the door.

"Sorry," she said when she opened it. "This was not the greeting I'd planned on. You may want to come back in an hour."

Spencer made the mistake of inhaling.

"Appears my afternoon snack didn't agree with the little man here."

Spencer smiled. "You made that big smell?" he asked J.J. "High five." He held out his hand and tapped J.J.'s fist. "Your daddy would be proud."

"Don't encourage him."

"What can I do to help?" Spencer asked.

Unprepared for the sweet offer, Krissy just looked at him, and to her absolute horror, she felt her eyes fill with tears. "I wanted tonight to be special. I bought a negligee." She reached for the bottom hem and held it out so he could see it. "One look at me and you were supposed to go crazy with lust and take me up against the door. Instead, here I am, holding a stinky baby. My new negligee is soaked and quite possibly as stinky as the baby."

She met his eyes again. "This stuff happens when you have a baby. And we're a package deal. So maybe it's a good thing you see what it's like early on so…" If you don't want to be a part of it you can back out now.

Spencer reached out and wiped the tears from beneath her right eye, then her left. "Tonight *will* be special," he said sincerely. "Only a little later than planned. And that sex against the door scenario you had in mind?" He shook his head. "Never would have happened, not tonight anyway. Tonight we're taking it slow. But greet me in that negligee without a stinky baby in your arms, any night after tonight, and you can count on some door pounding action."

The smile came to Krissy's face without her even thinking about it. "Good to know."

"Now what do we have to do to get the little guy settled?" Spencer rubbed his hands together.

"You don't have to—"

"I *want* to."

"Well, he needs a bath and his crib and changing table need to be changed."

Spencer hesitated. "I was thinking more along the

lines of me holding him while you handle the smelly stuff."

Krissy gave him a playful shove.

"Hey. I'm new at this. I need to work up to the gross stuff."

Krissy liked that he planned to stick around long enough to work up to the big stuff. "Come on." She walked to the bathroom.

Spencer followed. "I'm glad you're using the baby bathtub."

Krissy dumped out the dirty water and added fresh, warmer water. "Good call. Turned out I needed it after all."

As Krissy washed J.J. Spencer stood behind her, watching, and she didn't mind at all. Early on, she probably would have thought he was critiquing her technique, and he probably would have been. But now, it felt more like he was trying to learn by observing in addition to just keeping them company.

J.J. splashed.

"Wow. He really likes the water."

"Yeah. But it makes giving him a bath a wet undertaking." Krissy glanced over at Spencer. "I wonder if he'll be as good a swimmer as Jarrod?" Jarrod had been a member of their high school swim team.

"Time will tell." Spencer handed her a towel.

She laid it out on the bath mat then lifted a slippery J.J. from the tub, laid him down on it, and swaddled him up.

"Is that the towel I got you?"

Krissy nodded. "Another perfect gift. Thank you." She lifted J.J. and turned to Spencer. "Since you're here to help." She placed J.J. in his arms. "Give me a minute to clean out the tub."

That done, Krissy changed and dressed J.J. out in the living room, leaving him in Spencer's care while she tackled clean up and odor control. "I should have listened when you suggested I get a two bedroom," she yelled down the hall. Then she opened both of her bedroom windows.

When Spencer didn't answer, she went to find out why.

"Shh," he said, holding his fingers to his lips.

He sat leaning back on the couch with J.J. sound asleep on his chest, looking every bit a proud papa. Krissy's heart swelled, knowing deep down in her soul, that no matter what happened between the two of them, Spencer would always play a special role in J.J.'s life.

"I hate to do this, but I need to run the dirty linens down to the laundry room. They're stinking up the whole apartment."

He nodded. "But change first."

She looked down. Right, she was still in her negligee. Her wet, stained, anything but sexy at the moment, negligee. Sixty dollars, wasted. Oh, well, nothing she could do about it now.

When Krissy got back from the laundry room, she found Spencer in her bedroom, leaning over the crib, rubbing J.J.'s back.

When he noticed her watching he pointed at J.J. and gave her a wide-eyed, big-mouthed smile that seemed to say, 'Look what I did!'

"Great job," she whispered giving him two thumbs up. Then she added, "I'm going to take a quick shower."

He nodded.

Her lilac scented body wash smelled so good and the hot water felt so good, Krissy decided to take a little longer than a quick shower to relax and regroup and decide how to restart her seduction. On the verge of shutting off the water, Spencer knocked then opened the door.

"Wanted to run something by you," he said.

Krissy stuck her head out of the side of the shower curtain. "What's up?"

Spencer stared like a man hoping if he tried hard enough he could conjure up X-ray vision. "In my Internet travels I came across articles on breastfeeding women and sex."

Krissy fought a smile. "Oh, you did, did you?"

His eyes finally found hers. "I just want to make it clear that I am perfectly fine with you wearing a bra during sex. But listening to you in the shower gave me an idea."

"Oh, it did, did it?"

He nodded. "Leaky breasts don't matter in the shower, right?"

She liked where this was headed. "No they don't."

"I was hoping you'd say that." He whipped his polo shirt over his head. "Because I really..." he stared at that shower curtain again "...*really* want to see all of you." He unbuttoned then unzipped his pants. "Feel all of you, bare skin to bare skin while I make love to you, especially this first time." He shucked his pants, underpants and socks. Spencer Penn naked was absolute male perfection. Defined muscles, a light dusting of hair on his chest, and an impressive erection that she couldn't wait to feel inside of her. "So what do you think about slow, careful shower sex?" he asked. "Or start in the shower and finish on the couch sex?"

"I think you put a lot of thought into this."

He nodded. "I put a lot of thought into everything." He bent down, took a condom out of his pants pocket and held it up. "It's an affliction."

"It's not a *bad* thing."

"I'm glad you think so."

"In fact I like a man who puts a lot of thought into things and comes up with ideas like slow, careful, fully naked shower sex." She pulled back the curtain. "Get in here."

Never had a man seemed more eager to join her in a tub. "I was hoping you'd say that." Wasting no time he ripped the packet, rolled on the condom and pulled her into his arms. "God you feel good." He let out a breath. "I feel like I've been waiting a lifetime to hold you like this."

His hands roamed down her back to her butt, he squeezed both cheeks then pulled her close, bending then arching so his erection slid between her legs, front to back. And he began thrusting along her sex.

"That feels so good." Krissy rocked her hips, hoping her legs wouldn't give out. She planted her hands on his butt cheeks, then gave a squeeze and yanked him forward, holding him still so she could glide along his slick length, over and over again.

Spencer moved his arms to her back, squeezed her tight, and pressed her breasts to his chest as he swiveled from side to side. "I knew you'd feel like this. So soft."

A needy pressure built between her legs. Krissy found his nipple and sucked it into her mouth, still rocking.

Spencer sucked in a breath. "Next time I will last longer, I promise."

She sucked again, tilting her pelvis, bringing his tip to her opening.

"You ready?" Spencer asked.

"So ready."

He turned her so she was facing the wall. "Put your

leg on the side of the tub." He moved behind her, his front pressed to her back, as he positioned himself at her opening once more. "Talk me in," he said. "Let me know how you feel." He dipped inside.

Suddenly Krissy felt a little nervous.

Somehow Spencer knew.

"It's going to be good." He wrapped an arm around her front, loosely, not restraining her in any way, holding the weight of her right breast in his hand, as he dipped inside a little further.

The sensation familiar and yet different. "More," she said.

He pulled out and slid back in, deeper. Krissy's body stretched to accommodate him. "Again."

He pulled out and pushed forward.

This time Krissy pushed back, taking more of him.

Spencer sucked in a shuddery breath. "God how you test me." He pulled her close and started to move, gently, slowly.

Krissy moved with him, the rhythm perfect. Until she needed, "More."

He gave her more of him until she took all of him.

"Faster."

He picked up the pace, his breath turning into a pant by her ear.

"Harder."

"You're sure?"

"I'm sure."

He slammed into her from behind, over and over, caressing both of her breasts now, squeezing them, while avoiding her tender nipples, as if he somehow knew.

"You feel so good inside of me," she told him, meeting each powerful thrust with one of her own. "I need your hand." She removed it from her breast. "Here."

She placed it between her legs, didn't need to do anything more than that because it was like he knew exactly what to do.

"God you're good at this." He possessed her, controlled her, used her body, taking what he wanted, but giving so much more. Her orgasm started to build. "Please tell me you're close."

"Ready when you are," he panted in her ear, driving into her from behind, fondling her from the front, replacing the memory of every man before him with the memory of what he was doing to her right now.

"Now," she said, straining out her release. "Now." She came again.

Spencer let out a grunt and stiffened against her back. He pulled out, thrust in deep and held himself there, grunting again, kissing her ear, her neck, hugging her tightly. "I want to stay like this for the rest of the night."

"Not sure the hot water will hold out."

"Too bad."

Too bad indeed.

Krissy lowered her leg and Spencer left her body. She felt the loss of their connection immediately, missing it, wanting it again. Turning she threw her arms around his neck and pulled him down for a kiss.

He kissed her over and over, affectionate and caring kisses turning passionate. "That was so good. Just like I knew it would be." He turned off the water, reached for the towel on the hook, and wrapped her in it. "How do you feel?" He looked deep into her eyes as if trying to ascertain the truth there.

Krissy climbed out of the tub, reached inside the cabinet beneath the sink, and handed him a fresh towel. "I feel wonderful," she told him the truth, stretching. "I wish…"

"What?"

"My place isn't set up very well for entertaining men."

In the process of towel drying his head, he stopped and looked at her. "Good."

"Whoa." She held up both hands. "Down boy. I only meant, I have a twin-sized bed in a bedroom that I share with my baby. My couch doesn't open into a sleeper—" He started to speak. She held up a finger to stop him and kept talking, "which in hindsight may have been a mistake. Yes I probably should have listened to you. What I was trying to say, before you went jealous male on me," which she kind of liked, "is that I don't have any place where we can lie down together. Comfortably." To cuddle.

Spencer pulled her into his arms. "From now on, we'll use my place. I've got a nice big bed. We can get one of those portable cribs and set it up in the living room for J.J."

"Always thinking." She smiled. "I like that."

"As for tonight." He kissed the top of her head. "The couch is fine. When I get tired I'll head back to my place."

CHAPTER FOURTEEN

OVER THE NEXT few weeks, Krissy began spending more nights in Spencer's bed than in her own. His orderly apartment had turned disorderly. Baby stuff cluttered his living room, dishes sat in his sink, unwashed, and dirty clothes and towels seemed to materialize out of nowhere, draped on his couch, balled on his bathroom floor, and piled in the corner of his bedroom. And he didn't mind one bit.

It amazed him how quickly he'd transitioned from happily single bachelor to contented family man, how easily he'd fallen into the role of dad for J.J., and how much he'd grown to care for Krissy, in such a short time. She didn't nag, or complain, or question where he'd been or where he was going. She didn't call him throughout the day, didn't demand his attention, and really didn't seem to expect anything from him. She was smart and sexy, fun and most importantly, independent. She was the perfect woman.

He recalled a snippet from Jarrod's letter.

Look at her. Really look. Past her pretty face and hot body, beyond her flirty behavior and sarcasm, deeper, to the sweet, thoughtful, special woman she is inside.

In the last few weeks, Spencer had done just that. And it hadn't taken him long to realize how lucky he was to have Krissy in his life. He looked to the corner of his sofa where he had J.J. propped up beside him. "What do you think of the game, buddy?" Spencer pointed to his laptop screen where 'they' were watching NYC United play the Arizona Wolfpack, in Arizona.

J.J. smiled at the attention and shook his rattle.

During halftime Spencer called to Krissy who was in the kitchen preparing a lasagna for dinner. "How are you feeling about Patti and Bart's big news?" Their plans to relocate up to White Plains to be closer to Krissy and J.J.

"I'm actually looking forward to it." She walked out of the kitchen, drying her hands on a towel, and came to sit beside him on the couch. "I'm anxious to get back to work. With Patti willing to babysit J.J., it's the perfect situation for me. I think having them close will be good for all of us."

Spencer thought so, too, couldn't wait to have access to local babysitters he trusted so he could take Krissy out on dates and they could spend more time doing 'couple' things. "My friend Steve asked if we'd like to go out for dinner with him and his wife on Wednesday. She's six months pregnant, and they're fine with us bringing J.J." It'd be their first time taking J.J. out to a restaurant. Heck, it'd be Spencer's first time taking Krissy out to a restaurant.

"Wednesday doesn't work for me."

What? What did she mean Wednesday didn't work for her? He waited for her to explain. She didn't. So he asked, "You have other plans?" With who?

She stared back at him but said nothing.

"With J.J.?"

"Nah, I think I'll leave the kid home alone. He can't

walk or crawl yet, what trouble can he get into?" J.J. started to fuss so Krissy walked over to pick him up. "Of course, with J.J. I'm breastfeeding. I do everything with J.J. I go everywhere with J.J. He is always with me, twenty-four hours a day, seven days a week!"

"I'm sorry. Of course you'll be with J.J. Stupid question." Spencer moved the laptop from his lap to the coffee table. "So where are you going?" As long as Spencer wasn't traveling they spent every evening and most nights together. Exactly what plans did Krissy have that didn't include him?

She swayed on her feet, rocking J.J. while rubbing his back, appearing not at all eager to tell him.

Which made him want to know even more. "What's the big secret? Why won't you tell me where you're going on Wednesday?"

"It's no big deal and I don't want you worrying that—" She stopped mid-sentence.

"Don't want me worrying about what?" He sat up straighter.

"I knew you'd make a big deal about it, so I didn't plan to tell you until after I did it."

"Did what?"

Never one to back down, her eyes met his. "Introduce J.J. to my mom."

Her brain-injured mother who Spencer hadn't seen since her injury, but who he'd heard plenty of stories about back in the day. "Your mother? Who has violent outbursts?" At least she used to. "Who doesn't even know who you are? Why would you put J.J. at risk to meet a woman who doesn't even know who you are?"

"Wow. That was a jerky thing to say." Krissy walked over to J.J.'s diaper bag, picked it up and set it on the recliner. Then she started walking around the living room collecting J.J.'s things one handed. "Regardless of whether she remembers who I am or not, she's still my mother." Krissy wouldn't look at him. "*I* remember her the way she used to be, before the brain injury turned her into a different person. *I* want to introduce her to *my* son, not because it will mean something to her, but because it'll mean something to *me*."

He'd hurt her feelings, the very last thing he'd wanted to do. "I'm sorry."

"You should be sorry." She bent down to pick up J.J.'s blanket from the portable crib, balancing J.J. on her hip at the same time.

"Let me help you."

Before he could reach her, she whipped up the blanket, nearly toppling the crib over. "I don't need your help."

"Stop." He grabbed her by the shoulders, turning her around so she had to look at him. "I'm sorry. Of course you should take J.J. to meet your mother. I'll go with you." To ensure his godson's safety.

Krissy looked mortified at the thought. "You can't."

He can't? "Oh, yes, I can," Spencer said. "And to keep J.J. safe, I will."

Krissy looked ready to lash out at him, but she didn't. Instead she inhaled then exhaled and said, "I'm going to ignore your overbearing statement, because I know you said it with J.J.'s best interest at heart. But to clarify, *no*, you *can't* go with us. We won't be alone. Kira and Derrick will be there. We'll all make sure J.J. is safe."

"You'd rather have Kira and Derrick there than me? I have no say? After all I've done for you?"

Krissy went rigid. "After all you've done for me?"

"Taking you to Lamaze class."

"You mean forcing me to go to Lamaze class."

He ignored that comment. They both knew she had

to go. "Being with you in the delivery room, buying you things." He ticked the items off on his fingers, one by one. "Bringing you dinner, helping you with J.J., spending all of my free time with you, changing my whole life for you." The moment the last word left his mouth, Spencer knew he'd gone too far.

"Well. Tell me how you really feel," Krissy said calmly, way too calmly. He would have preferred it if she'd blown up at him.

"Right or wrong, that *is* how I feel," Spencer said. "We're close enough and I do enough for you that I feel I deserve a say in you bringing J.J. into an unsafe situation. And if I want to be there, I believe I have earned the right to be there."

"You believe you have earned the right?" Krissy glared at him. "Let's get something straight," she said her stance rigid and ready for battle. "J.J. is *my* son. *Mine*, not yours. If I want to take him to meet my mother, I will take him to meet my mother. While I appreciate everything you have done for me, I didn't realize you were under the mistaken impression your actions entitled you to certain rights where *my* son is concerned." She shoved J.J.'s rattle, a burping cloth, and a stuffy into the diaper bag.

"Out of respect and appreciation," she snapped, in a tone that didn't sound respectful or appreciative, "I will explain that since my mother's attack she has developed a severe fear of men. All men. Age, hair color, ethnicity, none of it matters. If a male comes near her she reacts. If she feels threatened, she flies into a rage and goes on the attack. Other times, like if she hears a male voice, it could even be on the television if she's not right in front of the screen, she'll bang her head on the closest hard surface until it bleeds. Or she'll stab herself with a sharp object, over and over until we can get it away from her. It's not something I talk about. Now you know. The reason you *can't* come with me to visit my mother, is because you're a man. It's not safe for you and it's not safe for her."

"So why does Derrick get to go?" Jeez. Even to his own ears he sounded like a spoiled child.

"Because he dresses like a woman, that's why."

"He dresses like a woman? That's the most ridiculous thing I've ever heard."

Krissy glared at him, again. "Yes. He dresses like a woman, so he can spend time with Kira while she's taking care of my mom, so he can help her and provide medical evaluation and treatment when Mom needs it." She pointed her finger in his direction. "If you tell anyone or tease him or say one unkind word to him about it, I will never forgive you. He's a great guy." Apparently talking about Derrick calmed her down. "He loves Kira, would do anything for her. She is blessed to have a man like him in her life." She hefted the diaper bag and slung the strap over her shoulder.

"Don't go," he tried.

"I don't want to intrude on your free time," Krissy said. "Your dinner is in the oven. Timer is set."

"Krissy..."

She reached for her pocketbook which hung on the back of a kitchen chair. The heavy diaper bag slid down her arm, throwing her off balance.

"Let me help you." Spencer reached for the diaper bag.

"Don't." She twisted out of reach. "Now that I know your help comes with expectations, I won't be so willing to accept it in the future." She turned to walk toward the door. "I knew you were like Kira, I just didn't recognize how much until today."

She said it like it was a bad thing. "What's that supposed to mean?"

"It means you do things for me, things I don't ask for, then, when you get mad at me, you throw them back in my face. If you didn't want to spend so much time with me, you shouldn't have. If you didn't want to buy things for me and J.J., you shouldn't have. If you didn't want to attend J.J.'s birth or drive us to Patti and Bart's, you shouldn't have." She opened the door then turned to look at him. "And for the record, no one asked you to change your life for me."

In the heat of the moment, "That's not exactly true," shot out of his mouth.

Krissy turned, slowly. "What did you say?"

Spencer regretted his words instantly and did not want to repeat them.

Krissy stood there, staring laser beams of rage in his direction.

Everything inside of him screamed now was not the time to tell her, that he should wait to explain after they'd both had a chance to calm down.

"Tell me," Krissy demanded. "You've got something to say, say it. Let's get everything out in the open, right here, right now."

At this point he'd do anything to be done with this fight, so they could talk it out and move on. So he told her the truth. "In his letter," Spencer explained. "Jarrod asked me to help you with J.J. To help you raise J.J."

Her eyes met his. "Jarrod didn't trust me to do it on my own?" Anger turned to hurt. She curled a protective arm around J.J. "He didn't think I'd be a good mother? That's the only reason you…" Anger flared back to life.

"That's the only reason you've been so nice to me? To worm your way into my life, so you can help raise J.J., because Jarrod asked you to?"

"No—"

"How could I have been so stupid to think you actually cared about me?"

"Krissy—"

"Well at least you got some great sex out of it, right? If you have to change your life for a woman you hate, and pretend to like her and care for her baby, because your dead friend asked you to, at the very least you deserve lots of great sex…as payment for all you've sacrificed."

"I didn't—"

"Don't you dare say you didn't enjoy it," she yelled. "I am one hundred percent certain you were at least happy to have me in your bed, and that you enjoyed yourself as much and as often as I did." Her eyes met his, full of challenge. "If you say otherwise you're a liar."

Spencer's nosy neighbor across the hall opened her door and stuck her head out.

"Come back inside," Spencer said calmly as he walked toward Krissy. "Let me explain."

"There's nothing to explain. Jarrod trusted me to give birth to his baby but not to raise it. So he sicced *you* on me, and you took full advantage of that." J.J. started to cry. Krissy bounced him in her arms as she fired off her parting shots. "As of today I am officially done with you. Stay away from me. Don't try to talk to me. Don't look in my direction. Don't even think about me. As of this very second, you are as dead to me as Jarrod is."

With that she turned and stormed away.

Spencer let her go. He had no choice. She was so

upset, there was no way they could have a rational conversation. With a nod to his neighbor he closed his door. He'd give Krissy a few hours to calm down. Then he'd go to her apartment to apologize...and tell her the whole truth.

CHAPTER FIFTEEN

KRISSY FLED SPENCER'S APARTMENT, his building, and his life. Then she loaded J.J. into his car seat in her car and drove. "How could I have been so stupid? To actually believe he cared about me?" Needing to hit something she pounded on the steering wheel at each slow moving vehicle in her way, each red traffic light that delayed her escape. She needed speed, needed to get away.

Of course she'd known their relationship would end at some point, but tonight's revelations had come out of nowhere, everything had been going so well. Or so she'd thought.

Jarrod didn't trust you, after all.

Spencer didn't trust you, either.

Krissy sucked in a breath. What about Patti and Bart? What had Jarrod written in his letter to them? Is that why they were moving to White Plains? To be closer to Krissy so they could check up on her, too? Because they didn't trust her with J.J. either?

Krissy's chest burned with hurt.

As if he could tell something was very wrong, J.J. started to cry. "It's okay, baby." But it wasn't okay. Nothing was okay.

And yet, as angry and hurt as she was, she slowed the car, knew she shouldn't be driving reckless. She was a mother now, a good, responsible mother, no matter what anyone else thought. Rather than flying into a rage or running away, she needed to find a way to *make* things okay, for herself and her son, starting with getting out of the car so she could dry his tears and hug him close and reassure him that he was safe and loved.

"A few more minutes, honey. Just give me a few more minutes."

Not wanting to return to her apartment ever again, and having no place else to go, she drove to Kira's.

Later that night, laying on a new twin bed in the extra room at Kira's house, alone in the dark, Krissy listened and watched the light on the baby monitor for any movement. Only in her second trimester of pregnancy, ever efficient, ever prepared Kira already had her nursery partially set up. So it made sense to put J.J. to sleep there, at least to Kira. But Krissy missed having him close, no longer liked being alone.

When she heard the front door to Kira's house open, she forced herself to sit up and wipe her annoyingly weepy eyes, then she forced herself to stand and walk and act like her world hadn't fallen apart this evening. "Hey," she said to Kira who was walking up the stairs, carrying bags of stuff she'd gone to get from Krissy's apartment, even though Krissy had insisted it could wait until tomorrow. "Need help?" Without waiting for an answer, she met Kira halfway and took the bags from her right hand.

"Feeling better?" Kira asked.

"Yes," she lied. "Thank you so much for letting J.J. and me stay here for a little while and for getting my stuff. I won't stay long, I promise." Just long enough to figure out her next move.

"Stay as long as you want," Kira said, planting a

kiss on Krissy's cheek as she walked past. "I need to use the bathroom."

From behind Kira, on the stairs, carrying the baby bath, the bouncy chair J.J. loved, and more bags of stuff from her apartment, Derrick said, "Don't think you have to leave because of me. Kira's family is my family." Kira had hit the future husband jackpot with that man, a keeper for sure.

"Thank you." When Derrick put down his bundles, Krissy went over to give him a hug. "At least I know J.J. will always have you to look up to and learn from." She hugged him tighter.

Derrick hugged her back. "I am going to be the best uncle in the history of uncles."

See, she didn't need Spencer. J.J. was going to grow up just fine. Krissy was going to be just fine too…as soon as the ache in her heart went away.

"I'm making tea," Kira said, joining them in the foyer. "Anyone else want?"

Derrick walked over to Kira and put his arm around her shoulders, but he spoke to Krissy. "She drinks tea before bed then complains when she has to get up in the middle of the night to pee."

Kira smiled up at him. "Sometimes you like it when I wake up in the middle of the night to pee."

Derrick gave her a very sexy smile back. "Sometimes I do." He kissed her.

There was so much love between the two of them. Despite her heartache, Krissy couldn't help feeling happy for her sister. No one deserved the love of a good man more than Kira.

"I've got an early day tomorrow," Derrick said. "I'm going to bed."

After another loving kiss for his fiancée, he headed down the hall.

"Come sit with me," Kira said, walking back into the kitchen. "Since you've been seeing Spencer, we haven't had much sister time."

Sister time sounded perfect, so Krissy pulled out a chair and took a seat at the counter. "As long as you know I'm still not ready to talk about what happened tonight." Aside from the humiliation of learning Jarrod hadn't trusted her to raise his son on her own and Spencer's actions had been motivated by an obligation to his friend and lust, rather than any real care for her, this was Krissy's problem, Krissy's life. And she'd deal with it on her own.

"That's fine," Kira said, carrying her mug of tea to the counter and sitting next to Krissy.

"What?" Krissy eyed her sister. "That's fine?" She hit the side of her head trying to clear a fake blockage from her ear canals. "Did you say that's fine?" She studied Kira's face, staring into her eyes, looking… "You must be an alien imposter," Krissy said. "Because my *real* sister would be questioning me and analyzing the information provided and telling me what I should do."

Kira smiled. "Derrick lectured me all the way home from your apartment." She dropped her voice to mimic him. "She has to fix this on her own, Kira. You can't solve all of her problems, Kira. She's a grown woman, Kira."

Yes, she was. "Have I mentioned how much I love my soon-to-be brother-in-law?"

"You and everyone else," Kira said. "While he's not always right, I think in this instance he is." She reached out and squeezed Krissy's hand. "Just know I'm here for you. I'm here to listen when you're ready to talk, to be a sounding board, if you want one, to give my opinion if, and only if you ask for it. I'll babysit. I'll pack up your apartment and move all of your things wherever you tell me to move them. I'll act as intermediary between you and Spencer so he can play a role in J.J.'s life, if that's what he wants, without you ever having to speak to him again, not that I think that's the best course of action, but it doesn't matter what I think. The decision of what path your life will take from here is all yours and yours alone."

With Kira's words fresh in her mind, the first major decision Krissy made was to cancel on Sunday dinner at Patti and Bart's. She felt awful about that, especially since she'd been the one to suggest starting them up again. But she wasn't ready to see any of them.

The following week, Patti called to say Spencer wouldn't be joining them for Sunday dinner and offer Bart's services to drive her and J.J. into and home from the city. Wanting to talk to them alone, Krissy agreed to dinner, but declined the offer of transportation. She was fully capable of driving herself into the city. And on Sunday, she made the trip without any problems. J.J. slept, traffic moved, she found a great parking spot close by, and actually wound up arriving twenty minutes early. Bart met her down in the main floor entryway so she didn't have to carry J.J. and the diaper bag up the stairs.

"Look at that big boy," Bart said as he hurried down the stairs. "He looks like he's doubled in size since I last saw him."

It'd only been two weeks, and they'd Skyped twice since then. "Thanks for coming down to get him." Krissy lifted J.J. out of the carrier she wore draped across her front and handed him to Bart. "Go to Grandpa."

Recognizing his grandpa, J.J.'s legs started to pump with glee.

"He's smiling." Which made Bart smile too.

"He's been doing that a lot lately." So had Krissy, she was moving on with her life and things were going well.

Up in the apartment, Patti greeted her as warmly as ever. "I'm so happy you came." She gave Krissy a tight hug. "How was your trip?"

"Not bad at all." Krissy set her bags on the floor then maneuvered out of the baby carrier. "But the downside of me coming by myself, is I didn't have enough hands to bring dessert."

"I know you like fruit salad," Spencer said from the doorway into the kitchen. "So I brought some. No bananas or strawberries."

Spencer.

He looked so good in his dark blue jeans and blue and white striped polo shirt. But Krissy forced her eyes away, turning to Patti who now held J.J. "You told me Spencer wasn't coming."

Spencer answered. "If you knew I'd be here, you wouldn't have come."

True.

"We need to talk," Spencer said.

Krissy looked from Spencer to Patti to Bart, who had conveniently positioned himself between her and door. "So you're all in on this." They were ganging up on her, and Patti and Bart had taken Spencer's side, which made it clear, whatever concerns Jarrod had shared with Spencer, he'd also shared with his parents.

"We're not taking sides," Patti said. "We're simply watching J.J. so the two of you can talk out your problems uninterrupted."

Spencer walked toward her, looking so serious, so

weary. "Give me fifteen minutes. If you want me to go after that, I'll leave."

Figuring the sooner he said what he'd come here to say, the sooner he'd leave, Krissy agreed. "Okay."

Looking relieved, Patti, who was still holding J.J., turned to follow Bart, who carried the diaper bag, down the hall to their bedroom. The door clicked closed behind her.

Spencer took a seat at the kitchen table.

Krissy grabbed a glass and filled it with water then she sat too.

"I've given this a lot of thought." Spencer held out an envelope labeled with his name in Jarrod's handwriting. "I want you to read the letter Jarrod left for me."

Krissy reached for it.

Spencer held it tight. "First, you have to promise to read it through from start to finish without getting angry or upset or asking questions. Second, after you're done reading, you have to agree to keep quiet and give me a full ten minutes to explain."

His expression dire, Krissy wasn't sure she wanted to read it. But curiosity got the better of her, and she nodded. "I promise and I agree."

With suddenly sweaty hands, she opened the envelope, took out the letter, and started to read.

Hey Spence,

If you're reading this, I guess I zigged when I should have zagged and I'm dead. Well, doesn't that suck? I hope I went out in a blaze of glory doing something heroic.

I know we're on shaky terms right now because you don't agree with my reason for joining the Army. But it's my decision, my life. And if my plan works, and Krissy and I wind up together, well, it'll be a happy life indeed. Sure, I'm not a fan of getting blown up in some foreign country, but if I do what I've been trained to do, I should be fine. Anyway, in the States, I could get killed simply crossing the street, right? No honor in that.

Now for the important stuff. If I know Krissy— and I know her better than anyone—she's probably waited until the last possible minute to give you this letter. So by now you can probably tell she's pregnant. Surprise! The baby is mine. I wish I could see her belly rounded with my child, wish I could be there to run to the store to buy stuff to satisfy her crazy cravings and hold her hand through labor and help her care for and raise our child. But obviously I can't.

In my absence, Krissy will try to do everything on her own, but she can't. She'll need help. And I expect you, my oldest and best friend, my blood brother since the third grade, to be there for her. That's why I made you the baby's godfather.

You're the best guy I know, Spence. I trust you to help Krissy raise my son or daughter the way I would have. Not because I don't think she's going to be a fantastic mother—because I know, without a doubt, she's going to be a fantastic mother. And not because I don't think she'll raise my child right—because I know she will. But I don't want her to have to do it alone. I don't want her to struggle and sacrifice, like so many single mothers do.

I know you had a crush on her at one point. I saw the way you used to look at her when you thought no one would notice, like you wanted to strip her bare and get down to business on the closest flat surface. Yet you never acted on that urge, at least as far as I know, out of respect for me, I'm sure. Another reason you're the best guy I know. Maybe I should have bowed out. I'm pretty sure she had a thing for you for a while, too. I'm selfish enough to admit, I liked it better when the two of you were fighting than when you were lusting after each other.

But things have changed. With me no longer in the picture, there's no one I'd rather Krissy be with more than you. I know you'll treat her the way she deserves to be treated.

If she's not in a relationship, or the guy she's with is her typical A-hole of a boyfriend, and if you're not in a serious relationship, I want you to turn on the charm and win her over. Dig deep. Remember how you used to feel about her before you two started fighting, reignite that old spark. Be nice. Be helpful. Be there when she needs you.

You were always so quick to see the bad in Krissy. Well, I got news for you, buddy. No one's perfect. Get over the past. Look at her. Really look. Past her pretty face and hot body, beyond her flirty behavior and sarcasm, deeper, to the sweet, thoughtful, special woman she is inside. Honest to God, I am giving you a gift, the life I always wanted for myself, a fun, loving woman who, if you let her, will make you happy. I know she will.

Wish I could be there when Krissy tells my mom and dad that they're grandparents. I get choked up thinking about it. Anyway, I know you'll do the right thing. Even so, I'll be watching. Love you, man,
Jarrod

So Jarrod *had* trusted her.

…because I know, without a doubt, she's going to be a fantastic mother.

Krissy's heart swelled with love. Then it deflated with loss because Jarrod wasn't here. Only Spencer was here—Spencer, who had only been a part of her life because Jarrod had asked him to be, guilted him to be.

And I expect you, my oldest and best friend, my blood brother since the third grade, to be there for her.

Krissy's eyes met Spencer's. "If you expected this letter to help your case, it didn't. Nice to know you're always so quick to see the bad in me."

"So much for you agreeing to keep quiet and give me a chance to explain."

Krissy crossed her arms over her chest, braced herself for what he was about to say, and glanced at the clock on the microwave. "Your ten minutes starts now."

CHAPTER SIXTEEN

KRISSY SAT ACROSS from Spencer, looking hurt and ready to hurl her water glass at his head at the same time. Letting her read Jarrod's letter had been a risk. But if they were to have any chance for a future together, there could be no secrets between them.

"To start," Spencer said. "The last time I saw you I acted like a total jerk."

"An adequate description." She nodded as if giving it further consideration. "A decent place to start."

"I'm sorry."

Her posture softened considerably.

"I need you to know that I wasn't being nice or helpful simply to get you into bed." He stared deeply into her eyes. "You have to believe me."

She stared back, but said nothing.

Not good.

"Sex with you has me thinking words like transcendent and unrivaled and unsurpassable. And let's face it, those aren't words I use on a regular basis."

She gifted him with a small smile. "I like those words."

He did too. "Why do you think that is?"

"We've got some crazy sexual chemistry going on."

"No." He reached over to take her hand into his. "It's because what's between us is deeper and more meaningful than just sex. My need for you is so much more powerful than simple sexual attraction. Regardless of what brought us together, I've come to care for you, Krissy."

She shook her head and tried to pull her hand away.

He held on tight, wouldn't let her go until he said all he'd come here to say. "Yes, in the beginning I got involved with you because Jarrod had asked me to."

"And probably because you thought I'd be a total screw-up of a mother."

Seeing her hurt made him hurt. "Back when you first showed up at my door, I'd had no idea you'd grown up to be such a responsible, committed, and capable woman."

Her eyes met his. "Thank you, Spencer. That means a lot."

"I helped you because it was the right thing to do, because you needed my help. But honest to God, I enjoyed spending time with you. Which is why, even after I assured myself you were a wonderful mother and you were taking great care of J.J. and really didn't need anything from me, I kept on stopping by. Because I *wanted* to, not because I felt I *needed* to. Because I started to care for you…again."

"Did you really have a crush on me back in high school?" She tilted her head. "You sure had an odd way of showing it." She seemed to give it some thought. "Because of Jarrod."

He nodded. "He'd been so in love with you for so long. I couldn't…"

Krissy squeezed his hand. "You're a great friend, Spencer."

Sometimes he didn't feel like one.

"But even so," she went on. "You shouldn't be expected to change your life, to take on responsibility for a woman and her baby, simply because your friend asked you to. Jarrod was wrong to—"

"No, he wasn't," Spencer insisted. "I'm glad he asked. I know I didn't sound like it, but I'm happy having you and J.J. as part of my life. I know I'm not his father and I had no right to—"

"I was wrong," Krissy interrupted.

What? "No."

"Hear me out," Krissy said. "I've given this a lot of thought. When we started sleeping together, I treated our relationship like I've treated every other sexual relationship I've had. I guarded my heart so you wouldn't break it, and I made sure to remain independent so that when whatever this is between us runs its course and we break up, I'll be just fine getting back to life on my own."

Spencer tried to say something but Krissy shushed him.

"My point is, you were right. You'd taken on a fatherly role for J.J. and I let you. It's obvious to me that you love him as if he were your own son."

"I do."

"So like I said, I was wrong to make the decision to go see my mom, knowing the risks involved, without discussing it with you first. Even though you're not technically J.J.'s father, you're the closest thing he has to one."

"Thank you. And I was wrong for throwing everything I've done for you back in your face, like Kira does. I was *happy* to go with you to Lamaze class, I *wanted* to be in the delivery room, and aside from leaky, smelly diapers and getting woken up in the middle of the night, I love everything else about being with you and J.J."

"You do take good care of us, just like Jarrod had asked you to."

Spencer's heart swelled with joy and pride and hope. "Thank you."

"So where do we go from here?" Krissy asked, avoiding contact.

"I'm hoping we can try again," Spencer told her.

She lifted her eyes to meet his. "I'd like that, too."

Thank you, God.

"But from today on, things need to change."

He didn't want things to change, liked them just the way they were.

"Don't look so worried," she smiled. "I mean change as in we need to do things the right way this time. Go out on dates, just the two of us. Get to know each other again. Have fun. Go out with friends, together or alone. Have lives that aren't dependent on one another. Create a relationship based on more than taking care of J.J. and having great sex."

He liked the sound of that.

"No more spending all of our free time together. One thing I've realized in our time apart is that I need to find a balance between me the mom and me the fun-loving woman I was before I became a mom. I need to make new friends and find things to do in my new hometown, which I've already started doing, by the way."

"I saw you've been spending time at an exercise studio on Maple Street."

"I'm taking a Mommy and Me class. We line all the car seats along the back wall. It's the cutest thing." She stiffened.

Uh-oh.

"How did you know I was spending time at an exercise studio on Maple Street?"

He could have tried to lie. Maybe something like, "I saw your car in the parking lot." But no, a future built on no secrets between them meant no secrets between them. He reached into his pocket, took out his cell phone, and accessed his Find Friends app. Then he turned the screen to her.

"Find Friends?"

"It's an app. I loaded it onto your phone."

"At the hospital."

He nodded.

"You've been tracking me?" This time when she pulled her hand away he let her.

He nodded again, waited for her to let him have it, felt everything slipping away. He'd lose her now for sure.

Surprisingly she didn't let him have it. All she did was ask, "Why?"

"I'd told you I would respect your privacy and not visit you without an invitation. I loaded the app so I could keep my distance but still see what you were up to."

Leaning back in her chair, she crossed her arms over her chest. "To make sure I wasn't going out drinking and partying all night?"

"No," he answered, staring her straight in the eyes, showing her he wasn't lying. It hadn't taken long for Spencer to realize how badly he'd misjudged her early on, and to know she was going to be a wonderful mother. "So I could feel close to you, without actually being close to you." He told her the truth. "If that makes any sense at all."

"So you know I've been staying with Kira for the last two weeks."

He nodded again. "Had you been alone in your apartment, I wouldn't have waited until today to try to talk to you."

Rather than yell and carry on like old Krissy would have, she sat calmly and quietly as if digesting all she'd just heard.

Spencer wouldn't allow himself to hope.

By the time she finally spoke, he'd been fully prepared to throw himself to the floor at her feet to beg for forgiveness.

Of all the things to come out of her mouth, "Thank you," the two words in that exact order, were the absolute last two words he'd expected to hear.

Had he misunderstood? "You're thanking me for spying on you?"

Her eyes met his. "I'm thanking you for telling me the truth."

The tightness in Spencer's chest loosened enough for him to take a deep breath. "I'll delete the app."

"Good idea."

He deleted the app. "And since I'm coming clean about my bad behavior..."

"Lord, help me." She shifted in her seat. "You mean there's more?"

"Might as well get it all out now, right? So we can start over with a clean slate."

"Why do I feel like I need a shot of something whiskey-like before you go on?"

"About that kiss in high school," he said.

She let out a relieved breath. "You pushed me away because of Jarrod."

"Yeah. And I got mean and obnoxious to keep you away."

Her lips curved into a small smile. "Or I might have tried again."

"When you wanted something, you were pretty persistent."

"And I'd wanted you."

"For the record, I'd wanted you too. If not for Jarrod, I would have claimed you as mine that night."

She stood. "How about claiming me as yours right now?" She straddled his lap.

Overcome with relief and gratitude, hope and happiness, Spencer threw his arms around her and kissed her like the world might end if he didn't do it thoroughly enough, prepared to sit there, holding her until the end of time.

She held him just as tightly, and kissed him back with equal enthusiasm, his perfect match in every way. So he eased back, to tell her, "You are what my life's been missing. You're fun and passionate, a wonderful mother, and thank God, kind and forgiving. You're laid back, you go with the flow and I need that in my life."

She countered with, "You're confident and sexy, dependable and smart, and you're going to make a wonderful father for J.J., I mean for as long as…" She broke eye contact, looking unsure.

"I'm going to make a wonderful father for J.J. period. End of statement."

"About my mother," Krissy started. "I want my children to know her, even though she showed little interest in J.J. when we brought him over."

He'd been wondering about that. "I handled that all wrong. Of course you should take J.J. to visit her, anytime you want. I trust you to keep him safe. But if you want me to, I will happily dress up like a woman to go with you, not for safety, but to keep you company when you visit or have to care for her. I'd do anything for you, Krissy. And I hope that one day, you'll feel blessed to have me in your life, same as you feel Kira is blessed to have Derrick in hers."

Taking his face in her hands and staring deeply into his eyes she said, "Baby, I already do."

EPILOGUE

Ten years later

KRISSY ENDED HER call just as Patti walked into the kitchen of the house she and Spencer had been living in for the past nine years, since right after they'd gotten married in a double ceremony with Kira and Derrick.

"The boys will be home in ten minutes," Patti said.

Krissy held up her cell phone. "I heard you talking to Bart. I called Kira. She'll be here with all the kids in half an hour." That would give J.J. time to open his two very special presents without the craziness of having his younger brother and sister, and Kira's two children running all around, wanting to see.

Krissy glanced at the letter from Jarrod and the velvet box from Patti and Bart that she'd set on the counter, trying to contain her emotions.

Patti opened the refrigerator door, drawing her attention, and once again, Krissy could not believe her eyes. "You outdid yourself this year." The race car cake Patti had created for J.J.'s tenth birthday celebration looked so realistic, Krissy hated the thought of cutting into it.

"Have to admit," Patti said as she took the cake and carried it to the center of their huge dining room table. "I had to do a few trial runs to get it just right. The people at Bart's work were happy to help us get rid of the duds."

This year J.J. hadn't wanted a big party. He'd only wanted two things, the letter from his dad up in heaven and to indulge his love of NASCAR and attend a race. For as much as J.J.'s looks and mannerisms, and his kind heart, were similar to Jarrod's, their son was most certainly his own person. His obsession with all things auto racing had caught everyone by surprise. But his very involved Grandpa Bart and his loving father here on earth, Spencer, had embraced his love of NASCAR, and went on to develop their own obsessions with it.

Ten minutes flew by in a blur of putting out drinks and food. Before Krissy knew it, the dog started in with his over-the-top happy 'My family is home' barking. A few seconds later J.J. ran into the kitchen to hug his grandma and then Krissy. "We had the best time, Mom."

Bart and Spencer followed, more slowly and lacking J.J.'s energy.

Krissy kissed Spencer's cheek. "An annual event?" she whispered.

"God, I hope not." He hugged her close. "I'm exhausted." They'd left at dawn and it was nearing seven o'clock in the evening. Thank goodness tomorrow Spencer had a day off from his work with NYC United, where he was now the head athletic trainer, so both he and J.J. could spend all of Sunday relaxing.

"Poor baby." Krissy went up on her tiptoes as she pulled him down so she could whisper in his ear. "I missed you today." Nine years of marriage and despite their crazy hectic lives, she loved him now more than ever. "I was hoping to show you how much."

He nuzzled next to her ear. "I'm never too tired for that."

A fact he'd proven time and time again.

"Can I open them now?" J.J. asked.

Krissy, Spencer, Patti and Bart all looked over to where he stood, holding the letter in one hand and the box in the other. The mood in the room instantly changed. J.J.'s excitement was almost palpable. But for Krissy, and she'd guess everyone else, this moment brought back Jarrod's loss once again. His son finally reading the letter he'd left for him would be bittersweet.

"What?" J.J. asked, with a look of frustration that so closely resembled a look Krissy had seen on Jarrod's face way too many times. "I took off my shoes and washed my hands and gave Grandpa Bart time to go to the bathroom."

Grandpa Bart laughed. "That he did."

Krissy smiled. The mood in the room seemed to lighten.

"Which one should I open first?" J.J. asked, eyeing the box then the envelope, trying to decide.

Bart stepped forward and pointed to the velvet box. "I think this one."

Without question, J.J. set down the letter and lifted the top of the box. As he studied the contents he looked confused, maybe a little disappointed even, until Bart explained, "This is your daddy's Congressional Medal of Honor. It was awarded by the President of the United States. It's the highest and most prestigious honor given by the U.S. Military, for extreme acts of bravery and courage."

"Wow," J.J. said with awe and a good amount of reverence. He'd been told the story of how his father had died during a hostage rescue mission when he'd remained behind to lay down cover fire, saving his team, a downed pilot, and ten civilians. But this was the first time he'd been told about the medal.

Spencer stepped forward. "We waited to give it to you to make sure you were old enough to understand and appreciate how important it is, and responsible enough to value it and keep it safe."

"I am." J.J. looked up at Spencer. "And I will." Then he turned to Krissy. "Can I bring it into school for show and tell?"

With tears gathering in her eyes and emotion clogging her throat, all Krissy could do was nod.

Leave it to Spencer to clarify, "On a day either me, your mom, grandma or grandpa is available to bring it into school for you."

J.J. nodded.

Slowly he set down the box and picked up the letter, staring at Jarrod's handwriting, like Krissy had done before opening and reading her own letter, like he'd done so many times since learning of the letter's existence.

He looked at Krissy for permission.

She nodded again.

A tear leaked down her cheek. If only Jarrod were here to see what a wonderful young man his son had turned out to be.

Spencer put a big, strong arm around her shoulders and held her close. Krissy looked over to see Bart doing the same to Patti, all eyes on J.J.

With the utmost care, J.J. used a letter opener to slowly and precisely slice open the top of the envelope, the ripping of paper the only sound in the room.

The envelope opened, J.J. reached in and removed the letter taking a quick look inside of the envelope before setting it down beside the box.

Then he climbed up on a stool in front of the counter, unfolded the letter and started to read. J.J. was at the top of his class in reading. Even so, Krissy couldn't help wondering if he'd be able to decipher Jarrod's handwriting, if he'd understand all of the words. He sat there reading, so quietly, not moving except when he finished one page and moved on to the next. Krissy could barely breathe, not knowing what Jarrod had written or how her son would react. The seconds ticked by like hours.

At one point J.J. smiled down at the letter, then he laughed, a snort-laugh, just like his father.

Then his face grew serious.

He sniffled.

Krissy wanted to run to him and comfort him. But when she made a move toward him, Spencer held her in place, shaking his head slightly. "He can handle it," Spencer whispered. So confident in the boy he'd raised as his own.

J.J. wiped his eyes then he smiled again and looked at Krissy. "Dad says hi. And that he loves you and wishes he could be here."

That's all it took. The tears she'd been trying to keep under control started to flow down her cheeks. She sucked in a hiccupping breath. Spencer rubbed her arms and kissed the top of her head.

"Oh." J.J. smiled. "He also said not to cry."

Krissy smiled through the tears.

"What else did he say," Patti asked, sounding hopeful.

J.J. jumped off of his stool and ran to Patti and Bart to give each one of them a hug. "That I have the best, most special grandparents in the whole world, which I already knew. And I should give each one of you a hug and kiss for him." Bart bent down for a kiss. Patti did the same. "He says he loves you."

That got Patti crying. Bart looked close to shedding a few tears, too.

J.J. walked over to Spencer, glanced at the letter and said, "Dad said you better be taking good care of me and teaching me to be a good man."

"Doing my best, buddy," Spencer said, messing up J.J.'s too long dark hair.

J.J. gave him a hug and Spencer bent down to squeeze him tight. The two of them shared such a close bond.

After releasing Spencer, J.J. walked back to the counter and dumped out the envelope. "Look," he said, holding up a baseball card. "My dad's favorite baseball card."

Bart said, "I was wondering what had happened to that. When he was young, like you, your dad used to sleep with it under his pillow hoping it'd make him a better baseball player."

J.J. seemed to like the sound of that. "I'm going to try that too."

Spencer whispered to Krissy, "It didn't work."

Krissy gave him a hip check.

"And look at this." J.J. held up a picture. "Dad in his uniform. A little one I can put in my wallet, someday, when I get a wallet. Like Dad has pictures of us in his wallet." J.J. held up the picture then read the back. "'To my special son. Love you always,'" he read. "'Dad.'"

Then J.J. held up a hundred dollar bill. "Dad says I can use this money to buy whatever I want, from him."

"You figure out what that is," Spencer said. "And I'll take you shopping."

"Thanks, Dad."

Sometimes it got confusing when J.J. talked about his dad, since he referred to both Jarrod and Spencer as

Dad. Each held a special place in his heart, and each one was equally special to him, Krissy made sure of that.

J.J. started to fold up the letter.

"Wait," Krissy said. "That was a three-page letter. What else did he say?"

J.J. laughed. "Dad said you'd ask me that."

He knew her so well.

J.J. continued folding the letter and carefully slid it back into the envelope. "Private stuff. Just between me and him." He looked her straight in the eyes and made a threatening face. "Dad said to mind your own business and no snooping."

"What? I don't snoop!"

Spencer started to laugh. "Oh, yes, you do."

Yes. She did.

"You'd better hide it good, J.J.," Spencer teased.

"Oh, I will." Their son ran up the stairs heading toward his room.

"Traitor," Krissy said under her breath.

An hour later Krissy stood in her crowded, noisy living room watching J.J. tear into the rest of his presents, his eight-year-old brother and five-year-old sister helping like they had every right to be up front with him. They were such great children, all three of them. She'd been well and truly blessed.

Patti sat holding Kira's youngest, seven-year-old, Isabelle in her lap. Bart sat with his arm around Kira's oldest, nine-year-old, Kate. As far as Patti and Bart were concerned, they had five grandchildren, each one more special than the next. It seemed like Patti was always baking for some party or celebration and Bart took off the whole week leading up to Halloween to make sure everyone's costumes were just right, and attend all of the school parties, of course.

Spencer came to stand beside Krissy. "Penny for your thoughts?"

"Just thinking about how lucky I am and all Jarrod has given me." Patti and Bart, J.J. and Spencer and the two beautiful children she'd had with him.

Her handsome husband crossed his arms over his chest and said, "I'd like to think I had a little something to do with all this, too."

"You had *a lot* to do with it," she said. "But by asking me to have his baby if he didn't make it back from the war, and by making you the godfather of his baby, Jarrod brought you back into my life." Krissy wrapped her arms around his waist. "And Patti and Bart." And more love and happiness than Krissy had ever thought possible.

Spencer wrapped his arms around her shoulders. "Hard to believe how much my life has changed since you showed up at my door a little over ten years ago."

Krissy looked up at him. "I hope for the better."

Spencer leaned down to kiss her. "Definitely for the better." He hesitated. "Do you ever wonder what would have happened if Jarrod wasn't killed? If he'd come back a war hero? Would you have…?"

Krissy put her finger to Spencer's lips to stop him from talking. "I loved Jarrod. I still do. And I wish he could be here with us. But I never loved him, or any other man, for that matter, the way I love you. You're the only man for me," she told him, squeezing him tightly. "You poor thing." Sometimes her laid-back attitude drove him absolutely nuts.

"I love you, too," Spencer said. "And don't worry about me. I can handle you."

He could, better than anyone.

He leaned in close to whisper, "Tonight I plan to *handle you*…for hours."

Krissy smiled, so happy, and absolutely loving her life. "I can't wait."

* * * * *

If you missed the first story in the
NURSES TO BRIDES *duet*
look out for
THE DOCTOR SHE ALWAYS DREAMED OF

And if you enjoyed this story,
check out these other great reads from
Wendy S. Marcus:

NYC ANGELS: TEMPTING NURSE SCARLET
CRAVING HER SOLDIER'S TOUCH
SECRETS OF A SHY SOCIALITE
THE NURSE'S NOT-SO-SECRET SCANDAL

All available now!

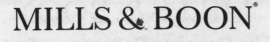

MILLS & BOON®

THE ULTIMATE IN ROMANTIC MEDICAL DRAMA

0816/03

MILLS & BOON®

The Regency Collection – Part 2

Join the London ton for a Regency
season in part 2 of our collection!

Order yours at **www.millsandboon.co.uk/regency2**